The Closer

Rowan Rossler

For all the boss babes.
And my financial mentors Darrell Ert & John Carter.

Closer

/klō-zer/

- A person who is skilled at bringing a business transaction to a close.

- The last part of a collection or series

Chapter One

JUNE

"For God's sake," I yell. "Somebody, move!"

It's nine in the morning, and my head is starting to throb. Ahead of me are three lanes of gridlocked LA traffic and a day spiraling from bad to worse. It's pathetic, really, my dismal time management. How can I be this late when I dragged my arse out of bed at dawn? Is it self-sabotage? Fear? Both, possibly. I had the entire Malibu morning at my disposal and bubbled too long in the hot tub memorizing every word of my upcoming Hail Mary speech because that's what you do when you have a date with the Devil.

There are no second chances.

I punch the horn again, and the Latina woman beside me in her Tesla rolls up her window like I'm a loose cannon with a Beretta in her glovebox about to go starkers. I fake a smile and wave at her—*Nothing to worry about. No, this is not the low point of my career.*

The reality? I might not have a career after today.

It all boils down to a meeting with Dallas Evener—nuisance in a suit and my arch nemesis.

I should clarify that Mr. Evener is not the Devil per se, but he is certainly no angel. If the *Wall Street Journal* crowns you the Dark Prince of Venture Capital, chances are your affinity for dirty deals trumps your philanthropic streak. When I escaped dreary London to stake my claim in America, I promised to keep my nose clean—no shady business. And up till now, I've honored that promise. June Allison, the proud lioness imbued with fierce ethics and virtue. I protect my baby start-up companies from leopards like Dallas who are always on the hunt for fresh meat to exploit.

The trouble is, today I'm a wounded antelope dripping a trail of blood. Easy pickings for a natural killer.

But I will not go down without a fight—if I make it there on time.

Finally, cars inch ahead. With the break in traffic, I peel off Lincoln Boulevard onto a side street. Instead of living large in Malibu or Beverly Hills like every other genius billionaire, Dallas resides in the Silver Triangle, an upscale area of stylish homes near the Venice Beach basketball courts where he allegedly shoots hoops with the locals. Despite the erratic layout of the neighborhood, I know this area like the back of my hand. After graduating from Stanford twelve years ago, I unpacked my suitcase of dreams in Marina del Ray, a stone's throw away. Back then, learning how to navigate the maze of streets in this area was a breeze compared to steering around the pitfalls of being a woman in a man's industry.

But parking around here is still a nightmare. I squeeze my Aston Martin between two SUVs camped near the end of his street and stand on Dallas's doorstep at a quarter past nine. I ring the bell, touch up my platinum-blonde waves, and breathe through the butterflies.

This is happening.

Today, I am officially eating my words.

Ten years have passed since our infamous meeting in his boardroom. After that fiasco, I licked my wounds and vowed to steer clear of him. Even though my start-ups always need cash, and Dallas has a rock-solid reputation for finding it, there are several reasons why I have avoided doing business with him.

Not that Dallas has needed me.

He is the most successful venture capitalist ever and stripped the title away from previous VC titans in less than a decade. Entrepreneurs desperate for his Midas touch offer their firstborns or sign their names in blood if it means he'll get involved.

And not one of them cares where Dallas gets his money from.

But I do.

And where the hell is he, anyway?

I ring the bell again. Another minute passes. Sweat starts to bloom around the pinched waistband of my skirt. The five extra pounds that cling to me like a lost child were joined by another four after I indulged in Paris last week, and all the seams of my Armani suit are crying foul. Just when I think this is all a ruse, another way for Dallas to get back at me, the door swings open to reveal one of the mighty engines behind America's capitalistic success.

6'2". Champion nerve. Still stupidly gorgeous. Powerful and unspeakably rich, dressed in James Perse lounge pants and nothing else.

Despite four-inch stilettos, I am forced to look up at him.

"Good morning."

"You're late," he says.

"Not according to the fifteen-minute traffic grace rule."

"My rule is to arrive fifteen minutes early."

His cunning hazel eyes bore into me, circling for a weak spot. A flush spreads beneath the silk of my blouse. Is this how we're starting? Me already on the back foot? And nice of him to dress for the occasion.

"Shall we get on with it now that I'm here?" I ask, adding a notch of crispness to my British accent.

He wordlessly waves me in without taking a step back. Forced to squeeze past him, an unmistakable whiff of male musk wafts off of him. A dark swirl gathers in my throat.

Dear God. Please tell me I did not interrupt him mid-shag.

Dallas toes the door closed, studying me in that penetrating way of his. "At long last, we meet again."

"You look well," I say. Meaning, damn you for not aging a day.

"You look nervous."

"Must be the traffic jitters."

He scans my face, and a tremor starts in my calves and travels up my body. Merely being in his presence rattles something deep in my thudding heart. He's always worn his midnight-black hair shoulder length to flip the proverbial bird at the conservative VC crowd. But I don't recall it being so lustrous.

"Nice place," I say, casting a glance around. He's a regular fixture on the party island of Ibiza, and this house evokes a similar Mediterranean vibe. Sleek and modern. Windows for days. All the right posh pieces are tastefully arranged in a great room heavy on beige and stark lines.

Dallas follows my sightline to a baby grand piano squatting in the far corner. "You play?" he asks.

"No. Do you?"

"Every day, when I can."

The notion of Dallas, a fine pianist, incongruously washes over me. Bashing on drums is the most I would have given him.

"My father ran a dance studio in Bellevue, near Seattle," he continues. "I pitched in here and there. Played the piano, helped the neighborhood ladies find their groove." His gaze, with its usual cut, clouds momentarily. Then, "Can you dance?"

My empty stomach tightens into a hard ball. Why on earth is he asking that? Knowing Dallas, it's a trap, so I answer carefully. "If the Macarena counts, then yes. Otherwise, I'm about as graceful as a gorilla on roller skates."

Dallas nods at this, eyes sharpening. "How unusual," he says. "I thought the Siren rarely makes a misstep."

Right. Here we go. The reference to my nickname, the Siren of Start-Ups, unsettles me more than his casual tone. Does he know? How can he? The story hasn't broken yet, but who am I fooling? Keeping a secret in LA is like trying to float in the sea with a bathtub chained around your neck.

"Coffee?" he asks. "Or would you prefer tea? I am partial to English Breakfast after my years at Oxford. I understand you're a fan."

Twice in as many minutes, he forces me to mask my surprise. How does he know what I drink? Or rather, who told him?

"I'll have whatever you're having," I say.

With a suit-yourself shrug, he pads into the kitchen. If I believe the foodie rumor mill around town, Dallas built his gleaming fortress of stainless steel to lure Alain Ducasse stateside to be his personal chef. Alain said no—a word Dallas rarely accepts but throws around with alarming frequency.

He fills a kettle at the sink, sets it on the base to boil, and prepares two mugs with teabags moving gracefully with a straight spine and smooth steps.

The carriage of a dancer.

I find myself thinking unprofessional thoughts again.

"Well, June," he says, "I'm all ears. And I can call you June, right? It feels like we should be on a first-name basis after all these years."

I almost buy it. Almost believe we are two chums sharing a cuppa and not masterminding how we plan to skin each other alive. But he would sooner give up his chauffeur and collection of Rolls Royces than consider me an equal. Case in point: he stays planted on the other side of the island, lest I forget who is in charge.

I set my handbag on the floor. "Can we skip the song and dance, Dallas? You know why I'm here."

"Why don't you refresh me on the details."

"If you read the deck..."

He glances at his nails, no doubt admiring his reflection in the buffed shine. "I don't give a shit about the deck. Tell me what you need."

I hold steady and lie through my teeth. "What we need is short-term financing until things get sorted out."

"Oh?" He tilts his head, and the crackling gleam in his eyes tells me I've just dug my own grave. "I heard that your business partner got caught with his pants down. Your investor freaked out and left you high and dry. You need money. Badly. The question is, what are you willing to give up for it?"

Calm and unhurried, but with the savagery of a hitman, he rips the rug out from underneath me. Not even five minutes in. *Of course he fucking knows*, I think dejectedly. The entire sad narrative of my current state of affairs just spooled off his tongue like the gloating ass had a week to rehearse it.

"I'm willing to negotiate," I say, tossing my script and hopes out the window.

He chuckles, only it sounds evil. "You need me, you pay. You knew that coming here. And a controlling ownership position is how this deal flies."

I clear my throat and try to recover from the shock of that. Is he off his rocker? No VC gets what he's angling for.

"Evener Equity now demands control of a company?" My voice rises with revolt. "Tell me who else has agreed to that hogwash."

"Speaking of hogwash," he lobs back, "the righteous June Allison would never skirt disclosure basics, would she?"

My face starts to burn. The legend surrounding Dallas is that he can walk into any boardroom and, in under a minute, assess who's in charge, who's faking it, and if any of the blokes are worth a dime of his precious investment money.

What was I thinking? I should have been up-front.

"I'm willing to offer a bigger fee," I say. "Fewer of your resources get tied up without day-to-day management. Less risk."

The kettle shrieks while his gaze frosts my skin, and I mentally kick myself in the arse. Rule #1 in negotiation is to let the other person crack first. But I have made a far graver mistake, judging from his fingertips, which press so hard into the counter they turn white.

"Are you giving me a lesson on risk?" he asks.

"Somebody needs to teach you a lesson," snarks a voice floating down from the heavens.

My head turns with Dallas's in mutual surprise. A pouty young plaything glares at us from her perch on the stairwell landing. Tall and lean, with black, sex-tousled hair, she thinks nothing about stomping into the kitchen to parade past us in a thong, boobs loose and high, bouncing under a crop top. She yanks open the fridge, takes a swig of milk from the carton, and slams it onto the counter as hard as a size double-zero can muster.

A loaded look passes between them before she says, "What?"

Dallas mercifully shuts the kettle off and observes her with a turbulent expression, like she's done something wrong. "I told you I had a meeting."

"Yeah, well," she says, tossing her mane of hair, "my agent just called. I have an audition at ten thirty. Can your chauffeur give me a lift into Hollywood?"

"No," Dallas says. "And don't slam the door on your way out."

Her eyes harden. I feel the tension in the room rise.

"Uh, hello? I give you head, and then it's, 'Sayonara'?"

"Language, please," he reprimands, as if she's a child, which, mathematically speaking, she almost is. "I have a client here."

With a withering once-over, Ms. Perky acknowledges my presence for the first time. Never has being fully clothed felt like such a disadvantage. And I did not sign up for a front-row seat to an imploding soap opera.

I reach for my bag. "Why don't we reschedule?"

"No, no, no," Dallas insists, motioning for me to stay put. "I committed. And this one here has to chase her dreams, right, Avery?"

"It's Ally," she sulks, her tone implying she has corrected him more than once. "And since I've had to do everything myself this morning, including getting myself off, why don't you make yourself useful and remove these." She thrusts her arm toward his face, and clamped between her fingers is a miniature golden key. I thought the jangly bit hanging from her wrist was a statement charm bracelet, but no.

It's a set of handcuffs.

Dallas, typically unflappable, looks unnerved as he snatches the key from Ally's fingers. "Where did you find this?"

"Dude, c'mon," she says with a dramatic eye roll. "Your bedroom is only so big. Like, maybe I watched where you put it?" Dallas frees her and Ally massages where the cold, tight metal gripped her for probably hours. She eyes my curves, this time suspiciously. "Are you really a client, or just next in line?"

"Hey," Dallas says, a bite to his voice. "Don't speak to her like that."

Ally spits a laugh. "Are you for real? Maybe she'd like to hear how you talk to me."

She whips the cuffs out of his hand and storms past me, one of her pontoon-sized feet punting my handbag across the floor. The buttery leather satchel soars like a football before clunking down on a sectional strewn with scraps of clothing.

"Sorry," she says in a scarcely credible tone and snatches up her skimpy wardrobe to dress in front of us. The spectacle of her squeezing into too-small denim is an unsung Cirque du Soleil act. She whips off her crop top to don her bra and stuff it with cleavage while Dallas tracks her every move, his jaw on a slow grind.

"I'm sorry, too," he says. "Nothing better than a woman stealing money from your wallet when she thinks you're asleep."

Oh, my. A night's worth of drama, thievery, and Lord knows what else simmers between them. The struggle on Ally's face is obvious: she wants to tell him to piss off and stuff his money where the sun doesn't shine. But she lacks the confidence. I almost feel sorry for her before realizing I'm in a similar position with him.

Minus the handcuffs.

Ally yanks on her lilac Uggs with a snort. "Like two hundred dollars would change things for you."

"It's the principle," Dallas says, irked that he needs to spell it out. "Some of us work for a living. And prowling for your next sugar daddy in a bar doesn't qualify as work, FYI."

Talk about twitch muscles. Or second-sense anticipation. Dallas snatches the handcuffs out of the air seconds before they crack against his forehead. Ally has an impressive arm. Better than I could ever throw.

"Your dick is the only thing decent about you," she mutters. "Good thing it can't talk."

Tromping across the travertine like a bull elephant on a rampage, she flings the front door open, and the closing slam says everything she didn't have the guts to. A small, jealous part of me is thankful for her whirlwind departure. I am demoralized by her perky breasts when mine will never stand so firm in their lifetime.

With a sigh, Dallas runs a hand over his hair as if a minor threat to his day—the milk gone sour—has been neatly resolved. "Where were we?" he asks.

"I'm not offering ownership," I say, seizing back the momentum. "And twenty percent on monies raised."

A sound of disdain blows through his lips. "Twenty percent is for amateurs. I can refer you to some if you want."

"Even without extorting me for a controlling position, thirty-five percent is a stretch. We both know that."

"And we both know you are the kind of woman who will bend over backward for your company," he says without missing a beat. "That kind of flexibility always intrigues me."

His resting superior face rarely cracks a smile, so I forgot about the dimples. He would be so attractive if he weren't an absolute wanker.

"Do you ever think of doing what's right for the business?" I ask.

"I do what's right for me."

"And yet you donate considerable sums to worthy causes."

He digests that with a deepening frown. "Are you suggesting I'm a bleeding heart?"

"I'm suggesting that maybe you have a heart."

His eyes taper with displeasure, and I dare him with mine. But any harebrained idea I might have that Dallas will concede defeat ends with the equivalent of a gun to my head.

"Ownership and thirty-five percent," he reiterates. "And if you walk out the door without saying yes, it will be forty when you come crawling back."

Frustration bubbles under my skin. I hate Dallas. Hate him more than the death of Queen Elizabeth. And I hate him for roughing me up just because he can.

"If I were a man, you wouldn't dare talk to me like this," I say.

He waltzes over, gleaming with optimism, and has the balls to leave nothing but a whisper-thin space between my ample C's and his greatness.

"If I get you this riled up hating me," he says, "imagine if you actually liked me."

I *pffft* in disgust. "I will never like you, Dallas."

He draws his shoulder blades together, and two perked nipples jut right into my face. I could stick my tongue out and lick them, which I am embarrassingly inclined to do because I did like him at one point.

And he's milking that for all it's worth.

"You know the drill, June," he says. "In our business, we never say never. And for the record, a man wouldn't come here all dolled up, assuming his beautiful face is all it takes to win me over."

Wait. Stop the world. Did Dallas just call me beautiful?

I search his eyes, but they shutter before I can confirm what I saw within their depths.

A flicker of emotion.

"I did my homework and called your bluff, sunshine," he adds. "Deal with it."

His beam of triumph feels forced because something shifted a second ago. But he'll never cop to it. Not when he can lord his authority over me.

The sunlit heyday of my Malibu hot-tub morning, when I was daft enough to think this could work, fizzles. I retreat to the sectional and snag my handbag, the burn of his eyes like a laser penetrating my skin. None of my plight bothers him in the least, and why should it? When Dallas hung out his shingle a decade ago at age twenty-four, the whispers were swift and malicious. Too pretty. Too young. Too full of himself. He grew a beard to lend gravitas to his youthful face and is giving The Rock a run for his money in the body department, but the crucial change in him is why he hosted this meeting barefoot and barechested.

America's youngest billionaire doesn't give a flying fuck what anyone thinks about him.

He is wealthy enough to make up his own rules and force everyone else to play by them.

"Call me," he adds, infuriatingly sexy with both arms crossed to show off his guns. "Anytime. Don't be a stranger."

His playful wink winds me up even more, but I will not give him the satisfaction. He can stuff his disrespectfulness up his arse if he can get it past the stick jammed in there. Like the last time we met, I will end this debacle with my dignity intact.

"Don't hold your breath, Dallas. And I'll let myself out."

Chapter Two

We Brits are known for our stiff upper lip. Thanks to my father, Frank, mine is made of concrete. Under his rule, the Allison household did not approve of flaky things like emotions. Mum cried in private. My scraped knees had ointment and a plaster slapped on them, but never received a healing kiss. If a boy called me a bad name, father said to wallop him one on the shins. I toughened up fast, to the point that every boyfriend has called me a variation of unsympathetic or relentless.

The thing is, I do care.

I'm just useless at showing it … unless pushed to the breaking point.

I strangle my steering wheel and scream bloody murder until the sound dies in my heaving lungs. Not many people can put me out of sorts, but on an irritation scale of one to ten, Dallas is an eleven. When I insisted on pursuing a business major, my father warned me about men like Dallas—vindictive types jealous of women and their success and eager to throttle me back. If I wanted to be at the mercy of men and clean up their messes, stick to being a housewife, he'd intoned.

Same shit, less hassle.

I never considered my father to be an oracle—a grim pain was more like it. We spent too much time with our horns locked; my entrepreneurial spirit at constant loggerheads with his misogynist Army sergeant view on life. Women raised babies or belonged in the kitchen, serving hot meals.

Is it any wonder I bolted across the Atlantic without a glance back?

Mum, of course, never intervened. A life of dusting under the doilies suited her just fine. But I could not fathom such tedium. I had a mission, a destiny to fulfill. I wanted to be the best at what I did, and I am.

If only I excelled at judging men's characters the way I do balance sheets, I might not be in this predicament.

Something the ring of my phone brings back into sharp focus.

I scrounge for the iPhone in my handbag. The 310 area code scrolling across the screen is a testament to how long Cliff Sassen, my soon-to-be ex-business partner, has called LA home. A renowned environmental activist, we met at a black-tie climate change fundraiser two years ago and bonded over our mutual passions of food and tech.

He had an idea. I had the ability to run with it.

We developed Green Time, a revolutionary system that uses blockchain technology to ensure traceability and transparency in the global food chain. In layman's terms, we help food get to people faster and cheaper. Last week, we had a tiger by the tail. Now, we're a giant turd steaming on the sidewalk.

I blow out a resigned breath and answer on speaker. "Hi."

"How did it go?" he asks.

I glance skyward, through the tinted glass of my moon roof, at the palm fronds swaying against a periwinkle blue sky. So peaceful. So demoralizing. When was the last time I took ten minutes to do nothing but daydream?

"Not well."

"Ah shit, Juney," he says, hearing it in my voice. "Can we meet and discuss?"

"I was planning to swing by on my way home."

"Uhm…" he starts. "I'm actually in Venice. I had itchy feet."

"You left the house?"

Cliff and I had planned to meet in the safety of his Pacific Palisades mansion, although I imagine tension is running high in the Sassen household. A wife who is clueless about her husband's side interest in girls younger than their two daughters is the kind of sticker shock marriages never recover from. My initial surprise has morphed into a quiet horror, and the news freaked out our lone investor enough that the conservative Christian fundamentalist from Montana yanked his full support three days ago. I had just closed that vital tranche of financing at the end of May, and we were set to rock.

"I have an outside table at the empanada place you like," he says. "I'm wearing a wig and hat, just in case."

A disguise? Jesus, this nightmare is real. "Okay. Give me fifteen."

We end the call, and I take a moment to gather myself and my bearings. I roared away from Dallas drowning in a soup of emotions and without a definite destination.

And look where I've ended up—my old parking spot in front of the Blue Moon Tavern.

Unlike most sixty-year-old relics in LA, the dive bar pool hall where I hustled day-drunk chumps has not had a facelift. Grime from the '80's streaks the windows. A dented Michelob sign still hangs crooked on the door. I sidestepped puddles of beer and blew off steam here back in the day, letting go of the frustration of establishing myself in a town that ushers every pretty face with a set of decent boobs to the casting couch. (Sadly, this behavior is commonplace in every industry.)

But I persevered, stuck to my ethical guns, and made millions. I splurged on a custom Brunswick pool table after my first big win, and now I crack balls across the purple felt with a limitless view of the Pacific from my Malibu estate.

The Blue Moon is a distant memory.

But I miss the unique texture of this neighborhood.

I fire up the car and scour my memory banks, trying to recall if Dallas lived in this area when we first met. If he had, I highly doubt he would have risked tarnishing his bougie Golden Goose trainers in a joint like the Blue Moon. The bottle of Armagnac we polished off in his office on that ill-fated afternoon a decade ago was three grand a bottle.

Beer on tap and a basket of curly fries?

I'm sure he'd rather face a firing squad.

Comforted by the fine roar of my Vantage, I ease away from the curb and head north to meet Cliff. But putting distance between Dallas and me isn't enough to quell the old, familiar feelings our visit conjured up. Sensations, tastes, and smells suddenly swarm me like a school of fish.

My insides buzzing and warm from the booze.

Dallas, tie loosened, and blazer shrugged off.

I kicked off my heels under his boardroom table.

The sparks flying between us were palpable, and we got comfortable.

I did, anyway.

By then, the winter sun had set, and we were the only ones left in his office.

In retrospect, I blame myself for what happened.

But he is to blame for everything else.

$

I CAN SPOT Cliff's stubby ponytail a mile away, but on the sun-filled patio at *Olé Empanada*, I got nothing—other than a dark-haired head-banger who windshields one arm back and forth.

"Juney," this weirdo calls out. "It's me."

Clueing into the wig, I thread past the rickety collection of tables to embrace yet another man who has screwed me over.

"That's quite the getup," I say.

"Good thing I love Hallowe'en. My bag of tricks is coming in handy. You look sizzling, by the way." Cliff grins, and a strange pang of sadness cuts through me. Blond and good-looking, sun-kissed and square-jawed in that California way, women of a certain age often mistake him for Robert Redford. He is a man who lights up the room, and the days always seem better when he flashes those bright teeth.

"Today is on me," he continues, handing over a crinkled plastic menu. "Go crazy."

I take a seat and skim the tropical drink offerings while Cliff, ever impatient, wastes no time digging for the dirt. "Did you walk out on him again?"

I sigh. Was it only twenty minutes ago that I killed our one shot at redemption? "Possibly," I say.

He raises his glass of lemonade in glass in a toast. "That's my girl. Don't mess with the Brits."

I laugh, brief and rueful, feeling a little looser now that the meeting with Dallas is behind me. But the embarrassment of it still hums under my skin.

"He knew," I say. "Every detail."

Cliff arches a brow. "Are you surprised?"

"No," I admit. "And I think I know who told him. But can you believe Dallas demanded controlling ownership?"

"Ouch. That is a surprise."

"None of this flies if you kill it. You are the majority owner."

His shoulders hunch, and I get the feeling Cliff considered this outcome long before I set a Prada heel on the patio. "If you want my approval, I'm saying yes."

"You can't say yes!"

My plaintive wail draws stares from a pair of twenty-somethings sharing a pitcher of Day-Glo green margaritas. *Yes*, I want to tell them. *I fell in love with the business and ignored the man attached. Yes, this is my comeuppance. Yes, do not follow in my footsteps.*

"Juney," Cliff says, and here it comes, him walking me off the ledge like he does every other week. "This is one of those times where you have to forget about the bad blood. I know that's hard for you. But why let this blow up? It sounds like he wants to help."

"And tear us a new one while he's at it," I grumble. "You won't be the one having to deal with him."

"True," he concedes. "But on the one hand, this might be good for you."

"In what universe?"

His eyes breeze past me to the early morning bustle of cyclists and rollerbladers on the boardwalk, living the California dream that's about to be snatched out from under him.

"Not to be the guy to dredge up bad juju," he eventually says, "but can you remind me why he dragged your name through the mud? I know it involved one of his companies."

A flutter of vexation ignites inside me. The only stain on Dallas's otherwise impeccable record is the sordid nightmare of ZedShed, the infamous cloud computing company that defied every odd. They raced to record revenues and the media fawned all over their plucky CEO, Sonny Burnett.

But no one, not even Dallas, suspected Sonny and his CFO of collusion. Before their high-profile arrests, those two weasels kept separate books, faked higher revenues, and bilked Evener Equity and their investors out of over ninety million. Dallas blamed me for ratting out Sonny when all we had was an innocent lunch because he wanted female representation on his board.

In fairness, the timing of our meeting looked suspicious. One week after our Beverly Hills luncheon, the ZedShed scandal rocked our industry. Dallas had major egg on his face and was livid.

"Guess who he took it out on?" I ask Cliff, who's listening to my rant with a look of sympathy. "After that, Dallas trash-talked me at every opportunity. He never once called me to ask if I *had* said anything!"

Cliff sighs and drains the remains of his drink. "That is harsh and childish. But you did smash his ego. I'm not saying what he did is right, but successful men are not accustomed to losing."

Before I attack that crap line of defense, a server shuffles over with a lopsided smile. "Yo," he says, grooving to the beat thumping in his earbuds. "A drink for the lady and a refill for youse?"

I ask for a gin martini and Cliff rises awkwardly from his chair, addled with a bad back.

"10-1," he says, movie code for bathroom break. "Sit tight, and we'll circle back to this."

While Cliff tinkles, my irritation slowly dribbles into a slurry of muddled emotions. The truth is, and I will only confess this under hot interrogation lamps with my chocolate supply threatened—I envy Dallas. He's the guy you hate, but secretly want to be. He possesses charisma in spades and uses his good looks to their full effect. Add on a near-prophetic ability to read and time the market … If anyone could build a bridge to nowhere and sell it at a premium, it'd be him. But if our recent clash proved anything, our business and personal codes of conduct remain staunch opposites. And I regretfully ponder the truth of that statement with a heavy heart. Once upon a time, I believed we could do great things together.

And the tiniest part of me believes Dallas probably agreed.

The faint glimmer of admiration rising in his eyes before I walked out was not my imagination.

Cliff returns from the loo a few minutes later, chatting up our server. It never fails to impress me how effortlessly he engages with people. Cliff became the celebrity ambassador for environmental activism through tireless campaigning and a knack for currying favors from famous faces and their bank accounts. Always at his brilliant and charming best surrounded by a crowd, I should have paid more heed to the starry-eyed, busty tree huggers who followed him around like a puppy.

After the server drops our drinks and grooves on over to another table, Cliff palms me a plastic baggie.

"Before I forget," he says, "I wanted to give you these."

I peer at the dark mass that looks like twigs collected from a forest bed. "What is it?"

"Mushrooms."

"As in drugs?"

"They are the least of my vices. But I can't risk having them around."

"My intoxicant of choice is alcohol," I remind him.

Cliff settles back into the chair. "Fresh solutions never occur on the levels where your problems lie. If you don't want to deal with Dallas, I get it. But what is the next step? This might be the right time to expand your mind, so give those a whirl. They aren't powerful. More like mushroom-lite."

What else did I expect from the counter-culture kid? Cliff grew up on a commune, frolicking with hippies while the sun shone on their bare arses as they harvested dandelions and peyote for the evening salad. I wager he spent a third of his life high. Something other than a sound mind had to explain the Grateful Dead cranking all day in his office.

I stuff the contraband into my purse, intending to flush it. "Thanks. But I need my wits about me."

"Speaking of that," he says, dropping his voice. "Are you around this weekend?"

My heart rate perks up. "Yes, why?"

"You might want to lay low. I made a deal with a reporter—a guy who owes me. He promised to publish the story on Saturday, the slower news day." He cracks a cryptic smile." "Kind of like an electric chair heating up slowly."

So it's official. Shit hitting the fan now has a date.

"I organized a meeting with our executives tomorrow," I say. "I'll pass on the warning."

"You know Mark is expecting triplets, right?" Cliff sucks lemonade through the straw, his bushy eyebrows raised to say—*you know what I mean.*

"Do not guilt-trip me, Cliff," I warn, prickling at his innuendo. "This is not my fault."

Mark Kendall is our vice president of sales, and his wife Sarah quit her job on the strength of Green Time's pending success so they could focus on starting a family. An infusion of cash needs to happen, or I have no choice but to slash salaries. It's killing me. I love my staff. They are my family. They mean something to me. This calamity is a massive hiccup for everyone.

"All I'm saying," Cliff adds, "is our people deserve the best. Don't let your ego get in the way of a solution."

I bite my tongue. Ego is a verboten word for Cliff, but he is not immune to other vices. Sober now for over twenty years, I wish he could have controlled his more damaging urges.

"Anything else?" I ask.

"Yes." His hand finds mine; our fingers curl together. "I fucked up big-time, and I will take whatever comes my way like a man. But I need one thing from you. Promise you will visit me in jail?"

A lump expands in my throat. In some distant land, I knew what the fallout might bring.

"Oh, God. Don't say that. You'll make me cry."

"Emotion is good, Juney. It's normal. You do not always have to be the strong one." His grip on my hand tightens. "Promise me, okay? I'll need to see a face that doesn't scare the shit out of me."

What happens to the likes of Cliff in jail is something neither of us wants to discuss. How will I react seeing him in a jumpsuit, hollow and grey, a scratched piece of plexiglass between us? A burly guard pretending not to listen to our conversation. Lawyers lurking in the waiting area with bad news.

"Yes," I say, caving under pressure. "I promise."

In the awkward silence, a gust of wind blows across the table. Cliff watches our napkins spiral to the ground like joint white flags falling in defeat. "We've had one helluva ride," he says in a sober tone. "I wish I could finish it with you. Do what you do best and make this happen. I'll be cheering for you from cell block nine."

Chapter Three

On the 350 days of the year when LA traffic sucks, I question living in Point Dume. My morning commute into Venice chewed through sixty minutes. Getting downtown during rush hour is a two-hour buzzkill on the motorway. I debated buying in Beverly Hills and instead paid dearly for an acre of Malibu waterfront. Travel times aside, I have zero regrets. The seaside calms me, and the space and light in my white-walled sanctuary swallow up some of my loneliness —a condition I've learned to live with.

I toe my shoes off in the foyer. The ivory marble underfoot feels warm thanks to the radiant heat I had installed during a renovation that transformed the east side of the house into a bank of windows. From here, I can see the patio. Bougainvillea covers the arbors that shade it and underneath sits a table smothered with delicate pink petals.

A knot of dismay tightens in my chest.

It's been months since I hosted a dinner party.

If I keep up this insane pace, it might become years.

Determined to pack away the crisis for half a minute, I beeline to the kitchen. The last of my stress melts away as I peel off the power suit and pour myself some chilled Chardonnay to end the day how it started.

Naked in the hot tub.

Perched on the edge of a cliff with a sweeping view of the Pacific, this is my spot to unwind. I set down my handbag and wine to remove the hot tub cover and start the jets. I considered leaving my phone inside, but I am married to it more than I ever was to my ex-husband. I sink into the bubbling water and begin scrolling through my messages.

Mum called again. I blew her off in Paris last week because any conversation with her is akin to banging my head against a wall. She understands nothing of my work, and her play-by-plays of the latest sitcoms tickling her fancy bore me to tears. And California does not have enough wine to fortify me against her inevitable breakdown once I tell her the bad news.

Mum adored Cliff.

I ignore her message and skip to the one that warms my heart. Vandana Hillman, one of my BFFs, confirming brunch this Saturday. I reply with a thumbs-up emoji and a gushing message on how much I miss her. She met Morgan, her yacht designer boyfriend, last fall on a business trip, and after a tumultuous start, fell in serious love. In true trailblazer fashion, she dropped a red-hot PR career, moved to Monaco, and started an interior design business. She and Morgan are a global powerhouse design duo and are dropping into LA this weekend to woo another potential client.

I can hardly wait to be reunited with her and our other bestie, Flynn Dryden. Our trio was formed at Stanford, living under the same roof in a Palo Alto rental. Vandana and I were roomies for the first year until she decided to rent out the spare bedroom. Flynn showed up, and the rest, as they say, is history.

Funnily enough, sweetheart Flynn has also messaged me. She's dying to know how it went with Dallas.

And yes, there's also *that*.

I did not arrange today's encounter with him.

Flynn's fiancé, Chavez Delgado, set it up.

The current darling of men's tennis knows Dallas through some random sports connection, and made a fortune investing in Leostrata, a tech company Dallas took public that became the biggest IPO in history.

Flynn, Vandana, Morgan, and I were all in Paris last week watching Chavez win the French Open. I threw them all for a loop by jumping on a flight back to LA in the bleary-eyed dawn of our drunken celebration party to deal with the 911 call from Cliff. I keep nothing from my besties, so they know all about the tragic ordeal. Flynn, in turn, told Chavez that I needed money. And because Chavez wanted to help, I swallowed my pride and said yes to the setup.

I warned Chavez not to spill any specific details to Dallas and just arrange a meeting, but Mr. Evener has a unique way of finding and exploiting weaknesses. No wonder he jumped at the opportunity to hear me out.

That predator had me hook, line, and sinker.

I ring up Flynn, and she patiently hears me out on the morning's spectacle. But the poor thing cannot get past the horror of the handcuffs.

"For the love of God!" she moans. "Does every guy in LA have to be a creepy douche?"

I chuckle and take a swill of wine. "I'm assuming I don't have to answer that?"

"I'm so sorry," she says. "What's plan B?"

I sink deeper into the water and shut my eyes. I am bone tired. "I don't know. Trying to find capital with this shitstorm looming will be close to impossible, and our company burn rate is astronomical. We can't afford to go months without a cash infusion. Plus, our official launch is slated for July. The timing is horrible."

In the background, I hear her Vitamix whip a smoothie into centrifugal submission. Alas, healthy living does nothing but make me crave a cigarette. I prop the phone against my ear with one shoulder and scrounge through my handbag for the Marlboros.

"If finding money is so hard, where would Dallas get his cash from?" Flynn asks.

"At any given moment, his hands are in several willing pockets," I reply. "Even if the market is tight, he finds cash."

And this is the suspicion that swirls around him. When Dallas first opened shop, the small fortune backing him was rumored to have dirty origins. He's been asked plenty of times about it but has never revealed where his initial funding came from. Since then, Evener Equity has raked it in on legitimate deals. ZedShed was his only wobble, and he overcame that, mainly because he has no qualms about tapping the ugly side of humanity for greenbacks.

"If, and I'm not saying you will," Flynn stresses, "but *if* you accepted his offer, does he guarantee the money? Is there an out for you if he doesn't pull it off?"

I fish out a cigarette and rummage for my Zippo lighter. "There is a time frame for the money raise. A way out, potentially. The problem is, he always delivers."

As soon as I utter those words, a warning bell goes off in my head. Something I need to look into.

"I know you well enough to know that you won't let this die without exhausting every option," Flynn says. "And forty million ... I mean, it's a lot, but not really in your world. Is there no one else to tap?"

Sure. Santa Claus. The Easter Bunny. A winning Powerball ticket.

Or Dallas bloody Evener.

"Tomorrow I have to drop the scandal bomb on my executive team. That should be the bee's knees." I shake my head, already dreading the fitful night of sleep waiting for me. "I pray that there's a hope in hell they know someone."

And where the heck is my lighter? I scrounge through my bag in a second, futile pass. Nothing. Strange. I don't recall taking it out.

"What about Morgan?" Flynn suggests. "He runs in some serious money circles. He'll do anything for Vandana, and you are an extension of her."

Morgan is a super talented yacht designer, top five in the world according to *Robb Report*. He lunches with billionaires regularly, and his family is one of those ancient Euro clans with a fortune that has compounded since the fifteenth century. But...

"I don't know him well enough to ask," I say.

"You mean you don't want to look vulnerable."

"I don't want to look like an idiot," I clarify. "His girlfriend's uni mate with a debacle on her hands coming round with a hat begging for money? No thank you."

Flynn sighs. She knows this side of me too well. "It's worth an ask," she insists. "And they fly in tomorrow, so it's good timing. Bring it up at brunch and see what he says."

"Is Chavez coming with you?" I quite like his fiery personality.

"Of course!" she says. "He loves you and Morgan. Warming up to Vandana slowly but surely."

Chavez with his rough and tumble background, tattoos, and in your face attitude rubbed Vandana the wrong way, at first. And her princess So Cal upbringing was a nasty reminder of the constraints Chavez had to rally past as a Mexican American trying to make his mark in an elite sport from the southside underbelly of Fresno, California. But kudos to him, because he is trying hard to align with Vandana.

"When do you two fly to London?" I ask.

"Monday," she says. "Grass-court season, here we come. Chavez rented this ridiculous house near Wimbledon. You're welcome to drop in anytime."

I gulp wine and it hits the back of my throat like a spray of acid. Am I forever destined to date losers? With Vandana now in Monaco and Flynn flying around the world with Chavez as his tennis coach, I have never felt more alone. Wallowing is so not me, but it fucking hurts knowing my besties have found true love and I haven't. A fortune teller I saw out of desperation last month said my time would come, but at this stage, I might as well pull a random guy off the street and buy him a house. Future ex-husbands are a dime a dozen in LA.

"Is Russ still causing you grief?" Flynn asks, careful but absolutely spot-on. She is a savant at sensing when my thoughts are about to slide into a dark hole, and my brief marriage is a black stain no amount of scrubbing can remove from my brain.

"We settled on a palimony amount," I say. "I doubt he will lift a finger to find a job for the rest of his life."

Flynn clucks in disapproval. "Really? Construction is booming. Contractors are in huge demand."

"Tell that to Mr. Ride Your Coattails. I had to swing past his condo to get a signature, and he was in his pajamas at noon drinking Old Milwaukee from a can."

Flynn wisely says nothing. Neither she nor Vandana sanctioned my marriage and looking back, I claim temporary insanity in saying yes. I should have known better than to marry a man who called a toilet *the shitter.* But Father had just passed, and I was feeling massively untethered.

Russ and I had met at a bookstore, in the travel section, and he'd seemed normal enough—a blue-collar worker with a taste for high-end vacations. (Or a taste for women who could pay for his high-end vacations.) We did get on at first. And only after our honeymoon in the Maldives did he start with the belittling—of my success, my dogged work ethic, how little time I spent with him. I stuck around longer than necessary because he was well-hung for a short man.

I do love a decent cock.

And there have been so few in my life.

But there have been a hell of a lot of pricks.

And speaking of that, an incoming text notification flashes on my screen. From Dallas. With a photo attached.

DE: I take it this is yours?

In the middle of his impossibly smooth palm is my Zippo lighter. A weighty brass fire-starter with *JA* monogrammed in ruby-red Swarovski crystals. How the hell does Dallas have it?

"Hey, Bella." Flynn snaps my attention back. "I don't mean to cut this short, but I have to pick up Chavez from physio. What should I tell him about the meeting with Dallas?"

I bite back a laugh. Would Chavez believe I walked out on the richest man in America?

"Tell him it's a work in progress," I say.

She snickers. "Sure. We'll run with that."

"Oh, wait," I say, suddenly remembering something else. "Before you go—Cliff gave me some mushrooms, Lord knows why. Do you want them?"

"Seriously?" Flynn's voice rises in disbelief, knowing full well I have never taken drugs in my life. She, on the other hand, has dabbled here and there. "I'd say yes, but Chavez would flip out. He's okay with me drinking here and there, but drugs, forget it."

"So he's not joining you at Burning Man anytime soon?" I joke.

Flynn bursts out laughing. Her multi-year mission to corral Vandana and me to join her in the desert has been an epic fail.

"Are you kidding?" she says. "He can barely cope if his sock drawer is out of order."

We chitchat briefly about what each of us plans to wear at brunch and then say our goodbyes. I immediately text Dallas back.

JA: Yes, it's mine. Where did you find it?

His reply lands within two seconds.

DE: On my couch.

Couch? Oh, right. It must have fallen out after quarterback Ally punted my handbag across the room.

DE: My assistant can bring it to your office in the morning.

Um, not! No one can be near my office tomorrow to hear the wails of sorrow. And I would sooner stop eating carbs than step back into the lair of Evener Equity.

JA: Can you leave it on your doorstep? I'll swing by tomorrow.
DE: Done.

I stare at the screen for a span of four shallow breaths and wait for the telltale dots. Wait for something less cut-and-dried to end our exchange with. But we never made it across the threshold where we sent funny or goofy or heartfelt texts to one another. Even after the debacle in his office, before he did everything in his power to smear my reputation, the most he offered were a few text messages, all of them variations of *Can you call me? Can we meet?* Never a *Sorry I was such an ass.*

And we didn't shake hands today. No contact whatsoever. It makes me a tiny bit sad.

My phone chimes with another message.

DE: Do you smoke cigarettes or weed?

My brows knit. As if that is an inroad to a meaningful conversation. And what is he implying?

JA: I have never done drugs.

DE: Of course not.

A riffle of annoyance washes over me. Texts can have a tone, and that one screams of a dig. I can see him grinning hugely, having a laugh at June Allison, the green-tech champion, carbon-neutral advocate, and keeper of the do-gooder flame. I secretly wish Flynn had pushed harder, dragging me to Burning Man against my will. What joy it would be to send Dallas a photo of me posing in front of the naked olive oil wrestling tent wearing a bikini and holding a joint the size of a baseball bat with the caption—*Kidding. I have done it all!*

Just as I'm forming a snappy, less drastic response, he beats me to the draw.

DE: I need a decision by Saturday, 7 p.m. My offer is dead after that.

I breathe deeply and try to will away the tension. Saturday, huh? I have two whole days to decide? Congratulations, Dallas. You have reached the bare minimum in the small, tender move department. My fingers fly across the screen in response.

JA: I'll let you know either way.

Thirty seconds pass, then a full minute, before I am certain he's moved on. I sink back into the liquid heat and stare at the cloudless Malibu sky. Cliff, Green Time, Dallas. All of it spools endlessly in my mind. I know whatever I'm feeling right now will pass, but I need a break. A time out. I need something.

And as if Dallas can read my mind, my phone chimes again.

DE: PS Weed might help you relax. :)

Is he bloody serious? Like I need life-balance advice from someone who can buy inner peace, no matter the going rate. And hello? As if a hundred-hour workweek isn't his norm. Or that a thousand unread emails don't keep him awake at night. What he does have is the ability to pound out his frustrations on captive starlets while I struggle to keep all the work I've done for the last two years of my life from flushing down the drain, and my only guilty pleasure is coming home to an empty house with a view.

What a tosser!

I chuck the phone onto a nearby deck chair and plunge beneath the bubbles. Warm water plugs both ears, and all sound deadens. Floating weightless helps reset my brain.

What am I thinking?

I refuse to do this deal with Dallas. His arrogance and reputation will be the end of me and Green Time. If a reality TV star became president and grandmothers gave birth to twins, surely forty-eight hours and sheer volition is enough to solve this mess without getting him involved.

Chapter Four

"Are we going to lose our jobs?"

The apex of this downcast afternoon in seven simple words. From the lips of Mark Kendall, with fear mounting in his eyes. Meanwhile, four other pale, shocked faces pin me to front of the Green Time boardroom.

"I am doing everything in my power to resolve this," I tell them, a sterile and useless phrase considering the atmosphere is as joyful as a baby's funeral.

Conchita, our whiz kid controller from Puerto Rico, lowers her glasses to give her infamous look of worry. "If suppliers force payment, we will be tapped by July. The bank could freeze our accounts."

"And who steps in for Cliff?" asks Mia, our savvy head of research and development. She's pretty, with a killer sense of humor and a flair for drama. "Having no CEO is like death."

Who can replace Cliff, aside from no one? His golden touch with celebrities was a one-of-a-kind gift. And ever since #metoo and other equality upheavals rocked the film and TV industry, that world is quick to distance itself from anyone or anything that reeks of that stink.

"I have no immediate person in mind," I say. "But to quell the noise, I'll step in as interim CEO and maintain my CFO status."

Kim Tate, a leggy redhead, resident cookie maker, and my assistant extraordinaire, raises a thinly plucked brow. "Lady. You will burn out faster than you already have."

"And with the July rollout, you and Cliff planned to tag team the tech events in Miami and New York," says Amir, our marketing guru, whom I wooed away from a competitor on the promise of a huge bonus. "You can't be in two places at once."

I hesitate, thinking I might just leave the room. I'm too exhausted for this conversation. At four this morning, after another sleepless night, I had higher hopes.

I take an audible breath, my face tense and determined. "Cliff has left me—us—with no other choice. And I have led many companies before," I remind them, more sharply than intended.

Mark sinks his face into both hands with a resounding, "Fuck!"

The gloom thickens. No one dares look at one another. Mark has pending triplets, but they all have mortgages and mouths to feed. I pace and try to shake off the jangling nerves. I refuse to consider everything we have built is now a sinking ship. The definition of leadership is to be the strong one, and my team needs something to grasp onto. I cannot destroy their weekend or their belief in me.

"There is one option in play," I mention, hating myself for bringing it up. "I don't love it, and it will mean a very different energy at the top."

Kim glances at me, questioning, a little judgy too. She seems to be asking, *Did you withhold something from me?*

Mark peeks out from behind his veil of fingers. "Who gives a shit about energy? We aren't selling incense. At this point, it's sink or swim. Hire Trump if he has the cash."

"We will never be *that* desperate," Conchita mutters, speaking for all of us.

"We are that desperate," Mark fires back. "And screw Cliff for putting us in this position. What an asshole. His poor wife."

Murmurs of agreement rise in the room. All the reverence they once had for Cliff up in smoke.

"Who is the bad energy guy? Or gal?" Amir asks, adjusting the elastic around his man bun.

A dull throb starts at the back of my neck. Will saying his name be a self-fulfilling prophecy?

"Dallas Evener of Evener Equity."

Mia's brows flatten into a straight line. "I thought you hated VCs."

"And don't you hate him?" Kim adds, since I'd bitched to her about Dallas last year on a Friday afternoon when we shared a bottle of wine over war stories.

"Hate is a strong word," I say, backpedaling. "And given our current time constraints, every viable option has to be considered."

Mark pushes the heels of his hands into his eyes and growls, "If he has the money, fuck your feelings about him or VCs. Do the right thing."

Amir, Mr. Proper, wags a warning finger at Mark. The rule here is to be copasetic and professional, even in the heated moments. But I let the F-bombs slide. I noticed the snappy, new suit and expensive shoes Mark strolled in with. All bought on credit because we were supposed to be rolling in dough next month.

"Duly noted," I say coolly.

Mark and I have warred before. We've survived the trenches on three other grueling start-ups, and my right-hand man could run this company one day if I let him. But the trick with Mark is to squash any petulant behavior he falls into when stressed. To not let it rile me.

I take a seat at the head of the table and steeple my fingers, resting them against my chin. "Trust me, gang," I assure them. "I hate dropping this news on a Friday. My entire weekend is committed to finding a solution. If you want to call it a day and go home, please do. I'll keep you all in the loop."

One by one, they stand, mumble something conciliatory, and file out with hangdog expressions. Mark remains planted in his chair. The space between us fills with silence and tension thicker than a steak at Morton's.

After a sticky pause, he asks, "How long have you known about Cliff?"

"He called me last week when I was in Paris. Why?"

His dark eyes sharpen. The consummate schmoozer, I get none of his love today. "And you're telling us a week later."

I hold his accusing gaze. "Without knowing the full extent of the situation, I—"

"Can the bullshit," he snaps, pushing back in the chair to stand menacingly, rigid as a light post. His cheeks are flushed. Lips mashed tight before he finally says, "I thought you were different. I thought you cared."

It feels like he's punched me in the stomach. I sit straighter to ward off the sensation.

"I am finding a solution," I say. "That is caring."

His brows raise in mock surprise. "Dallas is the venture capital king. Evener Equity wants in, and you're here crying the blues, twiddling your thumbs? What the fuck!"

He glowers at me, hands on his hips, full-fledged bitchy. Easy for him to point a finger when he has no clue to the backstory.

"Between you, me, and the fencepost, his terms suck," I say, keeping my emotions in check. "He wants a controlling position. If you want to be under the rule of a ruthless king, it just might happen."

What that means between the lines is Mark's status as the golden boy can be, and most likely would be, revoked by a less-friendly kingpin.

He takes his time answering. "I heard about the rift between you two. Everyone knows. You're always telling us to maintain positive relationships and not to let petty differences get in the way of bigger goals." He shakes his head as if the answer he's been looking for has been in front of him the entire time. "If you turn him down and we sink, I'm out. You and I are finished."

I can feel my heart pounding. Mutiny, right in front of me. And nothing I can do about it.

"That's a bit severe," I say, standing in an attempt to bolster my voice.

"No, it's not," he says. "I'm ready to take the reins of a company. You know it. I'm grateful for what I've learned working under you, but it's time to spread my wings. And if you let this company die because of *feelings,* then I've hitched my wagon to the wrong horse."

My eyes meet his. They are flinty and inscrutable, nothing like the shy young man who shuffled in for an interview and begged to work with me.

I clear my throat. It feels like I've gargled with sandpaper. "I see. So, after this weekend, if nothing happens…"

His bravado shrinks back a smidge. "Let's talk on Monday. And I pray to God that you're not like all the rest of them. In it for yourself."

He shoulder-barges past me, and the slam of the door behind him rattles the fillings in my teeth. Words fumble on my tongue, but what do I need to apologize for? Any fool knows not to hit the panic button until you fully understand a situation.

Too tired to fight, to stand, I lean against the wall with a dejected sigh. If there is a worse feeling than one of your soldiers plunging a knife into your heart, I never want to experience it.

$

AFTER EVERYONE ELSE HAS LEFT, I slink out of the office. I unlock my car with the key fob. The headlights blink, an interior light turns on. I reach for the door handle, my hand shaking. Mark's words cut deep, more than I let on at the time. And what does he expect? Yes, I have feelings. I'm a woman, for Christ's sake. But men revel in the double-edged sword that hangs over every female's head. And they perpetuate it in small, digging ways. They encourage us to be successful, but not more successful than them. Be nice, but not a pushover. Dress well, but we're asking for trouble if we dare be sexy. And never, ever show emotions because that shit is for babies.

Do I need to go on?

I slide into the driver's seat, shut the door, and stare blankly at the metal plate engraved with my name and mounted to the car park wall. I get it that men feel threatened by, or are scared of, me. Tight dresses, high heels, and making more money than them is a recipe for resentment. But the moment you compromise on who you are, you're in a downward spiral to misery. I am who I am. A ballsy Brit who loves form-fitting clothes as much as the thrill of a deal. Sorry, mates, if that gets under your skin. It's not a free pass for unprofessional shenanigans.

The very reason why Dallas and I toss darts at each other from opposite ends of Los Angeles.

The drive from El Segundo to his house is short by LA standards. Dallas texted me this morning with a photo of my lighter tucked behind the potted topiary on his doorstep. I never provided an ETA for my arrival because he is the last person I want to see. My plan is a thirty-yard dash. Car to door and back to the car.

I park down the street like last time and shake off a shiver on the sidewalk. It's chilly, as it often is close to the water when the June gloom hangs around. The light is low and flat, almost identical to the afternoon Dallas invited me to his office years ago. A decade has zipped by, just like that, but somehow it feels like yesterday when I stood in awe of the shiny glass empire of Evener Equity on a tree-lined street in Santa Monica. I remember staring past the soaring Doric columns flanking the entrance at the quote chiseled on a marble plaque high above the doors.

There are no failures in life, just results.

Elation soared in my heart when I read those words. I lived and breathed that principle. And I had high hopes for Dallas and me after our chance encounter at a Hollywood bar. We clicked right away. Both of us upstarts. Fresh off early wins. Two finance nerds talking deep into the night about valuations and the pathology of big deals, topics the average person would go cross-eyed listening to. How could I not fall in puppy love with him? Camaraderie like that comes along once in a blue moon.

And then…

I shut my eyes and try not to think of the tingle I felt yesterday looking at the photo of my lighter in Dallas's hand. I remember how smooth and soft his skin felt when it touched mine. How thoroughly besotted I was. How…

Stop it, June! Get the damn lighter and blast.

Right. It is probably best to draw a veil over that moment in my life. I was nervy; Dallas was in his element. All I need to do here is carry on. I beeline for his house, walking on tiptoes up to the door so the sound of my heels doesn't ring out. Thankfully, the only thing I encounter on his doorstep is the wisteria swaying in the westerly wind, and my lighter. An elastic band is wrapped around it, holding a business card in place.

A lump expands inside my throat.

It's a card for Mélisse, the Michelin-starred restaurant in Santa Monica where we were supposed to have dinner before the afternoon went tits up in his boardroom.

I snap off the elastic to skim his message written on the flipside of the card.

If you ever want any weed, the good stuff, call me. DE.

A thin, disturbed laugh leaks out. What does it say about me when two different men suggest I take drugs? And how can substances help wrangle a solution when every time I pull up a patch of yoga mat and shut my eyes, a fresh list of fifty things to do fills my brain? If I cannot control my mind in a regular state, how on earth am I supposed to manage it on another plane of existence?

But Cliff is right.

I need to find a solution.

For my employees to think I am uncaring is the cruelest thing imaginable.

I hurry back to my car and glance at the clock on the dashboard. Five thirty. Plan A is to waste ninety minutes of my life in Friday night traffic. Or…

I open my handbag and dig out the shrooms. Upend the contents to fill my palm. I sniff them, recoiling at the dank, musty smell. They look innocuous. Hell, I've munched through a plate of grilled portobellos four times this size. And Cliff said these were lightweight.

In the distance, just visible through the windshield, cars slowly motor up and down Washington Boulevard. My pool table has been out of commission all week while the felt gets replaced, and the itch to play hums on my skin. Why not eat some mushrooms, rinse them down with a frosty vodka tonic at the Blue Moon, and shoot a few rounds while waiting for a higher power to show me the way?

Plan B.

Go big or go home, right?

Chapter Five

AT FIRST GLANCE, NOTHING HAS CHANGED. THE OLD-TIMERS WITH whiskered faces nurse watery drinks and chew the fat. A permanent haze of burger grease hangs like LA pollution. Reviews cite the Blue Moon's vintage vibe as 'off the charts,' although I suspect they're generously referring to the faded decor rather than the floor, which is still covered in dust bunnies. Nothing has changed, save for me. And I feel the vibration of that in the dozen pairs of curious eyes following me as I approach the bar.

A Givenchy dress and winged Sophia Webster heels are seen here about as often as pork chops at a bar mitzvah.

A woman with green hair struggles with righting a beer keg behind the counter. After an impressive string of foul words, she telepathically clocks my presence, lifts her head, and smiles like her missing front tooth is the latest fashion statement.

"Well, I'll be damned!" she says, eyes lighting up with her smile. "Jumper June. It has been a long, hot minute."

I smile back quizzically, the pieces of who she is slow to triangulate in my mind. "Brenda?"

"New and improved," she says, flexing a decent bicep.

The former two hundred pounds of lovable Tennessee pride found a gym, even though she swore she would never set foot in one. But her trademark overalls and sassy attitude are in full flight.

"You look fab," I say. "Love the 'do. It matches your eyes."

"Oh, shucks, girl," she says, waving her hand coquettishly. "What's your secret, cos you get prettier every year. And you got that look on your face."

"Is it that obvious?"

Brenda chuckles and scans the half-empty bar. "No victims here yet, but I'll send them in for execution as they arrive. Tables are free, so take your pick. The usual to start?"

I smile back. "You remember?"

Nostalgia warms me, thinking of the good times we shared. Brenda offered me love advice, and I dispensed financial advice. She took it upon herself to be my mole, tipping me off to the drunk poseurs I could sucker into losing at pool.

And I tipped her back for the intel.

"How can I forget my favorite customer?" Brenda asks. "And not just cos you tip well." She winks and starts lining up a row of highball glasses. "Y'all get back there and destress. I'll be with ya in a minute."

The dingy, falling-apart charm of the windowless back room is what real estate agents would label a fixer-upper. The pool tables once had a nap, and the cues are more crooked than politicians. I roll the best of the worst along the worn felt, and it merrily *thump-thumps*. It makes no difference for a pool shark like me. I work with what I have.

And I have spent roughly two percent of my life hustling in this room.

I got this, as Vandana would say.

After I rack the balls, Brenda arrives with a tray of six fizzing drinks.

"You usually ended up north of four anyway," she explains off my surprised look. "The night's still young. Sip and savor." She lines up the glasses on one of the highboy tables clustered against the wall. "Holler if you need me."

Hmm. Do alcohol and mushrooms mix? Nebbiolo and risotto con fungi are a dream pairing that never fails, so why not? Besides, I feel nothing other than a disgusting taste coating my mouth. I rinse away the mushroom foulness with a deep drink of alcohol, swirling the vodka around like its mouthwash. Instantly, I feel better. Focused and ready. I step up to the table like I've done a thousand times.

Father taught me how to play pool, or should I say, he kicked my arse whenever he could. The only emotion he ever showed was a fist pump after every win. But his bitter frown on the day I beat him with a jump shot that became my namesake remains forever planted in my memory.

Men. All the same. They cannot handle a woman coming out on top.

I line up the break.

A rush of euphoria fills my veins.

June the Jumper.

It's time to fly.

$

THIRTY MINUTES LATER, I am playing magically varied shots and seeing everything in 5D. Booze must go hand in hand with mushrooms because I have downed four of the six drinks and feel invincible. Tight but loose. Business has picked up in the main bar area, and a lone Karaoke superstar warbles the lyrics to "Crazy in Love."

I block out all the noise to line up on the black ball. This baby is getting hammered into the far pocket. I can do this shot in my sleep.

I pull back, the slick wood of the cue caressing the skin between my fingers and thumb. The cue ball looks bigger than a beach ball. I can't stop grinning. I am an unstoppable force on mushrooms.

Seconds before I unleash, a gang of bros in loose shorts and basketball jerseys shuffle in noisily from the bar area. Two Black guys who have an affable charm about them. A muscled Latino inked with tattoos. The tallest fellow cradles a basketball in the nook of his arm and…

Dallas?

My heart stumbles. An intense desire to stop his eyes from piercing through me manifests into a slow-motion whiff of the cue. As it rises up and off my thumb and clatters onto the felt, the only thing missing is a *Noooooo!*

Dallas smirks. Of course.

"Hi," he says.

His buddies peer at me through the dirty light. On a good day, the kind of women who populate these beer-soaked floors are better known as broads. They cannot process me.

"What are you doing here?" I ask, not the stupidest question of the day, but close, given the beers and baskets of fries they've brought with them.

"I was going to ask you the same thing."

"I picked up my lighter and came here to shoot a few rounds." Why am I trembling? Stop trembling!

"You should have called," he says.

"That would've meant I wanted to see you."

One of the Black guys titters and nudges Dallas with his elbow. "This the one giving you grief?"

Without taking his eyes off me, Dallas says, "She's a piece of work, isn't she?"

"And a fine piece of ass," the Latino guy lisps. "You described her bang on."

The b-ball boys burst into raucous laughter, proud of their ability to act like idiots. Who are these homies? Simps that he carts around for validation? They position themselves on stools surrounding a highboy table like a show is about to start. Dallas and his crew have inserted themselves into my evening like he is trying to insert himself into my deal.

"I suppose that's the nicest thing you've said about me today," I say, challenging him to disagree.

Dallas shrugs, his smile practically glittering. "It's not my fault you're beautiful."

What? Am I hearing things? Yesterday, I swore his voice curled around the word when he said I had a beautiful face. And now it's happened again. I think. Or rather, thinking is just beyond my grasp.

Now that I've stopped playing, everything looks sparkly. I feel like I'm radioactive and glowing green.

Dallas tips his head to the cue I whiffed with. "Still on the learning curve? I could give you a few pointers."

His eyes dance all over me. I feel a prickly rush of want. Shorts and a wife-beater make him weirdly hotter.

"How kind of you to offer," I say.

"Why don't we play best of three?" He offs his beer glass onto the table and yanks a cue from the wall mount. "You win, I'll pay your bar tab. I win, we go back to my place for a drink."

I pin him with a look. "Perhaps I wasn't clear when I said I didn't want to see you. That also means I'm not drinking with you at your house."

Dallas dusts chalk onto his cue with a bemused expression. "What's it going to be then?"

A chorus of *Ooos* erupts from his peanut gallery. I know exactly what they're thinking—*Down the bitch and make her your bitch*. In another universe, where my back wasn't up against the wall and my employees weren't a step away from mutiny, I would place my usual bet. Walk out of here five hundred dollars richer. In the case of Dallas, I could milk him for a grand, easy. But the stakes are higher than my usual shark attack. And he's trying to milk me for way more.

Maybe I have low standards.

Or maybe I have none at all.

I march into his space with bravado. "Why don't you put your money where your mouth is? You win, we do the deal on your terms. I win, you get ownership and zero percent."

Dallas cocks his head. It takes a few seconds for the coordination of words and meaning to sink in. When the realization hits, a crafty gleam rises in his eyes. "Twenty percent."

"Ten," I counter.

"Fifteen."

"Twelve. And that's my final offer."

He laughs and glances at his friends, who smugly anticipate a swift beatdown. "Twelve it is."

"Shake on it?"

I stick my hand out and watch his smirk die on the vine. He searches my face as if I'm not of sound mind.

If only he knew.

"This is real, June," he warns. "I'm holding you to this."

I thrust my hand out with great determination or stupidity, take your pick. For a fleeting moment, his expression leads me to believe he's genuinely having second thoughts. Then he threads his fingers through mine, and I inhale sharply. My entire body feels as if it's opening up to some strange new sensation. Or that someone is tickling the inside of my tummy. Dallas watches my reaction, more curious than anything. I need to shake it off and focus because the edges of the room start to blur. How I react is critical because he is so going down.

I reclaim my hand, grab the triangular rack, and clunk it against his wall of pecs. "Rack the balls, please."

$

THE ART of the pool hustle is to fake out your opponent. Give them hope by missing no-brainer shots. Admire their skills while plotting five shots ahead to eventually wipe the floor with them. Dallas gallantly allows me to break first and I make a right mess of it on purpose. He struts up to the table to clear the triangle of balls that have barely moved and calls for the eleven into the side pocket.

Crack. Down she goes.

Hmm.

He hits with authority, more than most guys I scam. In less than a minute he's sunk three balls, narrowly missing a fourth. His boys are hooting remarks and order another round from Brenda who winks at me—*you got this schmuck.*

But do I?

The vodka tonic's have gone down like water and my head swims. I risk blowing one more shot, leaving Dallas nothing to work with. Thankfully, he flubs the bank shot. I line up my next shot, a difficult angle to kiss the eight into the side pocket. Half in shadows at the far end of the table, Dallas drains his beer. He says nothing, but I can sense the concern.

Too bad for him.

I suffered from nerves closing out Father the first time but have never looked back since.

By the time I jump the cue ball over the three to sink the black in the final game, Dallas and his cocky smile have disappeared. Like his posse, who slunk out to the main bar at the end of the second game to let their man die in private.

I drop my cue on the table, feeling nothing but pride. I never allowed him another shot since his botched bank attempt.

"Looks like we have a deal at twelve percent," I say.

Arms crossed, Dallas grumbles, "Disclosure isn't part of your vocabulary, is it Miss Shark?"

"I like to call it the art of negotiation."

I reach for my drink, but my depth of field has vanished. The glass crashes onto the floor in an explosion of diamond shards. Uh, oh.

Dallas looks at me with a funny expression. "Are you feeling okay?"

"I feel great. Why?" I ask, although I hear it now: my words slurring together.

"Because you've knocked back a few and your pupils are huge," he says.

I smile although it feels like my lips are sliding onto the floor. "And I still beat you. I hope that doesn't sting too much."

His face is moving in and out of focus, breaking up into little pieces. The pumping honky-tonk from the bar sounds like a marching band has taken up residence in my head. I mistake the tingling sensation in my body as lingering triumph, but when I take a step back, it's as if someone swapped their feet with mine. If Dallas and his lightning-fast reactions hadn't steadied me, I'd be sprawled on my arse. His warm hands grip both my biceps and he murmurs something that sounds like a question, remaining crouched and holding me tight, long enough that I understand he is waiting for some reply.

My words come out as thick as refrigerated molasses. "I'm, I'm fine. I just need…"

A whirlpool of fractals spins around like I'm in the middle of a rainbow tornado. I stand and stagger past him to feel my way along the wall to the loo. The music pulses in rhythm with my exploding heart. I hear him calling out my name, the sound of it becoming fainter.

Oh boy.

All I need is to close my eyes and rest.

Five minutes.

$

Boom, boom, boom.

The reverberations thump in my brain. They rattle up my spine. Stop, please!

"June? Can you hear me? It's Brenda."

Boom, boom, boom.

"Do you need help, hon? I can crawl under the door."

I feel like I weigh a thousand pounds. And what is that smell? My eyes flutter open, and for a few panicked seconds, I have no clue where I am. Then, my surroundings bleed into focus. Oh, dear God. Slumped on the throne with my dress hiked and knickers flopped around my ankles?

"June! I'm coming in if you don't say anything."

A weak croak slips out of my dry lips. "I'm … I'm okay."

"Are you sure?"

It takes supreme effort to stand, one hand on the wall for support. I kick away my knickers (not bending down to retrieve them feeling like this) and paw at the silver door latch. Christ. They design these things to be idiot-proof but they're clearly not mushroom-proof.

I eventually escape and stumble into a surprised Brenda.

"Woah," she mutters, wide-eyed at the tragedy of me. "Tippled back a few too many, huh? Time to get presentable. A guy outside is awfully worried about you. He asked me to come in here and check on you." She slings an arm around my waist and steers me to the sink. "Gotta say, that hunk makes George Clooney look like a hobo. I see him in here all the time with nothing but dudes. Not surprised you caught his eye."

Who is she talking about? And any man with 20/20 would run away screaming from this version of me. I am a pitiful sight. Face bedraggled and clammy, pupils the size of dinner plates. The pale blue silk of my dress rumpled beyond hope.

"I need to go home," I mumble.

Brenda dabs my face with a wet paper towel. "Sure thing, hon. I'll call an Uber."

We emerge from the restroom, and Dallas rushes toward us. "Jesus. Are you okay?"

Right. Dallas. We played pool. But why is he still here?

"She's a little rough around the edges," I hear Brenda say. "Not how she usually rolls. Can you watch her while I call an Uber? This number cannot get behind a wheel tonight."

"I can take her home," he says. "We know each other. We work in the same industry."

Brenda shoots me a guarded look and asks slowly, like I'm a five-year-old with learning differences, "Hon, do you know this guy?"

I squint at Dallas—a line of concern etched on his forehead, lips pressed together, and eyes soft for once. Something passes between us.

"Yeah, I know him."

"Is it cool if he takes you home?" Brenda sounds extremely unconvinced.

Suddenly exhausted and ready to crash, I mumble, "It's fine."

Brenda never doubted my word, so she leans into this disaster and wraps up the night.

"In that case," she says to Dallas, "her car is parked out front. You better move it tonight, they love to tow around here. And we need to exchange information before you go. I want your phone number and a shot of your ID. Text me when you get there. If I don't hear from you, I'm calling the cops. What's your name?"

"Dallas Evener. I'll send photo evidence of her safe at home if you need it."

"My handbag…" I squint at the floor, looking for it.

"I got it here, hon," Brenda reassures. "You go home and sleep it off. Catch you on the next round."

The collection of pixels that is Brenda disappears into nothing. It's just me and Dallas and a room spinning out of control. I lean against the wall to steady myself.

"Last I recall, you could hold your liquor," he says.

I stand there, eyes closed, lost in the outer space of my head. "I blame the mushrooms."

"Mushrooms?" He chuckles, almost to himself. "Is this your usual Friday night out?"

My brow furrows. "Didn't you tell me I needed to relax?"

Or was that someone else? Fuck, I can't remember. Even standing is too much effort. I slide down the wall onto my haunches. Breathe in a deep gulp of air.

"June, you are trashed. Time to go home, champ." Dallas crouches in front of me and says, "C'mere. Hold onto my arms."

He lifts one of my hands and then the other, encouraging me to grip his forearms. His muscles feel tight and warm, safe and able-bodied, as he slowly lifts me to standing. Overcome with sudden vertigo, I weave on my heels.

"Are you okay to walk?" he asks, the smell of beer on his breath making me light-headed.

"Sure," I mutter, and face plant onto his chest.

He stiffens but circles one arm around my waist to hold me flush against him. A lifetime seems to come and go, my nose buried in his wife-beater to inhale the sweet fragrance of his skin.

"Mmm," I mumble, feeling smaller than my already tiny frame wrapped in the curl of his arm. "You smell good. I remember you smelling good." I press the weight of my breasts against his warmth and feel, more than hear, the sharp intake of his breath. The soft flesh of my waist squeezes between his fingers. His chest quivers.

"What are you doing?" he whispers.

A foolish question when his thickness swells against my stomach.

Christ, a decent cock. Grade A. It fills me with urgency. I slide my hand between his thighs.

"I'm not wearing my knickers so … you know."

His supple skin tenses before he jerks his hips away. "June," he says, in a rough, strained voice. "Don't."

I lay both hands against the expanse of his chest. On tiptoes, wobbling, I crane my pursed lips higher so he can reciprocate. *Why not?* I want to ask. Am I not fantastically alluring and imminently shaggable? More importantly, were we not destined to end up here?

But nothing comes out of my mouth. Not words, anyway.

Something hot and liquid in my belly turns violent.

Oh, shit.

Chapter Six

DALLAS

"SHE THREW UP ON YOU?" PERCHED ON THE CORNER OF MY DESK IN A violet pantsuit, vice president of Evener Equity and self-proclaimed bad-ass Black woman Nikki Robichaux asks this with her nose wrinkled in disgust. "And then you drove her home in her car and put her to bed?"

She sizes me up in a way that suggests I might be suffering from a brain injury. More handsome than pretty, Nikki is the kind of woman whose gaze turns capable men into flustered idiots. She is also endlessly cynical when it comes to all things Dallas Evener and women.

I lean back in my chair and cross both sneakers on my desk. "What should I have done?" I argue. "Stuff her in an Uber and wave goodbye? She was totally out of it. Imagine if something had happened to her on the way home. I did the right thing."

"Lord almighty," she mutters. "And here I thought there was

nothing you could say to surprise me. Please tell me nothing happened at her house."

"*She* tried to kiss *me*, in case you missed that salient point."

She snorts a laugh. "Because that line of defense always holds up in court."

Think Kerry Washington from *Scandal* meets Serena Williams, and you get why I hired Nikki. She holds my feet to the fire every time. Mind you, the story of last night does sound dubious in the light of a new day. And I haven't told Nikki about the crazy parts yet. Don't think I will either, based on her reaction so far.

"Why are you making me sound like a criminal?"

"On that note," she says, "is now the time to ask how you know where she lives? Because it feels like the right time."

Under her scrutiny, I plead the fifth. But I know everything about June Allison, including everything I had to pay a private investigator for.

"You know what they say: keep your friends close and enemies closer."

She rolls her eyes, slides her butt off my desk, and wanders over to the bank of windows behind me in the only pair of sensible pumps Giuseppe Zanotti ever made. I hope she is admiring the view of Santa Monica. A silent, thinking Nikki scares me more than a start-up company with zero prospects.

Without looking at me, she says, "D-Man, how long have I worked for you?"

"Ten years. And forty-three days."

"And your obsession with June has been a thing that entire time."

I lift one eyebrow at her choice of noun. If forced to put my aberrant enthusiasm for all things June into words, *legally acceptable preoccupation* is the ideal way to describe it. God, she is an annoying, sexy bitch. Why does it have to be her, the lone bombshell in LA who embraces her curves instead of starving them into nonexistence? If I confessed that I get off solely by imagining her face on every woman I sleep with, would she finally fucking forgive me?

"Obsession is a bit of a stretch," I say.

Nikki studies me in silence. For those five seconds, we are warriors fighting the same battle. The only freak shows in the office on a Saturday morning.

"We haven't raised a single dime for our new fund," she says. "Even your slick ass needs a year to bag a hundred million. June needs forty of that like, yesterday. Call me crazy, but your game plan sucks in that there isn't one. You better rethink your strategy."

I respond with the focused patience that bugs the hell out of every jumpy entrepreneur eager for me to fulfill their dreams. "My strategy is unilateral and unwavering. Go after the gold. An opportunity like this comes around once a decade, if that. June's company checks all the boxes: patents, a viable market, leadership with smarts." I list these points off using my fingers. "It's a goddamned unicorn."

I chase the miracles, like everyone else in this business. But I never have, nor will I ever, go groveling. Not even to the Siren, the only woman—only person—who has picked more winners than I have.

A sore spot. More sore than I care to admit.

"And this has nothing to do with the fact we haven't had a monster hit since Leostrata?" Nikki asks, hitting me where it hurts. "That the bloom has come off the rose, and you are feeling the pressure?"

A muscle twitches in my chest. I need that reminder like the world needs another Hitler. "I am aware," I reply, "of all of that."

"Is that why you accepted less? Twelve percent doesn't come close to covering our costs."

"Generals do not back down with a victory in their sight line," I say, irritated that she needs me to spell it out. Not to mention, the word *less* gets bandied around here about as often as *yoga retreats.* More importantly, I haven't shared the news that Evener Equity got swindled into accepting less last night because we got our asses kicked at pool. "I know it's not my nature to take less," I add. "But June is up shit creek without a paddle. I can patch together forty mil if push comes to shove."

The cold truth? I would have better luck finding a rock to squeeze money out of. Tainted companies are like two-bit Vegas hookers, and no one wants to catch an STD. And the Cliff Sassen scandal is an infectious disease without an immediate cure. Not even my turn-a-blind-eye Russians will touch this one. But hell if I'm admitting defeat. Not before I turn over every rock.

Payback is an underrated motivator.

And Nikki has me figured out. She always does.

"Might I remind you," she says, planting her butt again on the Chippendale desk like my heated Sotheby's battle against a Hong Kong billionaire to own the slab of creaky wood means nothing, "there is no proof it was her who ratted Sonny out."

I open my mouth, only to snap it shut. This argument is as old as time. I have clung to my belief that June masterminded the sting operation that almost ruined my reputation. Never doubted otherwise until last night. Leave it to June, high as a kite, to create a whole new level of mess in my head. But I need to dig deeper to validate what she revealed.

In the interim, I run with my usual counterargument.

"Who else could it have been?" I ask Nikki. "And whose side are you on, anyway? She cost me—us—millions. We were this close to being permanently sunk. Not to mention, the next time we see Sonny Burnett, he'll be eighty. If he gets parole."

"He deserves to be in jail," Nikki says. With less thunder in her tone, she adds, "And I'm not saying our deals are squeaky clean when it comes to funding, but—"

"You knew what you were getting into from day one," I interrupt, weight behind my words.

Silence.

I might be a merciless asshole, but I have never lied to her.

"I did," she says, owning it. "And no one has ever accused me of being Snow Black. I had two kids, a deadbeat husband, and bills to pay." She shifts her weight from foot to foot as if juggling what to say next. "That being said," she continues, "June is not me. Word on the street says she is a straight arrow."

"This isn't about *her*," I grumble.

Nikki throws up her hands. "While you sit here and pretend denial is not a river in Egypt, I'm gonna go home, work out, and then get ready for my hot date."

"Man or woman?" I ask, quick to pounce on the change of topic.

Nikki hesitates. I only know about her recent pivot in the relationship department after I stumbled upon her making out in the parking lot with a woman she introduced as Susan, who looked suspiciously like a former Steve.

"A woman who identifies as a man."

"And your kids are cool?" I ask.

"Cooler than most of the tight-asses who work here," she says with a laugh.

"I hope it works out. You deserve the best."

She smiles, surprised. I don't show my appreciation enough. "Thanks, boss. Remember that in December when we talk bonuses. And by the way," she adds, "your hairstylist did a great job covering up that grey."

I run a hand self-consciously over my recent dye job. Salt started to creep in last year, and I hate to sound vain, but my life flashed before my eyes when it did. Thirty-five is eons away from old, but after you reach the pinnacle with nowhere else to go, that weight can make you feel ancient. One silver hair and my entire legacy came into question. Who would remember me, and for what? Would anyone show up at my funeral? What words would get chiseled onto my tombstone?

He was a cutthroat cunt who died with the most money.

Hardly the stuff of dreams.

I sweep the thought aside and thank Nikki for the compliment. "My hair has a reputation to uphold."

In a long, evaluating stare, her default expression of suspicion morphs into something more alarming.

Sympathy.

"Your hair has a better reputation than you do, D-Man. You have five homes scattered around the world and never spent more than a week with the same woman in any of them. Maybe it's time to rethink your nature. On every level."

I sigh and rub my temples. When Nikki starts to suggest that inner-life reflections will save me from myself, it's time to call it.

"Get the fuck out of here. Please."

"Love you too," she says, blowing me a kiss. Halfway out the door, she suddenly stops. "Oh, I almost forgot. While you were at the gym, a guy named Navarro something-or-other called? Said you know him and have his number."

My fingertips turn to ice against either side of my brain. I lick my suddenly dry lips and still choke on the words. "Navarro d'Amico?"

Nikki tilts her head. "Should I know him? His name doesn't ring a bell."

"I met him years ago," I say vaguely, fixating my gaze on the rug. Anything to avoid eye contact. "We both studied at Oxford."

In the awkward silence, Nikki senses there is something I am not saying; how strange the air has become. But she is wise enough to know when to let sleeping dogs lie.

"Ah, that makes sense," she says. "He sounded European. A bit la-di-da. Anyhoo, time to bounce. Do not bunk up in here all afternoon plotting, k? Later."

The door clicks shut, and alone, locked in my office, the bubble of emotion inside me feels familiar and disturbing. My legs are shaking when I pull them off the desk.

How weird is this? First Chavez, and now Navarro?

I rake both hands through my hair and move to the window, eyes not charting anything. Life was on its uneventful trajectory toward meaningless glory last week, and then my buddy Chavez Delgado calls. He owes me big-time for his payout on Leostrata. As it turns out, his fiancée Flynn is best friends with June. Chavez let slip that June's company was in hot water and asked if I would meet with her.

Duh, motherfucker. Does a pig live in shit?

That Chavez kid is savvy, but he also looks up to me, and I am smart enough to know when to play dumb. June funded her company with private equity, given her dislike for VCs. (Or for me, specifically.) So I asked Chavez, innocently, what was going on. My industry thrives on insider information, and since few can resist spilling it, Chavez gave me all the details I threw at June the other morning. The sick sense of vindication I felt when all the blood drained from her face proved my point. She knows better. Lie to me, and I will eat you for breakfast. The art of war and all that.

But then last night.

The things she confessed to.

The things she asked me to do.

Goddamn!

My fist lands with a *thud* against the window. Half of the things she muttered in the dark of her bedroom made my dick swell so hard it hurt.

And it still hurts.

I press my painful erection onto the pane of cold glass separating me from another endless sunny morning and force myself to think. For Navarro to surface at this precise moment leaves a strange taste in my mouth. The shady underworld he calls home has an endless mountain of cash in desperate need of laundering. A hundred million? If I asked for twice that, it would land in our accounts by noon tomorrow. A no-brainer on every level except one.

And June, tight-assed, virtuous, ethical do-gooder and current threat to my fucking sanity that she is, would find her mouth shaped into an O perfect enough for me to cram my shaft inside it if she knew Dallas Evener did have morals, corrupted as they may be.

Because once you get in bed with the mafia, good luck getting out without cement overshoes.

Even I know that.

This, however, is an unprecedented situation. A chance for a record-shattering deal to leave Leostrata in the dust and my name permanently etched in the stars as one of the greats. A chance to be in the same room with June without her looking at me like I am a piece of shit.

A chance to try again.

After a five-minute search, I unearth Navarro's phone number from a filing cabinet I keep locked 24/7. (I'm smart enough not to keep it on my phone.) He inked his number on a cocktail napkin years ago after an uncomfortable dinner at a Michelin-starred restaurant in New York, where the food was neither the draw nor the point of our meeting. A week later, he sent me a letter and a photograph.

I buried all three together because it felt safer—all my skeletons in one place.

I skim the one sentence Navarro wrote in his fanciful script, and before my morning burrito curdles in my stomach, I stuff the photo that accompanied the note back inside the envelope. Every ounce of anxiety he left me with years ago resurfaces. I walk with heavy steps to my desk, lower into the chair, and fidget with the napkin, folding and unfolding it, my blood pressure slowly ticking higher. Like Nikki, I also have a date to get to, although twenty more minutes pass before I decide to make the call.

Chapter Seven

JUNE

I AM, OF COURSE, LATE FOR BRUNCH.

Hungover and on edge in the aftermath of a night I remember nothing about. Dallas played a role, but the details elude me. I vaguely recall shaking his hand and a feeling of triumph after we played pool. But something I stumbled upon this morning in my kitchen sunk my heart. And all the little hairs on my neck bristle to attention the minute I set foot inside Luc's Brasserie.

The pending excitement of decadent foie gras Eggs Benedict?

I wish.

The egregious offense is my besties sitting next to each other.

The unspoken rule is that I sit between them. I am the mediator. The one who fluffs Vandana when the bluntness of Flynn cuts too deep. The caring soul protecting Flynn whenever Vandana's endless mothering of her reaches a crisis point.

And why are there two empty seats remaining at the table?

Vandana sees me first and waves. She has inevitably claimed the seat with a sweeping view of the celebrity landscape

"So good to see you, babes," she gushes, hugging me tight against her runway model frame.

Forever perfect, this morning Vandana has it dialed up to an eleven. Flawless makeup. Raven hair in her favored topknot ponytail. The latest Gucci number lint-rollered before she stepped out of the car to drop the jaw of every man because she makes Margot Robbie look homely.

Flynn butts in to steal me into another embrace. Chestnut curls flowing past her shoulders and toned legs showcased in a short emerald dress, she glows like any woman would if she were shagged nightly by Chavez.

And on that note, I cycle through hellos with the men of the hour. Morgan of the geometrically perfect face and sun-swept hair. Blond and dreamy. Almost inaccessibly hot. And then Chavez. His beguiling mix of Spanish and Mexican heritage created a pouty-lipped elegance his legion of female fans goes berserk over. Tack on the insane body of an athlete in his prime, piercing blue eyes that scream genetic anomaly, and the sexy swagger of a pirate … All I can say is my besties' baes are a duo of stunning contrasts who make a compelling case for three-ways.

Not that I ever would partake. My only experience with a ménage à trois ended on a strange note. Once bitten, twice shy.

"Is this where I sit?" I ask Vandana, pointing to my demoted seat assignment.

"Do forgive me," Vandana says, eyeing Morgan as one does when they are in on your secret, "but we are killing two birds with one stone today. Morgan has a new client—"

"Pending client," Morgan corrects, his lovely French accent floating like a feather in the air.

"Soon to be client," Vandana emphasizes. "And since he lives here *and* knows Chavez, we thought, why not invite him?"

In response to all our eyeballs landing squarely on him, Chavez treats us to an adorably perplexed smile. "Me? I don't know anyone in the market for a yacht."

Oh great, I think. I'm trapped beside a geezer who will mistake my silence as an encouragement to hear more about engines and fiberglass hulls.

Vandana suddenly snaps to attention, her gaze crossing the packed room of Hollywood power brokers.

"He's here," she says, breathless like the world's biggest movie star just strolled in and not...

"Dallas!" She waves to steal his attention from the hostess he's chatting with, completely unaware of Flynn and me quietly dying.

Her eyes swamped with mortification, Flynn mouths to me, "I had no idea."

Yes, our mystery guest is Dallas.

The Dallas who left his business card on my kitchen counter with *Call me* written on the back, followed by *I'll fill in all the blanks for you, partner.*

The Dallas who drove my wrecked arse home and ... ???

My stomach was in knots this morning, sitting on my deck, head in my hands, wracking my brain for any smidge of recall. To the best of my knowledge, Dallas didn't take advantage of me. Not in that way. I fingered myself and sniffed for semen. Checked for crusties on the sheets and my body. Dug through every garbage can on the hunt for a wad of sticky Kleenex. Nothing.

And because I did not call him and all the blanks remain unfilled, before he makes his way over and this brunch becomes a full-scale disaster, my only option is to hide.

But where?

My mind goes blank.

It's fight or flight.

I drop my clutch, and thank Christ that I'm short and wearing a dress with some give in it. Both are helpful to burrow out of sight under the table. But as soon as I'm one with the tiled floor and watching my friends rise to their feet to greet Dallas, fresh panic grips me. As if no one will question my disappearance. Or the scent of Angel eau de parfum wafting up from below.

Sure enough, Vandana pokes me with her stiletto, quiet urgency in her whisper. "June! What are you doing?"

"Hey, buddy!" I can hear Dallas greeting Chavez with a bro clap on his back. "Or should I say champ? Epic win at the French. I watched every minute of the match."

"Thanks, man."

Chavez then introduces Flynn as his fiancée, who pulls off a reasonably friendly greeting. Next up is Morgan, who thanks Dallas for making the time to meet. Vandana goes on and on about how beautiful his suit is before the toe of her shoe digs into my flesh a second time.

Dammit.

I missed my window to escape.

And now I have to play it cool. I take a breath to steady my nerves and tell myself this is not ideal, but neither is it necessarily terminal. I dropped my bag. No big deal.

Except everyone stares at me as I crawl back out and smooth the front of my dress. Every politician would pay good money for my fake and believable smile. Never mind that my face is aflame.

"Hello."

Dallas blinks. Then his half-amused smile spreads into a shit-eating one that barely fits on his face. "June Allison. What a surprise."

"Ah, shit." Chavez thumps the heel of his hand against his forehead. "I totally forgot to ask. How did the meeting go?" His eyes flit between me and Dallas while Flynn flushes bright red, clearly having said nothing.

"You two know each other?" Vandana asks innocently, when she damn well knows our history. Dallas says to me with a lift of his brow, *The floor is all yours.*

"We run in the same circles," I say.

"Of course," Morgan interjects. "Start-ups and venture capital go hand in hand, no?"

"Remember on my first trip to Europe, Morgan and I went to a yacht party in Genoa?" Vandana poses this question to me and Flynn. "It was Dallas's yacht. And now he's upgrading, or considering an update," she's quick to add, "with Morgan. Small world, right? How amazing that we're now all connected."

She beams and motions for Dallas to sit next to me. He lowers onto the chair, smiling like the cat who ate the canary. "I can't think of anything better."

"Yes," I say, inching as far away from him as I can while remaining in my seat. "Amazing."

Flynn signals with her eyes that if I need help, she'll do whatever it takes.

"You two should totally talk," Vandana blathers on. "June is always looking for money."

For once, I think, *please shut it.*

Thankfully, a waitress appears and hands out menus, reciting today's specials. She leaves with our coffee orders while Vandana skims the menu, oblivious to the tension radiating off me like solar flares.

"Everything they make is divine, Dallas," she says, "but we love the French toast."

I already know what I want but pretend to read all the letters swarming on the page. My heartbeat refuses to quiet down. The primordial, masculine mass sitting beside me smells rich, dark, and smoky. A tumbler of golden scotch on a crisp winter's night.

I reach for my water. My mouth is dry as dust.

"I was thinking about the mushroom omelet," Dallas says casually. "June, what do you think?"

Having just taken a monster sip of aqua, I start to cough, then choke, spewing droplets all over the table.

"Are you okay?" Chavez thumps my spine while I gasp and wheeze.

Vandana, brows knitted due to my streak of unbecoming behavior, cannot fathom why on earth Dallas is asking my opinion on omelets.

I hiss under my breath at Dallas, "Do not say *anything.*"

"From what I hear, venture capital is a challenging industry," Morgan says to Dallas. "What is the secret to your success?"

Dallas sets his menu down and crosses one leg over the other in a practiced, elegant motion. His suit is to die for. Cut from a shimmering blue-black fabric that probably costs a thousand dollars a yard.

"I love what I do," he says. "To help shape the destiny of the world through change, through the companies I fund … It's a powerful thing."

Morgan nods, impressed. Even I have to admit that is a gold-standard sound bite.

Chavez leans into the conversation. "It must be exciting to work with entrepreneurs and all their cool ideas."

"They can also be a pain in the ass," Dallas says, and I'm offended that he glances at me. "But yeah. The rapid pace, the energy and creativity that flows to me. It's addictive."

"Was your decision to stay away from Silicon Valley a deliberate ploy?" Vandana inquires.

"Yes and no," he says. "Don't get me wrong, the guys on Sand Hill Road are rock solid. But entrepreneurs do the death march from one office to the next up there, and you can't tell the difference between any of them. They all sound the same. Look the same. Pack mentality is a dangerous thing. Personality is key in this industry because entrepreneurs have a choice."

"Yes, they do," I say pointedly.

"But in the end," he continues, ignoring me, "it's not just about the money. They also need to ask: Do I want this guy on my board? Does he get the big picture? Will we have a good time together? You want to have fun while doing it."

"'Being a VC is the most fun you can have with your clothes on,'" I add. "Isn't that your famous quote?"

Dallas eyes me coolly. "One of them. *Time* magazine, 2021," he says, smiling at Vandana. "Man of the Year."

Vandana is agog. She can hardly stand it. Fame makes her world go round. "Morgan feels the same about yacht design," she says. "He wants his clients to enjoy every step of the process. We would be so honored to work with you."

"Where *do* you get your money from?" Flynn asks, forever the shit disturber.

Vandana frowns. Flynn might as well have asked the Pope how often he has sex.

Dallas rolls with it, smooth as vanilla cream. "Various sources," he says. "Pension funds, foundations, corporations. Tennis players, once in a while."

Chavez stretches his arm across the table to high-five Dallas with enthusiasm. "Leostrata, man. I owe you forever. Fucking best investment ever."

"And don't forget your shady Russians," I chime in. "Cartels, insider trading profits. The occasional dictator."

Crickets.

A dark and chilly universe of no sound.

Flynn stares at me wordlessly, and Vandana holds a slightly pained expression, her jaw so rigid a little muscle is visible.

Dallas assesses the situation and seems to wager he's best served by playing the gallant man. "If the markets started to ask where all the money comes from, the global economy would skid to a halt."

"In other words," I say, "forget about morals and ethics? Just have fun?"

Morgan's forehead creases with a thin line of *what is this all about?*

Shit. Now I have gone and done it. Overstepped an invisible mark. I attempt a smile, but it's tight like it has cost me.

Dallas's expression narrows. The period of humoring me is officially over. "Get your head out of the sand, June," he says in a patronizing tone. "Where have morals and ethics left you? With a company about to implode and no one in North America or Europe willing to touch it. Even the shady Russians," he uses air quotes for that, "won't take a sniff."

"But you have a magic solution?"

"I do," he says. "And I'll honor your counteroffer of twelve percent since you won fair and square."

"Won what?" Vandana asks, her bewildered look landing on an equally confused Flynn before they swivel their heads back to me.

I shift in my chair. Clear my throat. "Given the circumstances, I would like to reconsider."

"You knew full well you were taking me for a ride," he says. "And we shook on it."

The way his eyes sweep over me tells me I'm not getting out of this. Now Dallas chooses to live and die by the rules?

"And what exactly did we shake on?" I ask, tension digging into my body. "A pile of smoke? As of this morning, Evener Equity has no monies raised for a new fund. So where is this forty million coming from?"

After a moment of aggressive eye contact, he says, "We sourced a hundred million this week. The announcement of our new fund will happen once you and I ink the deal. Green Time is the flagship investment."

"Oh my God!" Vandana's pent-up stress erupts into a high-pitched squeal. "How perfect is that?"

"I can pitch in too," Chavez says, his eagerness to clear the air sweet and so unlike the festively edgy atmosphere he usually brings to the table. "My French Open prize money landed yesterday."

No. No!

Please, all of you. Stop talking.

I refuse to believe this. It is virtually impossible to raise that much money in a heartbeat and under the radar. When VCs go out to prowl for their next tranche of financing, word travels. Especially if Evener Equity is on the hunt.

But would Dallas have the guts to bullshit me in front of Morgan and Chavez?

Not a chance.

Which can only mean…

"Today?" It squeaks out.

Dallas looks me square in the eye. "That was the deadline. Do you plan to walk out on me a second time and have your company crash and burn?"

I can handle Morgan and Chavez suddenly forming a different opinion about me. And Flynn already knows I left Dallas and his offer in the dust the other morning. But I cannot bear witness to Vandana hovering near apocalyptic shock.

Before saying something truly regretful, I stand abruptly. "Excuse me. I need to use the restroom."

Chapter Eight

I storm past the waitress delivering our coffees, desperate for a place to hide. Flynn's heels *click-clack* behind me in a heated attempt to keep up. I shove the restroom door open, not caring that it clatters against the wall, cementing my Luc's reputation as an unhinged threat to decorum.

Why is it so easy for Dallas to get under my skin?

I'm hunched over one of the vessel sinks, fingers gripping the countertop, when Flynn pokes her head in.

"Bella?" she says softly. "May I?"

I find her eyes in the mirror and nod, deeply ashamed. Instead of throwing a consoling arm around my shoulders or telling me I was right, Flynn hangs out by the paper towel dispenser. The small silence grows.

"How much of a bitch was I?" I ask, hoping for a silver lining.

Flynn makes a cringey face and holds up her thumb and forefinger, indicating an inch.

Crikey. Someone flush me out of this place right now. "Thanks for lying," I say.

She inches closer with that warm, caring energy of hers. "I don't know where to start," she says, "but does any of this have to do with the mushrooms Cliff gave you?"

"I took them all last night," I confess. "And then ran into Dallas at the Blue Moon."

Flynn gasps, a hand covering her mouth. "All of them? Like, how many?"

"A handful," I say. "Give or take."

She bursts out laughing. "Jesus, girl. That is borderline overdose. What happened? Or do you remember?"

I glance at her with a bad feeling in the pit of my stomach. The scent of Dallas hung in my bedroom when I came to, and after a mini heart attack, fits and spurts of the evening tormented me, the full recollection just out of reach. A current charged through both of us at one point, I do remember that. Magnetic and electric. I can still feel the power of it rumbling through my blood.

"That's the problem," I admit. "I don't remember a thing! We were playing pool and then…" I shut my eyes, trying not to let my imagination get the better of me. "Dallas apparently drove me home. I woke up this morning in bed."

Her mouth falls open in shock. I could literally drive a truck inside. "Holy shit!" she whispers. "Did you sleep with him?"

"No!" I wail. "I mean, I don't think any funny business happened. And I haven't asked him because…" I sink my face into both hands, embarrassed to be so clueless and, as a result, at his mercy. "How is Vandana holding up?" I venture, rerouting the conversation. We've left our other best friend stranded to salvage the remains of my rotter behavior.

Flynn shrugs and tells me, "Holding the room together, as always."

This folly may etch a permanent black X beside my name in Vandana's book, and the idea of that guts me. I turn to Flynn for comfort, like I always do, and she hugs me, telling me it's okay as I let it all out in shuddering breaths.

"Men will be the absolute end of me," I mumble into her neck.

As she strokes my back, Flynn muses, "I know you hate being dependent on any man, but Dallas…"

I pull back, gearing up to remind her that the last time I was dependent on anything, it was diapers, when the door bangs open and Vandana swans in. If she had planned to unload on me with dramatic anger, Flynn stealing her job of being the confidante killed the momentum. Her lips mash together, and I can tell she senses she is not in the inner circle.

This is essentially death for her.

"How goes it out there?" Flynn asks, holding me protectively.

Vandana recovers and straightens her back, but the hurt rings in her voice. "As good as it can be."

I disentangle myself from Flynn and face the music. Vandana allows me to hug her, but she is stiff at first.

Will I ever live this down?

"I'm sorry," I say, leaning back onto the counter with a resigned sigh. "I apologize to all of you. I'm not handling any of this well."

After a beat, Vandana decides to defrost. "I can only imagine how difficult this Cliff thing is for you. I was in PR for a decade. I know a thing or two about breaking scandals and the stress they cause."

"The difference is, no amount of spin will save this," I say. "And there goes two years of my life."

"Or not," she says in a tone that suggests I did not think everything through. "Can we talk about this without you flying off the handle?"

I swallow hard and clamp my fingers tighter on the counter; my hands have begun to shake. "Go on. I'm listening."

"Remember a few months ago when you drunk-dialed me?"

I sneak a glance at Flynn, guilt threaded in my expression. The exact damage Vandana hoped to inflict with that comment. She needs to be our golden girl—the one we both turn to when life goes tits-up.

"I thought we agreed never to talk about that."

She carries on, dismissing me like she does when she has a point to make. "You wanted to cut back on the frenzy. Travel, find love again, enjoy life. Well, here it is on a silver platter. Dallas takes the reins and gives you some freedom."

I stew on that, feeling oddly defenseless. "I still own forty-eight percent of Green Time."

"Are you sure? He mentioned you two renegotiated the deal last night over pool?" Her arched brow cuts like a knife. Another thing I withheld from her.

Flynn masks a smile. Just.

"And," she continues, "can I point out that Dallas is the ultimate pot of honey *and* money? The wealthiest man in America and a serious babe."

There's a moment of hesitation before the realization sets in. I should have known. I should have smelled the scheme as soon as Dallas and his damn hair entered the restaurant.

"Was this a set-up?" I ask.

Vandana smooths her ponytail, her gaze dropping to the floor. "Not exactly."

As much as I love her, she mastered the art of being a meddler from her Republican whack-job mother. And while Vandana fancies herself a million miles removed from the scheming Ivy Hillman, the apple does not fall far from the tree.

"A man who drags my name through the mud for the better part of a decade is now boyfriend material?" I ask in disbelief. "Is that your conclusion?"

Flynn holds up both hands in a gesture of innocence. "I was not involved. I swear."

"June!" Vandana fumes, her exasperation catching me off guard. "We all know where your previous stellar picks left you. Forking out palimony to Russ. Cory left you with a trail of checks he forged your signature on. Stuart left you with smashed coffee pots." She's pacing on the black-and-white checkerboard tiles, winding herself up for the finale. "You could do worse than Dallas."

I don't agree or disagree, so she presses on.

"There's no need to state the other obvious point, but I will. Dallas wants to build a fuck-you yacht. Top-of-the-line everything. This is huge for Morgan. And me. I'll be the interior designer on record."

And there it is—the ultimatum.

"In other words, don't screw this up?" I ask.

Vandana's loaded stare at Flynn is indicative of one thing. Back her up.

"I mean, sure," Flynn admits grudgingly, once again painted into a corner with Vandana's forceful brush. "The guy poops gold bars and has a sexy CEO vibe. If that's your thing…"

"The last deal Dallas did apparently involved cartel money," I point out. "No blood on the tracks there."

Vandana sighs. She knows my point is valid but will not give me the satisfaction. To do so brings the success of her father's former shady automotive empire into question. Plus, the yacht world she glides through is not above scrutiny. Russian oligarchs do not build fortunes on ethical grounds.

"Strip away your personal feelings about him because you cannot be objective otherwise," she says, no longer on the attack. "If you work together, the company launches, you save face, you both make money. Is that so bad? I know you like to be on the right side of perfection, but you are in your line of work for the money." She points a warning finger in my direction. "Do not look me in the eye and say otherwise."

On paper, it sounds simple. Forty million in the door, joy and happiness commence. But it's never that easy. Every financing comes with hiccups. Last-minute changes and cold feet. Arguments.

Egos.

And that's when you're dealing with the devil that you know.

I throw my hands up in defeat. "Okay. Fine. I'll hear him out."

Vandana nods, pleased with me properly chastened and agreeing to toe the line. "Can we go back to the table and enjoy our brunch? And please, let Morgan and Dallas talk yacht shop. If you two want to butt heads over what happens next, all I ask is that you do so on your turf."

I cut her a sharp look. "I promise to be on my best behavior for an hour. When the clock chimes one, no guarantees."

Vandana leans in to kiss my cheek. "Thank you."

Our shared ambivalent look says more than meets the eye. We have history that no one knows about except us. But the memory fizzles away as Flynn reaches for my hand. She smiles, the message contained within it—*this too shall pass*. And it will. So it's time to take the high road because these two women are my rocks. Our collective bond is thicker than blood. They have carried me through the highs and lows and will do so forever.

Endpoint.

With the equilibrium restored, Vandana corrals us toward the door. Just before exiting, she offers me one last piece of advice.

"As much as I love your high voltage personality, please try not to be such a bitch."

Chapter Nine

———

WHILE FLYNN, CHAVEZ, AND I WAIT LIKE PLEBES FOR THE VALET TO bring our cars around, Morgan and Vandana slip into their waiting town car. Behind it purrs a gloss-white Rolls Royce Phantom. A liveried chauffeur scrolls on his phone in the front seat. Dallas paces nearby, earbuds in, on a call that started before we left the restaurant.

"That's a sweet ride," Chavez says, scoping out the ridiculous luxury that ferries Dallas to and fro.

"Nothing but the best for the dark prince," I grumble.

"Everything cool with you two?" he asks. "Shots were fired in there."

Thank goodness for Vandana. The former queen of PR was in fine form, post-bathroom huddle. Dare I say, brunch ended on a civil note. Not sure how long that will last.

"Welcome to the jungle," I quip. "Kill or be killed."

"You don't have to go through with this for us," Flynn reminds me. "Right, babe?"

"Hundo percent," Chavez agrees. "Nothing changes between us if you decide to walk away."

"Thanks," I say. "I appreciate you saying that. Unfortunately, I am short on options and he is the longest prick. I mean, stick."

Flynn stifles a giggle. "Freudian slip?"

The valet roars up with their Ferrari, and Chavez wanders over to greet him with a tenner folded in his fingers. Flynn hangs with me, chewing on a nail while we eyeball Dallas. The call is not going well, based on the stubborn line of his shoulders.

As I admire the cobalt finery of his suit, Flynn mutters, "Hard to believe he might become part of our group. What a fucking ego. 'Personality is key in this industry.' I mean, stroke yourself some more, pal."

I laugh. "Unbelievable, isn't he? Cocksure since day one."

"How do you survive around all that constant, big-dick energy? It must be exhausting."

My gaze lands on Chavez, chatting in Spanish with the valet. "Is that why you were yawning during brunch?" I tease. Flynn blushes and giggles, and neither confirms or denies that Chavez and his legendary stamina parlays into the sack. She doesn't need to. Some men just ooze their nature. Unfortunately for Dallas, all he oozes is slime.

"But to answer your question," I continue, "I'm damned if I do, damned if I don't. If I don't go toe-to-toe, I'm a pushover. If I scrap back, I'm a cow. My perennial state is lose-lose."

"Did you ever sleep with him?"

My head whiplashes in horror. "What? No! Who told you that?"

"No one," she says, stepping back from my intensity. "I remember you saying years ago, before he screwed you over, you two had this wicked chemistry."

Damn Flynn and her memory. And wicked is an understatement. What bubbled between us was hotter than lava. And then he had to go and ruin it.

"Any attraction I felt can be categorized as the misguided, hormonal rantings of a twenty-something. I can't sleep with anyone I have zero respect for."

"Not to play Devil's advocate," she says when poking at a hornet nest is her regular course of action, "but the fact he took you home and made sure you were safe? A guy only does that if he cares about you. That's my take."

I open my mouth to refute this, but there is a sliver of truth within her comment. And it makes me uncomfortable because it forces me to reframe my usual attitude toward Dallas. It's far easier to dislike him.

"We shall see," I say. "My take is that Dallas is in this for the money and glory. He has to play nice because I'm part of the deal."

"Fair," she says, knowing further discussion on Dallas will go nowhere. "But he does have some pretty sweet hair. That's about all I can give him."

Right on cue, Dallas pauses and sweeps both hands over his dark strands, a human highlight reel for the hair-care industry. His double-breasted blazer clings to his absurd physique like a tailor hand-stitched it on while Dallas posed nude.

He always had a killer body.

If only I could detach it from his personality.

Chavez comes round for a goodbye peck on my cheek. "Swing by tomorrow night if you can, all right? Last home-cooked meal for a while." He pinches Flynn's bum with a rakish grin. "Let's go, beauti-ful. Time to work off our brunch."

They slide into his Ferrari and peel away. It's wrong to feel jealous when they are so adorable together, but between them and Morgan spoon-feeding Vandana panna cotta on his yacht, something has to give. Where is my knight in shining armor?

"You have a minute?"

I jump as Dallas appears out of nowhere. "Christ, you scared me. What's up?"

"I just got off the phone with Navarro, my contact in Argentina."

Argentina? Navarro? Are we dropping into a South American soap opera? "Carry on," I say.

"He wants to meet both of us to break business bread, so to speak. I think it's a solid idea. Anytime you can get the entrepreneur in the room, it helps sell the company."

My brow furrows. "I'm not following you. I thought this was a done deal."

"We're good to go," he's quick to reply. "But for forty mil, the guy wants to meet. You know, the dog-and-pony show. What are the next few days looking like for you?"

Aside from fielding a shitstorm? Nothing. "I'm available. Tell me where I need to be and when and what ammo to bring."

Dallas nods distractedly. "Great. He's sending his jet to pick us up. We fly out tomorrow night at ten."

I feel my brain seize up. "Tomorrow? I thought he was coming to us?"

"He can't leave Argentina right now."

There is a caginess to his body language. A silent signal to not ask any more questions. I get the sense Dallas had the terms dictated to him.

"Who is this Navarro fellow?" I ask. "I need more information before hopping on a plane willy-nilly."

"I'll shoot you an email with his details," Dallas says. "His family's company is based in London. Cannistrá Capital." He scratches at his neck. "They keep a low profile."

Despite the hot sun on my face, a cold feeling coils in the depths of my stomach. I have never heard of the company. Or Navarro. And South America is where you go if you fancy cheap plastic surgery.

Or a kidnapping.

"Where are we staying?" I ask. For no real reason, I envision a dodgy motel with bars on the windows.

"Accommodations are covered. He has a castle and invited us to stay with him."

Right. Of course. Navarro is a princely kind of name that brings to mind grandiose structures. Still, I contemplate this unexpected wrinkle. "And we will have separate rooms?"

Dallas lowers his Vuitton sunglasses a smidge. "Are you always this paranoid?"

No, I want to say. *But it is hard to have your face so close to mine without feeling vulnerable.*

From the depths of my purse, an eruption of *pings* snatches my attention back to the here and now. And they keep on coming.

"Someone's popular," Dallas quips.

"Give me a second." I rummage in the dark hole of my handbag and peek at the frantic texts. My heart plummets. I see reporters' names. Online news outlets. The scandal has broken.

"Bad news?" he asks.

What kind of a daft question is that? The reason he stands before me in all his suited glory is because of bad news. Leaving the terror of my phone in the dark for now, I square my shoulders.

"We need to get this sorted. Fast."

He leans back, affronted. "I am sorting it out. And you're welcome."

Dammit. Me and my loose tongue running rampant once again. The shame of it spreads like fire across my chest. "What I meant is, this trip is not pool time and umbrella drinks."

"Who said it was going to be that?" he challenges.

More *pings*. An endless chorus of them. My teeth start to ache. I feel the world closing in, Dallas and his exalted aura bearing down on me. "I don't know!" I say, throwing up my hands. "I hear castle and jets and Argentina, and I'm not in control and—"

"Okay, okay," he says, gesturing for me to chill out. "Calm down."

Lips mashed together, I think, bloody hell. My histrionics are on full display. I need a good night's sleep. I need a break. I need this to work out.

I blow out a defeated breath. "Apologies. I'm at my wit's end."

Dallas studies me, at least I imagine he is, from behind his sunglasses. "Getting out of town might be a good thing. Switch up your routine."

"Let's just go and get the money," I say. "And why are you smiling like that?"

He shrugs and fights the widening of his smile. "I was going to say, don't pack the shrooms, but maybe you should."

I swallow hard. "What are you inferring?"

He tilts his head, and I remember how the strands of his hair kissed the tops of his tanned shoulders as he went about his kitchen making us tea. Shoulders wide and strong enough to hold two of me.

"You have no recollection of the other night, do you?" he asks.

No, in fact, I do not. And it's driving me crazy because I know something happened. "I drifted out here and there but otherwise, I had my full faculties."

"So, everything you told me was the truth?"

Dammit. A trick question. "If I said anything that made you feel uncomfortable," I reposition, "take it with a grain of salt."

He nods, dimples now in full effect. I know he knows that I remember jack squat. "Got it."

"And Dallas…"

"Mmm?" he says.

I pause, buying time to scrounge up the right words. His earlier harsh rebuke still stings. *Get your head out of the sand.* Dallas might be saving me, but at what cost?

"Promise you are not going to fuck me over."

I just need to hear it. If he says it, if it rolls off his crude but somehow delectable mouth, it will be a thing. A thing he uttered and is beholden to. You promise me this, Dallas, and I promise not to think about your perfect innie belly button and where the trail of hair beneath it leads.

"Fuck you over what?" he asks.

Even hidden by his sunglasses, I can feel his mocking eyes. The heart-stopping brilliance of them that witnessed Lord knows what in my wasted state. This is humiliating. One harebrained decision and this is where I end up. As the butt of his jokes. I can almost picture Dallas in my house, taking naked selfies, rubbing his stiff cock along the bristles of my toothbrush, living his best life.

"Send me all the information on Navarro ASAP," I say. "I need to know what I'm getting into. I will confirm by seven if this is a go."

He gives me a nod. "Done."

"Okay. Very well. Until then." After a few stilted seconds, I add, "And thank you."

The way he takes a head-to-toe gander at me scrambles my brain. Like the other morning, when, for a nanosecond, I projected myself cuffed and helpless on his bed. Prickly with need. Inexplicably I wanted him to fuck me at the same time he was fucking me over. A sure sign that I'm losing my mind.

"You look stunning in that dress," Dallas says. "Such a waste to hide it under a table." He spares me the full extent of his cheeky smile by walking away and waves jauntily in departure. "Talk to you at seven."

Chapter Ten

An afternoon of watching every media outlet sling mud at Cliff Sassen leaves me feeling queasy and uncertain. The sheer barbarity of how quickly people can turn on you. On top of it, the information Dallas provided on Navarro is sketchy. None of my contacts (ones brave enough to return my emails) have heard of, let alone done business with, Cannistrà Capital. The lone voice who offers any insight says the company primarily funds construction projects in Europe.

Their track record is solid, but so was Bernie Madoff's.

And tech is not their expertise.

So why are they coming to the table?

I pose this question to Dallas after swallowing my pride and calling him.

At 6:59 p.m.

To his credit, he does not crow about me caving.

"They want to diversify," he answers.

"I can't log in to their website without a password," I say. "Who else is involved in the company?"

"It's family-run," he explains. "They like to keep a low profile."

I gulp down the last of my DuMol Pinot Noir. Low profile? Is that their official motto? "Have you dealt with them before?"

After a long pause, he says, "We've tried over the years. The timing never worked out."

"What's Navarro's position? Is he the decision maker?"

"It's a done deal, June," he says, the first hint of strain leaking into his voice. "This is merely a meet and greet, like a hundred others you've done before."

I pluck another bittersweet truffle from the half-empty box beside me. At this rate, I'll be a full stone heavier by the time we wrap this up. I stare out my home-office window, at the sun sinking into the horizon. The sky is a riot of oranges and yellows slashed with blood red.

"How long will we be there? Two or three days, tops?"

Another pause. And then, breezily, "If you want, we can stay longer. Buenos Aires is the Paris of the South. Lots to see. And eat."

Has he gone full-tilt mad? Why on earth would I turn this into an extended holiday? With him, of all people?

"You are now the CEO of my company, currently involved in a major scandal. A vacation is the least of our priorities."

"Then we have a deal," he confirms.

"At twelve percent," I remind him.

"One of my guys can burn the midnight oil to get a short-form term sheet to you and Cliff. Is he around to sign?"

Whatever underground bunker Cliff is hiding in, he has Wi-Fi for sure. The man can play solitaire for hours. Perhaps he was training for this moment.

"I'll find him."

"I'll confirm the flight with Navarro," Dallas adds. "My chauffeur can pick you up tomorrow. Seven work for you?"

I feel the pull of two forces. Power and decisiveness turn me on, but I cannot be lulled into thinking this is a walk in the park. Dallas has me in a compromising position. "If we're flying out from the private aviation strip near LAX, that is in the opposite direction from me. I can take an Uber."

"It's no trouble," he insists. "Besides, the CEO and CFO need to catch up."

I chew on my thumb, mulling it over. Why not ride in style and comfort? One trip to the airport with Dallas won't kill me.

"Okay. I'll see you tomorrow at seven."

When I tumble into bed at midnight, the entire box of truffles sloshes in a tummy full of pinot. I toss and turn, unable to switch my mind off. This time tomorrow, I'll be in Argentina with my sworn enemy to wine and dine a stranger named Navarro d'Amico, who just happens to have no online presence. Not a single blip of information exists.

He might as well be a ghost.

My churning gut tells me something is amiss.

And my intuition, the one that has picked start-up winners for a decade, has never been wrong.

$

VANDANA INSISTED I text her a photo of Navarro's plane. Her sudden interest in aviation boils down to one thing—making sure my ride doesn't overshadow the sleek Falcon that Morgan owns. Unfortunately for her, big, in this case, is too small of a word. The Argentinian version of Air Force One hums like a giant black insect on the tarmac, lights on and ready to rock. My phone in landscape mode barely captures the jet in a single shot. Jesus. A small carbon footprint? Not for two people.

A pleasant, wiry member of the flight crew introduces himself as Christian and orders me to delete the photo. Then he asks Dallas and I to hand over our phones.

"Security reasons," he says after I ask why. "But you can use your laptops."

I turn to Dallas. "What is this all about?"

He shrugs, like it's no big deal, but I can tell he thinks this is odd too, by the way he ushers me forward with a stern, "Let's not make a scene, okay?"

We board the mothership, decorated like an ode to '80s excess. Purple velvet and shiny brass. Ashtrays! Christian leads us through the disco and bar and apologizes that the hot tub is on the fritz. (Yes, tragic news.) I promptly pick the largest of several private bedrooms, informing a dismayed Dallas that I plan to sleep for most of the flight.

"What about dinner?" he asks. "Navarro went out of his way to impress the resident foodie."

I am hungry. The last thing I ate was a wedge of toffee cheesecake at seven this morning. But I glimpsed the table set for two, cutlery polished and glowing on the white tablecloth. If I was coming off a thirty-day fast and delirious, perhaps I could tolerate an intimate dinner with Dallas. But drinking wine with a man who just last night I dreamt handcuffed me feels like a gigantic miscue.

I'm keeping it all about the money.

"Be a doll and have them box up the leftovers," I say. "I'll nibble on them in the morning."

His jaw squares. "Are you saving all your charm for Navarro?"

Hmm. I'm not sure what that's all about. On the drive to the airport, we had a reasonably pleasant conversation. Garden-variety chit chat about Green Time and how we'll move forward. Dare I say, I displayed some charm.

"Can we just power through this without unnecessary drama?" I ask. "I prefer to turn in early. I haven't had a good night's sleep in donkey's years. Tomorrow, when I am fresh as a daisy, I will shower the entire world with charm. I pinky swear on it."

Without me holding out my pinky for him to latch onto, he dumps his carry-on onto a nearby seat with a curt, "Fine. See you in the morning."

$

INSTEAD OF A FRESH DAISY, I wake up feeling like a rotten bouquet of weeds. I had a fitful night on the unfamiliar mattress and sleeping in pajamas instead of naked left a thin layer of sweat on my skin. A long, hot shower hits the spot. I linger on my hair and makeup until the plane lurches into the first stages of descent.

Only then do I make an appearance.

Dallas sits in the lounge, socked feet crossed on the ottoman in front of his chair. His steel-gray suit pops nicely against the crisp ivory dress shirt.

He looks up from the dense wall of text he's reading on his iPad and asks, "Sleep well?"

"Not great. You?"

"Like a rock." He reaches for his coffee and scours me in another head-to-toe that makes me feel undressed. "Your hair looks nice."

I styled it in soft waves for the Marilyn Monroe effect that works wonders with male investors. Nice, yes, but somewhere, the executives at Pantene are plotting to have Dallas and his perfect locks in their next advert. How does he get it so shiny?

"Thank you."

Christian appears from the galley, chipper as a Gen Zer who can function on minimal sleep. He takes my coffee order, not that I need caffeine. A thousand questions rattle like loose screws in my brain.

I lower myself into a chair opposite Dallas and ask, "We won't have to give up our phones at the castle, will we?"

He blots cappuccino foam off his lip with a napkin. The look he gives me is blank. I can tell the idea never crossed his mind.

"I hope not. We both need our phones."

The plane dips suddenly, and I grip the armrest until we cut through the thick soup of clouds. For South America, our summer means their winter. I packed a dressy pair of boots in case a formal dinner was in the cards.

Which reminds me…

"What's on the agenda for today?" I ask.

Dallas shrugs. "Not sure. Navarro likes to organize things his way. We follow his lead."

As Christian steams milk for my coffee, two things cross my mind. How little I know about Navarro and that Dallas has been on what qualifies as best behavior for him. He was an absolute jerk at his house

the other morning, and I expected more of the same: a take-charge attitude or some thinly veiled attempt to push me around. But he stressed
collaboration during our ride to the airport last night. How involved he
wanted to be. Have aliens taken over his mind?

"What's Navarro like?" I ask. "What should I prepare for?"

He sits with those two questions for a long minute before answering. "Very cultured and smart. He might come across as stiff at first but
give him a chance to warm up to you."

"How old is he?"

"Thirty-six."

"Oh. Close to our age." For some reason, I imagined him older,
well into his fifties. "Is he single?"

His brows knit together. "Why do you ask that?"

"I was curious if a significant other would be in the mix. Lining
things up in my head."

"Just go with the flow and relax," he says ironically. For someone
who claimed to sleep, the two black smudges under his eyes say otherwise. "Hopefully, you banked all your charm."

I let that slide.

In fact, we don't speak another word until we're landed and
unloaded onto the tarmac. The public airport off in the distance is
massive, and the city seemed to go on forever during our descent, a
reminder that Buenos Aires has a population five times that of LA. It's
warmer than I expected for winter. Humid, as well. Christian hands
back our phones and waves over a heavy-set man smoking near a
Mercedes G-Wagon. He crushes his cigarette under a boot heel and
limps over. He is about fifty, with a round face littered with acne scars,
and thick salt-and-pepper hair troweled into place with gel. One of his
eyes is lazy and it slants in the other direction than the bridge of his
nose does.

"Are you the Americans?" he grunts. His tone is exactly that of
someone who doesn't really care.

Dallas lifts his sunglasses. "Are you Battista?"

The man's one good eye leers at my bosom with shameless curiosity. "What's your name?"

"June," I say, politely, because he strikes me as a threatening fixture.

"This is all our luggage." Dallas points to our two roller bags.

Battista's craggy eyebrows lift. He is the sort of hired muscle that drags entitled douchebags into dark alleys to show them how to get their hands dirty. But he wears his newly appointed crown of baggage handler without a word, other than tossing our bags into the boot and opening the back door for me and not Dallas. The rich leather interior smells new and I feel settled now that we're here, the wheels in motion. I place my handbag beside me on the seat, adding my coat to the pile.

Dallas glances at the barrier I've constructed. "You're acting like I'm contagious. Is that man thing or a me thing?"

I feel something in my chest tighten. "That's a strange thing to ask."

"Weren't you married at one point?"

"What does that have to do with the price of beans?"

"It means you made an effort once. Found the time to let someone into your heart. Assuming you have one," he adds.

"Ha, ha," I reply. "And since I'm divorced, probably not the best person to ask about matters of the heart."

He fishes out his phone from his blazer and glances at the screen jammed with messages. Then he lifts his sunglasses to find my eyes and holds them with a steadiness that unnerves me.

"Despite what you might think, I do have a heart."

We're both silent for several seconds. Me, because a discourse on feelings is out of the question on a Friday afternoon in Argentina. He, well, I'm not sure why he continues to look at me with a strange light in his eyes. Or what he expects me to do with the emotion threaded in his words. Truth be told, I can't get past the intimacy of his earlier socked feet. How comfortable he looked. Like we were at home having breakfast.

Sidetracked by his emails, his preoccupation allows me to steal a look at his profile silhouetted against the afternoon sun that has cut through the clouds. His straight nose ends in a snub that is, for lack of a better word, cute. A few silver hairs shimmer in his beard. The passing of time impacting the arrogant invincibility of Dallas leaves a funny taste in my mouth.

I am not prepared for a humanized version of him.

Battista hoists his bulk into the car and advises us with his charming rasp that our journey will be an hour, give or take.

"That long?" I ask. "I didn't realize we were so far away from the city."

"He does live in a castle," Dallas reminds me. "They're typically not downtown."

Before I can think of a witty reply, a thick piece of smoked glass rises from a compartment built behind the front seats. It blocks off Battista from the back seat, prompting Dallas to mutter, "Thank God."

Then he makes a funny face that is so unexpected, it cracks me up.

Dallas side-eyes me. "The Siren knows how to laugh. There's a start."

"I laugh," I say, sounding more defensive than I'd like to. "Just not lately."

"Maybe it's time to change that."

Again with the eye contact.

I turn away awkwardly, under the guise of searching for my phone. Why won't my heart stop racing?

The question gets left in the dust because Battista punches the gas, and we're off. The airport disappears behind us, and I soon realize we're bypassing the city entirely. What a bummer. Chavez played a tennis tournament in Buenos Aires a few years ago and loved the energy. He texted the names of a few restaurants to check out if we have time.

The hour commute passes with Dallas and I silent and staring out of our windows for most of it. We roll through a lush rural landscape, but livestock and trees only do so much for me. Once the farmlands are dispensed with, we turn onto a smaller local road that funnels into a narrow dirt trail. The surrounding land is flat and unmaintained, not unlike barren lands where prisons squat. We lurch to a stop at an imposing gate, part of a rock wall that stretches as far as my eyes can see in either direction. I suppose if you have funds for a castle, you might as well build the Great Wall of China around it.

"Wow," I say. "This is impressive."

Dallas comes to with a yawn and mumbles something about needing a coffee. Since he wore sunglasses the entire drive, I didn't realize he'd dozed off.

The smoked glass hums open and Battista's stubby, yellow-stained fingers reach through. "Passports," he demands.

"For what?" Dallas asks.

Two burly men in army fatigues with thick necks emerge from a small hut to circle the Mercedes. The child-locked rear windows click open and silently lower to allow two dark barrels of terrorist-grade machine guns to poke inside.

Aimed straight at our heads.

I flatten against the seat with a shriek. "Jesus Christ!"

"What the fuck?" Dallas mutters, now fully awake.

"Passports," Battista drones again, his fingers wiggling like dry, callused worms.

"Why does Navarro need them?" I ask.

Battista's untroubled, empty face finds mine in the rearview mirror. "Entry requirement."

The guards jostle their guns with the menacing grunts of untamed animals. There is an uneasy comfort in their brutishness.

Dallas shoots me a look. This is not what he expected. "I guess we hand them over."

"Are you nuts?" I lower my voice. "Without our passports, we're screwed."

"Don't worry about it," he says.

"Then why do you look worried?" I whisper back.

Dallas rummages for his passport, collects mine, and hands over our tickets to freedom. The guns retreat, and the rear windows hum higher. Battista and the guards converse in a lyrical chatter that sounds like Italian.

"Do you know what they're saying?" I ask Dallas in a hushed voice.

He shakes his head. "No clue."

One of the guards radios a message on his walkie and the gate creaks open.

I can't take the entire property in, but the front of it seems to be wider than an entire city block. Three stories of imposing limestone, turrets, and Gothic architecture, which seem out of place in the Argentinean countryside. A castle from a storybook, surrounded by a soft, flawless lawn and a smattering of palm trees, tall and unmoving in the still afternoon. Beyond the vibrant greenery close to the house, a tangle of overgrown flora chokes the landscape.

The Mercedes rumbles up the hard dirt driveway. I look over my shoulder and our welcoming committee disappears behind the closing metal wall. As the castle looms closer, my heart rate thrums higher. I can't pinpoint why it has an eerie quality. Maybe it's an illusion, but particles of uncertainty seem to swirl around the building with the growing, violent momentum of a dust devil.

I whisper to Dallas, "Tell me you don't think this is weird."

He observes the approaching grand home of Navarro with his fist clenched and mutters, "It's a little weird."

Chapter Eleven

Battista hauls our bags up the marble stairs to the entryway, complete with imposing wooden doors straight out of the medieval ages. Ten feet tall and adorned with golden lion's head knockers. He shoulders one open and gestures impatiently for us to step over the threshold. I glance behind me one last time, unsure what I'm looking for. A sign of life among the shifting light and treetops skimmed by strange birds?

Inside, the temperature difference hits me first.

Mild humidity sucked into a chill that licks at the back of my neck. My shoes sink into a thick Oriental rug sprawled over the polished stone floors, and I feel small and trivial in the grandeur. Transported through time to an era of knights, kings, and epic battles. It smells of must and roses.

"Wow," I say. "This is the real deal."

My words echo high above us in the colonnaded walkway, where faded frescoes depict the usual assortment of bearded men and angels frowning hard at the debauched humans messing with their game plan.

Dallas rubs his hands together, blowing on them as he deadpans, "The only thing missing is a functioning furnace."

We follow Battista who leads us to a lush atrium—an indoor

garden feature popular in monied Latin homes. It's the centerpiece of the main foyer. Four hallways leading deeper into the castle converge here. Above the pretty flora and fauna is a direct line to the sky, topped by a glass dome perched high on the roof. Sunlight streams in, warming the chilly air.

Battista gestures vaguely at one of the hallways and says, "Navarro will be here soon. And Carolina is his housekeeper. She's running around somewhere. If you need anything, ask her."

Dallas tugs his wallet from his blazer and fishes out a crisp Benjamin.

"Thanks for the lift," he says, offering it in his outstretched hand.

For the first time, Battista displays a gesture other than a complete lack of interest. But catch it if you can. His greasy smile disappears as fast as it smeared over his face. He snatches the bill, stuffs it in his pocket, and mumbles grazie before shuffling back outside. I'm not sad to see him go. A little of Battista goes a long way.

I keep moving to stay warm and peruse a series of ornately framed paintings of nobles clustered on a nearby wall. Beneath the severe faces are brass plates inscribed with two different family surnames.

"How are the d'Amicos and Cannistrás related?" I ask Dallas. I did learn online that Cannistrá means basket weaver in Greek. How strange to name their capital company with a word inferring such lowly status. I doubt they amassed a fortune solely on making products with dried reeds.

Dallas ambles up behind me. "Not sure. You'll have to ask Navarro." He studies the paintings, the corners of his mouth turning down. "This kind of art does nothing for me. They all look miserable."

"How happy would you have been without a flushing toilet?"

"True," he concedes. "And night after night of wild boar and mead? Give me a burger."

He smiles when I look up. His dimples exaggerate the boyish qualities of his face. Can a man be sexy and cute at the same time? Apparently so. And why am I thinking of him in those terms? Because he stands so close that our shoulders graze? Not that I mind. His body heat is the warmest thing in here.

Far more welcoming than the grim expressions captured in oil paint.

Navarro's ancestors remind me of portraits in the oppressively sober church Mum and Father marched me to every Sunday in the London rain. I dreaded those outings. Mum patted my bum and whispered in my ear to go see the vicar, a gloomy, pock-faced fellow in a smelly robe who hung around in the confession booth.

"Run along now, June," she said, despite my protests of not having sinned. "You can never bank up too much goodwill from God. Imagine all your future sins."

How little faith she and my father had in me.

Even after I made it big, my father stuck his nose up at my American life. He considered me a traitor and refused to visit me in Malibu even though I'd bought the ranch-style house so he could trundle about in his wheelchair. *"Only a fool would buy a house miles away from a proper curry,"* he'd huffed over the phone.

A loud and piercing series of screeches startles us both and Dallas, eyes wide, skirts the perimeter of our surroundings for the source.

"What the hell was that? And *where* is it coming from?"

"I think it's a peacock," I say. And I'm sure the nerve-wracking sound seeped in from outside.

"What a horrible noise," Dallas says, shaking off a shiver. "It sounds like someone dying."

Peacocks and their otherworldly sound are an acquired taste, but Dallas seems spooked on a much deeper level. I'm about to ask why when our host arrives in a smashingly grand fashion.

Sweet mother of Christ, as Vandana's mother would say.

Navarro d'Amico may be cultured and smart but Dallas conveniently didn't mention he is also walking panty remover. Grown women are not supposed to feel waves of heat at the mere sight of a sensual smile, but anyone this handsome should be illegal. Locked behind bars with the keys tossed into the night. If all I have to do is convince Navarro to part with forty million dollars, I can think of several ways to start the process.

And not a single one of them involves him and me sitting down at a desk.

"Buonasera," he says, his dreamy accent giving me all the feels. "You must be June."

He's taller than Dallas by an inch or two. Slim, but nicely built. Golden hair curls around his ears and down the nape of his neck, showcasing his fine-boned, regal face. A trimmed blond beard adds a rogueish element to his sophistication, and prancing on either side of him like show horses are two powder-white standard poodles straining at blue leather leashes strapped around his broad hands.

"Yes," I say, finding my voice after first collecting my gasping heart from the floor. "Thank you for having us. This place is incredible."

"Piacere di conoscerti," he says, leaning in to kiss me on both cheeks. "Welcome to my home."

The silky pressure of his full lips, sends a shiver racing up my spine. I catch a scent of fire in his hair. A woodsy smell.

Navarro's gaze flits to Dallas. A chilly assessment? Or perhaps disinterested. Funny how I've forgotten all about Dallas standing beside me. It's hard to think beyond Navarro and the pale green of his eyes searching mine. How it felt like he was seeing right through me.

"How nice to see you again," Navarro says to him.

Dallas nods, no offer of a handshake. Only a stiff, "Hey."

Hey?

I steal a look at him out of the corner of my eye. His body language has shifted. But mine has as well. I respect presence, especially when it overwhelms me. At just past four p.m. on a Friday, a crimson blazer with tails feels like overkill, but leave it to an Italian to statement dress at any hour.

His dogs whine, eager to sniff the newcomers. With a tacit nod of understanding between us—I am a dog person—Navarro relents on their hold. They scamper around us, and Dallas snaps out of his mood, animated as he scratches behind their ears, talking baby talk. His genuine affection, the open display of it, catches me off guard. When I stood in his great room, the cold perfection of it did not speak to him as a pet lover. Or a man willing to display feelings so unabashedly.

The dogs seek me out next. They bark and dance, white puff-ball tails wagging in unison, pink tongues hanging out.

"These two are adorable," I say, gently shoving a nose out of my crotch. "What are their names?"

"Mimi and Rodolfo," Navarro says.

Dallas bites back a laugh. "I thought you hated *La Bohème*."

Navarro's lips purse ever so slightly. "I still do. Any story with star-crossed lovers depresses me. I prefer happy endings."

"So, you named your dogs after characters in a romantic tragedy."

After a thorny beat, Navarro's elegant fingers tighten and pull back on the leashes. The dogs whimper and immediately settle at his feet. He strikes me as a man who wields control as power. A haughty academic type who believes he is smarter, more interesting, and worthier of existence. Someone who will argue with you over the merits of Dante just to prove your inferiority. A man unafraid to wear monogrammed satin slippers.

"Would you prefer I call them Spot and Fluffy?" he asks, his brow raising to punctuate the sarcastic point.

"You can call them whatever you want," Dallas says, and I sense he's given up ground he didn't want to. There is some tension buzzing between them that I don't understand.

In the slow, languid way of a royal whose biggest question of the day is how to fill it, Navarro swivels his gaze to meet mine. "I understand you're a food connoisseur. My cook, Carolina, is top-notch. You won't be disappointed with dinner." He glances briefly at Dallas's trainers, unimpressed. "I hope you packed something appropriate."

Dallas ignores the dig. "What time is dinner? I have work to do."

"Seven. Aperitifs at six thirty. I'll show you to your rooms and collect you at six fifteen."

"What is the dress code?" I ask. Because there is one. And I want to be on the right side of it. And why is Dallas being so short with him?

Navarro stares at me like a curious cat—long enough that I touch my cheeks self-consciously. "Is there something on my face?"

"No, no," he says. "I apologize. The color of your eyes reminds me of my childhood. The seas around Capo Vaticano are a similar shade of blue."

"Where is that?" I ask, because I've never heard the name.

"Calabria," he replies. "Italy. The toe part of the boot. And if I may be so bold," he adds, "you have a lovely figure. I look forward to seeing you in a fine dress this evening."

My cheeks grow hot. Despite his eloquence, I feel like he expects me to show up with my breasts barely wrangled into a corset. Maybe I will. He has a gentle way of speaking that I like. Is that what knocks me off-center? Or is it the hem of his dress pants bunched on his left ankle? Although Navarro seems the type to embrace the latest fashions, ankle monitors aren't a trending accessory this season.

He clocks that I have seen it and smiles again, only this time it doesn't reach his eyes. But something else, something unsettled flares within their depths. The briefest thing. A speck. And then he glances at Dallas, who responds with a warning shake of his head, barely, like I'm not supposed to see, but I do.

What is that all about?

Dallas has kept a careful distance lodged between them. And his brief hello was a veritable mouthful given how quiet he's been.

Is he scared of Navarro?

Just an impression.

Chapter Twelve

THE WEST WING, AS NAVARRO CALLS IT, HOUSES MOST OF THE GUEST rooms. In the narrow hallway, the acoustics are different. Navarro's melodic voice crowds around us, hemmed in by the low, coffered ceiling.

"My office and bedroom are in the north wing," he explains like multiple wings are the most normal thing in the world. "The kitchen, dining hall, and salon are in the east wing. June, I put you in the tower room. I call it the Principessa Suite. The views are fantastic."

I increase my speed to keep up with Navarro's long strides. Dallas trails a few paces behind us, rolling our bags. We pass several doors without stopping. Animal heads line one wall, their frozen eyes unsettling.

"Is it just you and the staff here?" I ask.

"I have visitors once in a while," he replies. "Otherwise, the family business keeps me busy."

"A London base would make more sense, it seems. With your company headquarters there?"

He hesitates in the manner of someone reliving a sour memory. "London isn't the draw it used to be."

"Have you been back to Oxford?" Dallas asks.

"I never finished my schooling, as you know," Navarro says. "I don't feel the need to return to a source of unfinished business."

I'm dying to ask Dallas in private about their history. Years apart can rub the familiarity off someone, but he said they were uni mates. Those relationships create unbreakable bonds, not strained and awkward bites of conversation.

Navarro halts with the dogs so suddenly I almost crash into him. We're at the far end of the hall. A suit of armor stands sentry in a dark alcove. Looking back at where we came from, the atrium is a mere blip in the distance.

"This is your room, Dallas," Navarro says, gesturing at an intricately carved wooden door. It looks heavy, the iron hinges fearsomely forged. The type of door you'd expect to see in a Hollywood castle.

Dallas positions his Tumi in front of it. "Cool. I'll circle back," he says. "A tower room must mean stairs. I'll carry June's bag for her since you have the dogs."

"I can manage," Navarro insists.

Dallas refuses the brush-off. "All good."

I tell myself that he is being polite but can't shake the feeling that every exchange between these two is a power play. In retrospect, I'm grateful Dallas came along. Forty-eight steps up a tight corkscrew passage, and I am winded when we reach the landing. The dogs sniff around the fresh territory. It's warmer up here, and light filters in through ancient embrasures now covered in glass.

"This isn't much," Navarro admits, acknowledging the landing's worn rug and tight quarters. "But inside is a different story."

The question when I enter my room is: will I ever want to leave? Forget princess. I am upgraded to queen. Everywhere, gold and robin's egg blue. The wall coverings. Ceramics on the dresser. What looks like taffeta draped around the four-poster bed. And Navarro was right about the view. The single, tall window overlooks a formal garden in need of tending and from this height, I can see that the property stretches farther than I imagined.

Dallas scopes out the plasterwork on the ceiling. Sumptuous swirls that resemble buttercream frosting on a cake. "Marie Antoinette, eat your heart out," he says.

"This was built by Italians, not the French," Navarro corrects. "Far superior craftsmanship."

Indeed. This place makes Buckingham Palace look like a slum.

"I read that Argentina has a large Italian influence," I say.

Navarro nods, looking pleased. "Ah, a historian in our midst. Very true. Close to two million Italians immigrated in the eighteenth and nineteenth centuries. Argentine Spanish has a similar cadence to Italian."

I run a hand along the drapes, the thick velvet held in place with gold silken braids. Soft and luxurious. No dust. It makes me wonder if that's why we have yet to meet Carolina. The dizzying scope of this place is overwhelming, and she might be trapped in one of the other wings with a feather duster. Vacuuming the rugs has to be a two-day affair.

"Thanks for the tour," Dallas says. "June and I need to catch up on some stuff."

Such an obvious dismissal, and I swivel my gaze between them trying to gauge the man drama.

Navarro clears his throat, a sound of controlled annoyance. "Text me if you need extra towels or such. Or call. The reception is sometimes patchy on the lower levels. I'll return at six fifteen and escort you to the drawing room. Come along," he says to the dogs.

After they've departed, Dallas and I observe each other from across the room. Together in my boudoir, once again. Only this time I'm lucid.

"Are you always this short with your clients?" I ask.

He stuffs his hands into his pockets. "We haven't seen each other for a while. You know how it goes when you lose touch."

I cross my arms. "You were harping on me about charm. It takes two to tango."

"What did you think of him?" Dallas asks. "First impressions."

"He seems nice enough. Pleasant and well-mannered. Normal,

aside from living alone in a huge castle in the middle of nowhere with armed guards at the gate."

And infinitely fuckable, I don't add. The air in the room still carries his scent. A hint of smoke and spicy orange that warms my insides.

"Yeah," Dallas says, a non-answer if there ever was one. What is up with him? He is as still as a rock in a stream.

A thought runs through my mind just then.

"Did you notice the ankle monitor?"

"I did."

"Is that why he couldn't leave Argentina?" I press.

"I never asked why."

His pattern of answers frustrates me. He doesn't know. Or he never asked. Something in his demeanor tells me that he does know.

I come at it from a different angle. "I thought you two had a closer relationship. Mates and all."

He shrugs. "Things change over time."

So much for throwing me a bone.

"Can you try to be a touch more friendly until we lock in the money?" I ask. A reasonable request, given the circumstances.

For a long moment, Dallas stares at his reflection in a tall mirror, the silver edges tarnished with age. I get the feeling he is seeing past the glass and through the walls, into a place where secrets are held tight.

"Don't take his flirting to heart," he says. "Navarro is the great seducer."

I think about this. His tone. That he and Navarro come across as two roosters nipping at each other in the barnyard. My idea is not so far-fetched.

"Did he steal your girlfriend away at uni?" I ask, half-jokingly.

He shifts his eyes to meet mine, and bloody hell. Is it dumb luck that I hit the nail on the head?

"Yes," he finally says. "And I've never forgiven him."

Suddenly this in-the-bag deal is anything but. If Dallas carries a grudge this far into the future and refuses to play nice, we are doomed.

Time for a bath and a cigarette and alone time to prep for an evening of hustle.

"Unless there was something else," I say, "I'd like to freshen up. I'll meet you downstairs at a quarter past?"

"Perfect," he says, perking back up to the Dallas I know. Or who I think I know.

"I imagine we'll run through the details over drinks and dinner. Should I bring my laptop just in case?"

It's a legitimate question, but Dallas laughs like I've told the funniest joke in the world. "Definitely no laptop. He's Italian. Food is sacred."

"Then we have one thing in common."

Dallas shakes his head and says, "Trust me, you and Navarro have nothing in common."

$

WHILE THE BATH RUNS, I get the ugly bits out of the way. Wade through my emails and bring Mark up to speed. He says everyone—staff, suppliers—is on pins and needles, desperate for me to wave the flag of triumph. If anything is certain, it's that I have to pull my weight here. My first impression of Navarro that I didn't share with Dallas? I think he likes me. Might as well capitalize on that.

It won't be difficult for me.

He is impossibly hot. Like, scorching. No wonder he wooed away Dallas's woman.

I hop onto Google Maps and text Flynn a pin drop of the castle location. We talked last night before Dallas and his chauffeur arrived, and she made me promise to send her an update every day. Keep her posted on Mr. Snake Oil and his slippery ways.

Tasks complete, I strip and have one leg dipped into the tub when Vandana rings on FaceTime. Dammit. I debate not answering. She's checking up on me although she'll swiftly deny it.

I wrap a towel around myself and take a seat on the loo. "Hi."

"Hey, babes. How's it going?" In other words, have I screwed things up yet?

"So far, so good. We just got here an hour ago." Hint, hint.

"Great," she says, fighting back a yawn. She's on a balcony, waves breaking on the beach behind her. "Sorry. One too many glasses of champagne. We stopped over in Miami to meet a few clients, and just came back from a boozy brunch party in South Beach. What's your take on the money guy? Is he legit?"

God, what to say without giving myself away? "He's a very nice Italian man. Drowning in money. You should see his castle. It's nuts."

She frowns. "Italian? I thought he was from Argentina. What's his name? I wonder if Morgan knows him."

Morgan seems to know anyone staggeringly rich. It's worth an ask. Any intel will be helpful. "Navarro d'Amico."

"Hold on." Her image disappears as she presses the phone to her shoulder. "Morgan? I'm talking to June. Can you come over? We have a question."

We. Nice one. She is more wound up about this trip than I am.

Seconds later, a smiling Morgan peers at the screen. "Bonsoir, June. Comment ça va?"

"Bien, merci."

Vandana explains the lay of the land. "The financier they're meeting with in Argentina is a wealthy Italian. We thought you might know him. What was his name again?" she asks me.

I relay his name, thinking that it rolls off my tongue like butter. But Morgan's reaction is one of barely contained shock.

"Is he a blond-haired fellow? Tall and dashing?"

Hmm. A perfect summation. "Yes, that's him."

He glances at Vandana and then back at me. Right away, I know what's coming isn't good.

"What is it, babe?" Vandana prods. She senses it too.

"Navarro is a very powerful mobster," Morgan explains. "Deep in the 'Ndrangheta mafia."

All the blood drains from my face.

What I know about the mafia fits on the head of a pin, but I do know they don't come round to wish you well. They show up with guns and threats. Thrive on violence and bloodshed.

"The mafia?" Vandana whispers it before I have the guts to. Her eyes shift to meet Morgan's. "How do you know him?"

"I met him last summer," he says. "We were both guests on a client's yacht in Dubai. I found out who he was after the fact and couldn't believe it. He did not come across as a typical mafioso."

Meaning, Morgan has dealt with a few. No surprise. If Navarro's clan can cough up a hundred mil on a dime, yachts are a no-brainer.

But that's one thing. Dallas setting us up with the mafia is a whole other catastrophe waiting to happen. "What was the other word you said?" I ask. "It started with an N?"

"'Ndrangheta," Morgan says, before spelling it out letter by letter. "Italy has three main mafia groups. The Camorra is based in Naples, the Cosa Nostra in Sicily, and the 'Ndrangheta in Calabria. They are the most dangerous and very secretive, from what I've been told."

Oh, shit. Calabria.

The toe part of the boot.

"Shitty shit," Vandana mutters. "Do you think June should stay there?"

Morgan says nothing at first. Then, "I would check with Dallas. I can't imagine he would bring you into any compromising situation."

Is that the biggest joke of the day? The man lives and breathes controversy. And Morgan's unwillingness to get involved leads me to believe he will not make unnecessary waves with a potential big-ass client. This is my deal to sort out.

Christ! Forget about a relaxing bath. I need to jump on my laptop. Find out from the internet how deep the pile of shit is that I am now sinking in. I stare out the window at the thick band of mist that has rolled in with dusk. At first, a tall, dark form fifty yards away looks like another tree. Until it moves.

I squint and move closer to the window for a better look.

It's big, whatever it is.

"June!" Vandana says, alarmed at my expression. "What's wrong?"

The form disappears into shadows and I stammer, "Uh, nothing. I just saw something out the window." Was it an illusion? I can't see anything now. Strange. "I need to go. I have to get ready for dinner."

And wring someone's neck while I'm at it.

Vandana bites her lower lip. "I don't know. Maybe you call it a day and fly home? This is so not up your alley."

"I'll be fine," I lie as outrage rattles through me so hard my hands shake. Because there are no other options. And Dallas may never recover from my upcoming blast of anger.

I promise to send Vandana updates and hang up, taking another look at where the edges of the property meet the darkening sky.

This place. Suddenly, I can't wait to get out of here.

$

I MAKE my way downstairs at six p.m., contemplating every severe form of violence. I spent the last hour online researching the 'Ndrangheta and still feel nauseated. The endless articles were brutal. A sordid history of kidnapping and murder and drugs, much of it exported from the very country we stand in. And guess what? The mafia launder most of their money in jolly old England. Home of Cannistrá Capital.

Dallas, you lying shit.

I am beyond furious.

I pound on his door and am in his face as soon as he opens it.

"Look me in the eye and tell me you didn't know."

He steps back from my sudden spatial attack. "What are you talking about?"

"Do not fuck with me, Dallas," I growl. "In what world did you think I would say yes to mafia money?"

Realization washes over his features. He calmly grips my wrist and tries to drag me inside. "Keep your voice down, please."

I yank free of his hand and shout, "I will not! You know who he is, and you said nothing other than 'They keep a low profile.' Jesus, Dallas. Scum keeps a low profile too."

Dallas shrugs, doing an excellent job of pretending this isn't a calamity. "I said nothing for this very reason. I knew how you'd react."

"Did you now?" I scoff. "And did you also know we'd have ballistic-grade weapons shoved into our faces? I rather fancied a welcome glass of champagne."

He refuses my bait and shares his twisted logic. "We get this up and running, no one will give a shit where the money came from."

"I will!" I hiss. "My company is trying to improve the world, and this is a pit of dirty vipers. Do you not see the irony? And what are his terms? Horseheads and pinky fingers?"

Dallas rolls his eyes. "This isn't *The Godfather.*"

"Are you sure about that? How many people has Navarro killed?"

In my crash course on corrupt underground criminals, I discovered anyone with rank in the mafia has ended lives. Plenty of them. Killing is how you get promoted.

His expression darkens. "Why don't you ask him?"

"Have *you* killed anyone?"

I'm sorry, but I had to ask.

But clearly, it was the wrong question because Dallas steps out into the hall and forces me up against the wall.

His index finger presses hard between my heaving breasts. "Is that a real question?" he asks.

I am appalled at how unapologetic he is, and it takes a certain kind of entitled jerk to get pleasure from watching a woman squirm under his touch. I try to push him away, but he is a human barricade, and every inhale of his aromatic cologne sets my lungs aflame. His suit is as black as his hair, and they blend together in one seamless package, all of him begging to be unwrapped. Why does he have to look so amazing at this precise moment?

A traitorous rush of arousal reddens my cheeks, and his eyes skim mine with maddening confidence. The sudden uncomfortable temptation to work over his arrogant mouth weakens my resolve.

"I will feed you to the wolves if this blows up," I warn in a small, tight voice.

"Everything okay here?"

Navarro appears, silent as a snake. Dallas steps away from me, straightens his blazer, and has the nerve to say we're all good. Navarro's gaze alights onto me, questioning. I feel my pulse pick up at the sight of him. Luxury poured into a crisp tuxedo. Elegance outside, killer inside. I smooth my hair and the front of my dress.

"We were just hashing out a few things," I say, hating myself for playing along.

"Like an old married couple," Dallas adds with a smile I want to rip off his face.

"More like a divorced couple," I mutter.

Navarro's brows lift in surprise. Little did he know dinner would be served heavy on the sarcasm and bickering. But he is clever enough not to pick a side this early in the game.

"Well," he says diplomatically. "A feast awaits. Andiamo, as we say in Italy. Soufflés wait for no man. Or woman."

His eyes linger on me, drinking in my scarlet evening dress that shows more than a hint of cleavage. Like a layer of luscious crema hovering on an espresso, his skin is a similar rich shade of bisque. Smooth, and tempting me to stroke its softness. But his warm smile now has a treacherous feel, and how many men witnessed the curl of his lips before their brains splattered onto the sidewalk?

He winks at me, composed and imperious.

Dallas watches our exchange. It gives me endless pleasure to witness his irritation.

But it doesn't wash away my belief I have made a mistake coming here.

It feels like I have been set up for failure.

Chapter Thirteen

The mobster and the money maverick, with me literally stuck in the middle. Dallas and Navarro sit like kings at either end of a table long enough to be a lane in a bowling alley. *Dining room* doesn't do this space justice because the word *room* implies a cozy, infinite space. Not a vast rectangle that could house a small yacht. All that's missing is a carrier pigeon to transport conversational notes from one end to another.

Carolina arrives with the secondi, the fourth course in our formal Italian meal. She's fiftyish and slender with a pinched face. Silvery hair pulled back into a tight bun. A personality as frosty as the Calabrian liqueur she served earlier in the salon. Someone prone to communicating exclusively through the slamming of cupboard doors.

I half expected plates of brown slop served with her indifference, not transcendent Parmesan soufflé and tiny fried rice balls called arancini. Or the succulent herbed pork loin she drops in front of me. The combination of stress and starvation has created a hoover effect and our genteel criminal of a host watches me put it all away.

"You must have Italian blood," Navarro says. "My mother would sing your praises."

From the hinterland to my left, Dallas adds, "June's an accomplished chef. Her dinner parties are legendary."

"And since you have been invited to none of them, how would you know?" I ask.

Dallas tips his glass of claret with a thieving wink. "Word gets around."

Navarro chuckles and swirls his wine glass on the damask tablecloth. "You are still the same. Witty. One of your best qualities."

The booze has scuffed down the earlier rough edges between them but best qualities and Dallas? Surely, he jests.

"So, you two met at Oxford?" I venture, zeroing in on their past. "Were you studying the same discipline?"

Navarro nods and says, "I had hoped to pursue psychology, but my family insisted on economics. We met at a boring lecture and snuck out for a drink. Nothing like mischief and Guinness to create blood brothers."

"My taste for all things British comes down to those formative years," Dallas adds.

Navarro leans back in his chair. Is it the glow from the candelabras or did I miss that his eyes are so brilliantly light? Whatever the case, they bypass me and skip across the empty platters and peony bouquets to land squarely on Dallas.

"Is that why you insisted she come along?" he asks.

Like an infection coming to a boil, Navarro's question is an uncomfortable itch none of us can scratch away. Up until now, he's displayed the fine manners of a courtier. Over cocktails, he cozied up beside me on the loveseat, leaving Dallas alone and adrift on the brocade sofa. Warmed by the roaring fire, Navarro peppered me with questions about my family, and my time at Stanford, where my interest in tech and food developed. Everything I said seemed to impress him. We've been on smooth rails during dinner, getting more relaxed with each other.

Now it's just tense.

Never mind being referred to in the third person.

When Dallas breaks the silence, it's with quiet authority. "June is the mastermind. You know how important leadership is. Without her, the company will go nowhere."

Navarro tilts his head, those green eyes sharp as pins. "You mean without me."

In the long, loaded silence, something fundamental shifts. My prickly gaze falls onto Dallas who glances at the parquet with a certain traumatized fascination.

"Correct me if I'm wrong," I say. "But the last I heard, Navarro insisted I come along."

"Your acumen is not in question, June," Navarro is quick to explain. "And I am very pleased Dallas brought you here. A charming addition to the man party is always appreciated."

We've all had a lot of wine; Navarro pours with a heavy hand. And in the aftermath of that misogynist blather, I tell my drunken self to stay calm. Even if it means draining the last of the magnum to anesthetize myself. But holy fuck. Man party? There is only so much I can hold in.

It just slips out. I swear to God.

"I suppose in your line of work, women mend socks and ignore the chasm of their dull existence?"

Navarro's mouth puckers as if he's slammed a shot of vinegar. I can feel Dallas's eyes burning a hole in me.

"Don't mind her," he says. "June's been on a mixed bag of medication and is not her usual self."

I gape at him in disbelief. One night of mushrooms and he paints me as a medicated madwoman? "I am quite alright, thank you very much," I huff.

"I should state that the women in my family are critical and not relegated to menial tasks as you suggest," Navarro explains, a little too late. "Although I admit none are as utterly fascinating as you have proven to be."

A faint smile dances on his lips. Out of the corner of my eye, I clock Dallas toss his crumpled napkin onto the table in a disgusted manner.

"I don't mean to cut out," he says. "But I have a call that needs my input. It might take a while. Thanks for dinner."

"You're not coming back?" Navarro asks, surprised.

"Can't you push it?" I chime in.

"No," he says, addressing both of us as he rises from the chair. "June, I'll check in with you after. Otherwise, we can wrap things up tomorrow."

And he leaves without another word, narrowly missing a collision with Carolina, who's come bearing more goodies. She and Navarro have an entire conversation with their eyes.

"Dovrei abbassare il suo letto?" she asks.

"No, è capace di farlo da solo." Navarro finishes his wine with an air of irritation and asks, "Should we move on to dessert?"

I'm stuffed and knackered and would like to pack it in, but I can't bail. There is too much at stake.

"Coffee and dessert sound great."

"Dolci e caffè, per favore," he instructs Carolina, who disappears with her platter of fragrant green beans. Does she serve him endless dishes here, alone every night? The suffocating madness of that makes my skin crawl.

Navarro drums his fingers on the table, unamused by Dallas's display of rudeness. Little does he know how duped I feel.

"Is he like this now?" he asks. "I don't recall him being so testy."

"To be honest, we don't know each other that well."

"No? I thought you two had a long history?"

"It's a long and checkered one."

He dabs his mouth with a napkin. "I see."

I scoop up the last mouthful of creamed fennel from my plate, silently cursing Dallas. He never mentioned a call earlier. What is his problem? That I stood up for myself? Navarro picks up his chair like the gilded masterpiece weighs nothing and walks it over to sit next to me. His eyes seek mine and I feel my chest tighten. The brutality of criminal culture does not line up with Navarro's thick, flickering lashes.

"I apologize if my comment offended you. You are a remarkable woman. So accomplished."

The thrill of that compliment tingles through me. When he turns on the charm it's full on. It's like I'm sitting next to a pheromone factory.

"Thank you. It hasn't always been easy. Being a woman in a man's world," I explain.

"That, I understand," he says in a somber tone. "An Italian boy never escapes the expectations of his family."

His fleeting smile feels sad more than anything. From what I read earlier the tentacles of the mafia are nearly impossible to disentangle from. Once you're in, you're in. Does a life of endless intimidation demolish your spirit over time? Leave you afloat in isolation?

Sympathy is the last thing I should feel for Navarro, but I do.

And since Dallas left it up to me to mop up the evening, I will get the job done and engage my captive audience. Navarro stares openly at the swell of my breasts as if they are a lifelong candy supply for an unending sweet tooth.

The touch of my hand on his makes him jolt.

"Tell me about Calabria," I say.

$

AN HOUR LATER, I am spectacularly drunk. Giddy, as if I've taken some mildly euphoric drug.

A narcotic named Navarro.

I clutch onto his arm as he walks me back to my room. There is a comfort between us not attributable to the wine. He shared stories from his childhood and spoke fondly about his hometown of San Luca, nestled on the eastern slope of the Aspromonte mountains. He was an only child and doted on. Spoiled, he admitted, with a shy smile. He spent summers on the beaches of Tropea and foraged for mushrooms in the fall with his grandmother. For all intents and purposes, he had a normal upbringing. As normal as a member of the mafia can have. He never broached that topic directly, and the astounding Grenache he'd poured for me washed away my intentions to probe further.

We pass Dallas's room in silence. Is he locked inside and brooding? Or maybe he fell asleep, given his lack of communication since he abandoned us. I need to address his conduct tomorrow. What he's displayed so far is unacceptable, and his twelve percent might get knocked down to zero.

Navarro holds my hand while I attempt to climb the stairs half-plastered, offering his body as a midpoint rest stop. Chivalry is not dead, and neither is my libido. It's revving in high gear when we stand awkwardly in the tight confines outside my bedroom.

"It's been a lovely evening," he says. "Thank you for sticking around."

His attention rivets on me. I feel woozy and pulled to him like a helpless pin to a magnet. The last glass of vintage Grenache hit me hard. And he never had any, I realize. Just plied me with more.

"Give my compliments to your chef. The food was amazing."

"My mother instilled in me the desire to love a woman who is unafraid to eat," he says. "I hope this isn't too forward of me, but I find you quite irresistible."

His hand comes to rest lightly on my left hip. Delicious heat floods my skin. Pure, electric tingle. Is it an illusion, or is the landing squeezing around us, bringing us closer? My own laugh catches me by surprise.

"Perhaps you've been on your own for too long."

"Perhaps," he says, palming my ass.

My heart hammers wildly. How on earth is this happening? His eyes roam mine. Savage and hungry.

A two-footed wolf.

"June," he whispers.

I swallow down the lump in my throat. The only thing between us is the bald intention of his gaze. "Yes?"

"I want to do very bad things with you."

I feel his lips on my throat, the unholy pleasure of that magnificent mouth. I squeeze my eyes shut and tell myself, one kiss. An innocent drunken smooch, both of us caught up in the moment. Because, oh God, he feels so good. A solid wall of heat pressed hard against me.

The aching tension inside me erupts and I arch into him. The decisive connection of our hips seems to flip a switch in him.

His mouth claims mine in a savage possession, and he invites his tongue inside my slutty parting lips. Morals and ethics fly out the window, flagrantly thrown along with caution to the wind. His kisses are wild and fumbling, charmingly uneven as he moans into my mouth.

"Che cazzo! You feel so soft."

His slim hips pin me against the wall. Cold leaches through the limestone onto my spine while the warm splendor of his erection pulls me into a needy whoretex. I yank desperately on his shirt, and he thrusts his hand between my legs, groping around like a blind man in the dark. I want him to touch me everywhere. Words are unnecessary at times like this, but they leave my lips before I can stop myself.

"Fuck me," I whisper into his ear.

The blurred line disintegrates three seconds later when suddenly there's a sound of someone clearing their throat.

I push Navarro away with a weak cry of, "Wait!"

Imagine being clipped at the knees with a two-by-four. Helpless, with no ability to run and hide. Imagine the worst times ten million and that's what it feels like to be busted *in flagrante*. And I'd rather face a boardroom of mutinous shareholders whilst dressed in tattered underwear.

Face anyone, really, aside from Dallas.

Seeing him at the head of the stairs makes my stomach flip-flop.

Navarro abandons his hold on me and moves as far away as he can, braced for combat. I inch down the hem of my dress he shoved higher in his quest. My face burns.

"Don't stop on account of me," Dallas says.

Navarro immediately jumps in to save me. "I crossed the line. Not June."

Dallas stares wordlessly at him, but something passes between them nonetheless. "She was right there with you, friend," he says. "No need to take the fall."

Shamed and breathless, I stammer, "I … I drank too much. And the travel and stress…" I trail off, pitifully. Excuses are just that. Can't put lipstick on a pig.

"Yes, too much wine," Navarro eagerly agrees. He straightens his bow tie, and how I wish his pants weren't so obviously tented.

Dallas shoots him a murderous look. "Can you leave us alone?"

Navarro stands taller in the wake of the shifted dynamic between them.

"Carolina will be at your service in the morning should you be awake before me. Good night."

He gallops down the stairs, the sound of his brogues becoming fainter. Pinned by the cold gaze of Dallas, the weight of it pokes a hole into the spell I've been under.

An apology dances on my tongue, but he cuts me off.

"I expected more from you, June."

A blast of indignation surges through my drunken veins. I expect more of myself, but who is Dallas to point a finger? A serial womanizer who lied to my face and waltzed me into this situation?

"You left me high and dry," I remind him. "And since I serve no other purpose than being a charming addition to the man party, I figured, why not?"

His jaw settles into the usual arrogant line. "Those were his words, not mine."

"You told me Navarro wanted us both here. Those were *your* words."

"Clearly he now sees the value in my decision to bring you along," he snips.

"You didn't answer my question."

"Because there was no question."

Damn him to hell! Why does he have to make everything so difficult?

Hands parked at my waist, I continue to strike back. "What else have you lied about?"

He takes a step closer and clamps his hand around my wrist hard enough that I whimper. His steely expression could cut glass. "I am the wealthiest man in the US of A because I get shit done, June. I focus.

We are here on a mission. Keep your hands off of Navarro and your goddamn legs closed."

"Really?" I ask, ablaze with his attempt to lay down rules. "Dallas Evener giving me a lesson on sexual morals?"

Dallas refuses to back down. "I see it in your eyes, June. You know you fucked up, but you will never admit it because you would rather die on your recycled plastic sword in your pink bubble of righteous goodness than admit I'm right."

His breath feels warm and dangerous against my face. We are close enough to kiss without moving an inch, and it horrifies me to think this. Another slip in judgment? No, thank you. Not to mention how demoralized I feel because he is right.

I hate being wrong.

And I am very much in the wrong tonight.

I reclaim my wrist with a vicious yank. "It won't happen again. And I'm sorry."

Dallas watches me rub the red mark staining my pale flesh and offers no apology, and nothing changes on his face. But his voice is dark when he says, "I wish that was enough to scrape the image of you two dry-humping each other off my brain."

I try to focus on him but I'm drunk and weaving slightly. Fresh out of snappy comebacks.

He heaves himself toward the stairs and puts a point on the evening with a cold, "Have a good night."

Chapter Fourteen

DALLAS

THAT FUCKER!

Navarro has the nerve to pull off a stunt like that?

I rip my shirt off. It tears easily, buttons bursting from the fabric to scatter across the bedroom rug like pearlescent peas. I am seething, my fuse nonexistent. Gangsters aren't high on my most trusted list, and Navarro is as slippery as they come. His world is fighting dagger duels and taking blood oaths, and the last time I saw him interested in a curvy blonde with a mind sharper than both of ours put together was never. How dare he flex his meat against her?

And grope her ass like I want to.

Like she *wants* me to.

I slam my fist against the wall. The mirror rattles and reflects a crazed man, dark with anger and disappointment.

Pissed off with June and with myself.

Yes, I lied. Navarro didn't want her to come. He wanted me here alone. But I knew better than to do that.

I lurch to the fully stocked bar and drown a highball glass with the liquid gold of Macallan. I drink deeply, pulling my lips back against my teeth at the stringent burn of it. I'm light-headed from the wine but alert, nonetheless. We, June and I, need to be careful. It was reckless of me to accept Navarro's offer without asking more questions. I park my ass on the antique chaise lounge, darling and uncomfortable as shit, and curse my stupidity. Is this shaping up to be another painful learning experience at the hands of the ruthless master?

One of my New York buddies, Todd Shelby, disappeared before Christmas last year. He left behind a good-looking wife, Lauren, and a trio of sons. One month prior, his IPO tanked hard right out of the gate.

Investors were pissed, one in particular.

They expected a ten-bagger.

Ten million in, a hundred million out. Not the other way around.

Most guys in this business have more losers than winners. You learn to live with it. Fall off the bike and get right back on. No time for crying over spilled milk. Todd knew the drill. For him to vanish without a note or a peep to anyone? Not his style. When they found him weeks later, a carcass in the Amazon had more meat left on the bones.

Acid has a nifty way of destroying things.

When Lauren called to invite me to attend Todd's celebration of life, I lied and said I had a conflict.

A conflict with my conscience.

I am acutely aware of the text I sent to Todd last year. Navarro's contact details … with the caveat for Todd to watch his back.

Navarro is too high up now to get his hands dirty on that level, and some picciotti d'onore, a low-level soldier itching to climb the ranks, did what he was told. Navarro once said his people accept a certain amount of prison time as an occupational hazard.

The inherent problem is that Navarro told me too much.

I know more about the inner workings of the 'Ndrangheta than the Italian magistrates who stake their lives on ridding society of the mafia scourge. Omertà is the mafia code of silence, and I took a similar vow, promising to never tell anyone at Oxford who Navarro was. And I never did because I am a loyal fucker. Plus, Navarro played me like a puppet on a string with his passive-aggressiveness and intimate knowledge of what scared me the most.

He wasn't the only one who talked too much.

Over endless espressos and late-night study sessions spent poking holes in economic theories, I slowly revealed myself to him. All the pain. How Mom disappeared without a trace one summer. How I kept Dad's dance studio afloat when he spiraled into grief. I had to learn quick, or the business would be a victim of the school of hard knocks. Thrown into the deep end, I hustled hard and surprised myself. All the numbers started to make sense, and my skill at multiplying them grew day by day. In a few short months, I turned the entire damn studio around.

My newfound confidence did not go unnoticed.

The Seattle housewives with MIA executive husbands and time on their hands all liked me from the start—the dutiful teenaged son playing piano and stepping in to be their dance partner. Most of the perfumed old flesh did nothing for a horny teenager beating off every night to ripe centerfolds on pornhub.

But Mrs. Robin Cavanagh.

She was different.

I danced with all the women, but somehow Robin spent the most time with me. She was the sexiest thing. All curves and flame-red hair and this habit of winking at me to end her sentences.

One afternoon after class she asked me to help her put something into the trunk of her Porsche Cayenne. A bag of groceries that weighed three pounds. Whatever. I helped her. She was parked down the street. At that point, all the other women had gone home. I placed her Whole Foods bag in the back of her car and shut the hatch. Just my luck, a sudden Pacific Northwest downpour unleashed and Robin insisted we duck for cover in the car. I didn't mind. The black leather interior of her Porsche smelled like the life I wanted—rich and luxurious. She smelled nice too. Like flowers.

The windows slowly steamed up from our damp clothes and our

breath. I cracked a window, wondering when the rain would ease. In Seattle, it could take an hour or a week.

After an awkward silence, Robin asked, "Are you planning to take over the business?"

"Me?" I asked, like an idiot. Who else was she talking to? "No. I mean, I'll do what I can to help out, but I want to get an MBA. I like business."

She smiled. I liked her perfect white teeth. "You certainly have talent," she said. "Things have improved since you stepped in."

I felt myself blush. "Thanks. Numbers make sense to me."

"And people?"

"Uh…" I fidgeted with the ring on my finger. The one Mom left behind for me—my grandfather's wedding band. "Not so much."

Robin leaned forward to catch my eye. Hers were always twinkling with mischief. "Maybe it's just women that don't make sense to you?"

She called that right. Guys were easier to hang with. I didn't have to interpret shit. The chicks at school said one thing and did the other. And Mom… If she wasn't on her meds, watch out.

"I never understood my mom," is what I said.

"Do you miss her?" she asked.

This landed on my heart in a way I didn't expect. I stared down at the floorboard wishing it would open up and suck me out of the car. Dad refused to talk about Mom, but Robin and I always had this ease between us. I didn't entirely know what to do with it, other than it made me more aware of how blue and bright her eyes were and how my body responded when hers pressed against it.

But where was she driving this conversation?

"Yeah. I miss her a lot."

On any other day, with any other woman, the buck would have ended there. The last thing a seventeen-year-old wants is to get touchy-feely. When I think back to that moment, with the fogged windows and rain falling like bullets on the roof, it's obvious Robin had a game plan.

And I fell for it.

She made it easy to fall for her.

When the rain did ease up, half an hour had passed. We were still cocooned in her car. Talking with Robin turned out to be as satisfying as dipping her during the tango. I'd blabbed about my dreams to become a millionaire, and she said she could steer me in the right direction. Her husband was a serial entrepreneur with a huge Rolodex of contacts.

Her intention to help eventually panned out, but not in the way either of us had planned.

But I wasn't thinking about a future with her on that Friday afternoon. An hour was the most my ADD brain could look ahead. And why look beyond the button on her blouse and how it had come undone? Or the jiggling swell of flesh underneath when she laughed at one of my dumb jokes. She noticed me notice, and a pause hung between us, heavy as the innuendo, before she smiled and the walls of her car seemed to fade away.

Some nights, with too much Scotch swirling in my veins, I swear I can feel the heat of her hand pressed hard on my thigh like it was yesterday.

"You're so very handsome, Dallas," she said.

If silence could be measured—ten being so goddamned quiet I could hear my soul sinking into hell—that period when my tongue could not find a reply to save my life was a clear eleven.

That was the first time I whored myself for money.

And I won't lie. It got easier every time.

I pound the last of my drink and set the cut-crystal glass onto the rug. Even a smooth vintage Highlands blend can't get rid of the sour taste in my mouth. Dad texted me earlier, asking if I would come home for his birthday. I missed his seventieth, delivering a keynote to a humorless room of Russian officials who played chess with their citizens as if they were actual pawns. And I forgot to text him later, busy as I was getting serviced by one half of a perestroika twin set who came complimentary with my hotel suite.

God, my lack of priorities.

I drop my head into the curtain of my hands and never want to surface from the darkness.

Seattle holds a lot of misery for me. If I can avoid it, I do.

I have avoided most of my limitations.

At some point, most of us reach a place where we're afraid to fail, where we instinctively stick only to what we're already good at. My skill is winnowing a million pitched ideas into the precious few that make rich people richer. This expertise has brought me wealth, bucketloads of it, enough to build an impenetrable fence around my heart. The downside of such a fortress? My heart remains a forever tidy and barren space where nothing ever changes.

Or allows me to feel better.

Navarro knows all about this fear. And he is not above twisting my soul around his finger to gain the upper hand.

A light rain starts to patter against the window. It takes me a couple of tries, but I eventually stand and stagger over to stare into the blackness. Goddamn it! Will June ever forgive me? That woman holds onto a grudge tighter than I do. I dragged her here hoping for a reprieve so we could unpack our baggage—pick apart her stoned ramblings and set the story straight about Sonny.

And ask her point blank if she meant what she had said about me.

If it's true that she wishes things could be different between us, I would have handled our meeting last week entirely differently. Put on some fucking clothes, for one thing. Conduct our business in the office, instead of my house. But no, genius me, the vindicative one, I wanted to intimidate her. Flaunt my body like I didn't give a shit. Make her sweat with my home-court advantage. Why I picked up a tart like Ally the night before is another question for the ages. The brat refused to leave before June came over and promised to stay quiet upstairs.

Jesus. I must be getting soft if I start believing the babble of a twenty-one-year-old.

I stumble to the bed and flop onto it spread-eagled. My heart thumps heavily inside my chest. June looked smoking hot in her dress tonight. Such a babe and effortlessly brilliant. How did I fuck things up so badly?

It's fine, I think, bleakly. *I'm fine.*

Fucked up, insecure, neurotic, and emotional.

Lord almighty, as Nikki would say. Time to get it together, D-Man. Do not get sucked into Navarro and his games. I know what I need to do. I accepted this gig not only for his blood-soaked money.

Navarro and I need to set things straight.

It's been a long time coming.

Chapter Fifteen

I WAKE UP HEAVY-HEADED WITH AN UNEASY SENSATION OF BEING watched. But the room feels too silent, too empty. I yank off my eye mask and prop up on both elbows. My gaze bounces feverishly around the room, but I don't process what I'm seeing on the first pass. The human brain handily bypasses the obvious on occasion, a phenomenon called inattentional blindness. When our attention is focused on one thing, we fail to notice other, unexpected things—like the giraffe quietly munching on its breakfast and staring at me through the window.

What? I cuff away the sand gritted around my eyes. Is this another hallucination?

I wrap the sheet around me and slide off the bed. The rug under my toes feels cool, like the air. I inch closer to the window, my heartbeat skidding back down to normal levels. It dawns on me this is the lumbering shadow I saw last night. A giraffe.

And it sure is cute.

Its whiskered snout looks velvety to the touch. The giant black eyes are gentle and fearless. But when I reach for the window latch, both its ears rotate back and flatten before it lumbers away. I quickly open the window and poke my head out. It saunters north, to the rugged landscape in the distance, visible in the clear sunny morning. The long, elegant strides of the animal remind me of someone else.

Shit. Last night.

It all comes crashing back. All my unsavory actions. And no surprise, when I cross the room to check my phone, not a single message from Dallas. I'm ashamed to face him and Navarro.

I haul myself into the bathroom to shower and think.

As warm water rains down on my body, I struggle to make sense of what came over me. Yes, I was drunk, but also too glowing and aroused. Too open. Had I not experienced the mushrooms I might not know any better, but it felt like I was high on something. I towel off and trowel on makeup, my mind looping through the final hour when it was just Navarro and me. At one point, I went to the loo. And he'd cracked another bottle of wine after I returned. He plied the Grenache on me but never took a glass himself.

Off bottles of wine do occur.

But typically, the taste is a giveaway.

The wine tasted like syrupy goodness. Sweeter than normal? It's tough to say. And I can't entirely blame the alcohol. The wine didn't whisper *Fuck me* into Navarro's ear.

I make a grim face in the mirror. My only hope is that our host has short-term memory loss or is very forgiving.

By the time I venture out to face Dallas, I'm feeling a tad better. Dressed in what Flynn calls my pinup look—hair clipped to one side with lips lined scarlet red, the look tied together with a black cashmere sweater dress. Looking presentable bolsters my courage to knock on his door. After several minutes with no answer, I conclude he's up and at 'em. Doubtful he's asleep. It's ten in the morning here, and West Coast finance types like us are up early for the market open.

And then I hear the music drifting down the hall.

The faint sound of piano playing.

Navarro mentioned the piano during dinner last night and asked if Dallas still played. I follow the melody through the foyer. The sliding doors to the main salon were shut when we arrived yesterday, but they're open today. A three-foot gap that I peer through. Light pours in from several tall windows, drenching the room in warm sun. It's a sophisticated space designed for social gatherings, with furnishings clustered around the perimeter of the room because the focal point is a grand piano smack in the middle of the gleaming wood floor. Dallas plays with his back to me, lost in the haunting melody.

It's funny when you see someone in a completely different context from how you know them. Dallas could be the main event at Carnegie Hall, that's how good his playing is. I feel the vibration of his soul as much as the music itself. Some musicians merely play their instruments. Dallas caresses the piano, coaxing illicit, dreamy sounds out of it like the moans of a lover. He's barefoot and shirtless, dressed only in lounge pants. The hazy light accentuates the deep ridges of his back muscles as he tickles the keys.

I could stand here all morning and listen. But then an itchy sensation in my nose intensifies. I try to contain it but can't hold back the sneeze.

Dallas immediately stops playing, and I feel a rise of disappointment as the notes dissolve into the still air.

The silence is painful.

Without turning around, he asks, "How long have you been there?"

"Long enough to be impressed. Who's the composer? I didn't recognize the piece."

"Ludovico Einaudi. He's Italian."

"It's incredible," I say, the flurry of notes still fresh, dancing on my skin. "You play with so much emotion."

He spins around to face me. His hair is mussed but shining in the sunbeams. It's concerning to mentally debate whether he's more attractive half-naked or in a suit. Combined with the beauty of his piano playing and framed in this opulent room, I feel strangely intimidated.

"Speaking of Italians," he says in a flat tone, "I haven't seen Navarro this morning. Did he end up in your bedroom after all?"

My cheeks burn with embarrassment. "Of course not," I say. "And I wanted to apologize again for what happened. I think the wine might have been off."

He cocks a brow. "So, the wine is to blame."

"I'm not making excuses for my behavior, but—"

"But you are."

My instinct is to back away from his accusatory gaze, to put more space between us so I can safely keep my emotions bottled up and not let them spill out in a tremulous fashion, like my voice sounds. "Why are you making this so hard for me? I wasn't even supposed to be here."

"I would say Navarro is damn thrilled that you did come along."

My heart twinges. He has every right to be a hard-ass. "You know him better than me. Will this be an issue? Do you think he'll renege?"

He laughs, but it has no humor in it. "Is that your big concern?"

"Yes. One of them. And I could tell you were upset."

He rewards my honesty by prowling closer. I didn't know lounge pants could be sexy, but they make a strong case clinging to his hips.

"Why do you think that was?" he asks.

"Um, well…" My face glows with heat and awareness. He has never looked at me this way before. "I mean, obviously I screwed up."

He takes another step forward until he is looking right down at me. "Do I need to handcuff you to my bed to make sure nothing else happens?"

My heart drops. I try to recover from the shock of his words and fail. "You travel with some?"

"This time I did."

There's a bluntness to his statement. The realization comes to me slowly. I said something about handcuffs when I was high. That's the only answer here. It explains his reaction to me and Navarro. It explains why he's looking at me with that strange light in his eyes.

"Just say the word, June. I'll make it happen."

He squares his shoulders, the charge between us trapped and more electric because of it. Control was, is, and will forever be his hallmark.

That's why he made me come to his house the other morning instead of meeting at his office.

But he has to be joking, right? Because otherwise…

"I should find Navarro and make peace," I say. "Set things straight."

I also need to ask him if my pearl earring somehow got tangled in his clothes. I could only find one this morning.

"June," Dallas says, commanding what little space there is with his voice. "You need to be careful around him. Keep your guard up."

I search his face. The concern etched onto it. Nobody says what they really mean, so why would he?

"Are you jealous of us?"

"*Us?*" he repeats, incredulously.

So much for plucking ideas straight from the air without running it through the fire first. Now I'm committed.

"If didn't know you any better," I venture, "I'd say you acted very jealous."

Something shutters in his face. Full lockdown. "You don't know me at all."

"I know—"

"You know what you've read," he interrupts. "The gossip, the articles, the whispers around town. We had a brief encounter a decade ago, and that is your only frame of reference for me. You don't think I've changed since then? Are you the same person you were ten years ago?"

After a tepid pause, I say, "No."

"Exactly. Do *us* both a favor and don't make any judgments on who I am."

His defensiveness stokes a fire in me. "You made my life very difficult based on a single rumor you never bothered to substantiate. That is its own form of judgment."

"And what?" he says, waving an arm from left to right. "You would have picked up the phone when I called to ask about it? You never replied to any of the texts I sent after you stormed out of my office." He lifts his index finger. "Excuse me, *one* reply. 'Go fuck yourself.'"

"What did you expect?" I fling back. "There was no humility. You berate me for not apologizing to you and a sorry never formed on your lips. All you asked is if we could talk."

"Isn't that what humans do when they're trying to fix shit?" he says, dangerously close to anger. "They talk."

That he believes I overlooked his attempt at relationship repair is concerning. I need to right this ship.

"I came to the conclusion that I am the farthest thing away from your type," I say, primly. "And I still am."

He scoffs. "How do you know what my type is?"

"Based on your history, ten years younger and five sizes smaller than me. Zero self-esteem."

His eyes narrow into slits. That was a low blow, considering the flock of rejects I've attracted. And Dallas wastes no time setting the record straight.

"Last I heard," he lobs back, "your ex-husband tapped you hard for palimony. Not exactly a shining example of self-reliance there."

I draw back, like a boxer signaling for a time-out. Where does he get all his information from?

"I never claimed to be perfect in the love department."

"Do you even know how to love a person?" he asks. "Something else besides work?"

I snort a laugh. "Dallas, come on. We're both workaholics."

"Is that why you find me so detestable? Because I'm just like you?"

The problem with this conversion is that I don't know where to go from here. It's too intimate. Too raw. I am not ready to face old demons or mistakes I regret.

"You left me high and dry last night," I accuse. "During drinks, I gave you ample opportunity to jump in and close the deal. Get a firm commitment. Why am I paying Evener Equity if you sulk on the sofa and say nothing?"

He runs a hand over his hair in irritation. Truth be told, he never had a chance to jump in. Navarro dominated the conversation.

"Navarro is a different breed," he explains. "I don't need to close him."

"And yet he snaps his fingers, and we fly to Argentina. He could have just wired us the money if it's a done deal. And I could have stayed in LA, apparently. What's up with that?"

The muscles in his arms flex, both fists clenched into tight balls. This is where he needs to come clean. Admit to his subterfuge. If his scheme involves him, me, and a set of handcuffs, I need to hear it from the horse's mouth.

The longer he says nothing, the more his entire being betrays him. His swagger drops a notch and he looks past me, at some random place on the wall that won't extend this argument.

"Go find Navarro and grovel for forgiveness," he says. "I'm going back to my room. And since you have so little faith in me, I will close him over breakfast. I'll meet you in the kitchen."

He storms forward and I grasp his wrist. "Wait…"

Dallas pins me with a look. "What?" he asks, sounding fatigued.

My mind rushes. What do I want to say? That our pasts keep bumping up against the present, and I don't know what to do about it. That I've forgotten what it's like to patch things up with someone because I've let all the relationships in my life slip away without a fight and instead bury myself in work to survive?

Adrenaline floods all through me. I feel sweat gather in the pits of both arms.

"Uhm … I don't recall you ever mentioning you played piano."

His expression blackens for a second. Then I see something entirely different pass over him—a wash of sadness.

Oh, June. That clunker statement is your best attempt?

No wonder he shakes free of my hand and brushes past me with a toneless, "You never gave me the chance."

Chapter Sixteen

LAST NIGHT, THE CASTLE HAD A SPOOKY FEEL. MOONLIGHT FILTERED through the stained-glass windows and cast eerie shadows on the walls. Every nook and cranny whispered and screamed of history and close calls. Oodles of atmosphere as thick as the silence. The trek to the dining hall took an eternity.

Everything feels different in the safety of the morning. Brighter and less daunting. I'm in the paneled drawing room in no time, feeling an odd mix of emotions as I stare at the gaping jaw of the fireplace, big enough for two people to stand in. The night began here with me respectable and perfectly mannered, sipping aperitifs. Then Navarro mania hijacked my libido.

Standing here, replaying my mistakes, the tiny seed of doubt in my chest grows. The confusion that almost undid me last night becomes something else.

Fear, maybe.

At how sluggish and thick I felt, unable to control my basest desires.

I set those shaky thoughts aside and scour the drawing room, peering underneath the loveseat and rummaging between the cushions. I scout the perimeter of the vast dining hall and find nothing. Huh. My

Bulgari clip-on earrings aren't jewels to brush off as a casual loss. They were a treat to myself after my first company—an app that paired food shelters with events that had leftovers to donate—got bought out by Microsoft for a tidy sum. Flush with millions, I snagged the Malibu property and a few things my heart desired. Vandana insisted I also buy a watch, but the limited edition Chopard has very little control over whether or not I show up on time.

Time management is another thing I need to work on. That impossible task holds more appeal than the formidable endeavor of clearing the air with Navarro.

But I can't evade him forever.

I retrace my steps to the atrium and hang a sharp right to the north wing. If he's not in his office, I'll abort the mission. No way in hell will I knock on his bedroom door. Not when I can still feel the hot grope of his fingers on my arse.

I pass a parade of famous paintings mounted on the walls—Klimt, da Vinci, Dali, no doubt originals—and speculate on what a working day entails for a mafia man. Does he create spreadsheets on kidnap victims? Check in on drug runners? Tweet selfies with the hashtag #gangsterlife?

Or he could spend his time doing things as mundane as speaking to clients on the phone.

Navarro steps out from his office into the hall, iPhone glued to his ear. He's facing the other direction and doesn't clock my presence. But I feel his. Six feet something of authoritative existence. The crisp white dress shirt buttoned to the top. Pleated charcoal trousers and oxfords so shiny they reflect what little light seeps into the dark recesses of Navarro's end of the castle. I still recall how silky soft his mussed blond locks felt in my grip of madness.

"Yes," he says, to whomever is on the other end of the call. "Thursday at the latest. Is that possible?"

While his phone companion speaks, Navarro mumbles agreeable sounds.

Then, "The unexpected addition will not pose a problem. I'll make sure of it."

He turns on his heel and blinks. I wave, like an idiot.

"My guests are awake," he says calmly into the phone. "Ciao, and please say hello to everyone for me." He hangs up and tucks the phone into his shirt pocket.

"Buongiorno," he says, and his amiable greeting settles my nerves a smidge.

"Good morning. How are you?"

"Wishing the evening could have ended differently. And you?"

He smiles, and a flush grows along my chest—from embarrassment, or maybe the pleasure of remembering.

"About that…"

He's staring at my hand, where I'm furiously twisting my ring. "Does last night change your opinion of me?" he asks.

"No. And I hope it won't damage your belief in me. Us. Me and Dallas," I quickly add. "That should never have happened."

"And yet it did."

His shimmering green gaze locks me in place. The glow. The hunger. The hunt. He reminds me again of a two-footed wolf.

Does a wolf have any natural predators?

Or does it hold everything in the natural kingdom in its sway?

I clear my throat. "As Dallas mentioned, I haven't been feeling myself lately."

A laugh slips out of his lips. The deep belly sound reverberates along the walls and spills back onto my skin like a brush of fine silk. "Has anyone told you that you're a horrible liar?"

His confidence is unshakeable. Does it stem from an upbringing where violence secures your lifespan? A deep-rooted satisfaction in knowing how to get what you want? He steps closer and his energy, the dazzling force of it, pushes me back.

"What is your relationship with Dallas?" he asks.

"Strictly business."

He is quiet, waiting for me to elaborate. Then, "Nothing bubbling under the surface?"

"Anything you see bubbling is a clash of will and ethics."

"I felt your will last night. Tried hard to dissolve it."

His eyes search mine, looking for an answer I'm not sure how to deliver. It's difficult to look at him. Lots of violent emotions cloud my brain. "My actions were very inappropriate."

"It must be hard to hold back the way you do," he says, skipping over my weak protest. "What I see is a wild woman desperate to run free. All she needs is the right person to open the gates."

He trails one long, elegant finger down my arm leaving a buzzing line of stars in its wake. I square my shoulders and do everything in my power to stand stoic and unaffected as my insides melt into jelly.

I have never known a man to be literally intoxicating.

But I have to say no to all forms of mind-altering things.

"Sorry," I say, brushing his hand away. "I can't. This isn't right."

His eyes, the line of his jaw, harden into pure ice. "So, there is something between you two."

"Dallas has nothing to do with this," I lie. After witnessing him sculpt air with music that left me aching, and the frankness of his emotions left me reeling, the long-buried part of me that once wanted him has bubbled back to the surface with a vengeance.

"Why are you so loyal to him, when he has treated you so poorly?" Navarro asks.

"Do not confuse my sensibilities with loyalty to Dallas," I bristle. "The only reason I'm here is because he was not up-front with me. I would never have agreed to this."

Navarro smiles thinly. "This, meaning me?"

"What you represent," I clarify, careful in how I address the madness he is part of. "We live in very different worlds."

"Not so different," he suggests. "We both run businesses at the end of the day."

His ambitious comparison almost makes me laugh. "Forgive me for stating the obvious, but I would call murder a major difference. Insurmountable, actually."

"Ah," he says, notably unconcerned. "That is your issue."

I can't believe I blurted that out like it was nothing. Am I insane? Perhaps not as insane as him though, responding so casually to death.

"You have killed people, right?" I ask, and never in a million years did I dream of asking someone that question.

After a pause that seems to go on forever, he says, quite formally, "Only when necessary. And it might be beneficial to view my work as how I better the planet. Not everyone is good for this world. I make the requisite adjustments."

"Adjustments?" His warped perspective keeps getting funkier. And it's one thing to be told about the mafia. It's quite another to have someone admit to your face they have snuffed out lives and not show an ounce of emotion while doing it. "Is that Italian for murder?"

"What did it feel like to kiss a murderer?" he asks, genuinely curious, it seems.

What did it feel like? Like decadent chocolate mousse drizzled with raspberry coulis. Or foie gras dolloped with oozing crème fraîche. A never-ending, fattening sin that might be the death of me.

"That's also inappropriate," I whisper.

His eyes flicker back and forth between mine. Sizing me up. "After all is said and done, would you come with me to Italy?"

My heart starts to hammer. "What for?"

"You and I would make a great team. And there is far more money in my business than yours."

I don't know what to say to this, at first. He isn't joking. After letting it sit for a beat, I ask, "Since when does the mafia allow women to participate?"

"How does the saying go? Behind every successful man is a strong woman."

Well, how about that? It's a toss-up whether his male entitlement or arrogance is the most injurious, but if he hoped to win the game, he just lost, big time.

"We have a saying in America that might not translate for you, but let me be clear: I do not ride bitch."

He laughs again, before swooping in to plant a kiss on my forehead. "Can we have a drink together tonight after dinner? Just you and me?"

The wrongness of that sends a jolt up my spine. There is no deal.

No money has changed hands or bank accounts. And a drink together is an old-school way of saying Netflix and chill. Even though floating around in a giant castle with giraffes, peacocks, and poodles does lend an air of frivolity to the circumstances, this is not a drunken sorority free-for-all. Riding the cock of a potential investor is first-class, monetary whoring, and Navarro will not be a one-night stand forever in the rear view of my walk of shame. Soon his face might stare back at me on monthly Zoom calls. He may fly into LA for investor updates. Plenty of serious moments await, and the last thing I should be thinking about is how we once fucked like animals.

"Just one drink," he repeats softer, which makes it somehow louder.

A less crappy version of myself knows the correct answer, except nobody ever said I was perfect.

"Okay," I say. "One drink."

Chapter Seventeen

When we arrive in the kitchen, Dallas nurses a coffee at the farmhouse-style table. He eyes us over the rim of his cup and wears his silence like a heavy crown. Carolina pulls fresh croissants out of the oven while Navarro chats her up in Italian. I'm stunned to hear her laugh and discover that she can smile without her face cracking into pieces.

I sit next to Dallas with low-level guilt rolling through me. I explain through eye contact that Navarro and I smoothed things over, but I'm not sure he's buying it.

"You slept well?" Navarro asks, settling in at the head of the table.

"No," Dallas replies. "I slept like shit."

Navarro massages tiny circles on his forehead with his fingers. "I think we all went a little overboard."

That is a generously mild way to describe our frenzied groping, but I'm grateful he's trying to spare me the shame of it. It's funny how he seemed larger than life looming over me in the hall but is humanized in this kitchen massive enough for a bevy of servants, chefs, and their assistants to run about and never collide. I could roll out a pie crust as big as a car tire on the island. Precious heat floods out of the oven, and the warm air smells buttery and decadent.

Too bad we're not here under different circumstances.

This is a foodie's dream kitchen, and I would run hog wild if the waxen and sullen Carolina would allow it. Her sharp, dark eyes follow mine as I scope out the milled cabinetry. A shadow of a frown crosses her face. Maybe she senses competition.

"Would you like a coffee?" she asks me, presenting a platter of croissants on the table.

"A cappuccino, please."

Dallas raises his tiny cup. "I'll take another espresso while you're at it."

He's nicely put-together in a cashmere jumper and jeans. Not a stitch of jewelry except for the burnished band of gold on his left middle finger that he's worn for as long as I've known him. A warm panel of sunshine falls over the table, and I'm struck again by how shiny his hair is. And how badly I want to touch it.

I would also like to fill the silent void. At this flinty pace, breakfast will drag on like one of those art-house documentaries Flynn insists will enrich our souls.

Dallas beats me to the draw, thereby establishing beyond any doubt that he hasn't forgiven me for last night. "June is a little antsy about your commitment after yesterday," he says to Navarro. "She'd like to hear from you that the money is confirmed. When should we expect it?"

My cheeks redden. I feel like a child who whined for three helpings when everyone else had one. Dammit, Dallas! Yes, I wanted some breathing room. But did he have to bring it up in that context?

Navarro, idly thumbing through a magazine, lifts his gaze. I sense Dallas has broken an unspoken tactical barrier between them.

"The wire should arrive tomorrow," he says. "I put everything in motion on Sunday."

Dallas awards me a good hard look. "There you go. I'll follow up with Nikki after breakfast."

"Do you need anything else from us?" I ask Navarro, meekly, because I'm still dying inside.

He shakes his head. "I have faith in the team. With you two at the helm, I expect great things."

"To reconfirm," Dallas says, "you cash out before the IPO. We'll make sure to sweeten the pot."

Dallas explained last night that he wants us to go public and plans to froth up the market for a high valuation. And he was adamant that Cannistrá Capital cashes out before the IPO. I felt a twinge of apprehension, because any deal I do gets executed with some respect for my partner's intelligence. If Cannistrá sticks around and all goes well, they'll make a minimum of thirtyfold on the investment. But Navarro agreed to the terms.

Odd, to say the least.

"Yes," Navarro says, distractedly, like some of the shine has come off his morning.

Carolina delivers our coffees and generally seems a little stressed, like she knows every day involves a mile-long, thankless to-do list.

"Grazie," I say, careful to inflect on the A and stretching out the ending to make the E-A sound like Navarro taught me last night. Foreigners tend to pronounce it like *taxi* with a G.

"Prego," she replies, and disappears into the pantry with her shoes scuffling along the tile.

Graceless as a lawnmower.

"If you two have any requests for dinner tonight," Navarro says, "please let me know."

"Actually…"

Before Dallas can finish his thought, his phone lights up on the table. I catch a glimpse of the Lock Screen photo, and how cute! A smiling Dallas with two puppies in his arms. But he whips the phone off the table as if I've spied a dick pic.

"Hey Natalie," he says, an apology embedded in the greeting. "You're probably wondering where I am. A last-minute trip popped up and I forgot to call." He rises from the table and hustles to the mudroom at the rear of the kitchen for some privacy.

Natalie. Another woman in his long line of conquests? Or judging from Navarro's dark look, the woman who came between them? I help myself to a croissant and liberally coat it with apricot jam, pretending not to eavesdrop on Dallas's chatter.

"Did you see Giorgio this morning?" Navarro inquires. "He was making the rounds."

I pause mid-bite. "Is Giorgio the giraffe?"

"Yes. He usually hangs out by the acacia trees on the north end of the property."

"Why do you have a giraffe?" I ask, because the truly powerful rarely need to put on a show.

"A client from Dubai gifted him," he replies with a shrug. "I quite enjoy his company. Such a beautiful creature, vero?"

His eyes fix on mine. Where he kissed me on the forehead is still warm. An oddly touching gesture, and one I don't want to be enchanted with but find myself being, nonetheless. Never mind that gifting a wild animal is highly impractical. Like giving the gift of herpes.

"Does he have a companion?"

"No," Navarro says. "Lonely and looking. It's been hard to find him a mate."

He leans forward, elbow on the table, chin resting on his upturned hand to watch me intently. Is my heart the fastest-racing one in this room?

"Give Ralph and Myers a cuddle for me," Dallas says, returning just in time to pop the cozy bubble that settled around Navarro and me. "I'll see you next week."

"Do you have secret children?" I joke after he hangs up.

It's so obviously nosy, but it doesn't faze him.

"I volunteer at an animal care center in Carson," he explains. "It slipped my mind to tell them I was unavailable this week."

"Carson?"

Packed between two of LA's roughest neighborhoods, you don't end up there unless you've taken a wrong turn. His Rolls would get keyed within five minutes.

"I wanted to be anonymous," Dallas says, in answer to my disbelief. "Ditch my world for half a second. While I'm there, I'm just another guy who loves dogs."

On cue, Mimi and Rodolfo pad over to Dallas to indulge in a morning ear scratch. Navarro takes it all in with a bemused expression. "You always had a soft spot for animals," he says.

"Some of us care," Dallas says without looking up.

"Says the merciless billionaire."

Dallas pivots his head. The way they hold each other's gaze feels perversely intimate.

"I didn't grow up rich and entitled," he says. "I had to scrape my way through life."

"Up until a point," Navarro replies, and for the first time I hear aggression in his voice, a glimpse of something menacing.

Dallas pushes back with a stern, "I worked my ass off. No one handed me success." As the static between them threatens to engulf us, he steers the conversation into a different lane. "Anyway, circling back to dinner. To celebrate her hard work, I want to take June out tonight. I snagged two seats at a famous tango hall." His head swivels in my direction. "You'll love it. It's a great experience."

"Tonight?" Navarro repeats. "What about dinner here?"

After a moment of pinched silence Dallas says, "We'll eat at the club. They make a mean steak."

"But I can't join you," Navarro stresses. Clearly Dallas has forgotten his manners and the ankle monitor.

"You said the money lands tomorrow. We have to fly home and get things moving. That means tonight is our last night. Gotta make hay while the sun shines. Can Battista drive us there and back?"

Navarro appears to consider this for a moment. He breathes through his nose, slow and controlled. But not before a hurtful glance in my direction. "That can be arranged."

"Cool. We need to leave here at six."

Dallas flashes a tight smile and I can't figure out what's going on here. We just got confirmation on the cash, and to abandon Navarro would be the height of rudeness. But Dallas is hell-bent on doing just that. And hello? How about asking me instead of telling me the plans?

But when he plants his hand onto my knee in a territorial fashion, I read his scheme for what it is: a non-negotiable. He gave me what I wanted, and I need to return the favor. I'm not opposed to a night out. In fact, I'm relieved to escape the castle because the drink I agreed to with Navarro will only head in one direction. He made that abundantly clear.

And I would like some alone time with Dallas to unpack our unfinished business. The conversation we had in the salon still swirls through my head. I blamed him for everything, and one hundred percent, he needs to shoulder it for starting a smear campaign against me. But I'm responsible for not accepting his attempts to right his initial wrongs. Our path might have been different if I had given him a chance.

A night on the town won't change an entire decade, but it feels as good a place as any for a reboot.

So I finish my breakfast with one man's hand warming my skin, another in a snit while reading a magazine, and convince myself that somehow all of this is going to work out.

Chapter Eighteen

I meet Dallas in the atrium at ten past six. He's thumb-scrolling on his phone amidst the ferns and birds-of-paradise, looking very dapper in a brilliant black suit with satin lapels. I'm decked out in a sexy, flapper-style dress, evening coat draped over one arm. Dallas does a double take, tracking my curves with a sweeping once over. I feel the attention as if it were his hands caressing my skin.

"Wow," he says. "That fits you like a glove."

"I figured when in Rome, might as well go with the color du jour. Red is the tango, right?"

I twirl so the beaded hem of my dress flares out, and I warn Dallas that is the full extent of my dance moves because he looks encouraged.

"You look great. Don't go changing."

I blush and wish I could stop, but better to gain a few watts of radiance than five more pounds.

"Battista's waiting out front," he adds, grinning that little sideways smile of his. "We should blast."

He offers to help me into my coat, and I joke, "A full hour with Krusty the Clown? Oh, joy."

"You watch *The Simpsons*?" he asks, more puzzled than anything else.

"Here and there. I prefer *South Park*. Cartman is my favorite."

"Interesting. I would never have guessed that about you."

He adjusts the collar of my coat, and the shimmer of his touch against my neck warms a spot deep within me.

"Maybe you need to leave your ivory tower to mingle with the proletariats now and then," I say.

He bursts out laughing, and this is what I remember the most. His devil-may-care, Armagnac-soaked laugh that loosened my inhibitions and made me believe in love. That my world could be right again after years of endless wrongs.

"I watch March Madness sitting in my underwear with a cold beer," he says, his hazel eyes twinkling. "I think we're even."

He wraps a hand around my forearm and squeezes gently, setting off a giddy reaction in my chest. We cross the foyer to step outside, and cool night air washes over me. It's a nothing sky, black and starless. After a long morning and even longer afternoon chained to my laptop, I'm ready to blow this popsicle stand. One can only suffer through so many Zoom meetings before contemplating life after death.

And I'd love to remove the niggle of doubt at the back of my mind.

The howling silence we left behind in the castle tells me all is not perfectly squared away. Navarro promptly disappeared after breakfast and did not come around to see us off. Dallas reassured me again earlier that Navarro's word is as good as gold, but until Nikki confirms the wire, I can't fully relax.

Dallas helps me navigate the stairs in my heels. Battista hunches like a troll in the idling Mercedes, cigar smoke skulking out of his mouth. After we settle in the back seat, Dallas informs him that he has to hang around until the show finishes to drive us home. In response, the glass barrier rises to cut off further communication.

Dallas and I share eye rolls.

Whatever.

We secure our seatbelts in unison, and when the backs of our hands touch, static electricity erupts with a blue crackle. We both jump, me laughing, although it's at a much higher pitch than I'm used to emitting.

Dallas smiles, and God, those dimples.

"A spark to kick off the night," he says. "Feels about right."

The way he looks at me. A rush of arousal heats my skin. It is completely irrational, although maybe not. There is a reason why I fell hard for him. He made me feel special and, more importantly, understood.

My heart starts to race with something I can't quite name.

I smile back at him, hoping that he can't tell the effect he has on me.

$

An hour later, we are firmly in the trenches of Buenos Aires, a pulsating and cosmopolitan metropolis that oozes old-world elegance. Battista weaves in and out of insane traffic like a madman. July 9 Avenue is a major thoroughfare, the widest boulevard on the planet. My last count is fourteen lanes, all of them jammed with zooming taxis and buses packed to the tits. The sprawl alone makes the 405 in LA look like a country lane.

I crane my head in every direction, awed by the diversity streaking past my window. "Look at the buildings!"

Skyscrapers mingle with baroque finery butted up against neoclassical masterpieces. No wonder the capital of Argentina is called the Paris of the South. It feels like Europe. A wilder version. The unpredictable and saucy middle child. Fishnets and stilettos.

Dallas soaks it all in from his side of the car, fingers drumming a restless beat on his thigh. "I love the vibe. It's a late-night city, like New York."

He's right. I can almost taste the kinetic energy.

This is something else.

And so is our final destination.

Club Duende is a famous tango hall in the upscale Recoleta neighborhood. Dallas knows the owner through an old dance connection, and the man scored us last-minute prime seats for the show. As Battista pulls up to the spired facade of the private club, my skin hums with excitement. The crowd! Flawless, sexy minxes flaunting acres of skin. Chiseled men dressed to the nines. A smiling doorman in a top hat escorts Dallas and me up the red-carpeted stairway into a sumptuous interior like La Scala in Milan. Royal-red velvet and gold everywhere. Soaring archways. A sense of history.

I snap a few photos and group text them to Flynn and Vandana with the caption—*Night on the town!*

"Who are you texting?" Dallas asks, trying for casual.

"Vandana and Flynn."

"You all seem very close."

"They're the siblings I never had. I'd be lost without them."

"I get it. Only child syndrome. We hold on hard to the people we love." Dallas crooks his arm for me to slide mine through. "Better not lose the most stunning woman here," he says with a wink.

Hot awareness seeps up my neck. Another profound breakthrough occurred on the long drive into the city—a conversation with Dallas where we aligned on something other than mutual frustration. With a rescued company imminent, our shot at the gold, the thrill of it, fizzed through every question. Can the launch date be pulled? Do we head-hunt fresh board members? We rose above our history and rekindled the shared ambition that brought us together in the first place. It felt like he was trying to mend trust.

And tonight also feels like the proper date we never had.

I link my arm with his and say, "Lead the way."

He steers us through the crowd to a velvet rope draped between two stanchions in front of an entrance marked *Privado.* A smartly uniformed usher checks off *Evener* on his clipboard of names. Then he draws the heavy curtain back, allowing us to enter.

Right away, I love the intimate room.

Couples crammed around cocktail tables. Dirty light. A frisky vibe more speakeasy than formal dance hall, where at any given moment one of the men will pour a shot of whiskey over the twin towers of his date's bosoms and lap it up. Lined along the wall where we entered are curtained private booths like the ones Vandana splurges on for poolside primping at Caesars Palace in Vegas.

Dallas nudges me forward. "Ours is the biggest one. At the end."

I can feel eyes on us on our short walk to the booth. Dallas looks smoking hot in his tux and trainers with silver-sparkle stars. Movie star hair swept back and shining. And my flapper dress is note perfect. The only thing missing is a rose clenched between my teeth.

We scooch onto the half-moon of velvet sofa circling our table, and a slim waiter arrives to inform us that our steaks will be forthcoming with the wine and that the show will start in an hour.

"I had to preorder," Dallas explains. "If you don't want the Wagyu I ordered for you, I'm sure they can whip something else up for you? And one bottle of wine to start," he adds in a playful tone. "I got your back. No tattoos you will regret in the morning on my watch."

His eyes dance all over me, and okay, enough already.

"Will you please come clean with me?" I ask. "What happened after you drove me home?"

He tilts his head. "I thought you had all your full faculties."

"Maybe I lied."

"Where do you want me to start?" he asks. "With the vomit?"

I pale. My hand shoots up to cover my mouth. "Not *on* you?"

"Your friend at the bar helped clean me up. Good thing I'm washable."

I smack his bicep with the back of my hand. This is horrifying. "How could you not tell me that?"

"Because I knew it would gut you," he says, and my heart stutters with his sincerity.

I take a nervous sip of water because there's more. I can see it in his face. An entire evening's worth of folly and shame waiting to bite me on the arse.

"And what else?" I prod. "I need to hear it all. The good, bad, and the ugly."

He slings an arm onto the top of our sofa. Not quite touching me, but close enough that heat penetrates through his suit onto my skin and brings with it a cloud of his seductive cologne.

"You asked me to lie on top of you."

I shut my eyes briefly. "Please tell me you didn't."

"What if I did?" he asks, all flirty-like.

"You could claim you were only following orders, I suppose."

A smile quirks his mouth. "For the record, I didn't. Although it killed me not to."

"What was the worst thing?" I ask. Not that vomiting on someone could be misconstrued as anything good.

"Hmm," he says, mock-thinking, fingers drumming on my shoulder. "The funniest thing is when you asked me what my middle name was."

"Why did I ask that?"

He laughs. "I have no idea. You were very stream of consciousness. And after I told you, you said it was the most pretentious mouthful of vowels you'd ever heard."

I sink my face into both hands. At this rate, maybe I don't want to know everything. I sneak a look at him through the screen of my fingers. "What is your middle name?"

"My full name is Dallas Diamond Cole Hollyer Evener."

I burst out laughing and am embarrassed how I can't stop. "Sorry, but I wasn't far off then in my assessment, was I?"

"It is a mouthful," he concurs. "My mom and dad couldn't agree on names, so they slapped them all on me."

He smiles ruefully at first. Then it becomes sad, cooling just slightly, like his eyes before they tear off mine. I can see his Adam's apple move up and down with a hard swallow.

What just happened? Did I cross a line insulting his name? Or did the mention of his mom and dad throw him off? He is right, in that I know nothing about him, other than what he revealed in a week of rambling phone calls from New York a decade ago. He'd flown there the morning after we met in the bar.

Before we met one last time at his office.

Dallas gives me a sideways glance. "Did you narc on Sonny Barnett?"

"No!" I exclaim. "Did I say otherwise?"

Dallas doesn't know me well enough to understand I'd rather eat salad for an entire year than lie, but he clocks my body language, the indignant straightening of my back. After a beat, he flicks imaginary dust off the cream-colored tablecloth.

"On the contrary, you repeatedly said it wasn't you. I just wanted to match up the story now that you're lucid."

Now? What does he think I was doing for the past ten years? Sniffing glue on the boardwalk? I have the same phone number, for Christ's sake. He could have called.

"A decade later you decide to ask me this?"

"A decade too late," he corrects. "And pardon me for being a vindictive motherfucker. Not my best quality."

I absorb that, and all the implications of having to rethink his nature.

"Is that an official apology?" I ask. Best be sure before I commit to a whole new world of Dallas.

"It's one of them."

He blows out an audible breath and looks vaguely at the dance floor. The room is filling up. Spanish chatter, animated and drunk, floats around us.

A long silence ticks past before he says, "There's a lot you don't know about me, and I don't want to get into it tonight. It's also not an excuse. I acted like an idiot with you. You had every right to walk away."

He reaches for my wrist. The same wrist his hand circled when we were drunk on Armagnac and well past good manners.

I feel a rush of memories. A dropping-away sensation in my stomach.

On how that afternoon turned on a dime.

We'd been having a dandy conversation about management and how picking the right teams was critical. He'd said a person's human capital is as visible to him as a painting on a wall. And because I was still reeling from my latest breakup, unsure of myself after months of being told I was a workaholic and not fit to be a girlfriend, I longed to hear what he thought of me. After I asked, Dallas looked at me straight on. I still remember how my heart pinched at the good fortune of being someone who could soften the intensity in his eyes.

And then he said, "What I see is an incredible rack. And I'd love to see more of it before dinner."

Insert the world's longest, most heinous-sounding record scratch, and it would not do the disgraceful moment justice.

"Come again?" I said, out of reflex.

"Again?" Dallas laughed long and mightily at my unintended joke. "I'm a simple man, June. Once is enough, although most women prefer me to post higher numbers. Just like my investors."

A sick feeling intensified and took hold of my stomach. "Are you for—"

"June," he interrupted, leaning forward to encircle his hand around my wrist. The warm touch of his skin almost made me forget the nightmare of what came next. "It's Friday night. Time to switch it off." He tipped my wrist to check the time on my Chopard. "I have reservations at Mélisse for seven. How about we fuck on this table first? I always wanted to do it in here."

Suffocated in filth.

That's what it felt like.

The gulf that opened up between us felt irreversible. I couldn't get out of there fast enough. And it took weeks to scrape the slime of those words off my skin.

I drink in long, steadying breaths, my chest and back rising and falling as I try to collect myself. It feels like the world is exploding all over again.

Dallas tightens his hold around my wrist. He knew the danger of bringing this up and is prepared. He won't let me walk away this time.

"June," he says, slowly, carefully, his voice a little thick. "I'm sorry, and I should have said that. Please forgive me. I was twenty-five and stupid and scared. You blew my mind with how smart you were. How smart you are. I realized too late that you are the perfect woman. Perfect for me."

I squirm in the fabric barely containing me. Me, perfect? A stubborn roll around my tummy and jiggly underarms, no matter how many full wine glasses I lift? He fingers the spaghetti strap of my dress and the thicker bra strap beneath. My heart starts pounding in my ears so loudly that I can't hear the canned music.

What he's saying without saying it is that he wants me. Wants us.

And I'm so dumbfounded my tongue refuses to work.

"Can you forgive me?" he asks.

His fingers walk up the nape of my neck to weave into my hair. He uses that hand in my hair to pull me closer to him. The press of the room closes in on me as Dallas waits for my reply. But I can't form the words because his fingertips slowly massage my scalp and steal my breath away. I feel the sting of surprise tears but defiantly blink them back. He behaved badly that day, but the memory of everything that came before shimmers like gold. We search each other's faces. There is something comfortable about our silence, an understanding embedded in it. Is this where we kiss and make up? Because it sure as hell feels like it.

We are so completely and wholly in the moment our waiter clears his throat a few times before he snaps our attention. We pull back, flustered with the interruption. The young buck, no more than twenty, carries a bottle of wine in the crook of his arm. His smile says he's seen it all.

"Dinner will be out shortly," he tells us. "May I serve you some wine?"

"Yeah," Dallas says, sitting up to push my wine glass forward. "I'll let the lady have the honors of tasting."

The waiter pours a taster and I do the swirl and swish. Malbec can often have a bite, but this one goes down smooth.

"It's delicious," I say, and offer the last swig to Dallas, who concurs. He chats amicably with the waiter as he fills both of our glasses.

After he departs, Dallas raises his glass for a toast. His eyes are soft, falling on mine. "Thank you for coming," he says.

I clink his glass and take a deep pull of liquid courage. Maybe tonight I will blame the wine because, in my mind, the dirty dishrag that it is, I think, *But I haven't yet.*

Chapter Nineteen

DINNER FLIES BY. OUR STEAKS ARE THICK, SEASONED, AND memorable. The wine is smooth, and our conversation never hits an awkward patch. The oppression and strangeness of Navarro's world are only an hour away, yet it feels like we exist on an entirely different planet.

One I am enjoying immensely.

I feel warm and squishy. I blame the steak and the wine, and Dallas, whose arm has snaked around my shoulder.

One good pairing inevitably leads to another.

He tops up my wine and says, "After the main dancers, the floor opens up for amateur hour."

I squash his hopes with a head shake. "I hope I was clear. In no universe will you drag me onto a dance floor."

"I'll ask you later in case you change your mind."

"Why would it change?" I ask, skeptical and also worried. His smile is pure mischief.

Before he can respond, the lights dim, and murmurs of excitement ripple through the air. A curtain at the front of the room furls upward to reveal a small stage and a cluster of musicians—a piano player with two violinists and a burly man seated on a tiny chair, leaning on the pleats of his accordion. The dissonant cacophony of instruments tuning up serenades the arrival of the dancers.

It's showtime.

Dallas's arm tightens around me, this time in a completely different fashion. Before it was casual. Now it's possessive, intense. Like what unfolds in front of us. I'm embarrassed at how turned on I am by the dancers. Bodies pressed tightly against each other, and the drama of leg flicks and dips—I feel the seductive thrill of their deep lunges, every sharp swivel of their hips. A spotlight prowls after them like the police chasing a fugitive, and the exotic-looking woman owns her dress, slit to the waist. My soft body would spill out of her tiny costume, but she is alive with confidence, eyes only for her partner: a consummate Latin lover with a dress shirt stretched tight to emphasize his buff physique.

They drip with sensuality.

The tango as tawdry burlesque?

And the music is its own thing, a ribbon of seduction wrapping around us like a hot summer night. Dallas stirs beside me, his leg pressing hard on mine from hip to knee. He smells sweet and spicy—a cupcake made with single malt. A recipe I should have tried at least once, now that I think about it.

When the dance floor gymnastics finish, the crowd erupts into thunderous applause.

"They were incredible," I say, leaning into him. "Can you dance like that?"

He raises a brow. "Do you want to find out?"

"Not really." But yes.

The room slowly brightens, and the musicians pack up, smiling and chatting with one another in that content way of artsy types who never have to worry about companies and failed reputations. Canned tango music drifts over the loudspeakers, and couples take to the floor in heated embraces, far less skilled than the performers but too drunk to care.

Amateur hour is on.

Dallas's eyes roam over the crowded floor. I can tell he's itching to get out there.

I elbow him gently. "Why don't you ask one of the women to dance with you?"

He shakes his head. "It's not like high school prom. There's a protocol with tango. It's called Cabeceo."

"What's that all about?"

"You make eye contact with a woman first and wait for them to give you a quick nod. Once they do, you're good."

His gaze lands directly, forcefully onto mine.

"Oh, no," I say, holding both hands up in protest. "I told you, I can't dance."

"Nothing fancy to start," he insists. "I promise." He reaches for my hand, his pulling no match for my resistance.

"I will bring shame and embarrassment to this entire club," I claim, quite accurately. "You need a capable partner. Go on. I'll cheer you from the sidelines."

"June," he says, refusing to be shut down. "You are the most capable woman I know. Don't be scared by something you've never tried."

He bum-slides out of the booth and waits for me with his hand outstretched, not giving me an inch. "Five minutes," he says. "You can survive five minutes."

I can survive nuclear war too, but who wants to live through that? And I'm not prepared to show the world how a stumbling water buffalo makes mincemeat of the world's sexiest dance.

Does he not see the absolute fear in my expression?

"You'll be in the arms of a professional," he adds, going the extra mile to sell it. "It makes all the difference."

I sigh and capitulate. I did eat an entire crème brûlée for dessert, and not just a tiny ramekin either. A few spins on the floor could qualify as a workout of sorts.

"Fine," I say. "Five minutes." I scooch out and point to a patch of floor beside us darkened from a burnt-out light bulb overhead. "But we dance over here, where no one can see us."

"You're afraid," he teases.

"I'm realistic."

He takes my hand and tows me across the floor, assuring me he won't go crazy as he positions our arms and hands and walks us through the basic moves. Explains the steps and the rhythm. Quick, quick, slow. Leg flicks. Variations that make me more nervous.

"Listen to the music," he says. "And follow my lead, even if it kills you."

Locked in a stuffy formal position, worry surges through every vein. Russ once said I was four left feet dragging around a bundle of bricks. Not that he was Fred Astaire.

And then we start moving.

Me as nimble as a concrete statue.

"Stay loose," Dallas whispers into my ear. "Feel it, don't force it."

Through some miracle, I don't botch it completely. Not when Dallas holds me tight.

Like, very tight.

Are we supposed to be this close?

He feels so familiar. Is it a buried muscle memory of his biceps carrying me into my house like a stoned rag doll? (Apparently, I couldn't walk.) Or maybe it's the furnace that is Dallas burning hot onto my skin at this very moment. He moves so fluidly. We float effortlessly in our little space. I feel a glow of pride, but let's be realistic. We are moving at a quarter of the pace that the pros did. But a junior version of the tango is still the tango. A tightrope of flirtation. Sex while standing, as sensual music cascades into every crevice of my soul.

I slowly find my groove, and after a few minutes, muster the courage to try a leg flick.

Success!

"Oh my god! I did it," I say, breathless and feeling strangely nervous. Anytime I've overcome the odds, the invisible bar I set for myself pushes higher.

Dallas feels my frame relax a fraction and takes the opportunity to draw me even closer. "Hold on," he murmurs.

Very slowly, he dips me, holding onto me like I am precious cargo. What a freeing sensation to hang in space. It seems inconceivable that not a single muscle of his fatigues with the effort of holding me horizontal. And yet he holds me, strong and unmoving, far longer than any dip requires.

To the point I have to ask, "What?" Because a question hangs in his eyes.

"The other night, you said you wished things could have been different between us."

I smile weakly. My mushroom monologue. The gift that keeps on giving.

"I guess I *was* out of my mind," I joke, my only defense because the way he's looking at me sets my heart aflutter.

His voice transforms into a quiet, urgent tone. "I'm asking for real, June. Is that how you feel?"

My throat is so thick I can't verbally respond. His pupils are so huge only a thin hazel ring surrounds them. Then he leans forward, and before I can process what is happening, his mouth is on mine.

And I'm kissing him back.

A marvelous, scary, wonderful feeling bursts inside me. It's not just any kiss. It's hot and open-mouthed, our tongues in a passionate flurry of arousal and need. My entire body responds, and have I ever experienced anything so electric? Around me, I can hear the soft sounds of the club: couples chattering, music on the speakers, laughter. And it fades away until I am aware of nothing except the force field we're creating. A jolt of desire from fingertips to heart.

It's a miracle of performance and timing as he lifts me in one flawless, effortless move, never once breaking the kiss. He pulls me flush against him, my fingers tangling in his hair to steady myself. I can smell the exertion on his skin and feel his cock pressing hard between my legs. We are as close as two people can be with clothes on in a room that has gone silent. Or maybe my mind has gone blank and blocked all sounds. Dallas breathes heavily, head nestled in the darkness of my neck. The rise and fall of his chest against mine is like a melody written in heartbeats. Not a word passes between us because our bodies are saying it all. Anyone can plainly see the want between us.

Now what?

Dallas runs his fingers through my hair and kisses the tender flesh of my neck. The commotion in my heart settles when he lifts his head. Framed by the dark curtain of his hair, his eyes are a fresh, shining shade of bronze. They cast a spell as he stares through me, into the locked-up places of my heart.

"Hey," he says his voice barely a whisper.

I swallow past the lump in my throat. His singular taste hums on my lips. "You certainly know how to kiss."

He chuckles. "Better bring my A-game for the Siren."

God, I've dreamt of this. Cried over it never happening. But is it outlandish to sleep with him? Will he disappoint me again? If he does, it's impossible to walk away this time. We are in the trenches together.

"I don't want to play games, Dallas."

His fingers dance along the back of my neck, and I realize with a tightening of my heart that he's gently unraveling a knot in my hair. "You deserve the best, is what I meant," he clarifies.

Ten years later, defying every odd, we're here, heading straight into the unknown. I tell myself to relax and run with it, but when I've spent countless nights wondering how things could have been different, and now the answer is being served up on a platter, the first thing my efficient, numbers-oriented brain wants to do is to reject the long-shot odds.

As if he's reading my mind, Dallas murmurs, "You tell me what happens next."

Our heads swivel in unison to our empty booth. He said earlier that closing the curtains signals the staff to leave you alone. The naughty thrill of it sends my head spinning, but as liberal as Paris of the South is, I gather Club Duende member guidelines do not encourage public lewdness. And I learned from Vandana that the embarrassment of being splashed across the internet as a naked sensation comes with a price.

Dallas finds my eyes and, with heart-breaking sincerity, says, "I don't want you to feel cheapened, okay?"

My heart pounds and aches at once.

A brief sentence, and it says more than a nine-hundred-page novel ever could. Maybe this is how life works—people can and do change. We don't stay the same forever. But is this too early in the game for us? Who knows? Honestly, I need to stop analyzing. The already soaked-through Parisian silk of my knickers threaten to sag to the floor. And from what I can tell, Dallas is packing, and I'm in the mood to unpack.

Cock is like oxygen. You don't miss until it's gone, and it has been out of my life for far too long.

"Should we find Battista?" I ask and hope that's enough of an answer.

Chapter Twenty

If I believed in fairy tales, I'd say castles are magical places where princesses get rescued by manly princes and live happily ever after. But there is no magic going on here. In the dead of night, the d'Amico home feels like a graveyard. Entrails of fog skim the palm trees. No lights warm the inside. If Navarro wanted us to get a taste of what it feels like to be left behind, utter blackness pretty much sums it up.

Dallas shoves the front door open. Inside, the silence is palpable, like the cold flood of air. Chillier than the shifty once-over Battista honored us with when he picked us up at the club. Was it that obvious? Did we have scarlet letters of sin painted on our foreheads? We played it safe on the drive home and crammed into our respective corners of the back seat. Not touching each other almost killed me.

"My room?" Dallas asks.

I study his face in the dimness. I've had an hour to process what transpired between us and what will follow.

"Uhm … do you have anything?"

His expression falters, just for a nanosecond, before he says yes. Is he asking himself the same questions I am? Is this madness, what we're doing? What happens after? His hand finds mine, our warm fingers settling. It feels like I'm floating down the east wing hall, and I push aside my uncertainty. We've both made mistakes. I'm sure we'll make many more. But tonight, it feels like we righted a wrong, and that's all that matters.

Dallas fumbles drunkenly with the door—pulling instead of pushing—and rolls his eyes at me once he figures it out. He flicks the light on and allows me to enter first. If my room is a bone-china teacup ringed in gold and sipped by a princess with her pinky extended, his is a tarnished goblet with mead spilling over the rim, fisted by a rake.

The air hangs thick with the musty scent of polished wood and aged tapestries. A massive four-poster bed dominates the room, its canopy draped with rich, plum velvet that whispers of royal extravagance. Beams crisscross the ceiling and a single stained-glass window curves into a gothic peak. Outside, the castle grounds are bathed in the soft glow of misted moonlight.

Dallas helps me out of my coat and hangs it in the wardrobe. He undoes the laces of his trainers and kicks them off. I feel a pinch beneath my belly button.

Something about him in his socks.

The domesticity of it is endearing.

"Drink?" he asks. "I have it all."

"Some sparkling, please."

He fixes two glasses of water while I scan the room. Where to sit? The bed feels too presumptuous, so I curl up in one corner of the sofa and wish I could call on the servants to draw up a fire. Both nipples have perked from the chill and I can't do a damn thing to hide them. Dallas hands off my drink and sits facing me, one leg tucked underneath him. His gaze is piercing as always, but with an undercurrent I can't put my finger on. It adds another layer of mystery to the room.

We sit for a moment in silence before he says, "Thank you for tonight. All of it."

"I enjoyed myself," I say, the most lukewarm reply ever considering he titillated every cell in my body with his five-alarm kiss. Can I let my guard down and just be for a change?

He runs a fingertip along the curve of my shoulder. It feels as if he's gearing up to get a formal announcement out of the way.

"I want to make love to you," he says, with a frankness that disarms me. "But I like certain things to be in my control."

"The handcuffs?" I venture, without having to think about it, because I have indeed thought about it. I scoured an embarrassing number of BDSM articles after the morning at his house. The psychology behind restraint during sex fascinated me because it's not cut-and-dried across the board. Some enjoy the power play. A few get off on the degrading aspect. Other pleasure seekers try it once, just for kicks. I touched on one article that analyzed trauma and how it can manifest into kink. When I think back to Ally and how irked Dallas was … It didn't feel like he was angry at her per se; more that she had escaped.

"Are they…" I pause, unsure how to phrase it. "I mean, do you need them?"

"Are you asking if I need them to get off?"

"Do you?"

He finishes his water and sets the glass on the floor. "No."

"But you still want to use them."

"Is that okay?"

I glance at his bed, envisioning myself cuffed to the spirals of wood. The helplessness is part of the appeal, truth be told. My sense of self-preservation is wildly excited at the thought of submission. I ran the bedroom show with all my past lovers, and it gets a bit dull when men do as they're told and have no imagination.

Sometimes a woman wants nothing more than to be conquered.

"Do we need a safe word?" I read about those. The most common safe word system is the traffic light analogy where *Red* means stop, *Yellow* means careful, and *Green* means go.

Dallas shoots me a quizzical look. "If you want one. Otherwise, I'll stop if you tell me to. I promise."

I think about that. "Can I hold onto the keys in case you have a heart attack?"

I'd read about that in a Stephen King book. I don't fancy the misery of being trapped with a corpse as my bedmate. But I'm glad Dallas finds it funny because his laugh breaks the strange tension that has built up.

"You can have whatever you want," he says and leans in to brush his lips against mine so tenderly that it feels as if we've been together like this a hundred times. "Why don't you get comfortable on the bed and leave everything to me?"

He wanders into the bathroom, and I feel my confidence drop off a smidge. The thundering beat of my heart sounds like a tribal drum. Okay, then. We're on. I dim the lights until they cast an ethereal glow. I damn near need a footstool to mount the bed and scale it like it's Kilimanjaro.

The bed linens smell like vanilla and the sweet whiskey-tinged musk of Dallas. They're smooth to the touch, a luxurious weave of high-end cotton. I feel like a virginal princess on her wedding night in this regal sanctuary. The thrill of consummation pebbles my skin with goosebumps, and I wriggle out of my dress before I get too comfortable. Removing things will be tricky once the cuffs are on. I undo my bra next and position myself in one of those campy boudoir photo poses to make my boobs look perkier. Hand behind my head, and my body stretched out.

Too much? Too little?

Think of the bright side, I tell myself. Instead of a salacious tryst in a public venue here, with the door shut tight and lights dimmed properly, I won't sound like a dog in heat, panting and whining, trying to hold it all in.

This is…

A low whistle echoes in the room. Dallas has returned. Shirt untucked, he holds two sets of cuffs in one hand and several condoms in the other. His eyes roam up and down my body with an awed and hungry sweep.

"Jesus," he mutters. "You're a goddess. I don't know where to start."

A powerful urgency douses the last of my doubts. A ten-year wait to sleep with someone might be an underrated commodity.

"I think you do," I say and beckon him closer with a Mona Lisa smile.

Chapter Twenty-One

"Is there enough give?" Dallas asks. "I didn't tighten them
too much?"

I blow out a shaky breath. "I'm all right."

Arms stretched overhead, I feel like a trussed Christmas goose. Shackled and ready for basting. One set of cuffs binds both wrists, and a ring from the second pair of cuffs circles the taut chain. The other one fastens me to the spindled headboard. My short wingspan made it impossible for Dallas to use the spired posters of the bed. The man has his act together when it comes to restraint; focused and unflappable.

His lips press against my pale skin. "Your wrists are so tiny. So delicate. Very unlike your personality."

I zero in on his eyes, wicked twinkling topaz gems that they are. "Excuse me?"

He chuckles and palms me the keys. "As promised. But it's up to you to hold onto them."

I feel as fragile as the ancient, warped window glass and fear I might shatter into a thousand glittering pieces when Dallas gets started. He grips my chin between his thumb and forefinger and lifts my mouth, pressing his to my spreading lips for a kiss so damning and brief that I whimper at the tortured brevity of it.

"I'm so ready for you, June," he says.

"Are you going to take your clothes off?" I ask.

He laughs and scoots off the bed to start unbuttoning his shirt. "That's kind of how it works."

My head is clear, but the edges of the room grow dim as he fiddles with every button. His graceful fingers can coax magic from piano keys. Will I soar as high and bright and loud when they touch me?

He flings the shirt onto a solitary, high-backed chair and unbuckles his belt, giving me a curious look. "Why are you smiling?"

"I'm watching a man disrobing like it's a performance. That's a win for most women."

He whips the belt from his waist. The audible *crack* of leather sends apprehension rippling over me like a shockwave.

"Is that part of tonight?" I ask.

"Not a chance," he replies. "Violence does nothing for me. I've never even been in a fistfight."

"For the record, it looks like you could win."

Dallas is the antithesis of a no-neck gym rat. Sculpted, yes, but built like a luxury car. Detailed with fine, exotic lines. Ripped biceps and cut abs, hard muscle without a trace of fat. And just the right amount of hair dusted over his pecs.

"I do like to win," he says. "But tonight, it's all about you."

He shimmies the fine wool trousers past his hips, and they puddle onto the rug.

A thrill rockets through me, followed by a wave of surprise.

For some reason, I imagined him a briefs wearer. Not tighty-whiteys, but something to keep his balls snug and controlled. I do like the striped boxers though. They quaintly resemble a circus big top tented by his erection. And above the waistband, his darling innie belly button whorled with soft, dark hair. Oh, to swirl my tongue around in that private hole. I forget about the manacles until their cruel bite holds me back.

"It's unfair that I can't touch you."

He smiles. "I know."

"But you can bring yourself to my mouth."

"I could," he drawls, as if legitimately considering my request.

And slowly, he slips himself free of the boxers.

Damn, damn, damn.

I can't unsee this spectacle.

I told myself years ago that he had a mini prick, a pinky finger of uselessness I wasn't missing out on. But scratch that. His cock is heavy and smooth and weighted down by a glistening, thick head. A meaty, purple vein bulges underneath the length long enough to maraud but manageable in the throat. It's rude to stare, but Dallas is so unapologetically *male*.

He climbs onto the bed, grinning as he straddles me, knees on either side of my hips. I am breathing unevenly. Nervous. A blushing nude. A hungry hum of energy spills off of us, excitement and anticipation curling through the room.

"You have beautiful breasts," he says, tracing a line with his finger down my throat, between the damp V of my bosom. "Absolutely perfect."

He circles my nipples until they stiffen into fat nubs of aroused flesh. They feel enormous, throbbing with every heartbeat. I jerk on my bonds, a jingling reminder nothing is in my control.

Oh, God. The tease.

This is so addictive.

"How does it feel not to be in control?" he asks, cupping the soft flesh of my breast into a painful, peaked mound.

"I'm a little frustrated," I admit. "This takes some getting used to."

"Lucky for you," he says with a lazy, wicked smile. "I have the perfect cure."

He shuffles backward and settles between my legs. My willpower dissolves into shudders as his fingers dance along my inner thighs, voyaging higher. I muffle a cry. It's criminal what the smallest of touches can do to me.

"Mmm," he mumbles. "Someone's ready to go."

He grabs handfuls of ass to arrange me into a better position. I feel dizzy, swamped with desire, the cuffs amplifying everything. Very gently and purposefully, he spreads my folds, planting his face deep into the wet center to inhale deeply. My rear end clenches, my body drawing taut as a drumhead.

"Oh, God," I whimper.

Looking over my bits, beyond my belly, and up through the valley between my breasts, his eyes find mine.

"June," he whispers. "You fucking smell like life."

Relief, silly as it is, washes over me. Like every woman, I feared a spin on the dance floor might have left me musty or smelling like off clams.

"I don't know how long I'm going to last," I say, a high, strange note in my voice.

He nips at my quaking inner thighs. "We have all night, champ. All you need to do is relax."

Story of my life. And one that unravels into a debauched second act when the warm, wet tip of his tongue flicks my clit. The room seems to tilt a little: a combination of my lightheadedness and the sensational ache. I arch against him to grind against his mouth in forbidden complicity. He's awakened something in me that has been dormant for far too long.

He latches onto my swollen nub and suckles like a babe on a teat. I shut my eyes and steel myself. He said earlier he didn't know where to start. Start. End. Middle. What do those words even mean? He pushes me to the end of surrender in an endless cycle of punishment. Tongue-fucking me with tormenting accuracy. Every delicious stab is a shock-wave of pleasure.

Five minutes feels like an agonized hour before I cry, "Enough! Slow down!"

My arm muscles scream. The smallest hairs tingle. The thick, musk smell of my desire makes my head spin.

Dallas pants in a heavy, ragged rhythm, his breath hot on my bits. "June," he whispers. "Come for me. Let it all out."

He buries his tongue like there's a prize in the farthest reaches of my womb. I'm spiraling higher to the apex of desire. Shudders of pleasure roll through me in great waves, my hips bucking and begging Dallas for the bliss of completion.

Seconds away from the point of no return, I feel the air shift. A rush of cool flits over my peaked nipples. For a single, pulsing moment dots fill my vision. That's why I don't see him at first.

But then Navarro steps out of the shadows, and my heart leaps into my throat. He jams his hand in his pockets with a pinched expression, like he's dad and Dallas his renegade son, cavorting with the local harlot.

"Dallas!" I whisper through clenched teeth.

His eyes, half-lidded and dazed, find mine. My body has tightened like glass, and he senses it. "Everything okay?" he mumbles.

"Why is he here?" I don't know why I sound frightened, but Dallas sees the fear in my eyes and whips his head around so fast I'm surprised it doesn't pop off.

"What the fuck!"

He leaps up from between my legs, and the speed at which it happens is both impressive and merciless. I was seconds away from rapture. Dallas fumbles the sheet over me and shouts, "You ever hear of knocking?"

"I did," Navarro says, calm and cool, he of the fine suits and leather shoes. "But I guess you didn't hear."

"No shit, Sherlock!" Dallas scrapes his hair back, eyes wild. We're panting like sprinters. I am crimson with shame. "Jesus Christ," he says, "what do you want?"

"I need to talk to you."

"Can it wait until the morning?"

Navarro's mouth puckers into a tight cupid's bow. "No. We need to talk now."

Dallas lets out a heavy sigh and his shoulders sag. Is this a dream? Because in what reality does he not assert himself? And there is something else. You can lie about a lot of things, but you can't lie about what you do on instinct. And I don't miss that Dallas, for all his blustering, hasn't covered himself up. And I don't know what I'm supposed to understand there.

"Fuck! Okay," he says tersely. "Give us a minute, please?"

I wouldn't call it mocking, but there is a superior fire in Navarro's eyes when they land on me. Like someone who hates to lose has just scored a win.

"I'll be in my office. Meet me there."

And as stealthily as he infiltrated, Navarro retreats, the door clicking shut behind him.

The mother of all awkward silences hangs between Dallas and me before he sinks his face into both hands. He's shaking and appears rattled to the bone. I can't think a straight thought, let alone avoid getting trapped in a permanent loop of pointless thoughts. What the fuck was that all about?

"Is he mentally okay?" I ask, a viable question, given how Navarro's chin wobbled when he spoke, and an eerily sad light seemed to take over his entire being.

Dallas drags his fingers down his face and mutters, "I don't know what his deal is."

"I'd say he's pissed about tonight. We shouldn't have gone out."

Dallas doesn't reply, and something in his body language reads cagey. Like maybe Navarro barging in and demanding to talk isn't a surprise. He jumps off the bed, yanks open the cupboard, and drags a T-shirt over his head. Rips a pair of jeans off the hanger and stuffs one leg in and then the other. Zips up and swoops the hair off his face in an aggravated gesture. His eyes are dark, hollowed out.

"Is there more here than you're not telling me?" I ask.

He pauses. "Like what?"

"You, running off in the middle of the night to talk with Navarro."

A little muscle works around his mouth. "Give me an hour," he says, slipping on his trainers.

An hour? What can they possibly talk about at one in the morning that needs an hour?

And, hello?

"Can you unlock me, please?" I ask, exasperated and a little annoyed. Does it end like this after everything that went down between us?

Dallas frees me, but his movements, everything about him, feel checked out. Mind elsewhere. I sit on the bed and try to breathe calmly. This situation reeks of weirdness.

"Do you want me to stay here?"

His eyes flash and then flatten into a strange, lost expression. "Yes," he says. "Whatever happens, do not leave until I get back."

Chapter Twenty-Two

DALLAS

THE MIDNIGHT CHILL PENETRATES MY JEANS AND SETTLES LIKE BLACK ice in my bones. I shiver, wishing I'd thrown on more than a T-shirt. How can Navarro stand it here? After two days, I'm ready to climb the walls. Ready to clear the fuck out. I pass through the atrium—nothing but a dark sky overhead at this time of night. Midway down the north-wing hall, a soft glow of yellow spills out his office door. Light at the end of the tunnel? Or the light you see before life as you know it snuffs out?

You never know with him.

And I dread what's waiting for me. I get the distinct impression Navarro is at the end of a rope that might find its way around my neck.

I hear the crackle and hiss of logs in his office, and my steps instinctively slow. Anxiety claws up my throat. I collect myself with a deep breath and step inside his man cave. Burning timber rages in the fireplace, casting an otherworldly orange light on the quotidian details. A desk in the far corner with two monitors on it and nothing else. Behind it, a bookcase filled with leather-bound first editions, no doubt alphabetically arranged by author's last name. Navarro the neat freak. Everything is in perfect order.

Everything, that is, except him.

He sits slumped on a majestic wingback chair in a pose of sulking tragedy. The hard lines around his mouth say nothing and a hundred things all at the same time. In a stuffy, proper room where deadly business is the order of the day, I lower into the chair next to his, facing an inferno that also burns within our souls.

A long silence passes.

"What was that shit?" I demand. "Do not play fucking games with me."

His lips purse like the petulant child he can be. "I might say the same thing."

"Clarify, please."

He taps a finger on the worn leather armrest, the gesture betraying increased agitation. "Did June mention she and I had planned to have a drink earlier this evening?"

I shoot him a perilous glance. "Since when—"

"Nothing has changed," he snaps, with the sudden ferocity that makes him so brutally efficient at what he does. "But *I* need to make a change. Why do you think I'm here with this on?"

He gestures to the ankle monitor I forgot about. Or, truthfully, I opted not to ask about it.

"Is that courtesy of your father?" I ask.

Rafaelle d'Amico and I have never crossed paths. Not sure I'd be sitting here if we had.

Navarro takes a deep breath, reclaiming the control he momentarily lost. "Since we last spoke, I have risen in the ranks. You know my passions have always run high, and I did my best to contain them. But not enough around the giovane d'onore. The honored youth are the future of our organization, as you know." He states this as a simple, agonized truth; he is a man locked in the permanent purgatory of a battle he can never win. "Rafaelle suggested I should come here to oversee the cocaine operations," he finishes, with only a hint of sarcasm.

"And fix the unfixable at the same time?" I ask.

A glint of wariness comes into his eyes. "Yes."

"Hence the security."

"To keep me inside," he says with a hollow laugh.

I lean forward, elbows on my knees, hands curled into a resting spot for my chin. Navarro shared his struggles with me from the start. I was the only confidante he had.

"June is against everything you stand for," I tell him. "It would never work out."

"My mother will love her," he insists, and the hope in his voice fills me with sadness.

"But *you* won't."

"I can try," he says, bristling. "She'll make it easy. Easier. She's unlike any woman I've ever met."

His refusal to see the big picture, his denial of it, exhausts me. "Frame your wild fantasy in reality for one minute. If June went to Italy with you, do you think she'd embrace the role of your beard? Stuff cannoli with your mother night after night while you maim and destroy and then come home to a lie? Both of you would be miserable."

Navarro cuts me a look. "And you will make her happy? Or is it that you want me to remain unhappy?"

"That is an idiot thing to say."

He picks again at the armrest. "She told me nothing was going on with you two. A lie, obviously."

I stare straight ahead, feeling my eyeballs crisp in the hot, dry room. Did June say that? Up until tonight, it was the truth. But I cannot imagine those words leaving her lips anymore.

"It's complicated," I say, the word a pale attempt at summarizing the distress I created. "At one point, it should have happened between us. But I fucked things up. Then I tried to right the wrong and bungled that too. When one of our companies imploded, I convinced myself June sabotaged me, so I returned the favor. I turned bad into worse and lost an entire decade with her. But there was always something between us. From the very start. You know how precious that is."

I glance at him—the distinguished profile burned forever on my brain.

"ZedShed?" he asks. "Is that the company?"

I tilt my head. Why did he pluck out that detail? "How do you know?"

He shrugs. "News travels."

"June had nothing to do with it, as it turns out."

"You're certain?" he asks.

"Yes," I say, unsure why his voice has a pressing quality. "Why?"

He scratches his neck. In the hazy light of the fire, I see it—his mangled right hand. I'd forgotten about the injury but not the story behind it. A politician held hostage high in the Aspromonte mountains attacked him years ago, tearing out skin and bone with his teeth. The last thing the man ever ate.

"Is that why you brought her here?" Navarro asks. "To avenge your misguided behavior and capture the fair maiden?"

Always sharp with his words, they cut deep this time. Unfairly so.

"You know what it's like crawling through life on autopilot," I say, my voice tense. "June is the real deal. I hope we can put our collective stupidity behind us. Maybe I can find happiness again. With someone who sticks around."

Navarro returns his gaze to the fire. "Is she also protection?"

I ignore his implication. "She knows the company inside and out. In case you had any questions, I wanted to be prepared."

Heaving a sigh, Navarro rises from the chair to fix drinks at a silver bar trolley camped next to the fireplace. He sloshes amber liquid into two crystal tumblers from a bottle that defines our tumultuous history. He sets his glass on the narrow table between our chairs and waits for me to take the offering from his outstretched hand.

"I hope you still enjoy Armagnac," he says, the green glow of his pupils searing through me.

I palm the glass and mumble, "Thank you." He seems so much taller when I'm trapped in the chair.

And then he moves behind me, his feet whispering on the thick rug. My shoulders tense out of reflex as his hands rest on either side of my throat.

"You're still not married," he says.

I shut my eyes, trying to block the avalanche of emotions. "Don't. Please."

"It says something."

"It says I'm going to die rich and alone. Halle-fucking-lujah."

Untroubled by my pity party, Navarro begins to massage the tight cords of muscle along my neck. He knows every old sore spot and works them over with increasing vigor. So much strength in his willowy body. No one ever sees what's coming.

"Your vindictiveness with June," he says. "Did you learn that from me?"

"Learn from the best, right?" I half-joke.

It's a truth if there ever was one.

Men of honor in Navarro's world specialize in either business or violence. Navarro the chronic overachiever considers himself a multitasker.

And I have never forgotten the blood.

So much of it.

I'd just turned twenty, and Navarro and I had been enjoying a quiet dinner in the London flat owned by his family when a junior 'Ndrangheta henchman barged in with a suspected traitor and delivered him for justice. The snitch might have escaped alive had he not glanced at Navarro and me, the intimate table set for two, and muttered something in Italian that sounded cruel.

Navarro went ballistic. A hurricane unleashed.

Nonplussed with the fellow unconscious and bleeding out on the floor, Navarro brushed blood from his knuckles, straightened his blazer, and smoothed back his hair. The swift and sudden rage that had ballooned in his eyes retreated like a tide, leaving behind a swath of evidence of who he truly was. Navarro nodded curtly at his soldier, who dragged the inert guy into the kitchen for later disposal. The henchman then joined us for dinner, laughing when he thanked

Navarro for all of his guidance because he had learned from the best. I remember how I pushed lasagna around on my plate after, my stomach in tatters. The tomato sauce…

Navarro stops grinding on my muscles.

The fire pops and hisses.

"That night was unfortunate," he admits, knowing the exact event under discussion. "You never finished your meal."

I laugh, on the inside. Reflection but never regret. Classic Navarro.

"It made me wonder what happened to people who did more than whisper rumors," I say.

Navarro clears his throat. "No one else at Oxford knew who I was except you."

"I know. I never told anyone. And I never will. I promised."

His fingers move higher to dig into my scalp. I groan from the pleasure of his kneading strokes. He still has the magic touch. And I can't deny there is something comforting about this. About him. Our old, complicated connection.

"I appreciated that about you," he says. "I've never forgotten your loyalty."

And very gently, like a spring breeze changing direction, Navarro brushes a kiss against my neck.

Lingering and soft, but with intention behind it.

Adrenaline knifes through me.

I grip the armrests to prevent my hands from shaking because the old memories have started to crowd in. He smells like the Acqua di Parma cologne I never could bring myself to wash out of our Marks and Spencer sheets. I endure the trail of kisses he dusts higher along my throat better than the stirring between my legs. For all his violent tendencies, he was always tender and patient with me. When my learned instinct clenched against the mass of him demanding entry the first time, he taught me how to breathe through the worst of it. In the end, I craved him like an addict jonesing for crack.

Navarro nuzzles my earlobe with an aching hum deep in his throat.

"After me?" he whispers. "Was there anyone else?"

The longing curling through his words splits the heart June accuses me of not having wide open. My dick strains painfully, reaching for the mouth that created an emotional shitstorm every time it sucked me into its forbidden darkness.

A dreadful attack of vertigo washes over me. I squeeze my eyes shut and mumble, "No."

For a split second, the thudding of my heart seems to fill the room. I cannot navigate the tightrope of our past without falling, and an explosion in the fireplace miraculously spares me from the plunge.

My eyes pop open.

A half-burnt log has collapsed and spewed a smoldering chunk of wood onto the rug. Navarro rushes forward to scoop the ember back into the fire with the refined grace that caught my attention in the first place so many years ago.

A quiet elegance seemed the key to his entire personality when he strolled into the campus coffee shop with the last of Oxford's summer heat swirling around him. For an American never exposed to the sophisticated ways of European men, his linen suit and man purse made me feel like a chump in my ripped jeans and high tops. He instructed the barista twice on how to craft his espresso and kept tucking an errant lock of golden hair behind one ear while he waited. Oblivious to the hot stares of every nubile co-ed mesmerized by his presence, he downed the coffee like a tequila shot.

On his way out, he caught my gaze and smiled. I returned it nervously. He was, is, and always will be, a beautiful man. A few days later, we crossed paths at a dull lecture on supply-side economics. Navarro sat beside me and introduced himself. During my first term at Oxford, my first time away from US soil, I felt alone and disconnected. The Brits spoke my language, but their version of daily life had yet to make sense.

Navarro changed all that.

He changed everything.

And not all of it for the better.

After tending to the fire, Navarro sits back in the chair and drains half his drink in one gulp. Aside from a few beads of sweat on his forehead, he appears unfazed by the electricity that crackled between us seconds ago. But he always was the master of cool. When your day job involves assassinating people, it comes with the territory.

"Is Rafaelle still at the top of the food chain?" I ask, carefully reapproaching his dilemma.

His brow settles into a flat line. "Until I am deemed fit to take over."

"And if you're not?"

He flashes a bittersweet smile. "How do you say it in America? Fake it until you make it?"

"You can't fake who you are forever," I say quietly. "It will eat you alive."

Another silence passes. Then, with frank misery, he says, "So I have lost you for good."

The yearning within the depths of his eyes stops the earth from spinning, the entire fucking universe from existing. It feels like my insides are shredding into pieces.

"Remember the good parts," I say, my voice low and wavering. "That's what I do."

A lone tear spills down his cheek. He wipes it away, and I can tell he's embarrassed that he's ended up here.

"Everything about you is good," he whispers. "That's the hard part."

He tosses back the remains of his Armagnac, washing his bubble of emotion back down into the dark pit where he stores it under lock and key. A stillness settles like a hand muffling a scream from someone's mouth.

"You will move things along with her?" Navarro asks this without looking at me. The resignation threaded in his question pricks my heart.

"That's the plan."

In the waning strength of the fire, the emerald shine of his eyes turns dull and accusing. I've weathered the storm of that look before, on a snowy night in New York City. Navarro materialized out of the blue five years after his disappearance and wanted to meet.

At a private table in the exclusive hush of Le Cirque, we caught up over filet mignons. He explained the situation, leaving gaps in the story I knew not to fill. The details didn't matter anyway; I'd made up my mind. But the giddy rush of our singular connection caught up to my willpower. I let his hand graze mine. He dabbed sauce from the corner of my mouth using a finger. His jittery energy registered as nothing more than the after-effects of a dizzyingly fine Bordeaux. But minutes before our strawberry Napoleons arrived, he stopped fidgeting with his napkin and summoned the courage to ask if we could reunite.

I will never forget how the light in his eyes faded when I told him things had changed. With power and money comes scrutiny. All the morally antiquated Alpha males who funded my projects would kick my ass to the curb if I showed up at a dinner with Navarro on my arm. I couldn't risk everything I'd built up.

And the wretched conflict that left me strung out and hollow on that bitterly cold New York night once again churns violently in my stomach. Navarro mirrors it by spinning his empty tumbler in tight circles on the side table.

Round and round and round.

There is no breath anywhere in the room.

"I wired the money from my personal account," Navarro finally says. "There will be no trace or connection to Cannistrá."

"But?" Because it's there, hanging like a guillotine.

Navarro's long, elegant fingers squeeze the crystal glass like the throats of countless men who have crossed him.

"All the contacts I gave you," he says. "They paid off in spades. You're a rich man because of me. I would like one small thing in return."

The glow from a final dying ember nullifies to ash. I sit in the shadows, absorbing my fate in silence. Somewhere, in the darkest place of my mind, I wanted to believe the timing of his call was a lucky coincidence. But a sixty-billion-dollar underground empire of drug trafficking, money laundering, murder, and mayhem does not rely on coincidences.

And from what he just said, I can do the math.

Cruelty and hope cannot reside together peacefully in a man's soul.

They are on opposite sides of a war. Navarro decided what side of the battle he would fight on long before I set foot in Argentina. And the repercussions for him being a turncoat will be severe.

I feel his hand grasp mine. He arches one eyebrow and waits.

Time passes, measured in agonized seconds, before I hang my head and say, "Tell me what you want."

Chapter Twenty-Three

JUNE

My eyes pop open. I'm freezing. I can see my breath in the air. The sky outside is dark, the clouds a midnight blue. It feels late. I fumble for my phone on the nightstand and stare dumbfounded at the screen. Nine a.m.? The hour of game shows starting up on the telly or when retirees come home from doubles tennis and eat prunes with their yogurt. Not when June Allison wakes up, unless I've crawled into bed in a fitful state.

Dallas asked me not to leave his room, and I might have stayed if he had bothered to answer any of my increasingly distressed texts. I gave up at three in the morning, drowning in ceaseless thoughts.

And still no replies.

I burrow under the duvet and try to make sense of things. Is this the definition of 'different,' according to Dallas? A cold shoulder after intense intimacy? Why would he pull a stunt like this?

The only answer is Navarro.

And what the hell is up with him?

Who wanders into a friend's bedroom as a Peeping Tom? The embarrassment of him witnessing Dallas buried between my legs is one thing. Not to be the focus of it is entirely another. Something changed in Navarro's face last night. A mask dropped. He stood in the shadows, mesmerized not by me cuffed to the bed, but by Dallas in the buff.

I struggle to get a definitive handle on him, but I sense something slippery, swimming just outside of my grasp.

And Dallas has been strangely withdrawn around Navarro since we arrived. He's tiptoed around any digging questions about him. Last night, his chatter about things being different between us, the idea of a much-improved version of Dallas on the menu, lifted my heart. But actions speak louder than words. And being dropped like a hot potato mere hours after opening my soul and legs crushes me.

I lie in bed, overwhelmed with confusion. A hundred questions burn a hole in my brain. Dallas better be prepared for an interrogation. If he tries to feed me BS or dance around the answers, how can I trust him with my company?

Or my heart?

$

To my surprise, Dallas is in his room. He opens the door seconds after I knock. Bundled in a robe, the blankness of his face feels deliberate. And a complete contrast to his blazing eyes.

"You promised to wait for me," he says.

I snort a disbelieving laugh. "Good morning to you too. And I did wait. Until three in the morning. I assume you received all my unanswered texts?"

Dallas digests this, giving me nothing other than an awkward lean against the door. The oddity of this is instantly clear.

"We got to talking, and the time flew by," he says, and I can tell he's trying to sound breezy. Something to counter the heaviness about him that has not been there before.

"That's all you have to say?" He cannot be this daft.

"There's a change of plans we need to discuss."

I feel a wave of illness. A crash of defeat. His voice. The resigned sound of it. He gestures with a tilt of his head that I should come inside, and I slip past him to scour every inch of the room, dismally aware I'm on the hunt for clues. But besides his open laptop on the desk and the heavy drapes drawn back, nothing has changed since I gave up hope and slunk out of here in the witching hour. So why do I grapple with the strange sense of being in a dream?

Dallas stands very still, hands jammed into the pockets of his robe. His eyes are unreadable.

"What is going on?" I ask. "I need you to tell me the truth."

After a sticky silence, he says, "Navarro wants out."

I suck in my breath and hold it there before my question trickles out on the heels of a quiet gasp. "Out of the deal?"

"No. Out of the mafia."

It's not as if I believed this day would suddenly revert to normal, that all we'd have to do is get cleaned up and rally. But the magnitude of what Dallas just uttered is beyond the scope of my comprehension.

"Is that even possible?"

"Very few have done it successfully," he says.

A light dusting of chest hair is visible in the V of his robe. The stub of a nipple. I can still smell us in the air and how he made me forget everything except the drowning pleasure.

Fuck!

No wonder I stick to business. Lust is so damn confusing.

"And this involves you somehow?" I ask, because it feels like it does.

Dallas lowers himself onto the end of the bed. I can't entirely parse why something like dread flickers in his eyes. "Navarro views me as a neutral confidante. I'm the only outsider who understands the complicated knot of his family."

"What does that mean?" I press. "What has he asked you to do?"

"Once the money lands, and it should be today, you take off and get things on track. I'll be in LA Monday or Tuesday."

Something cold rises in my chest. He's dodged my question. And I can see it in his face—the haunted lines marring his normally smooth forehead. Fishy is only the beginning.

"This company is my sweat and blood," I remind him. "I need to be in the loop on everything. If you've made any concessions…"

He's quiet for so long that I think he might not answer. Then, "Whatever the deal is between Navarro and me has no bearing on Green Time or us. And when I say us," he clarifies, "I mean us from last night. Me and you together. I meant it when I said I want to give us a shot."

I say nothing at first because his bald statement catches me off guard. So many emotions are running through me right now.

"If that's the case, we need to be open with each other. It's admirable that you want to help out an old friend, but Navarro is a mobster. Not that I qualify as an expert, but from what I've read, anyone in that culture has to be strategic in their dealings. Their survival depends on it. What do they call that code of silence?"

"Omertà," he says.

"Right. The mafia protects their family, themselves, at all costs."

Dallas drops his gaze to stare at the rug. I get the sense he is in the process of crushing something deep within himself, and helping Navarro is part of this twisted story. Has Dallas taken more than dirty money? Has he taken a life or two? He claimed his manicured hands weren't big on violence, but why else does he look so guilt-ridden?

"He needs my help to make this happen," Dallas states, emphatically, like he remembered he drank the Kool-Aid. "It's a one-time deal."

"Why you?" I ask. "He must have a laundry list of contacts who operate on his level."

"He can't risk exposure. One person from his network rats him out, and he's done."

"Does he plan to be on the lam for the rest of his life?"

"He's up against centuries of legacy," Dallas says, skirting an answer for the second time. "His father holds one of the highest ranks, and Navarro is expected to take over. It will be impossible for him to leave after that happens."

I cannot fathom the intricacies of Navarro's world—a rich and complex repertoire of symbols, traditions, ranks, and rituals. The pressure that comes with all of it would drive the sanest person around the bend. And for him to abandon it must come with a hefty price.

I digest this. Or try to connect the dots pinballing inside my head.

"What about his ankle monitor? I assume from that someone considers him a flight risk."

"He's been here for months and played by the rules," Dallas says, and it sounds like he's repeating whatever story Navarro told him. "This weekend is his first chance. Battista, Carolina, and all the guards have stuff going on."

I cross my arms. This all sounds too convenient. Has Dallas thought any of this through?

"Fine, sure, no staff around. But how does he disappear if he's being tracked?"

"We'll get the monitor off," he says, like all he has to do is wave a magic wand.

His mind is made up. I can feel it at the center of his strange calmness. But why is he blowing this off like it's nothing?

"He's giving us forty million dollars and then vanishes into thin air?" I pause, hoping the absurdity of that sinks in for him. "Who do we report to after the fact? The mafia isn't in the business of handouts or freebies. And what if they find out you helped Navarro defect? They kill people like you!"

"The money isn't coming from Cannistrá," Dallas explains, unruffled by the shrillness in my voice. "Navarro has private numbered accounts all over the world. This transaction will never exist in the 'Ndrangheta books. Once Nikki confirms the wire today, we are off to the races. We kick ass. This is what you wanted," he reminds me. "What you worked so hard for."

I search his face, the sincerity written all over it. How can I argue that point? But there is another reality to contend with.

"You realize we can't do a thing without our passports."

"I know," he says and eases himself to his feet. "Navarro gave them back to me last night."

Tucked beside his laptop is a manilla folder. Within it, our passports. I take mine from his outstretched hand. Flip through it to ensure all is well.

"Did they send a copy of these to his family?" I ask. "If so, it looks bloody suspicious if Navarro disappears right after we leave. That puts us both at risk."

"I asked about that," Dallas is quick to say. Every answer thought of, or so it seems. "The protocol is that every guest leaves their ID at the gate. He didn't want the guards to suspect anything, and they would have if we'd breezed right in."

I stew over everything for a long beat. The invisible money trail, the passports. Whatever the plan is, Navarro mapped it out well in advance. But for Dallas to risk his livelihood on a chum from Oxford who happens to be next in line to oversee the world's most powerful mafia baffles me. Family is who you risk it all for. Or a lover.

One hundred percent, Navarro is not the former. And the latter seems borderline impossible based on Dallas' reputation of bedding half the women in LA as a side hustle. But sexual fluidity isn't out of the question. At one point, my preferences swung both ways. I'm tempted to ask Dallas but stop myself before I do. Why would he drag me here if they have an intimate history? He could have traveled solo.

It makes no sense, he and Navarro in that way.

But nothing makes sense right now.

My muddled thoughts leak into my expression, and Dallas reads it. He gestures for me to sit on his lap. I sink onto his muscled legs and lean into his protective warmth. He kisses my forehead, cheeks, and the tight line of my mouth. The lightest of kisses, nothing close to the weight growing heavier in my heart. Another conflicting signal in this topsy-turvy morning.

Outside, the light suddenly darkens. It feels like the sky will open up at any second.

Dallas tucks a lock of hair behind my ear, his expression so adoring I feel a knot in my chest. "I have a Zoom board meeting at ten. It will take a couple of hours," he says. "Why don't you have breakfast, catch up on work, and come find me? This time, I'll lock the door."

Chapter Twenty-Four

Wolves are nocturnal.

So why did I expect Navarro to be in his office this early? The door is shut and locked. I press an ear to the solid hunk of wood and hear nothing but my racing heart. Instead of breakfast with a stilted Carolina, I detoured here to confront Navarro because the anguished look on his face last night haunts me. And Dallas roped in to help him escape? It does not sit right with me. I need to clear up a few things niggling at the back of my mind.

In the dead calm, a faint vibration of music echoes in the darkness at the end of the hall. His bedroom. Do I risk it alone? Do I have a choice? With measured steps, I slink closer as covertly as I can. The hall smells of mildew and his scent—the distinct smokey orange that is strange and unsettling. Like the ominous music taking shape. A slow, building whirlpool of minor-key notes.

Beethoven's Seventh Symphony.

The allegretto.

The door to his room is ajar, and I steal a look from the safety of the hallway. It's a clubby, gentleman's space. Tasteful and strikingly tidy with rich burgundy rugs and wainscoted walls. Oatmeal-colored sheets pintucked perfectly at the corners with two pillows fluffed against the slab headboard. Instead of a cozy vibe, I feel nothing but isolation in the bare, elegant bones of his room.

I hear Navarro before he comes into my view.

He hums to the foreboding melody like it's a feel-good piece. As the allegretto soars into wailing violins and cellos and the thunder of a symphony in full flight wash over me, it's nothing like the sensation of witnessing a half-nude Navarro.

Holy mother of God.

The vision is impossible to wrench my eyes away from.

I have yet to see him without a shirt buttoned tightly around his neck, sleeves down and cuffs impeccable. And his golden, gentle features never hinted at this: a torso without an inch of unmarked skin. Inked onto his rippled stack of abs, over pecs and traps and scapulae are fierce, primitive tattoos of crosses and sinister creatures. The muscles underneath are so defined and daunting that they cannot be real. My mind rewinds to the conversation Dallas and I had ten minutes ago. How can Navarro escape the mafia when the tableau on his skin marks him for life?

The longer I stand there trying to reconcile his fine manners and brutalist sensibilities, time seems to slow down. Navarro, sensory creature that he is, perks his head. His eyes latch onto my slack, pensive face reflecting on him from the handsomely framed mirror he stands in front of.

He observes me, not moving a finger. A quiet, tranquilizing stare.

My toes curl inside the leather of my vintage Fendi heels. Navarro asked me what it felt like to kiss a murderer, but this is what it feels like to look into the soul of one.

He pauses the symphony playing on his phone. The loud silence is deafening.

"Buongiorno, principessa."

I swallow past the dry cotton clogging up my throat. "Hello."

"Please, come in," he says.

"I can wait for you out here."

"Nonsense," he says, sounding vaguely annoyed. Or maybe just tired. "You've gone to the effort of tracking me down. Might as well finish the task."

All the confidence I felt on the way over trickles away. It takes every ounce of courage to put one foot in front of the other. I hover near the door just in case, trying not to stare at the flower tattoo that curves lovingly around one hip bone jutting out from the waistband of his pleated trousers. A gladiola. Not a predictable rose. Where have I seen that before?

Navarro whips a pressed dress shirt off his valet stand and buttons up, keeping me firmly in his sightline. He raises an eyebrow in silent question.

"I just wanted to say thank you," I say, trying to keep nerves out of my voice. "Dallas said we can expect the money today."

"He wants you to fly home tonight. It's unfortunate you will be leaving so soon."

"I offered to stay, but we have a lot of work ahead of us."

"Good thing you are so capable, vero?"

He expertly knots his bowtie next and fingers his thick hair into a stylized coif—the entire stunning package of him defining the word sprezzatura. A beat of silence passes. All the while he stares at me.

"Come and sit with me," he finally says.

He takes a seat on a bench at the end of his bed and lays a hand beside him. I have a sensation of free-falling the closer I get to him. Navarro as a living thing is a black hole of energy, sucking me and all my will into his darkness. I perch on my sit bones beside him, the bench hard and unforgiving. It's difficult to breathe. The same smoky essence that drifted out of Dallas's hair when he kissed me earlier floats around us with suffocating intensity.

Navarro's mouth curves into a distant smile. "What would you like to know?"

It seems like an innocuous question. But he's addressed the reason why I'm here. What is my mission?

"You and Dallas seem to have a tangled history," I say.

His look is quizzical. "Is that a question or a statement?"

"I know what it's like with uni mates," I say, sidestepping the answer. "My dearest friends were my Stanford roomies. They are like sisters to me. Closer than family."

"The bonds of our brotherhood are similar," he admits carefully. "We are very close."

"And yet you two seem ill at ease around each other."

His gaze flits away before landing back on mine. "You play the game well, June. I can see why you're successful."

"So, there is a game?"

Navarro folds his hands neatly in his lap. "Great chess players can see many moves into the future," he says. "That is how they win."

I look straight into his inscrutable eyes. It hit me out of the blue when I walked over here—I have an inkling who gave Dallas his initial pot of money. The one he never talks about. That money spawned a lot of good in this world, but the problem with dirty money is you can try to scrub it clean, but the stink of origin remains.

And karma eventually comes full circle.

"Winning means someone else has to lose, right?"

"Forty million is your prize," he says. "Hardly losing. I suggest you walk away with that and consider yourself lucky."

Getting inducted into a special club is how he presents it. Rejoice in the festivity and back the fuck off.

But that is not my style.

"I'd prefer it if Dallas could walk away with me."

His spine straightens, and he breathes in and out of his nose. I can tell he's strategizing on what to say next. "Have you seen him this morning?"

"I think you know the answer to that."

Navarro steadfastly maintains his composure. "It has been an honor and a pleasure to meet you," he says. "How unfortunate we never crossed paths earlier."

Seductive tyranny is what his smile evokes—a professional-grade weapon unleashed in case I am not clear that this conversation is over.

But is anything ever over? We can pretend that our pasts don't lurk in a dark corner. Ignore them like the stains on the sofa we cover up with a throw pillow. But last night, Navarro inadvertently played his hand. Whatever he and Dallas talked about in the wee hours of this morning had something to do with their collective baggage.

"When the dust settles, you should visit LA," I suggest, shifting gears. Another test of what Dallas told me. "Meet the rest of the team."

"We invest as silent partners only," he reminds me. "But I appreciate the invitation."

"Are you sure? It must be hard. Living here alone."

I rest my hand on his thigh and feel the muscle beneath it jump. His mouth clamps tight, and he considers me for a moment. What else do I have stored in my quiver?

"I have my family," he says. "Therefore, I am never truly alone. And the condition here is temporary. Like most situations in life." He removes my hand from his leg, delicately, like a surgeon might lift out a kidney. He presses a kiss against it. "I believe it's time for colazione, principessa."

He burrows both feet into the slippers precisely lined up on one side of the valet. Elegant feet, I decide, with their high arches and trimmed nails. I follow him into the hallway, where he locks the door and slides a brass key into his pocket. His movements remind me of a dancing king cobra—slow and hypnotic, never in any rush. He'd be the guy driving PCH on a Sunday afternoon in an old-school roadster, cruising without a care in the world. Maybe he could find a new life there. Become a Pilates instructor. Run a food truck and serve arancini. It's easy to disappear in a city of four million people.

"You might enjoy Los Angeles," I say. "Keep it in the back of your mind."

Navarro clears his throat and starts walking. "You'll be in good hands with Dallas. He is quite fond of you."

My head snaps up to meet his eyes. "He said that?"

"I sensed it. Before last night," he adds, flatly.

He's walking fast and I'm rushing to keep up with him. Or maybe I'm trying to outrun my embarrassment. "I'm sorry you had to witness that."

A disappointed sound hums in this throat. "I'm sorry an invitation wasn't extended."

I stumble, my feet suddenly not moving in sync with each other. Before I can formulate a response to what he just said, Navarro steadies me, his warm hand reassuringly gripping mine.

"Careful," he says.

The most loaded word of the day? He is dangerous, that I know. He and his bloody castle are like a heavy atmosphere sinking around me, silently imposing their will. An intravenous drip that fills my veins with a drug I'm slowly succumbing to. I cannot align with what he represents, and when he intertwines his fingers with mine, it only compounds my confusion.

I shouldn't have accepted his money. I should have hightailed it home as soon as I found out who he was. Except it's too late. The wheels are in motion. But where are we headed? A cobra only dances for so long before it strikes.

In the not-so-distance, a clap of thunder rumbles.

"Let's go find Mimi and Rodolfo," Navarro says, tugging on my hand. "Carolina took them for their morning walk, but I believe they've taken a shine to you and Dallas."

Chapter Twenty-Five

THE STORM TURNS INTO A BITCH'S BREW HALFWAY THROUGH breakfast. Gusts of wind hammer the palm fronds sideways. The rain falls so hard that it bounces off the patio. Every time the sky brightens with a brilliant flash of lightning, Mimi and Rodolfo snuffle and whine, burrowing closer together on their daybed.

Carolina delivers cappuccino refills for Navarro and me, informing us that the airports might shut down today.

"How severe is it?" Navarro asks.

"Forty millimeters of rain expected today with high winds and lightning." She glances askance at me. "Is she still scheduled to leave today?"

So far, Carolina has tolerated me as a mid-level orbiter. But referring to me in the third person is especially cold. I'm tempted to wave my arms and say, *Hello. I am right here.* But to what end? Polar bears would move to the tropics before she and I became besties.

Navarro assesses the misery outside. "I guess we have to play it by ear."

"Is it okay with you if I have to stay another night?" I ask.

He glances at Carolina. A silent conversation passes between them. Then he says, "Not a problem in the slightest."

But something in his tone sounds like this is less than ideal. Is he worried the menial duties of making coffee or arranging an airport transfer will fall on his pampered shoulders? Carolina leaves this afternoon to attend a funeral in Mendoza, and Battista is already gone, halfway to Uruguay for a wedding. The guards have booked the weekend off. Soon it will be just the three of us and a storm that shows no sign of abating.

I help myself to a second pastry from the platter Carolina left on the table. Low-level tension hums through me. A helpless feeling, similar to what grips you at the airport when your flight gets canceled. The dark skies make me yearn for LA and the parade of beautiful days, although the idea of being home this time tomorrow, the very concept of home, grows indefinite at the edges.

My phone pings, and a text from Dallas pops onto the screen.

DE: Still stuck on my Zoom. Any chance you could bring me a coffee? No rush. :)

A warm, fuzzy feeling spreads through me. This is what couples do. Bring each other coffee.

JA: No problem. Give me twenty.

Dallas responds with three emojis: the dancing man, the peace sign, and a coffee cup.

I smile to myself. Navarro sets aside the magazine he's been flipping through—*Grazia,* a European fashion rag—and asks me what's so funny.

"Nothing," I say. "Dallas is on a Zoom call, and they can get pretty boring."

"Does he have anyone to replace him at the company?" he asks.

I gauge his tone. I'm not entirely sure I understand why he's asking. "He has no intention of stepping down as CEO, if that's what you mean."

A clap of thunder right overhead frightens the dogs into another round of whimpers. Navarro reaches down to soothe them, murmuring in Italian.

"I'm curious if he has a strong second-in-command," he rephrases.

"I believe Nikki Robichaux is his vice president. She sounds very capable."

I see his face change. And it makes me think I've supplied information I shouldn't have.

"Ah, yes," he says. "I think he's mentioned her before."

Carolina interrupts us and asks if we need anything else. She has a full morning of laundry to get to before leaving.

"Can you make a latte to go?" I ask. "Dallas is tied up and asked me to bring him breakfast."

Her mouth twitches. It's the end of civilization when people don't sit down for a proper breakfast. She marches back to the coffee machine, briefly silenced by this affront. I scrape a spoonful of froth from my cappuccino and decide to cut her some slack. Maybe she needs this job, even if she hates it. Because who in their right mind signs up to be a housekeeper in a cavernous pile of limestone to dote on a gangster?

Another howl of wind rustles through the shrubbery surrounding the patio. A streak of lightning turns the sky violet. It's a right mess out there for planes, people, and animals.

"How does Giorgio fare in a storm?" I ask Navarro. "Does he have appropriate shelter?"

Navarro shrugs. "He'll be fine. A giraffe is quite hardy, as it turns out."

"And the peacock?" The thought of all that glorious plumage drenched to the bone makes me sad.

"Battista built him a shelter. He used to be a carpenter, back in the day. His tool collection is quite impressive. He insisted on building a workshop to house them all," he says with a laugh. "It's the ugly little shack near the front gate."

As I try to recall if I'd seen this shack when we first arrived, Carolina sets a creamy latte on the table. In a cup and saucer.

"We don't do to-go," she informs me, before spinning on her heel to swan off.

God. If she loosened her bun and tried a red lipstick, she might almost be pretty. Not to be in the path of her bridling resistance for the rest of today is a small win.

Navarro rises from his chair, finishing what's left of his coffee. "Scusa," he says to me. "But I have work to do as well. Tell Dallas to keep an eye on the weather, and I will do the same. Hopefully, our plans stay on track."

The dogs jump to their feet, and Navarro encourages them to say goodbye to me. As they yip and prance and lick my hands, a smile brightens Navarro's face.

"You are a true animal lover. Mimi and Rodolfo will miss you terribly."

"It might be time to get a dog," I admit. "I've always wanted one."

"You should. Pets are therapeutic. There when you need them and exceptional listeners."

"Cheaper than a psychiatrist?"

He laughs. "Exactly."

His good mood is another layer to the endless paradox he is. Part of me wants to delve into every nook and cranny of his psyche. The other part screams to leave well enough alone.

"Arrivederci," he says and wanders out of the kitchen with the dogs trailing him.

I offer Carolina a kindness by tidying up. I collect plates and cups from the table and set them in the sink. Wipe down the counters. The fierce wind has ratcheted up to full throttle, and the screen door leading out to the patio bashes against the frame. I walk to the far end of the kitchen and latch the door back into position. Satisfied it will hold, I turn around and, for the first time, notice a small alcove. Recessed within it is a roughly hewn door.

Strange.

A simple door compared to the finery everywhere else, and a novelty hard to resist. *The Lion, The Witch, and The Wardrobe* is my favorite childhood story, and it fueled my fascination with doors and what lurks behind them. I palm the doorknob, shocked at how chilled the metal is. An icy lick of air bites at my ankles, and I jump back with a yelp. The door frame isn't snug to the floor, and cool air smelling of stale water and grime trickles out. I shimmy the knob. It's locked.

"What are you doing?"

My heart leaps into my throat. I spin around. Carolina, the resident vampire, has emerged out of nowhere. She clasps a broom staunchly in one hand—South American gothic, right down to the dour expression. My legs tense with an impulse to flee, but I take a calming breath instead.

"I, uh, I heard the screen door banging and latched it," I explain. "And then I saw this door and thought it might be the loo."

The firm set to her mouth deepens. "Do you always snoop through people's homes?"

"I wasn't snooping."

A defiant edge has cut into my voice. All the evidence Carolina needs to prove I'm a liar.

"I don't have time to make Dallas another coffee," she says, a laughably inaccurate statement given how she handles the espresso machine. "You should take it to him before it gets cold."

"Of course," I say with a tight smile. "I'll be on my way."

There's something I don't like about her, but if asked, I'd be hard-pressed to come up with anything other than she's a right hag, which feels judgy. Maybe she showers her friends with affection and expensive gifts? Whatever. I don't have the time or inclination to warm her up.

Just before I slip past her, she reaches into the pocket of her starched uniform to reveal my lost earring. "I believe this is yours. I found it in Navarro's bathroom. Were you in there?"

I tamp down the guilt ballooning in my stomach. Technically, I only set foot in his bedroom.

"No," I say, plucking the earring from her hand. "And I asked yesterday if he'd seen this."

Why would Navarro hold onto it without saying anything? Does he have an earring fetish? Did he plan to pawn it? For no apparent reason, I imagine him creating a voodoo doll in my likeness.

"It's not advisable to stay here any longer than you need to,"

Carolina says, her words carrying an undertone of a warning colder than wherever that air came from.

We regard each other in a state of uneasy silence.

Trust me, Carolina. If I could jump on the next plane, I would.

"Duly noted," I say, and hightail it out of there, stopping only to grab two croissants and the coffee.

Chapter Twenty-Six

DALLAS

I excused myself from the Zoom meeting thirty minutes ago, citing another call, when the real story is I needed some self-care. My exhausted brain was desperate for a breather and a block of alone time to process the twists of fate that slammed me against the Navarro wall. I hate how much power he has over me—that he can bend me like a rubber spoon.

But as I told myself before I dragged my ass into bed a few hours ago, this is it. The great seducer has had the last hurrah. The era of me being his yo-yo is over.

Do you want to disappear? I will gladly help you.

And end this fucking story once and for all.

"Dallas?"

My ears perk up. It's June. She knocks softly on the door and says, "It's me," like I need an introduction. She's the only thing preventing me from losing it.

"Give me a minute," I call out.

I hop off the bed and yank on my jeans. Flip open the laptop and empty my earbuds from the charger. Make it look like I was busy on Zoom instead of stroking myself. On the way to the door, I pause to tidy my hair in the mirror. Nikki says I could rock a ponytail, but my b-ball crew would laugh me off the courts. The last thing I need is to look like an earnest fucking poet out there.

I open the door and the remote thought I had earlier, that my life could have a happy ending, magically returns. June is as beautiful as the night I met her in that bar on La Brea. A Wednesday night notable for absolutely nothing other than her laugh.

"Hey," I say. "Good timing. The call just ended."

"The coffee's not hot," she says. "But the croissants are crisp."

"Thanks," I say, relieving her of both. Most of the coffee has sloshed into the saucer. I hold the door open with one foot and follow the sweet line of her swinging ass walking into my room. June the forensic investigator scours every inch of the premises with those ice-blue eyes like she did earlier. Can't say I blame her. Would I trust me?

"Was Navarro awake?" I ask casually without paranoia.

"We had breakfast together," she says. "This storm is set to get nasty. Conditions might shut the airport down. I might have to stay."

Rain sleets sideways on the window and the gloom of the fog turns the day into soup. Nasty is an understatement.

"Are you okay with that?" I ask.

She rubs her bare arms. An igloo retains heat better than this pile of rocks. "I don't think you should stay and help Navarro. You should fly back with me."

I set down my breakfast. I can see on her face that she's working through a lot of emotions, not all of them because of me.

"June. I already—"

"You cannot..." She pauses. Then, with more control of her voice, she adds, "I went to his room before breakfast. To talk."

Oh, shit. Is that why she's trembling? "Please tell me you kept your mouth shut about what I told you."

"I did," she says slowly, meaning, she didn't. "I kicked the tires, so to speak," she admits. "I'm sorry. What you rambled about last night didn't sit well with me."

I sit down heavily on the bed. "What did he say?"

"He talked about chess games and how to win. That I should consider myself lucky to walk away with the money."

I search her face and fearlessly hold back the visions that haunt me in my dreams. The blood. The broken bones. Navarro showed me a taste of his other world because he needed me to understand, but I cannot involve June any more than she already is.

"Don't read too much into what he says. He can be cryptic. It's part of his personality."

She's not buying that, based on the wringing of her hands. "Has Nikki called?"

"Not yet," I say. "But she knows to hit me up right away. C'mere." I steer her between my splayed legs and wrap her in my arms. "It's going to be fine. We have our passports. I help him this weekend, and we're done. We never have to deal with him again."

"I don't know," she says. "This feels dangerous."

I want to tell her how incredible she feels in my arms. That the reality of her trumps every night of filthy masturbation. But my phone rings, and June slips out of my embrace so I can answer.

"It's Nikki," I say, my heart beating fast. "Hold on." I unplug the phone from its charger and pump up my enthusiasm as I answer. "Hey, what's up?"

"It's crazy here this morning, D-Man," Nikki says. "The Dow cratered a thousand points."

"Yeah, I saw that. How are the short positions doing?" In the background, I can hear phones ringing and excited chatter. The Evener Equity investment portfolio always loves a good market meltdown.

"We're raking it in. And now that the money is here, when are you coming back?"

I glance at June, anxiously hanging on every word. "Did you say we have the money?"

"Cleared and banked. Should we send out a press release?"

I give June a thumbs-up, and her hand flies to her mouth. Oh, that mouth. The things I have yet to do to it.

"Uh, no," I say. "Hold off on that for now." I drop my voice an octave and walk over to the window. "Where did the money come from?"

Silence. Appropriate, I suppose. I never ask that question.

"Belize," she says. "The usual no-name deal. Why?"

"Just curious."

After a beat, she asks, "Why are you not jumping for joy?"

"It's great news," I say, too bright, too fake. "June is here with me. She's thrilled."

Nikki breaks into a howl of laughter. "Oh, you dirty fucking dog. I get it. Is she everything you fantasized about?"

"June will fly back tonight, weather permitting. A crazy storm has blown in and the airports are shutting down," I say. "I'm hanging around here until the weekend. I'll be in the office Tuesday or Wednesday."

"Nice cover-up, boss," she says, snickering. "Do your best not to screw it up, all right?"

"Appreciate the vote of confidence."

She tuts good-naturedly. "You know I'm happy for you. What's more important is you being happy with yourself."

"Thanks for the check-in," I say. "Give the team a high five. I'll be in touch."

I hang up. June is motionless and unblinking. "It's done?" she asks.

"In the can. And Navarro said last night the money would come from Belize. Nikki confirmed it."

She joins me at the window and almost topples me with the force of her hug. "Thank you," she mumbles, her breath seeping through my shirt to warm my chest.

It hurts to breathe. It hurts to think. I want to drag my mouth over hers. Cup her breasts. The growing mass between my legs is the payback for her presence, and I can't let a good opportunity go to waste.

"Now the real work starts," I say. "But we can celebrate first."

I kiss her hungrily along the pale column of her neck. Ravage her mouth next. I was denied the right to come properly and savagely last night. No blessings of appropriate downtime to process the life-altering win of getting June into my bed. So, I'm going for it. And she's kissing me back, the hot wetness of her mouth open for me to tongue.

Then she suddenly pulls away, leaving me desperate and gasping for air. Seriously, what is happening to my heart?

"Hold that thought, okay?" she says. "I should tell my team the good news. Get everyone sorted."

"Good idea," I agree, thinking *Fuck 'em all*. "How much time do you need?"

"A couple of hours?"

I gently reach out, my hands cradling the contours of her face. The act is tender and intimate, two words no one would ever use to describe me, but reflective of what I want to convey and what words alone can't articulate.

"We did it," I say, and steal one more kiss so I can have her taste on my tongue while I shower and touch myself. "Tell your people the good news and come back ASAP."

$

An hour later, I'm lying in bed day-drinking. Naked, showered, and remotely hopeful. I checked in with Navarro via text. We talked about the weather and the implications of June staying another night. Mostly, I wanted to test the waters—make sure June didn't spook him. Navarro was his usual arrogant and spoiled Italian mama's-boy self. He had the nerve to ask if June could cook us dinner.

You mean for the man party? I texted back.

God, for someone so worldly, he could be so clueless.

Anyway.

All seems to be okay. As okay as an ambush in waiting. That's what this weekend feels like. The storm is just delaying the inevitable and I'd rather get it over with. I take another hit of whiskey and let the burn build on my tongue before swallowing. Lightning bursts in the sky, a flash so bright I shield my eyes. A punishing boom of thunder follows with more fat drops of rain.

The fucking rain. I hate it. Give me a desert, and I will live there forever.

The last time a storm cloud of noise broke over my head while drinking in bed, I lay curled in the arms of Robin Cavanagh, the winter light pale on the shore of Lake Washington, and a bottle of warm Chardonnay pressed against my jewels. We were a month away from her breaking off our affair. Did I see it coming? Nuh-uh. Not with the lazy afternoons and sex so bombastically good, I had no energy for porn. She said, *she fucking said,* she loved me, and I stupidly believed that her, the yacht and five cars, and the ten-room mansion on Mercer Island would all become mine.

Because her marriage to Dick Cavanagh was on the rocks.

Her douchebag husband spent weeks on the road, managing companies in Europe. Construction was where he made his fortune, one of the many details I unearthed during my all-too-frequent internet stalking. He had close-set eyes that reminded me of a rat. I thought about what it must have felt like for Robin to face those eyes. During breakfast. During sex. And what man scurried all over Europe building shit, while leaving his marriage to crumble into ruins?

It made no sense to me at the time.

But his being away gave Robin and me the time we needed. I thought we could make it work. But seventeen-year-old me couldn't see past the raging hormones. I didn't think any of it through. That she had a fertile womb and never asked me to use a condom. That I was underage, and she could be in serious shit. She said all she cared about was us, so I told her I would work three times harder to pull my weight.

I swallow the mouthful of whiskey. Close my eyes. I almost had her words chiseled above the Evener Equity doorway.

"No fortunes are ever made honestly, Dallas," she said. "Forget the dance studio. You are so much more than that. The next step for you is education. The best money can buy. You are clever and have a bright future."

I buried my face in the softness of her boobs. Something about a woman confident in her curves cranked every lever inside me to ON.

"I can't afford college," I said. "Not the good ones."

She massaged my scalp with those long fingers, the nails always painted a shiny shade of pink. "That's where I want to help."

And she told me about her good friend George over in England, who worked at Oxford, and had I heard of it? I had no clue. At that point, my only frame of reference for the world was Washington State University. Robin went on and on about how wonderful Oxford's campus was and that we could trust George to be discreet. Imagine four years in England, she said, wrapping one leg around mine. Just you and me.

Good old George. He took Robin's money, all four years paid for up-front, no questions asked. Robin booked our first-class plane tickets. She paid for my dorm room to keep up appearances, but rented what she called a *flat* nearby. She watched me smile self-consciously for my first passport photo at a drug store in Everett. We were supposed to leave in August, shortly after I turned eighteen.

She called me on the morning of May 29 while I was in class.

I knew right away something was wrong.

She usually made it a point not to bother me at school.

To this day, I don't want to believe that she never saw us in England together. That she'd planned it all only for my benefit. That she never fucking believed in us because she was dying.

The worst part was Robin saying we couldn't see each other anymore. That Dick had flown home to look after her during her final days, and that, please, I had to understand why.

But the heart isn't so understanding.

I begged. I pleaded. And she said no.

Breast cancer took her a month later. Boom, gone.

After she died, I couldn't handle home, the studio, Seattle, my reflection.

I did what she wanted me to do.

Fly to England and get smart and rich.

I snag the whiskey bottle by the neck and pour another glassful.

Not my usual deal, loafing in bed on a weekday, but I'm taking the time to think about shit other than where the next million is coming from.

Like, where would life have taken me if Robin and I never crossed paths? One thing is for sure, I wouldn't be stuck in an Argentinian castle with my ex-lover and sick to my stomach because I whored myself for the money again.

Bizarrely, Navarro is the only person who knows about Robin. One night when the demons caught up to me, I told him everything while he cuddled me in bed. I don't think he cared much for the story. He never liked hearing about me and other people.

One day, when everything between June and me is where I always wanted it to be, I'll tell her about Robin. She reminds me so much of her. Strength and beauty and full-figured lushness my dick cannot get enough of. But June is special in her own brilliant ways.

If only I had half of her virtues and ethics.

Maybe all her goodness will rub off on me.

Maybe with her help, I can get out of this predicament in one fucking piece.

Chapter Twenty-Seven

JUNE

Move over, New Year's Eve. You got nothing compared to the dance party on my laptop screen. My executive team hoots and hollers, shaking their booties with the blindingly good news. I smile too, dazed but very, very relieved. I can sleep soundly tonight in my principessa bed without grinding my teeth into oblivion.

"Should I set up any meetings or calls for next week?" Kate asks. She's eager to put all the shaky energy behind us. And bake some more cookies in celebration.

I glance at the sky, dismal and rain soaked. "Not yet," I say. "Let me land first and get sorted."

Mark throws me a virtual fist bump. "I knew you could do it!" he gushes, and I don't have the heart to remind him he, in fact, did not think this. "Backed by Evener Equity." He speaks in a hushed, revered tone. "Do we get to meet Dallas?"

The revelry grinds to a halt. Amir, Kate, Mia, and Mark hang silent, faces expectant and awestruck, waiting for my reply. To meet

Dallas is to meet a legend. He's the biggest star in our industry. And I can, blushingly, attest that he's larger than life not only in a business sense. Christ, his cock is near-perfect. A blunt instrument I need deep inside me while the tantalizing torture of captivity spirals me into a delirious state of no return.

"Well?" Mark prods, snapping my attention back. "Do we?"

"At some point, yes," I say, mentally shelving my graphic thoughts. "He has a seat on our board and is keen to make this a huge success."

Another round of joyous high fives. Amir can't stop smiling. Mia whispers something to Kate, and they dissolve into girlish giggles, no doubt in stitches over the other half of Dallas's legend. When they find out about us, what will they think? What will my industry think? I can tell you right now, the gossip will explode and follow one tried-and-true narrative—that I slept my way to success. The swift, baseless, and inevitable judgment irritates the hell out of me because there is no way to explain that our destinies merged in mutual consent without eliciting eye rolls and "Uh-huh. Sure."

"What about the investor?" Kate asks. "Is he cool?"

Navarro, cool? A blazing propane torch couldn't melt his steely nerve.

"He prefers to be hands-off and won't stick his nose into the day-to-day. He has other business interests to focus on."

There you go. Couldn't have positioned it better myself.

"Wow," Mark says. "Most investors are needy bastards."

"Or are giant pains in the ass," Amir adds.

My phone buzzes with a message from Dallas.

DE: Almost done? :)

I smile. He's been on my mind this entire time.

"Sorry to run, team," I say. "But Dallas and I have more work to do. I'll keep you posted."

I shut my laptop and lie back on the satin bedspread. Tension drains from my shoulders and I feel profound relief. Green Time will launch. The team has renewed faith in me. My reputation is saved. All these positives and yet the prospect of what lies ahead, the weeks of stress and sixteen-hour days, the road map I've followed for years, rings hollow. This does not bode well for my future.

Or maybe it's time to redefine my future.

Will Dallas be a part of that? He already is when it comes to the company, and last night he consumed my senses with unspoken intensity until everything faded into the background. The world outside ceased to exist before Navarro showed up.

I bite my lip, staring up at the ceiling.

Navarro. He's mercurial, a human version of shifting sands, leaving me off-balance and grasping at straws. I haven't put the possibility aside that the wine was off, and when I think about it, something about him seems off in general. He strikes me as a tragic figure, harboring immense sadness beneath his eloquent exterior. Complicated as fuck.

And I would similarly describe Dallas as such. I have known him as brimming with confidence—too much of it, for the most part. But I sense a certain measure of loneliness. Silent and self-contained. The need for handcuffs is a dead giveaway of issues, a boatload of them, but who am I to call the kettle black? Russ harped on me to see a therapist to get over my own control issues. Is that why I felt a connection to Dallas that transcended words? Bound and helpless. Vulnerable, together.

My buzzing phone interrupts my bubble of introspection. I suspect it's an impatient Dallas, but it's Mum with another message. She's all panicky over Cliff and begging to be filled in. A funny taste fills my mouth. After two weeks, I can't hold her off any longer. She might send the cavalry.

I pop in my earbuds and call her.

She answers on the first ring, with a relieved, "Junebug! I've been trying to reach you. I'm worried sick. Is this rubbish about Cliff true?"

"Unfortunately, yes." I shut my eyes. Here we go.

"That is absolutely crummy. How could he do that to his wife and daughters? And to you? How are you getting on?"

"It's a long story, but I'm in Argentina. The company will be fine."

After a pause, she says, "Luv, I didn't ask about the company. I asked about *you*."

The feeling begins in my stomach and radiates out. A sensation I have no words for. The caring in her voice. I charge through life with my sword, all the little battles and tragedies so important, and one line from Mum does me in.

"It's been horrible," I say, my voice wavering. "So much stress. Everyone in my company blamed me. But I got it sorted."

She clucks in sympathy. "Oh, Junebug. I don't understand why you push yourself so hard. It's unhealthy."

Normally, this is where I'd get my back up. Argue her into a corner about the discipline it takes to succeed. That it requires sacrifice. Long hours and working weekends. Brushing off holidays. She always believed I was mad, pushing myself to the brink. But I had to.

I needed to prove my father wrong.

In retrospect, that bit me in the ass.

Once I beat him at pool, he became scared of me beating him at everything. Earning more and achieving more, both of which I did. It's why he refused to visit me. He was quite fine, thank you very much, staying put in their cramped, dark London flat. I remember when he said there was no nobility in my work and that my trendy LA life had brainwashed me into believing I was better than the average person.

Average, meaning him.

My vision blurs with hot tears. Mum had insisted his pneumonia was standard issue and I didn't need to fly home. Two weeks later, I hopped on a plane for his funeral. Did I need more of a sign to slow down after that? Instead, I threw myself into work.

"Believe it or not," I say, "I have been second-guessing how much more I have left in me."

"It's about time," she says, surprising me with her ardent response. "Me and your dad were always worried about you. So driven. And with all your relationships falling apart, it's as if you didn't want to see yourself as the problem."

"What?" The shock of Mum, a newly minted armchair psychologist, fizzes through me. "Now you sound like Russ."

"That fool," she grumbles. "Why you married him, I'll never understand. Such a lout. And a ginger! Ugh."

He and Mum never got on. If you refuse bangers and beans, you refuse God, in her eyes. And she was right—he was a ginger wanker, in the end.

I sigh, happy to find common ground with her. "One of the many lessons I'm slowly learning is to set the bar higher with men."

"Good," she says, more assertive than I've ever heard her. "I know it must be a struggle. It's not easy being a woman. Not at your level. And your dad and I knew we couldn't stop you from chasing your dreams. But at what cost?"

A lump expands in my throat. I can see her clearly in my mind. Comfortable in the leatherette recliner, a cozy mystery in her lap. A cuppa nearby on her tray and the telly on in the background. Feet tucked into knitted slippers. The reassurance of that scene breaks something inside me. I promised myself never to be that doddering housewife, and yet Mum is content as a clam, aside from wishing that her only daughter might drop in every now and again.

"This whole business with Cliff turned me inside out," I admit. "I think I'll take a step back after this. I found a solid partner to help out. He's very talented. I won't have to carry the whole load."

"Do I know him?" she asks.

I'm quiet, wondering if I should fess up. I did blubber to Mum about Dallas years ago in a rare, vulnerable moment, but I doubt she'll remember. More important matters fill her day, like settling the debate about what comes first on the scone, the jam or the cream?

"Dallas Evener," I say, and his name rolls off my tongue without bitterness for the first time in a decade.

I hear the squeak of the recliner as she sits up. "Are you pulling my leg?"

"No."

"Isn't he one of the richest men in the world?"

"How do you know?"

"Because you told me about him. How heartbroken you were when things went tits up. I've kept him on my radar ever since. He's very handsome and single, last time I checked. You need a man like him and not a Russ who drags you down to their level. Every cup of tea needs a proper biscuit, Junebug."

That she knows so much about Dallas throws me for a loop. That I and Mum are chatting about my lackluster love life is an even bigger shocker. Chatting, in general. After Father passed and she moved to Vancouver to be closer to me while remaining in the safety of the Commonwealth, she found it hard to make friends in a city not known for being friendly. She clung to me at first, and then I stopped taking her calls. Texted when I had time, which was hardly ever.

And she kept a stiff upper lip when I should have sensed the forlorn hope of a mother wanting to connect with her only child. Jesus. It crashes around me all at once. The companies I've poured my heart and soul into while neglecting my own Mum.

Neglected boyfriends, husbands, and to an extent, myself.

I feel a rush of all the time that has passed.

"Let's do a proper catch-up once the dust settles," I say. "I'll come to Vancouver and spend a good week."

"That long!" She makes an indeterminate sound of surprise. "I would love that if you could manage it. A new neighbor is on me constantly, asking when you'll visit. She's into finance and all that stuff I know nothing about. Any chance you could bring Dallas with you? I need a new crush now that Cliff is on the outs."

I chuckle at the thought of Dallas amidst her Manchester United bobblehead doll collection and listening to her endless stories about the Queen. "I'll see what I can do."

We chatter on about the weather and the tea drinkers' plight in Vancouver—a city obsessed with coffee. Just before we hang up, she says, "Junebug, I know things were hard with you and Dad. He never showed it, but trust me, he cared. He was proud of you, but too proud to get off his high horse and show it. And I'm just a lady from the country, happy with her petunias and East Enders. I will never under-stand your world." She laughs self-deprecatingly. So bloody English.

"Was I ever a bitch?" I ask. Full cringe, because I already know the answer.

"Sometimes," she says, with a tenderness I don't deserve. "You were a bit intimidating, luv, all that passion. But I will always adore you. That's what mums are for."

Chapter Twenty-Eight

I arrive at Dallas's room an hour later and feel like a new woman. Or at least a re-arranged one. I spent the last sixty minutes FaceTiming with Vandana and Flynn because my besties always set me straight. They happily picked apart where I might have gone wrong with Dallas years ago, and more importantly, they brought my short-comings into focus.

I ditched my parents to prove I could be successful and paid dearly for it when my father disowned me. I dated guys who would never eclipse me because I feared losing control. And since Dallas was an equal, the imbalance left me vulnerable. So I blamed him for every-thing because it was a way to protect myself. But fault and responsi-bility are different. He tried in his own way to apologize; he knew it was up to him to fix what he screwed up. But I was responsible for being a bitch and not accepting his olive branch as my own twisted form of revenge.

God, to have it all spelled out to me was humbling.

And then poor Flynn had a heart attack after hearing what had tran-spired so far in Argentina.

"You and Dallas?" she said in utter shock. "It's been what ... three days?"

"Technically, we have not slept together if penetration is the bench-mark," I said, keeping mum on Navarro and his strange behavior thwarting our attempts because that would open a whole can of worms. Flynn takes on worry too readily, and she has a full plate with Chavez, a hothead prone to the occasional meltdown.

"She held out longer than I ever have," Vandana joked, not-so-secretly pleased because she would tell everyone later that her match-making brought us together.

I smile and knock on Dallas' door. It's early days, but this time, it might work out between us. At the very least, we can start with the sleeping together part.

Dallas flings the door open and greets me with nothing on except a bathrobe and a radiant smile. "I was wondering what happened to you."

"Did I miss the party?" He smells like a pub and looks a bit loopy.

"No," he says, reaching for my hand. "You're right on time."

He pulls me inside, kicks the door shut, and flattens me against the wall. And then we're kissing like one of those Hollywood movies where the lovers end up together after being apart for years. It's a dance of tongues and synchronized breaths. A kiss that is more than a meeting of mouths; it's a fusion of souls. I grip the expanse of his back, the taut muscles coming alive under my touch. His tastes and scent heighten, adding to the sensory overload of our bodies pressed together.

When we come up for air, he holds me close, our foreheads touch-ing. Or at least as much as they can with our height disparity. Damn Mum and her stumpy Viking genes.

"What was that all about?" I ask. His whiskey breath tingles on my tongue.

His eyes, pools of emotion, lock onto mine. "I'm happy to see you. How did it go with the team?"

"They're excited to meet you. I felt like an afterthought."

"That won't happen here. You're the main event."

"Am I staying another night?" I ask, reconfirming a text he sent earlier. Based on the howling wind that rattled through every crevice in my room, not even the birds were flying tonight.

"Yes," he says. "And I forgot to mention Navarro asked if you could cook dinner."

"Really?" I brighten at the thought of running free in that kitchen sans Carolina. "I'd love to."

He makes a funny face like I should reconsider. "Maybe you can dial back the enthusiasm? I warned Navarro you might be offended."

"You should be chuffed with the idea," I tease. "To tell the world you ate one of my dinners."

He can't help smiling at that. "I'd rather tell the world I ate you."

His hand slides between my thighs. He slips his thumb under my knickers, zeroing in on my still-swollen magic button. It becomes wetter with every delicious circling stroke. And just like that, I am hot everywhere. Christ, we haven't made it out of the entryway, and already I'm weak at the knees.

"That feels so good," I groan.

I can feel the heat of his erection pulsing through the robe. I find him behind the wall of terrycloth and wrap my fingers around his satin skin.

"Oh, fuck," he mutters, his eyes squeezing shut.

I start to pump him with slow, sensual moves. "Did you lock the door?"

He flutters a sigh. "Not yet."

"I think we learned a lesson last night, didn't we? Safety first."

After a hard swallow, he says, "What you're doing is very unsafe."

"I was wondering how I'm supposed to eat you if you keep locking me up."

He spirals a finger into my channel, capturing my gasp with a kiss. "Special circumstances can be arranged. At my discretion."

"Ah, how convenient, Mr. Evener."

Muffled laughter buzzes in his chest. "Nothing about you is convenient, June. You hammered me down to twelve percent, embarrassed me in front of my crew, and you're a do-gooding ballbuster who refuses to back down on virtually anything."

"Hmm," I muse. "Buttering me up now, are you?"

"Don't say butter," he moans. "*The Last Tango in Paris* is one of my favorite movies."

"An erotic drama? What a surprise." I palm his balls, loving the feel of their swollen weight.

"You are the surprise," he says. "I secretly hoped you were this kind of woman."

I raise an inquiring brow. "Slutty?"

"I was going to say *adventurous*."

He bites back a smile, popping his thumb in to join his finger and teasing me with rapid, tiny pulses. It fills my veins with fire. I ride his hand, bucking my hips. I want him in every way possible.

"Keep going," I mumble, doing the same with him as we slowly get each other off.

He leans closer and kisses me—hard, hungry, and penetrating. I lose myself a little. He's making this so easy.

"You are a siren," he murmurs, his lips humming on mine. "I just want to crash on your shores. I don't care if I drown."

"And if I give you the chance," I whisper back, "what becomes of me and the dark prince?"

He's breathing faster, his fingering of me less precise as I bring him closer to the peak. "They fly back to LA and live happily ever after."

"Is there such a thing?"

He pulls back a little and stares down at me. A burning awareness radiates in the depths of his eyes. "We'll never know unless we try. And we've wasted so much time already. You and I speak the same language. We are twins. You know it. I know it. Can we just get over ourselves and make it happen?"

Dallas's breath is warm on my face, his hand at a standstill under my dress. I have one hand in his hair and the other curled around his smooth manhood. The strange thing is that all of this feels so familiar. But I look at him with my full attention to make sure I'm not imagining this.

"I think it already is happening."

He smiles and kisses the tip of my nose. "Hold on."

In the time it takes for Dallas to lock the door, I shut my eyes and savor the electric energy coursing through my body. Things will get wilder and rougher soon, with no time to process anything beyond planets colliding and stars filling my brain.

I lift my eyelids to find Dallas in front of me again—robe splayed open so I can admire what's staring me in the face. Many inches. The excessive kind. Thickness that I'll have to get used to.

"You're trapped inside with me," he says, a hint of challenge in his voice.

With him this close and smelling so good, my path is clear. I might be locked in his room, but I'm not locked up. Yet. I lower to my knees and swirl around the slick tip of his cock with my tongue.

Eyes a little wild and breathing erratically, Dallas grits out, "You get five minutes. And then I take over."

I search his face, but he's dead serious. "Now I'm on the clock?"

"Four minutes and fifty-nine seconds."

"Can I do anything I want in my allotted time?" I ask.

He marshals his words carefully. "I'm not sure I should say yes to that."

"It doesn't matter," I say and drop sweet kisses on the creamy bits of his inner thigh. "I think I'll just run with it."

I take him all at once for the shock value. Relish the jerk of his hips and the *thud* of his skull connecting hard with something more unforgiving than me.

His hands dive into my hair, and he growls, "Fuck. Me!"

Maybe later, I think to myself, smiling, but not too hard, because teeth and a blow job are a dreadful combination. But I love giving head. It's one of the only times when men no longer hold all the power. When they become begging babies—bodies strained to the point of snapping and goo in their heads instead of brains. A woman can ask for anything, and she shall receive, so it crosses my mind, strangely, fleetingly, to ask why Dallas was buck naked as he argued with Navarro.

But I reach behind him to grip his ass instead. I speed up, and Dallas paws uselessly against the wall instead of my hair—thank you for that. I can feel his thighs expand, growing warmer, heat pouring off him.

"Oh, June," he whispers. "Goddamn."

He's on the brink. I can smell it—that extra squirt of pheromones. With the finish line in sight, I pop him out of my mouth like the mean girl I am.

His eyes smash open, and he cries, "What? What's wrong?"

I pretend to look at a watch on my wrist. "I believe my five minutes are up. So sorry."

Dallas is in a daze as I rise to my feet, not quite believing I've left him dangling. Or rather, very upright.

"You…" he sputters.

"I never promised that I wouldn't fuck *you* over," I say.

I give his poor cock a squeeze and waltz over to the bed, take a seat, and cross one leg over the other. With minimal fanfare and maximum sass, I tell him, "I'll just be over here if you have any plans for revenge."

Chapter Twenty-Nine

DALLAS

THERE'S a subtle dance between excitement and nervousness. Compound that emotional push-pull with a dick so hard it could hammer nails and yeah, I need a breath or two to calm the fuck down. June holds court on the bed like a British sovereign waiting for the commoner to approach. What a cheeky little wench. She needs to be overthrown, in the best way.

Blue ball me at your peril.

I swagger over, robe flapping open, her pink lipstick artistically smeared in my pubes. Standing over her gives me a fine view of the plunging neckline of her dress. I've learned enough of a lesson never to utter the word *rack* around her again, but man. Those tits of hers. I could live three lifetimes buried between those bundles of sweet glory.

"You need to change your mindset," I say. "Revenge sounds cruel."

She looks up at me from under her thick fringe of lashes. Fake? Yes. But the rest of her is one hundred percent real. Her parts move like nature intended.

"I'm not above pain," she states. Testing me is what it feels like.

"Everyone has a threshold, June. But I'm not interested in breaking yours."

"Why not?" she asks, genuinely puzzled.

Placing a finger beneath her chin, I lift her gaze to mine. "Because I never want to hurt you again."

Her chin trembles and she swallows hard. Damn. Did I finally say the right thing? I'll never win the prize for Soliloquy of the Year, but I can string a sentence or two together when needed.

"That's incredibly touching," she says, her voice shredded. "And kind."

"I told you I had a heart."

And will you embrace it? is what I want to ask because the chemistry crackling between us is a palpable force.

With a ghost of a smile, she says, "I stand corrected."

Her slowly dilating pupils and how they swallow up the ice-blue irises make me want to blow past our thresholds and storm the gate. I did hope, like every guy does, that she was a woman open to the occasional round of debauchery. But this good fortune? I could be a card counter wiz in Vegas and still not beat the odds that June would be cool with my particular needs. In retrospect, had I played my hand the right way ten years ago and taken her out for dinner first, chances are we might've fucked on the boardroom table after the fact.

Does that absolve me from being a prick? Not a chance.

But the moment I spied her in my favorite Hollywood bar, decent thoughts flew out the window. It's not every day you meet your match, and mine was a blonde bombshell in a tight suit who kept pretending not to notice me notice her.

"What are you thinking about?" June asks. "You have a nostalgic glow about you."

"Do you remember the night we met at the bar?"

She smiles as I trace my finger along the sensual line of her jaw. "Your date didn't fancy you buying me a drink. I know that much."

"Your date was way beneath your pay grade. I had to save you."

"You assumed I needed help?" A small, knowing smile lifts one side of her mouth.

"Everyone needs help at some point."

She tilts her head. "Even you?"

"Especially me."

I caress the soft lobe of her ear between my thumb and forefinger. Intimacy feels right with her and not some foreign thing beyond my grasp.

"What can I do to help?" she asks.

Let me rock you from the inside.

"I want you to undress while I watch."

Her eyes come alive, sparkling with humor. "Getting lazy in your old age?"

"Ouch. You might have to pay for that."

"I'm already paying you too much," she says, flipping her hair as she stands to confront me in that superior manner. It's a complete turn-on because no one ever challenges me except Nikki.

"I'm not renegotiating. But I will happily wait for the show."

"I see," she says with the cutest smirk. "In that case, can you unzip me?"

She lifts her hair and turns, waiting for me to get busy. But I'm preoccupied with her full ass in that dress and how it makes my dick cramp. The hottest Formula 1 driver in the world would crumble if they had to navigate her curves. Do I go fast or slow with the zipper? Since speed kills, I inch the zipper lower in slow motion. She shrugs the dress off her shoulders to expose her silky lace bra and shoots me a coy look over her shoulder.

"I can take it from here."

I hop onto the bed and hunker down. The handcuffs are ready to go on the bedside table. I had two hours to prepare and fantasize but also curse those damn silvery rings. It guts me how badly I need them. The last woman I slept with sans hardware was Robin, and I have genuinely forgotten how to be with someone and not restrain them.

Can June change all that?

I think she can, eventually.

She is a deity amongst all the dumpster fires I've fucked and forgotten.

And look at her go.

Heat builds inside my body watching a bona fide seductress ease a designer number past the curve of her hips. She shimmies three square inches of panty down her petite legs, and damn—words fail me. Not a bad thing, because talk is cheap at a moment like this. Also, my brain is about to explode. I'm goddamn salivating because I can smell her pussy from here. She arches her back to unhook the bra and my dick gets harder, if that's humanly possible. Some guys are ass men. I am one hundred percent a boob guy. June's mind is her pièce de résistance, but those mountains of cleavage tumbling out of their confines are a strong runner-up.

She spreads her arms with a flourish, a smile lighting up her face. "I believe I'm done."

"Are you kidding me?" I laugh and motion for her to join me on the bed. "We haven't even started."

A beautiful sight she is, scaling the bed, those heavy tits hanging with perked pink nipples that are begging for some love. Forget about control. How am I not going to come as soon as her tightness sucks me inside?

"Let's swap positions," I say, and make space for her to lie down. I snap the cuffs on her tiny wrists, and the electric tingle in my gut drives me crazy. My mind and body are forever at war.

She exhales slowly and, apropos of nothing, asks, "What time is dinner?"

"Not until six," I say.

Plenty of time to demolish you.

As if she can read my mind, she says, "I don't know if I'll survive hours."

I slip off the robe and position myself between her legs, spreading them wide. My face is inches from her glistening nub of pleasure.

"I think you can," I say.

My tongue tip grazes her outer folds, and she shudders violently. I alternate between sucking her clit and finger-fucking her until she thrashes like a caged animal.

"Hold on," she pants. "I need a minute to recover."

I take a breather as requested. No harm in stockpiling my energy before I crank her to the breaking point. Extract every last ounce of willpower. Dismantle her completely.

I have plans, June. Not to worry.

A minute later, I'm back.

My dick throbs, swollen beneath me as I lie flat on my belly eating her up. I can feel her clit harden into a tight bud. Clock the agony on her face. She's almost there, the sweet, pained conclusion seconds away. I'm relentless, pushing her higher and higher to the precarious edge until she plummets.

"Fuck!" she moans.

What a vision she is, swept away in waves of pleasure. I lap up the torrent of her coming apart, and she fills my senses so completely that my surroundings seem almost irrelevant. In the aftermath, she slowly returns to earth, body sheened in sweat and twitching from post-orgasm tremors.

Her eyes slowly peel open, and she looks down at me through her heaving breasts. "Dallas," is all she says.

I nibble on her trembling thigh. "Present and accounted for."

She laughs—a weak, whimpering sound. "I need you to fuck me. Now."

My heart starts to beat double time. I can't explain how she makes me feel. She's a firecracker who understands my world, because it's her world, too.

And she's an unholy beast in the sack.

I don't need to be asked twice.

I sit up and sheath myself while she watches. With one hand flush against the mattress to support me, I hover over her and use my free hand to angle my dick onto her clit. I draw sweet, slow circles until she begs me to enter her. I push in ever so slightly. She's hot and needy. I clench my ass and think of the worst thing possible to put the brakes on my momentum.

"You can start slow if that helps," she offers.

"Slow?" I offer her a wry smile. "I might have to go backward."

"I just want this moment to last."

Sweet and anxious and full of yearning, her expression catches me off guard. I feel a shiver of something in the air between us. Like if I fuck this up, the next stop is eternal damnation with no chance of parole.

"June," I whisper. "You are everything. I'll try my best."

Best meaning, I hilt myself because easing in is a recipe for disaster. My balls smack against her ass, a gasp of surprise spills from her lips, and sweet Jesus. It's like losing my virginity for the first time all over again.

I apologize for the swift intrusion and promise to honor her request. But her thrusting hips tell me otherwise, and we find our rhythm as June's sweet warmth contracts tightly around my dick. In no time at all, I can feel the burning and twisting up inside my balls. I burrow my head into the dark safety of her neck and breathe in the secret scent of her skin.

Slow, I tell myself. *Slow*.

But I always was a horrible listener.

Chapter Thirty

JUNE

"Hey, sleepyhead. Time to get up."

I stir awake in the big, warm bed to find Dallas propped up on one elbow, gazing at me with a smile the size of Arizona.

"Hello," I say, sounding self-conscious in that after-the-first-time way. I sit up and squint out the window at a black sky. The rain has slowed to a drizzle. "What time is it?" I ask.

"Five," he says. "We've been summoned to the kitchen for six. Unless you've changed your mind?"

Oh, right. Dinner.

"No, it's fine. I'm happy to cook. I just…" I trail off, unsure how to convey the complexity of my feelings. Our lovemaking was a master-class in losing control, and we skimmed the dark edges of infinity before spiraling into an abyss of sweet, aching arousal. And after, he whispered apologies, thank-yous, and sweet nothings that lifted my heart. His touch made me remember all the things I used to be.

No wonder I've slept until dark. Revenge takes its toll.

I sink back into the soft feather pillows with a contented sigh. "A night like this is perfect for staying in bed."

Dallas snuggles closer. "We can cut out early. Have dessert back here." His mouth brushes mine with a sweet, soft kiss. He tastes naughty, the tang of me mingled on his breath. "You drive me crazy," he whispers. "I'm sorry if it got too wild. Do your wrists hurt?"

"They're a little sore." I smile. "But not as sore as other places."

The intensity in how he shagged me … I sank into myself, clawing through endless layers, until I hit bedrock. To have him wage an assault on my most sensitive area and unable to touch him was sublime torture. But my cries only fanned the flames. He ignored my pleas and answered with punishing thrusts, leaving me mute, swallowed up by his fullness. I felt the blood rush to all my damaged places, and he rocked tight against me until we both came undone.

He seemed fragile and untouchable in the moments after, the light bouncing off his cheeks, his hands shaking as he freed me from the cuffs.

It had crossed my mind before it went blank with desire, and the safe, quiet space we find ourselves in fuels my courage to ask.

"Have you ever tried role reversal?"

On his flawless, impassive face only his eyes move, taking me in. But I can feel the thunder of his heart.

"The handcuffs aren't for fun."

"I wasn't—"

"I'm damaged goods," he interrupts, the blunt reality of that statement amplified with brusqueness. "Full disclosure."

Pain runs underneath his voice, like a dark shadow. I'd guessed, randomly, that something old and deep-rooted lay at the source of his needs, and this reconfirms it.

"We're all damaged, in some ways," I venture because it is true. And because I don't know what else to say.

His eyes flick off mine to contemplate dead space on the wall. Does a faint flicker of shame register in his squared jaw?

"My mom left us when I was seventeen," he finally says, his voice gruff. "She just up and disappeared one night. No note, no nothing. I don't know where she is. If she's even alive."

"Oh my God." I touch his leg under the duvet. He looks wilted and lost. "Dallas, that's awful. I'm so sorry."

"After she left, I had a couple of severe heartbreaks. They fucked me up. I deal with loss by preventing it. No one leaves me unless I okay it."

He strokes my hair absently but with aggressive strokes that I imagine reflect what's churning in his mind. To speak the truth and finally have it out in the open feels monumental, like he's never voiced this to anyone. All I can hear is his ragged breaths, with more and more time in between them before he says, "I understand this might not be what you signed up for, so no pressure. I'm not pushing you to anything more than one day at a time."

I track his eyes, uncertain. He's just opened up and feels compelled to give me an out. But it's for all the wrong reasons.

"Okay," I say, slowly. "Understood. The same goes for me. No expectations. But maybe we need to be open to anything. Whatever that entails."

His brow furrows, like maybe I've said the exact wrong thing. Then he buries his face into my hair and whispers, "I just want to go home and be with you."

The walls around my heart crumble. I planned to ask Dallas tonight if he would forgo the help-Navarro-escape deal he got lassoed into. Maybe I'll bring it up during dinner prep because it appears to be weighing on him, among other things. For now, I wrap my arms around his warmth and marvel at how the universe works in strange ways. I had many expectations for this trip, but Dallas Evener stripping away his pretenses after he stripped away the last vestiges of my modesty? Ninety-nine on the One-to-One-Hundred Impossibility Scale.

$

THE AIR VIBRATES DIFFERENTLY TONIGHT. It's still bloody cold in this draft magnet of a home, but my heart is warm as we walk to the kitchen. I'm excited to cook.

Mimi and Rodolfo greet us first, bounding toward us with exuberant barks. They know Dallas is good for a solid chin scratching session, which he gladly administers. They're so cute with their whimpers. And they seem to animate Dallas. Navarro coolly regards the scene from a stool at the kitchen island, forever stylish with a kelly-green bow tie and emerald cufflinks shimmering on his starched cuffs. He pops his book shut. Nietzsche—*Beyond Good and Evil*. Some light revolutionary reading before dinner.

"Buonasera," he says.

Dallas replies with a chin nod. "Hey."

They exchange an uneasy glance. The same tension I felt when we first arrived crackles between them, and Navarro's gaze feels loaded with disapproval when it cuts to mine. Is it obvious me and Dallas shagged ourselves silly? Should we have made more of an effort to engage with him on our last day? But then I remember today is only *my* last day. I hope Dallas changes his mind and joins me on a flight home.

"Any requests for tonight?" I ask Navarro. He's uncorked a bottle of wine and is decanting it into a delicate blown-glass creation.

"You have free rein," he says. "Carolina stocked the pantry before she left. And I can help. I'm not entirely useless in a kitchen, despite what my mother might say."

Dallas rinses up at the sink. "Your mother did all the cooking. You just sat there and had plates placed in front of you."

Navarro stands there for a minute and sets down the decanted wine. "I can do more than burn toast."

"You didn't have to eat it," Dallas says, pointedly.

"I didn't want to hurt your feelings."

Dallas dries his hand and chucks the towel onto the counter. "So you kept buying more bread."

Navarro sighs. It feels like an old argument, never to be won. "Relegate the basic tasks to him," Navarro says. "And we should be fine."

Based on his eye roll, Dallas is a long way away from a town called

Fine. I don't know if I'll ever crack their dynamic, but they are as bad as nattering girls.

"As long as your respective manhoods aren't threatened, I could use some help from both of you."

Mimi and Rodolfo trail after me as I pluck Carolina's apron off its peg and tie it on. Hard to believe the two dogs are better behaved than the men I'm about to cook for.

$

AN HOUR LATER, the steaks are cooked and resting. I crack pepper over the salad and check once more on the fingerling potatoes crisping in the oven. Dinner has come together perfectly, despite Dallas. The basil I asked him to chiffonade came back hacked to smithereens, and for a man who owns an impressive collection of Shun knives—I remember them hanging from a magnetic holder in his kitchen—I was frightened that a fingertip might end up in the salad.

Meanwhile, Navarro excised fat from the steaks with surgical precision. I kept glancing at his hand, the missing half-moon of flesh. It looked like something took a bite out of it. At this point, I don't want to know, and I'm not one of those types who can blurt out questions like Flynn. She can ask a stranger about their disfigured face in such a heartfelt way that before you know it, they're sharing every detail about a gruesome accident like it's no big deal. If I asked, they'd move farther away and tell me to mind my own beeswax.

Whatever, I think, taking a mouthful of wine. We all have our strengths. And based on how perfectly Dallas folded the napkins for the table, that might be his true calling.

He's disappeared to the loo and is still gone when Navarro returns from the wine cellar with two dusty bottles. He inhales the fragrant air and crowds me against the island.

"It smells fantastic in here. And you do, too."

He leans over to plant a kiss on my cheek. His sweet manners stab at my heart. How can someone so gentle kill in cold blood? I smile and say thank you, aware of every inch of him and how close he is. But what is that scent? My nose twitches. Is it my imagination that the damp, old smell wafting around him is familiar? I feel a pinch in my stomach when the recognition hits—the frigid air that licked at my ankles earlier. That section of the vast kitchen remains in the shadows, but did Navarro go there to fetch the wine? I was busy chopping rosemary to finish the potatoes, although I have a cold hunch that the answer is yes.

Navarro sweeps dust from one of the black bottles and presents it to me as a sommelier does for approval. "This one is for you and Dallas."

I glance at the label and do a double take. Romanée-Conti Grand Cru? Some of those bottles sell for six figures.

"Are you sure? You must have a glass with us."

"I'm not a Pinot Noir fan," he says. "You two enjoy it."

"That's very generous of you."

"It's the perfect way to end the trip, vero? Good food, wine, and friends."

I assess his wistful smile and the grand kitchen, trying to make sense of a world I will never understand. Will his decision to defect lead to better things? Can someone on the run ever be happy?

Dallas returns a minute later and slides in beside me, blissfully unaware that he kisses the same cheek Navarro's lips landed on earlier.

But Navarro notices.

And his eyes glow like he's lit up from within.

$

To mark the end of dinner, hailstones the size of walnuts crash out of heaven to pummel the patio pavement. Navarro glances over his shoulder to gauge the ruckus. He sits across from Dallas and me, his back to the storm. The dogs whine quietly, hunkered together in their bed.

"Good thing you're not flying in this," Dallas says, slinging his arm drunkenly around my shoulder. He's had a lot of wine and been chatty and handsy. Navarro, on the other hand, was upbeat and talkative during prep and fell silent when we started eating. He sawed morosely at his steak while Dallas and I talked excitedly about Green Time and our plans over the next few weeks. Is it too much for Navarro to be an integral part of the company but also completely removed?

"What time do you want to leave tomorrow?" Navarro asks.

"Whatever works best," I say. "I'm flexible."

Dallas nuzzles my neck. "Maybe not too early."

He helps himself to the last piece of focaccia after Navarro and I decline it. Chewing thoughtfully, he draws circles on my thigh with his palm. "Did you have any plans for dessert?"

"I saw some cream and dark chocolate in the fridge. Perhaps a mousse?"

Navarro raises his hand like he's back in grade school. "I have a suggestion."

Dallas snickers, although not unkindly. "Let me guess … Cannoli?"

Navarro folds his napkin in a perfect half, then halves it again. His face lights up with that strange glow, the fathomless emerald of his wolf eyes alive and glittering. I'm feeling the wine, but even if I was stone-cold sober, nothing could prepare me for what he says in his posh, velvety accent.

"I would like to sleep with both of you."

A blistering bolt of lightning turns night into day. An explosive *crack* follows, and then the slow, creaking sound of a tree smashing to the ground. The dogs leap from their beds and start barking into the night, wet noses pushed against the window.

Dallas blinks, the drunk smile sliding off his face.

Thunder booms overhead, and the kitchen lights sputter off, shrouding us all in black.

Chapter Thirty-One

In the time it takes for the generator to kick in and the lights to flicker back on, my remaining saliva has transformed into glue. Dallas and I sit motionless in our chairs, smothered by the immense silence.

Dallas finds his voice first. "What the fuck? Are you out of your mind?"

"It's not what we agreed to," Navarro replies with an eerie calm. "But why not?"

I feel all the color drain from my face. Three words leave my lips in a piteous creak. "Agreed to what?"

"June is not part of our deal," Dallas warns.

"What deal?" My head swivels between my dinner partners.

Navarro is about to say something, and Dallas snaps, "Don't."

A quiet doom settles over the table. Mimi and Rodolfo skitter nervously around their master, spooked by the storm and the rise of tension in the room.

Navarro's eyes taper with accusation. "You haven't told her. I assumed you told her everything."

"Shut up!" Dallas hisses in a way that feels like a final warning.

"Why?" Navarro asks. "Are you ashamed that we were lovers?"

It feels like the earth is widening beneath me, about to swallow me whole. Holy shit. Nothing made sense, and suddenly, it all makes sense.

The tension between them.

When Navarro walked in on us—the look on his face.

Is that why Dallas evaded my eyes the morning after?

As this mind fuck of information rolls over me, I am conscious of Dallas's tense jaw and of his silence. Navarro watches every reaction play out on my face. Did they stay up all night brokering me like I was chattel? Or sleep with each other while I hardly slept? Navarro's cavalier request blindsided me, but why did I not put more faith in my gut instincts?

I push back in the chair and stumble to my feet. My first thought is that I drank too much. My legs feel heavy and thick.

"Whatever you two have concocted does not involve me."

"It's a little too late to back out, principessa," Navarro says, eyeing me as I wobble in my heels.

Dallas glares at him with simmering rage. "I need to talk to June. Alone."

Navarro steeples his fingers in front of his mouth. The thinking man's psychopath. "All I'm suggesting is we go with the flow, as you liked to say when we first met. A slight adjustment to our original plan."

"Tell me what is going on," I say, doing my best to stay calm. The normalcy of the evening is slipping away and I'm uncertain what will take its place.

"No adjustments," Dallas says. "None."

Navarro appears to consider this. "Unfortunately, you don't make the rules here. And it would be such a shame if something happened to Nikki's two children over a simple matter, vero?"

A hot surge of nausea wobbles me. This isn't a suggestion. This is blackmail. And this is my fault, because Navarro asked me earlier who Dallas's right-hand person was.

"You motherfucker." Dallas speaks with disgust so severe I doubt I would ever be able to match it.

"An Italian boy does not use that term," Navarro says, offended. "And there is no need for such language."

Dallas leaps up from his chair. "You're doing this to get back at me. Because I turned you down in New York. You see I have a real chance to be happy and you can't handle it." He jabs a finger across the table at Navarro, punctuating his words. "I moved on because you left me no choice!"

Navarro rises from his chair and soothes the yelping dogs. I can tell his mind is made up. And he's made our minds up for us.

With a *you fix it* gesture directed at me, Navarro says, "Perhaps you can talk some sense into him. I'll be in the salon, waiting."

In the long, chilly silence after Navarro leaves, Dallas stares blankly at nothing, chin squared and trembling, holding back anger and lord knows how many other emotions.

"This is not happening," he says. "I won't let him do this."

I think back to Navarro's fumbling kisses in the tower. How he said I felt so soft. The full, lush feel of his lips on my cheek a scant forty minutes ago. The electricity of it. I realize I'm mistaken to believe I didn't play a role in this.

But that does not wipe out what Dallas neglected to tell me.

"What happened the other night?" I demand. "The truth this time, please."

"Everything I told you is the truth," he says. "He wants to leave the mafia." After a loaded pause, he adds, "What I didn't tell you is that he wanted something from me. For the money. It was supposed to be just us tonight."

I do the quick math. "So, you two … back at Oxford."

His face flushes pink. "No. I mean … yes. For a while. Back then."

"And there was no girlfriend at uni that he stole away from you," I say, not bothering to pose it as a question.

Dallas responds with a curt head shake. Then, "The only thing he stole was my soul."

I suddenly feel so aware of the invisible wall between them since we arrived. Dallas was scared of Navarro for an entirely different reason than I imagined.

"You loved him."

"Yes," he admits wearily. "But the dynamic was incredibly unhealthy."

"Because he had the upper hand?"

"The obsession went both ways."

Of course it did. If I've failed to offset the thrumming, unsettled force of Navarro's presence in three days, four years of uni with him must have been debilitating.

I hold Dallas' gaze. "Is he bi? Why does he want to sleep with both of us?"

"I don't want to burst your bubble, but Navarro likes men. He always has. He's never slept with a woman. This is all to prove he has power over me. He wants to hurt me emotionally and you are the perfect bargaining chip."

"Why does he want to hurt you?"

Dallas throws up his hands in frustration. "Because I broke his fucking heart. And he's never gotten over it."

"Are *you* bi?" I ask. A less intrusive question might be preferable but, like I said, holy shit. And I'd kind of like to know.

"Navarro was the only one," he says tersely.

It's impossible to have a clear train of thought. Too many emotions swirl inside, muddling all the pieces into soup. But one thing pokes up like a swollen log bobbing in the ocean.

"Did you bring me here to make him jealous?"

I might as well have suggested we murder the president, is what Dallas's baffled look says. "That is the last thing I wanted you here for."

"Then why?"

He laughs, a losing-it kind of laugh. "Why? What happened between us in the past three days was everything I always wanted! Why did I bring you here? I'll tell you. Because you lay in your bed stoned out of your mind and told me how hurt you were by what happened between us. How you thought I was the man of your dreams. That we were two sides of a perfect coin. That you wished things were different. What am I supposed to do with that? Walk away? I have feelings too."

His outburst stuns me into silence. I think about the heartbreak I felt all those years ago. How it sprawled for days on end with no relief or escape. I never once assumed he might feel the same.

That, however, does not change the fundamentals.

"He just threatened the lives of Nikki's children. What does he plan with us? And where does that leave Green Time?"

I mean, where do I even start? This is beyond fucked up. I spent an hour today with my team getting everything back on track. I cannot renege. This cannot fail.

But my options boil down to either public or private disgrace.

"Let me go and talk to him," Dallas says, not sounding confident in the slightest. And why should he? Our petty issues of safety and business decorum will not side-track Navarro from getting what he wants.

"Before you do," I start, and then stop to take a steadying breath. Am I really about to say this? Apparently so. "If we were to go ahead with this, what guarantees do we have that he doesn't screw us over?"

His mouth drops open. "You can't be serious, June."

"What choice do we have?"

At first, I chalk Dallas's terse silence up to him floundering for rational reasons to escape this situation. Then he sags cheerlessly against the table.

"You want to sleep with him."

It's not as if I haven't dreamt of a half-drunken fuck with Navarro. And Dallas busted me swallowing our host's tongue. But the script has flipped considerably.

"Oh, for Christ's sake, Dallas! Jealous at a time like this? I could be in my hot tub sipping a nice Pinot Grigio right now instead of trapped in a bloody castle with a three-way on tonight's menu and wondering if I'll be alive at the end to tell the tale."

"I told you, Navarro would never hurt me physically. Or you."

"Great. But a mental mind fuck halfway to China is just dandy?"

I pace around the island trying to rid myself of nervous energy that claws up my throat. Something suspect is fueling this. Beyond their broken love. Dallas owes Navarro. And if it's what I think it is, there is a whole lot more here at stake than a frolic between the sheets.

"He's the source, right? The dirty start of Evener Equity?"

Dallas gives a startled blink and fidgets with his ring. "Not him directly," he concedes. "He gave me a bunch of contacts."

So here we are. The sword hanging over Dallas's head now looms over me, and the entire evening is thrown on its head. And will a gangster who considers murder an acceptable way of tidying up the world put the brakes on manipulating Dallas after a simple ménage à trois?

Fuck.

Forget Cliff and all the other problems I thought I had.

This is what it means to be in over your head.

Chapter Thirty-Two

"ARE YOU SURE ABOUT THIS?"

Twenty minutes later, we're standing outside of the salon, Dallas asking me for the fifth time a question I have no interest in answering. I'm not sure of anything anymore, to be honest. My head feels like a balloon. I stumbled twice on the walk over here. This dopey sensation reminds me of the first night—the lure of Navarro, and me transferring saliva without shame.

"Let's get this over with," I whisper back.

This room shimmered with sunlight on the morning I found Dallas creating magic in here on the piano. But now it's heavy with shadows, pierced only by the one floor lamp Navarro bothered to turn on. He sits beside the fireplace in the most sumptuous velvet chair. Dallas and I shuffle closer, serfs in deference to a king who might say *Off with their heads* as easily as *I want to sleep with both of you.*

This vast, lavish room was built for special gatherings, but none, I imagine, quite like this.

"You've thought things through?" Navarro asks. One leg is crossed over the other, and his folded hands perch on a knee.

"Yes," Dallas says, at the same time I do, which seems to amuse

Navarro. Dallas side-eyes me and adds, "But we'd like there to be some parameters."

Navarro answers carefully. "Such as?"

"Condoms."

"Of course."

"Nothing weird."

"Whatever that means."

"With June," Dallas clarifies. "Nothing degrading."

I blush just as I did fifteen minutes ago when Dallas forced me to discuss boundaries. Checks and balances to ensure I am emotionally safe. As safe as I can be falling down a rabbit hole.

"And we want a time frame," he adds. "Two hours max. June wants to leave first thing in the morning, storm conditions pending."

A calculation flickers in Navarro's eyes. "How very unromantic and American, fitting everything into a time slot."

"I mean it," Dallas warns. We might be captive cargo on Navarro's erotic ship, but he can't steer us off the end of the earth. "This can't drag on for hours."

Navarro's nostrils flare. My first thought is we've pushed it one demand too far. "Understood," he says.

And to add my voice to the conversation, I say, "We want your word you will not harm Nikki or her children. They are innocents in all of this."

Navarro gazes at me with a sort of forensic curiosity. "That's very noble of you."

"Don't fuck with me, okay? This is your chess game, not mine. I just happen to be a pawn."

A small laugh catches in Dallas's throat, but his poker face is as good as they come.

"And a very beautiful one," Navarro says, eyes softening, or rather, he appears less in shock after absorbing my verbal blow. Nothing fazes him, it seems. He stands and stretches, as if preparing for the upcoming physical performance. "The dogs have settled for the night in my room. And since you two have settled into Dallas's room, that feels like the best choice. Andiamo?"

$

T HE THUDDING in my chest gets louder the closer we get to the bedroom. My regular nights don't involve forty-year-old vintage wines, and now I wish I'd capped my consumption. I have a real-live case of the shakes.

The allure of sexual exploration has always burbled in my soul, but what will I do with dueling penises?

I suppose God did grace me with two hands for a reason.

Bloody hell. Mum was right after all, about my future sins. But there are not enough confession booths in the world to save me from this one.

And here we are.

Dallas opens the door and shuttles me in first, pushing on the small of my back. None of us said a word walking here. Dallas tight-lipped, Navarro checked out, eyes straight ahead. And me, wondering what sordid hump fest awaits.

"Should we start a fire?" Navarro asks amiably. He turns on the lights but thankfully dims them. The ambiance is the last thing on my mind, and I'd rather not be on display under a bright spotlight.

Dallas plunks himself defiantly into the occasional chair by the window. "Go right ahead."

I wedge myself into the far corner of the sofa, and Navarro frowns at our opposite seating arrangements. But he can't credibly claim that his feelings are hurt. I mean, c'mon.

"You two should be on the bed," he says.

"Clothes on or off?" Dallas asks.

Navarro flits his gaze to mine. For the first time, he seems a little nervous.

"The circus ringleader needs to step up to the plate," Dallas reminds him. "We're just the performers."

"Yes, I know," Navarro says, flustered. "Off then, please. And can you bring me the handcuffs?"

Dallas shakes his head. "No fucking way. I told you, nothing weird."

"If it's not weird for you to use them, I should be afforded the same grace," Navarro snaps back. "I have agreed to all your terms. This is mine. Do as I say."

I can see Dallas's frustration rising like boiling water, Navarro slowly turning up the temperature. "Only one of us is cuffed at a time," he grumbles. "And we hold onto the keys, not you."

Navarro unknots his bow tie and tosses it across the room; his version of *yes,* given his lack of verbal response. Dallas storms into the bathroom, and Navarro glances sideways at me like I'm a flower he doesn't know where to put in his arrangement.

"I apologize for all the undue stress," he says.

I open my mouth and a stream of nonsense spills out. What the hell? My fingernails glint like candied lacquer, and why is my head throbbing?

Navarro steps closer, his eyes raking over me. "Are you feeling okay?"

I instinctively take a step back. But my legs are heavy as stone, and I'm suddenly falling, helpless, Navarro catching me in his arms before I hit the floor.

Now cradled in his embrace, I feel trapped and question my impulsive decision to sanction this crazy train. My breathing turns shallow, and I give in to the strange heaviness inhabiting my body.

Navarro pushes hair off my forehead and kisses me tenderly on the brow. "I'm so sorry, principessa. I'll explain later."

His features have started to fuzz around the edges. I blink but fail to bring them back into sharp relief. The tiny pinhole of remaining light gets smothered, and the last thing I hear is Dallas shouting, feel his hands on my face. The weight of the earth drags me to its center, and I understand, a little too late, that Navarro is apologizing for something entirely different than this.

Chapter Thirty-Three

I AM COLD. SORE. MY EYES SWIM IN THE DARK. BUT WITHOUT SEEING a thing, I know where I am. The sense of smell is linked closely with memory, and I can never forget the ancient air that swirled out from under the closed door in the kitchen. The same dark, dank smell wafting off Navarro last night infiltrates my nostrils and settles like sour milk deep in my heart.

Wherever that air was coming from is where I wake up. Slumped like a rag doll against a jagged wall and wearing what feels like one of the plush cotton robes from Dallas's bathroom. Otherwise, I'm naked. I swallow or try to. My throat feels like it's lined with steel wool. A handcuff on my right wrist secures me to something on the floor.

What is going on? And where is Dallas?

His name spills off my lips with a trembling release of breath.

From the murky dark beside me, he answers in a thick voice. "I'm here."

His fingers fumble onto mine and our respective handcuffs clank together. Whatever I'm attached to, he is as well. I pride myself on keeping calm, cool, and collected in the face of disaster, but if there is ever a time to freak out, it's now.

"What's happening? How did we get down here?"

Snippets of memory drift in and out. I remember lying listless in Navarro's lap. A kiss. An apology before darkness took over.

"Navarro must have carried us," Dallas says. "After you passed out, he admitted to putting a sedative into the wine. That's how he used to subdue his kidnap victims. I passed out later."

Kidnap? Victims? I don't know which word is worse, but at least I know I wasn't losing my mind.

"So, that first night," I say. "There was something in the wine."

"Probably. A test maybe. I'm sorry, June," he says, his voice bleak and on the verge of cracking. "This is all my fault."

I try to control my racing thoughts, but a feeling of utter panic reaches up from my stomach and grabs my throat until I cough.

"What does he want?" I ask.

Before Dallas can answer, footsteps sound overhead. We're underneath the kitchen, I know that much. This is where that strange door leads to. And that crafty bitch Carolina had to have known something was up because why else warn me not to stay? No wonder she cleared out of here. I bet Battista and the guards are in on this, too. All of them having events over the weekend was a pile of BS.

And now the steps are coming closer, moving down a set of stairs. Tiny hairs on my arm flicker to attention. To be reduced to this—chained and helpless, strength sapped with muscles cramped from the cold. Even if I could run, how far would I get?

I hear the sound of a key turning, the bolt sliding. I'm holding my breath, a film of nervous sweat on my skin. The door swings open and two seconds later, a flash of searing brightness illuminates the room. I duck my head to shield myself from the sudden glare and take panicky stock of our surroundings—a twelve-by-twelve, windowless hell of stone walls and a dirt floor lit up by six bare bulbs recessed in the ceiling. A massive rock with a ring bolt drilled into it sits between Dallas and me, our cuffs attached to the rusted ring.

For a moment, it feels like the air contracts around me.

Navarro stands before us, carrying a fancy silver tray laden with pastries, coffee cups, and an urn leaking the aroma of coffee.

"Buongiorno," he says in a strange, flat voice.

His posture bleeds tension, and I'm trying to wrap my head around Dallas and me chained up like animals while he's gussied up in a suit and tie offering breakfast.

Dallas is less analytical. "What the hell is this all about?" he shouts. "Unlock us. Now!"

Navarro purses his lips and says, in a louder tone, "I cannot. But the least I can do is feed you."

He shuffles toward us and rests on one knee to set the tray down. Dallas boots it with a swift, vicious kick that sends dishes, food, and coffee flying, our breakfast raining down with a clatter around a wincing Navarro.

"We are not eating anything, asshole," Dallas growls. "Not after you drugged us."

Navarro looks at him with crushed despair. "You have never called me that."

"Maybe I should have. Because it kind of sums you up. Whatever demented plan you have set in motion, June is not part of it. You have to let her go."

"You insisted she come along," Navarro argues like I'm not even here. "You left me no choice."

"Navarro!" An unfamiliar voice bellows down from the kitchen.

Navarro rises awkwardly and brushes dirt off his pressed trousers. "Down here," he calls back. To Dallas, he says, "You have a visitor." Then, his voice drops to a whisper. "Play along, okay?"

Heavy steps start to clunk down the stairs. Tremors squeeze my ribs, stealing away air. What is going on? It feels like we're actors in a performance, but for whom are we on stage?

"Who is it?" Dallas asks, parroting my thoughts.

"Someone who's been wanting to meet you for a long time," Navarro says, his voice petering out as the stranger ducks his head to enter.

A chill goes right through me.

This man is not here to light our path to glory. He's a thug dressed in Brooks Brothers lost on his way to a party in the Hamptons. Sinister and privileged. The skittish eyes of a rat. Flynn would generously describe his aura as a black stain, and a smirk I can only describe as evil spreads over his face as he locks eyes on Dallas.

I can tell from his expression he knows who this guy is.

"If it isn't the dark prince," the man drawls, with an accent that sounds Midwestern by way of Boston with a detour through England. He drops a salacious look on my boobs. "And aren't you a juicy plum? Too bad you landed in this dirtbag's orchard."

He slings an arm around Navarro's shoulder, who flinches and drops his gaze to the dirt. "My plane just made it here in time before they shut everything down last night. For-tu-i-tous!" he sing-songs. "Kind of like our dinner here a few weeks ago, right?" He gives Navarro another ominous squeeze. "I've been doing business with this family for decades," he explains, although to whom isn't clear. "All that time, and no clue this punk knew who'd been fucking my wife."

The man comes to crouch in front of Dallas. He's blandly handsome with a thinning grey combover and the body of an ex-football player brought on the field for brawn rather than brains. He gathers a loogie in his mouth and hocks the yellowed blob onto Dallas's chest.

"Dick Cavanagh," he says, "in case you don't remember my photo on her bedside table."

Dallas wipes the spit from his chest with his free hand. "What's the endgame, Dick? What do you want? Money?"

Dick (an appropriate name for a bald male intruder) snorts a laugh. "I got money coming out of my ass. But I should send you an invoice for the Oxford tuition she purloined from my account. *My* money set you up, you fuck. The dumb, ungrateful cunt never worked a day in her life. Buried her in a cardboard box, just to prove a point."

The savagery of his disdain. It makes me cringe. What woman in her right mind would pair up with this letch? He's a swath of unfortunate smells—fried meat, old socks, and cheap cologne—and I can never warm up to a man who wears a pinky ring.

"She was right," Dallas says, refusing to keep quiet. "You're a dick in every regard."

Dick's eyes narrow into slits. He has remarkable composure, but I suppose you need that when dealing with the mafia.

"And what about you?" he sneers. "The innocent piano player and dancer? The good son helping out his father's business while doinking the clientele? Give me a fucking break." He shakes his head in a remembering way. "I should have smelled her lies a mile away, like I smelled your spunk in her hole. Robin spent way too much time at that damn dance studio. She fed me some story about your Dad and how distraught he was when your Mom pulled a Houdini act and disappeared. Robin said she and all the other trophy wives were just *helping him through it*." He pauses, and something dark moves swiftly across his face. "I always thought she was fucking your dad. Never thought she'd dip into the underages. What were you, seventeen?"

"If you want to have at me, I'm all yours," Dallas says. "But June has nothing to do with this. Have the decency to let her go."

Dick considers this. For the briefest moment, my flagging hope revitalizes.

Then he laughs cruelly, glancing over at Navarro. "You love it when they start to beg, don't you? That's what Rafaelle told me. Oh, the quiet desperation." Back at Dallas, his smirk calcifies. "I want what every man wants when his property is violated. Revenge. I had half a mind to put a bullet in your two-bit brain, but there's something satisfying about prolonged mental torture. Maybe it's the sadist in me," he says, sounding creepily nostalgic. "I'm tickled pink to have you rot in here until your last shitty breath. Hopefully, she goes first."

Dick stands, both knees cracking like gunfire. "Say the last rites," he instructs Navarro. "I'll meet you upstairs. We need to book it. I need to be in London by ten a.m. Nice meeting you, girly," he says to me. "And nice tits."

Dallas waits for the sound of Dick's footsteps overhead before he freaks out on Navarro. "How the fucking hell does he know about me and Robin? You were the only person I told!"

Navarro inches closer. He radiates intensity and speaks in a hushed, secretive tone. "Dick and Rafaelle were here a few weeks ago. For some reason, my time at Oxford came up over dinner. When Dick found out you were my roommate, he had all sorts of questions. How did we meet? How did you end up at Oxford? I told him you had a patron, a woman from Seattle who paid for your tuition before she died of cancer. I had no idea Robin was Dick's wife. You'd never mentioned her last name."

"And then what?" asks Dallas. "Dick finds out from you I was the one sleeping with Robin, and you concoct some scheme to bring me here for slaughter? The sacrificial lamb?"

"Rafaelle had a gun to my head," Navarro insists. "And I don't mean that metaphorically. Our business is a brotherhood, you know that. Dick is family. I had no choice but to set this up."

"You always have a choice," Dallas scoffs. "And you decided to trade our lives for yours."

Navarro steals a look at the ceiling and then lowers his voice to a whisper. "It looks like that on the surface, but I need you to listen. Please. I need your help."

"You want our help?" Dallas laughs in his face. "That's fucking rich. What you need to do is get June out of here. You are crazy, but you are not a monster."

From the way Navarro's features tighten up, I can tell Dallas has hit a nerve. The smarter idea is not to vilify your captor, but file that nugget away for another time.

"You don't stare at this face every morning in the mirror and question your sanity," Navarro says in a dismal monotone. "It is impossible to find joy. Every day exhausts me. I need out, and the only way I can get out is with Dick. My father trusts him." He lays a hand on Dallas's shin and speaks with so much tenderness I forget to be scared of him. "I had weeks to plan this. Everything is running smoothly. You must know I would never sell you out. You are my one true love." He turns to me and speaks with similar, heightened emotion. "And Principessa, you weren't supposed to be here. I did not mean you any harm."

Dallas flicks his leg to rid himself of Navarro's hand. "You fucking sedated her and me. You don't think that's harmful? What about your three-way deal last night? Like that won't give June nightmares for the next century."

"With the storm and both of you here, I had to think on my feet," Navarro explains. "And…" he pauses, like what he has to say next is hard. "I wanted to experience a woman. Once. But with another man involved. It was perfect with you two and—"

"Perfectly messed up," Dallas interrupts.

Navarro takes a deep breath. "I know it was wrong—threatening Nikki's children and using the sedatives. Old habits die hard. But I needed to subdue you."

"And what if Dick had pulled a gun on me?" Dallas demands, and rightly so. "Did you ever think about that possibility?"

"Have you forgotten what I am capable of?" is Navarro's biting response. "I would never have let that happen."

"Navarro," I say, interjecting myself into the conversation. If there is a sound plan where I don't breathe my last breath in this room, I want to hear it, all of Navarro's fuckery to date be damned. "What has to happen now?"

With the first whiff of solidarity, Navarro's shoulders relax. "I leave with Dick," he says. "Give me a few hours, and I'll come back. I need your help to arrange a private flight out of South America. Our company plane isn't an option, and I can't stay here unless I disappear into the jungle. Our network on this continent is too sophisticated. They'll track me."

"You plan to hide out in LA?" Dallas has a legitimate reason to sound concerned. "The American mafia is alive and well. They'll find you if they want to. And you in LA put June and me at risk. Not happening."

That narrative stings, judging from Navarro's crestfallen tone. "Why would I live among two people who will torture me every day when they look past me at each other?"

"Where do you plan to go?" I ask.

"I don't know," he admits, and for the first time, sounds uncertain.

"Yo, Navarro!" Dick shouts from upstairs. "What the fuck is taking so long?"

Navarro yells back, "I'm on my way. Just locking up." His attention rivets back to us. Those eyes. Surreal and swirling. "Will you help? All I need is a few hours."

Dallas side-eyes me with a look that asks—*are you feeling adventurous or doomed?* My silent reply says—*it's a crap shoot.*

"Leave us the keys to the handcuffs," Dallas says. "If anything happens to you, we're fucked."

"I can't," Navarro answers with infinite weariness. "You are my guarantee out of here. If you leave me stranded, this whole plan was for naught." He rubs his temples, agitated. "I cannot live another day in this world, Dallas. It ruined my relationship with you. I want another chance to be happy. As slight as that prospect is, it will never happen if I stay here. You have my word. I promise I'll come back."

Dallas slumps against the wall with a defeated sigh. "When you called me, you didn't care if I needed money, did you? And wanting me to stay the weekend..." He trails off and a mournful silence follows.

The sound of a heart breaking.

With pain in his voice I will hear in my head forever, Navarro says, "All I ever wanted was you."

Dallas bites his lip. For a fleeting second, I think he might cry. "You sure have a shitty way of showing it."

They regard each other. Two casualties of war with no clear winner. I don't know what, if anything, happened between them last night or the other night. But one thing is clear. No man has looked at me the way Navarro silently pines for Dallas.

After a heavy pause, he gathers himself and seems in no hurry, walking at his usual languid pace to the door that might seal us in here forever if whatever he has planned goes tits up. Before stepping out into the hall, he glances over his shoulder.

"L'amore non è senza amarezza, ma io ti amerò per sempre," he says, sounding all but demolished. And then, "I'll leave the lights on."

Dallas said he doesn't know Italian but by the way his face crumples, those words are crystal clear. I want to ask what they mean, but it's impossible to breathe. The door shuts behind Navarro, and a rake of shivers crawls over my skin. My legs feel like anchors. I can't think.

My brain has stalled.

After four days of experiencing a lifetime's worth of emotions, I am frozen, unable to process the idea that I may never experience freedom again.

Chapter Thirty-Four

DALLAS

IN THE STALE gloom of the dungeon, I scrape a second line deep into the limestone wall with a pebble. Yesterday I bloodied a knuckle and left a rash of skin on the rock as a souvenir. Practice makes perfect, I think, morbidly. The two rough and jagged markers I etched stare back at me like fangs. Teeth sunk into my flesh, my life draining away. In the movies, prisoners mark their time this way, and I get it now. When the meaning of time becomes lost, the need to capture it becomes all-consuming. Here, even more so. The human body can survive for thirty days without food, but only three days without water.

I can't say how much time has passed, but it feels like two days since Navarro promised to return.

A barren emptiness fills me.

I am a goddamned moron for thinking he could ever be harmless. Self-preservation and his bloodied family ties govern Navarro's psyche so that not even an eternal love can infiltrate and pry it loose.

Fuck!

I never believed he could do this to me. Treat me like an animal and leave me to rot, like so many of his victims. And to involve June…

She slumbers on the floor, her breathing the only sign of a sane world. She asked me at some point yesterday to stop apologizing. Fair enough. How many useless *sorries* does one woman need to hear?

But I couldn't stop talking. I had to fill the space.

When the mind is devoid of distraction, emptied but somehow full of a million screaming thoughts, and you have no choice but to face the ugliness of who you are, it is humbling and terrifying. I have dissected every minute of my life in this bleak jail. The stupid grudges I held in high school. My emotional deflection tactics. The mythologized version of my life—beautiful but useless, winning at things that don't matter.

For years, greenbacks were the only way I kept score. To track my trajectory farther and higher until my competitors were specks on the horizon. If God or whoever is in charge wanted to play cruel and deny me love, so be it. Success would be my revenge. A towering mountain of it.

All of it completely pointless. Almost two decades lived in vain.

And my crowning moment?

I take advantage of June and her desperate situation.

Lasso her with a lie so she comes here for my benefit—and I use the term fucking loosely. (Hard to position the Navarro sedatives and seduction shit show as any form of a win.)

And with all this bearing down on me, I had to run my mouth to shut my brain off.

I told June everything to unburden my soul. Yeah, I know. Another shining example of selflessness brought to you by Dallas Evener. But she listened, and never interrupted as I laid out the entire chain of events that brought us here. Mom leaving. Me taking over the dance studio. The affair with Robin and how she set me up at Oxford. My chance meeting with Navarro.

Most of her questions surrounded Dick.

I answered what I could.

One of the benefits of loving Navarro is that I had to read between the lines so often that I became a savant at putting together the pieces. From Dick's bitter gloating monologue yesterday, I deduced he and Cannistrá were thick as thieves when Robin and I were together. Too many parallels. Dick spent weeks in London. His business was construction, and Cannistrá specialized in bribes and coercion and strong-arming the Italian government to build shit while Team Rafaelle skimmed half the profits.

Also, he and Rafaelle were similar in age. Old-school criminals in their coats and their ties.

Robin had claimed to be clueless about her husband's business, but I wonder about that now.

Fortunes are never made honestly, Dallas.

Tattoo that on my ass and call it a day.

And speaking of tattoos, the one Navarro flashed last night distressed the hell out of me. He asked me if I liked it, and yeah, with my brain swimming from drugs, I mumbled yes. What else was I going to say? But to have DALLAS inked on his dick is like perpetuating a disease. He will never be free of me, nor I him, and I guess that's his fucking point.

Even when he disappears, he leaves his mark.

I remember waking up that Sunday morning in our Oxford dorm room gripped with fear. Long before I drummed up the courage to open the closet only to find it half-empty, the funereal silence told me everything. Navarro used to buzz around in our kitchen at some ungodly early hour, excited for the day and the simple pleasure of a meal with me.

I stumbled out of bed, my lungs collapsing.

Instead of freshly made espresso on the counter, he'd propped a note against the infamous toaster that burned his breakfast for three and a half years. An hour passed before I unfolded the single piece of paper. I hoped for an explanation, a timeline, a number where to reach him. (His old number was already disconnected.)

At the very least, I expected the words *I love you.*

I suppose in his way, the list of contacts he left behind was his version of a love letter.

But that didn't erase the hurt.

I close my eyes as memories froth to the surface.

The endless rainy nights I lay in bed barren and defeated, too prideful to cry, my mind pushing back on the inevitable. Weeks went by. Then months. Nothing. It killed me to admit it, but his first love could never be me. His soul belonged to a complex, violent family structure forged centuries earlier in the feral clans of Southern Italy. Trying to track him down would be a fool's game. Even the least sophisticated mafioso could remain undercover for years.

After Mom called it quits, the death of Robin, and Navarro's disappearing act, I vowed never to let anyone get close to me. For the nights I needed a girl like Ally, LA had no shortage of actresses on the make willing to play by my rules. I filled my empty life with disposable women. No one would break my heart again.

Because inside me, not visible to anyone, is a fear of being abandoned that has never gone away.

And then June Allison came around.

I fell hard, swept away by her damn accent. It reminded me of Navarro and our time in England. But mostly, I felt like I had met my twin. (One I could dive into bed with and have it not be creepy.) So, what do the dark prince and eternal idiot, namely me, do? I pull the ultimate creep move and have my ass handed to me.

Deservedly so.

June did the right thing walking out on me ten years ago. And I could cry in my spilled milk that she should have answered my half-assed apology texts, but what self-respecting woman would want a follow-up to such a shitty first act? I treated her irresponsibly, not brave enough to bare my soul for fear of rejection. I sank into a depression after, unsure if I could ever open up with anyone again.

In retrospect, I blame Navarro for how I reacted to June's dismissal of me. Yes, he did so much during our time together. He showered me with money and gifts and filled me with a sense of belief so all-consuming that it became my trademark.

But his vindictiveness also rubbed off on me.

I wanted to crush June for ditching me and got creative in my attempts to discredit her—spreading rumors, lies, and ill will like butter on hot toast. At the same time, pathetically, in complete contrast, I'd secretly hoped every time I trash-talked her it would rile her enough to call and chew me out. And when she didn't, I just tried harder.

No one ever accused me of being a slacker.

June stirs beside me, a delicate whimper escaping from her lips. I pull myself out of the toxic trip down memory lane and watch her breathe, wondering how I could have been such a disrespecting twat.

Earlier, whatever the hell that means down here, she'd whispered, "There is still so much beauty to see in the world."

And, reading between the lines again, I understood the flip side of that comment and hated myself for putting June in a position to go there.

I'm hanging on by a thread not to go there.

The gravestone I wondered about a few days ago hangs in front of me like a house of horrors mirage. Will Dad mark my grave like an unknown soldier? Will he shed a tear? I send him money once a month, a nameless, faceless, and substantial wire transfer, but he still lives in the same house. Drives the same car, even though I bought him a Tesla and had it shipped to Seattle with a red bow on the hood. Eighty grand of Elon Musk finery sits in his garage like a museum piece while he putters around in his '95 base model Camry.

I shut my eyes and try to bring his face into focus.

Was it eight years ago when he last visited me?

What I recall with absolute clarity is how he squirmed uncomfortably during the six-course meal at Providence on Melrose. My date, another skin-and-bones actress, pounded back the Ciroc and simpered mindless Hollywood gossip while I bragged about my latest deal and how much money I'd made. Dad just nodded and picked at his escargot. *What a hick*, I thought, *he's not even using the snail tongs.*

He tried to make a joke of it. Said he poured salt on snails to kill them before they destroyed his garden. But I saw the truth in his eyes. His son, now full-on bougie and snot-nosed populist, forcing him to eat snails?

Fuck him, I thought at the time. Go back to Seattle to rot in the rain with your snails. He could go to hell if he had no appreciation for how I turned my life around.

I guess the feeling was mutual.

"I wish you the best of luck," is the last thing he said before hopping in an Uber and leaving me to my grandstand life.

One of the eight million things I've promised myself I would do if we get out of here is to call him. Book the first flight to Seattle and tell him face-to-face I'm sorry for being a cunt. I will bring Nikki a hundred white roses and tell her to vacation for a month in my St. Tropez villa that I've been to once, because she has worked her butt off and never complains.

And I will get down on one knee, I will crawl over nails, broken glass, and used syringes, and beg June never to leave me.

If she'll have me.

If we ever get out of here.

If, if, if, if, if.

Goddamn, it's starting again.

I yell in my inside voice, *Stop! Please brain, just shut off.*

All I want is to drift into a restful sleep and stop my thoughts from eating me alive, but I'm scared shitless that I might never wake up.

I rub the throb growing in my temples and cling to the future that gets dimmer and dimmer every minute.

Not *if*, I remind myself.

When.

Chapter Thirty-Five

JUNE

EVERYONE HAS A BREAKING POINT. HARD TO BELIEVE A FLAKY PASTRY is enough to push me over the edge.

Ah, good old starvation.

It makes delirium so much more fun.

I am hungry enough to eat the rat nibbling contentedly on the croissant lying just out of my reach. Dallas apologized yesterday for many things, including kicking the breakfast tray. The aroma of fine Italian coffee rising from the damp dirt floor seems to have caffeinated him via fumes alone. He finally fell asleep on the floor an hour ago. He's motionless, although I doubt his mind is at rest. If his constant stream of babble is any indication, it's been spinning endlessly.

But I appreciate his intent.

Men will admit to cheating on their taxes before copping to weakness, and Dallas is doing a remarkable job of masking his despondency. If my former lover abandoned me so cruelly, I would not be able to hold it together like he is. He carved another line on the wall while I fitfully slept, as if marking our lost time would somehow extend it and allow for a Hollywood-style, save-the-day finish.

The reality is we are screwed.

I promised God earlier that I would do things differently if he spared our lives. That's how quack my thoughts have become. Talking to God. Another male who never listens.

And like the damp stones leaching heat out of this torture chamber bit by bit, my belief in Him and seeing the light of a new day has equally diminished.

Even my secret fantasy I allowed to run amok in my mind just to fill the time now seems laughable. Flynn and Vandana know where we are—I sent them the pin drop. And my not touching base for two days is for sure on Flynn's WTF radar. But if either one miraculously shows up, how do they get through the Great Wall? That beast is twelve feet high and four feet thick. The attached gate is a modern marvel of impenetrable steel. Vandana can wield a hair dryer like nobody's business, but scaling a wall with kitten heels? Even slim, athletic Flynn can only jump so high.

And oh, Christ.

The bloody peacock is at it again.

If my lungs weren't holding my breath hostage, I would scream, *Stop wailing like a banshee, please!*

Because it upsets the dogs every time that bird starts to squawk.

I can hear Mimi and Rodolfo overhead in the kitchen. Nails clicking on the tiles. The doleful whimpers. How could Navarro abandon them, too?

And then suddenly, the dogs start barking. Loud and out of control. Excitement or panic? I can't tell. Both sensations crackle on my skin as I perk my ears. Holy shit. Footsteps. Voices. But whose? Navarro wouldn't dare return with a visitor. Please don't be that pasty lump Battista or the goon brothers. I'll even take effervescent Carolina for a hundred, Alex.

I lick my dry lips. Summon moisture into my throat.

"Hello!" My voice cracks, not carrying. I swallow again and try harder to project. "Help. We're down here!"

Dallas stirs awake. Dazed, one eyebrow hitched lazily in question. In a thick voice, he asks, "What? What's going on?"

I point at the ceiling. "Listen! People."

The moment he hears the commotion, he scrambles to sit upright. "Hey!" he shouts, his confident voice instantly commanding and louder than mine. "Can you hear me?"

Silence. Did the outburst scare them off?

Then, "Oh my God, Morgan! Did you hear that? It's coming from downstairs."

Rampaging relief courses through me. Vandana and Morgan? It cannot be. I feel an almost imperceptible shift in the air like the upstairs door is opening to suck a draft of air through the inch of space under ours.

"June! Dallas!" Morgan yells. Our names are the two most beautiful things I will hear today. "Are you down there?"

"Yes!" We scream at the same time.

Dallas faces me with hollow and shattered eyes. But as long as I live, I will never forget that smile. Or those dimples running free. "It's a goddamn miracle," he says.

To comprehend that life will carry on? A dizzying sense of gratitude makes me light-headed. And what is my priority with the world opening up again? I use my one free hand to fuss with my hair.

I must look atrocious but Dallas, eternal champ and liar, says, "You look great."

Morgan pushes on the door so hard it almost flings off its hinges when he tumbles in. Vandana is right on his heels and comes to a dead stop when she sees us. Her hand flies to cover her mouth, but a cry of despair leaks out anyway.

"Oh, June!"

Most of the drama Morgan witnesses in Monaco are magnums of champagne going to waste. Or two women showing up at a gala wearing the same dress. This? He blinks repeatedly as if he expects to see something different every time he opens his eyes.

Vandana snaps out of her shock and rushes over to hug me. "I'm here, babes. We're here. It's going to be all right."

Morgan jumps into action, peppering Dallas with questions. "What do you need? Water? What about these cuffs? Do you know where the keys might be?"

"We definitely need water," Dallas says. "But I have no idea where the keys are. There might be something in the kitchen you can use. A chisel or something with a sharp edge. And a mallet or sledgehammer, if you can find one. You'll have to pound away on the links until they break."

"Okay," Morgan says with steely resolve. "I'll go look."

Vandana eyes her departing boyfriend nervously. His moisturized hands create yachts in the safety of an air-conditioned office. The idea of a sledgehammer and precision blows may be a concern.

And then I remember.

"Wait!" Morgan wheels back around and I say, "Navarro's driver … he has a workshop. It's near the front gate. He used to be a carpenter and has all sorts of tools."

"When did he tell you that?" Dallas asks.

"Is it locked?" Morgan inquires, keeping me on track.

"I'd find a rock or something in case you have to smash a window."

"You stay here," he instructs Vandana. "They need water and food."

Morgan's out the door like a superhero on a mission, running up the stairs two at a time is what it sounds like. The dogs bark again as if to ask who are all these people and why are none of them feeding us? Interesting that they don't come down here. Like they know it's bad juju.

Filled with relief but still stunned, I ask Vandana how they found us.

She tucks a lock of lank hair behind my ear and says, "Flynn called me freaking out because she hadn't heard from you. Your phone went straight to voice mail, you didn't respond to her emails, and no one in your office had a recent update. She begged me and Morgan to fly down here and make sure you were okay. Thank God the pin drop you sent was accurate."

Face pinched and a grim set to her mouth, Vandana is shaken to the core. She caused me inner turmoil once, so I guess the playing field has been leveled.

"Thank you both for coming," Dallas says, "from the bottom of my heart. Our hearts," he quickly corrects, flashing me a sheepish look.

With the time to properly scan our surroundings, Vandana sees the furry remains lying between us and drags her eyes back to mine with a green expression. Dallas had impressively killed another rat with one hand, but neither of us could bear the thought of a rodent as our last meal.

"I'll go get water," she says.

$

WE'VE CHOWED through several apples, a box of crackers, and a gallon of water when Morgan shows up sweating profusely and carrying an armload of tools.

He sets everything in front of Dallas for review. "I collected every-thing I thought could help."

"That for sure," Dallas says, pointing to the mallet. "And the chisel is perfect. Put the edge there," he instructs, pointing with his free hand to the middle link of the chain on my handcuffs. "On the weak part of the link."

There is a pause as we all take in the moment. I confess, the sight of a chisel and a weighty mallet strikes fear in my heart. I pray Morgan's swing is as accurate as his designs.

"Turn away from it, June," Dallas warns. "In case shards fly."

Every vicious blow sends reverberations up my wrist to the base of my skull. After several strikes and no action, my hope deflates.

And then the motherlode. A chink in the armor.

Dallas whoops and says, "You got it! Whack that same place again, and we're gold."

A few more successful hacks, and I can obliterate all those empty hours that had extended before me in a place that was utterly neutral on the question of whether we lived or died. I hold my hand up in absolute wonder as Morgan repositions the chisel to free Dallas. Between his newfound calling as savior muscle and Dallas's surprising tool prowess, Vandana and I may have a pair of rednecks on our hands.

Vandana helps me stand, and I wobble and weave, finding my bearings.

"Do you want to change or shower before we go?" she asks.

"We need to grab our bags and passports," Dallas reminds me.

Morgan is on a roll, pounding the living daylights out of the chain. When it snaps apart, Dallas staggers to his feet. Without a second thought, we come together in a fierce, desperate hug. The denouement of our bold rescue floods through me in a numbing wave. When your life flashes before your eyes, something irrevocable takes place. Dallas apologized many times yesterday for bringing me here and involving me in whatever scheme Navarro had concocted. But as he burrows his head into my neck and showers me with kisses, it is with immense recognition that fate has dealt him the mother of all wins with me.

When we pull out of our embrace, Morgan and Vandana stand there, stiff and silent. How we got here is still a question, and thankfully, they both know better than to ask at this precise moment. How can I explain, with any accuracy, what it felt like to be trapped behind glass while the world slipped away?

Dallas and I endured a situation no one can ever understand.

"Let's get the fuck out of here," Dallas says.

Holding my hand, he guides me up the stairs into the kitchen, where Mimi and Rodolfo barrel toward us. I lavish all the care I have left within me on these two fluff balls.

"Oh, darlings," I mumble. "You must be starving." I glance up at Dallas. "We can't leave them here. It's too cruel."

Vandana asks Morgan, "Can we fly with animals?"

Morgan shrugs and says, "Pack them up, we'll deal with it at the airport." He and Dallas break off to hunt for our bags, leaving me and Vandana to corral the dogs. We pass through the atrium and the foyer. It all looks so different. But who knows if I'll see anything the same way again?

To step outside and feel sunlight on my face is indescribable. The temperature dropped since the storm blew through. The bright afternoon is cool and windy. At the bottom of the stairs, an SUV is parked askew.

"How did you get through the gate?" I ask.

Vandana steadies me as I move gingerly down the stairs in bare feet. "It was open. Why?"

Did Navarro leave it that way on purpose? Who knows? I don't have the bandwidth to imagine tomorrow, let alone what far-flung ideas Navarro envisioned.

We load the dogs into the boot and wait in the back seat for Morgan and Dallas. The words between us have dried up, and I am acutely aware of how ripe I smell.

"Holy shit!" Vandana points at the immense figure in the distance. "Is that a real giraffe?"

Funny how Giorgio reminds me of Navarro. Long legs. Power in his size and silence. Liquid, haunted eyes that hold so much mystery.

"Good thing the gate is open," I say. "He needs to escape."

Vandana can't believe what she's seeing, the day bending into non-reality every minute longer she's here. "What kind of a person has a giraffe?"

"It's a long story," I say, and isn't that the truth?

Twenty minutes later, we are packed up and moving. People, dogs, bags, and passports. As the SUV rumbles down the driveway, I catch Dallas watching me in the rear-view mirror. Does he sense my guilt? That I made a mistake not revealing I overheard Navarro on the phone the other day? Based on his commentary, confirming a Thursday arrival, etc., all points lead to Dick being on the other end.

Not that I knew the depths Navarro could sink to.

I don't want to linger on the memory of him, but I can't bring myself to believe he would not come back for us. Which can only mean one thing. The master chess player orchestrated one hell of a game, but even the greats stumble once in a while. And my gut is telling me that Navarro got fatally outmaneuvered.

Chapter Thirty-Six

"C'MON, MAN," DALLAS SAYS, AT HIS MOST CONVINCING. "A BILLION pounds of cocaine gets smuggled through here every year. No one will notice two dogs."

We've overcome one massive hurdle only to smash into another at the private aviation facility. Enrique, the burly, brick-headed customs officer, sports a gun on his hip and an untainted allegiance to protocol. The dogs cannot travel without proper health certification. We're all itching to get out here, but none of us has the heart to leave the dogs' fate up in the air.

"I'm going to call Natalie," Dallas says and whips out his phone. Enrique watches him talk and pace, having no idea the smelly weirdo in a bathrobe has the power to complicate his life big-time.

"Who's Natalie?" Vandana asks, and I explain that Dallas volunteers at an animal shelter. I don't mention Carson because such a place does not exist in her rarefied world.

Two minutes later, Dallas ends the call and circles back to us with good news. "Nat can sort out the paperwork, but she needs someone on the ground here to help coordinate."

All eyes fall back onto Enrique. He shrugs with a gesture of *Who, me?* Without a word, Morgan strolls to the lone ATM and returns a minute later with a wad of bills most commonly seen during a drug deal. We have a winner. Enrique pockets the bills, now smiling and accommodating. He agrees to stickhandle the vet and look after the dogs until they can be shipped. He and Dallas exchange contact information, and we bid a teary farewell to Mimi and Rodolfo.

I get the sense the airport staff are relieved when our motley crew disappears onto the tarmac. They will never see my face again, that's for sure. Argentina is on my permanent no-fly list.

I duck my head to enter Morgan's Falcon jet, and my first thought is how tiny it is in comparison to the Navarro show. Dallas jets around in similar luxury in his Gulfstream, so the dimensions should feel familiar to him. But when he steps inside, his face drains, and his jaw flexes. The Falcon's low ceiling is disturbingly similar to the claustrophobic oppression we escaped. In hindsight, customs holding back the dogs is a relief. Two more jumpy creatures in this confined space would make me climb the curved walls.

We settle into our seats and Vandana launches into mothering mode, plying us with pillows and cashmere blankets. She's still jittery like a bird and trying not to show it. Her golden lifestyle makes me forget that every once in a while, she too has to deal with hard and dark things beneath her glossy surface.

Morgan buckles up and offers us the bedroom. "If you prefer to sleep, it's all yours."

Dallas sweeps his hair back with both hands. "I need a drink. And then a shower. How about you?" he asks, his hand skimming my knee.

"Same," I say. "In reverse order."

The pert flight attendant hovering nearby swoops in, and Morgan orders an entire bottle of scotch. I stick to water. I might not touch alcohol ever again. I also have zero interest in checking my phone. For all I know, the world is on the brink of nuclear war. After such intense tunnel vision, every ounce of energy sapped from wrangling flyaway thoughts and emotions, readjusting to the real world is jarring.

We taxi to the runway, and my eyes roam over the scraggly trees in the distance, wondering if Giorgio has hightailed it to freedom. When we left the castle, I fought the temptation to steal one last look. Of all the bible stories I suffered through in Sunday school, the tale of Lot's wife frightened the living hell out of me. A disobedient woman turned to salt over curiosity? It seemed highly unfair. Mum explained it later, and her voice rang loud in my mind.

"It's a reminder to live in the moment," she said. "Forget about the past and look forward."

So, I didn't look back at the castle.

But I look back now.

Something knots in my stomach.

Navarro's plane is camped at the far end of the terminal, sleek and motionless like a Jaguar waiting in the tall grasses to pounce. The image splashed across the tail triggers a jumbled reaction because now I understand why it looks familiar. The identical flower is tattooed seductively along Navarro's left hip.

Dallas picks up the shift in my body language. "What's up?"

"Nothing," I say, because I can't talk about Navarro without losing it. "I'll be happy once we're in the air."

Vandana scans me with wary reserve. "I'm going to stay with you in LA for as long as you need, babes. And you can't say no."

She sets her hand on mine but stays silent, holding space for me to consider this. The warmth of her skin remains on mine as the plane swings into its final position for take-off and the engines rumble to life. When the sprawl of Buenos Aires disappears through the chop of low clouds, she winds our fingers together.

I choke back the rising swell in my throat.

She is always there for me, and Flynn, too.

On the drive to the airport, I FaceTimed with Flynn. God, she was a wreck. She knew something was up, as if the sight of me sitting in a car in a bathrobe and two poodles gleefully panting in the boot didn't give it away. I artfully dodged her probing questions, and she figured out that the truth would be told at a later date.

Still, she said she'd ditch England in a heartbeat if I needed her. But I know Chavez needs her more.

Right now, I'm just grateful to be going home.

And my best friends are to thank.

$

I wake up in the morning and feel as heavy as a bag of flour. I slept hard. No dreams. Point Dume is as quiet as a tomb at night, and judging from how high the sun sits above the rolling waves of the Pacific, it has to be noon or later. Vandana and Morgan escorted me home last night, and the murmur of their voices in the kitchen this morning makes me smile. I smell coffee, but it's not enough to get me out of bed. Not even the power of a new week inspires me to move, and I'm the lady with a *Thank God it's Monday* sticker on my laptop.

Eventually, I have to face the day.

An entire business chomps like a filly at the starting gate, waiting for me to ring the bell and thunder away. My staff are ready to rock. Suppliers and early-adopter clients are eager for the show to start. It's all there waiting for me, and I can't be bothered. I hope this is short term and nothing chronic. After our bumpy midnight landing in Los Angeles, Dallas and I parted ways, both of us in a peculiar, drifting state, yet also silently aware of the steep challenge now facing us.

Professionally and personally.

"June?" Vandana follows up her greeting with three soft knocks on my bedroom door. "Are you awake?"

I sit up and drag the sheet around me. Scrub the sand from my eyes. I could use a cigarette, but my breath already tastes foul. She'll have to deal with it.

"Yes. Come in."

Vandana pokes her head in and smiles. "Morgan made a fresh pot of coffee. Do you want some?"

"Not right now. I just woke up."

She leans against the door frame, fit and glowing in her head-to-toe Lululemon. Her hair is perfect. She's an absolute stunner sans makeup. No wonder every man wants to sleep with her. Hell, I slept with her once.

"Dallas called an hour ago," she says. "He'd like to talk to you."

"How is he?"

"Concerned about you. We all are." Her brow furrows as she

surveys me and the bed, for once not a makeshift office. I often work from here for the first hour of the day, earbuds in, and laptop balanced on crossed legs with twenty screens open in my browser. Smothered by ironclad timetables. Vandana has seen the real me in action and never not in motion like this—with kneecaps knocking against my chin and my hair a raging disaster because I slept on the wet strands.

I pat the patch of mattress next to me. "Stop being a stranger and snuggle with me."

Her tentative smile shifts into something looser. She joins me in bed, and I inhale the signature Vandana smell, a sweet bouquet so tempting you want to stick your nose closer for a bigger whiff.

"Any requests for breakfast?" she asks.

"Are you cooking?" I ask in mock horror.

"Sorry, miracles don't count as requests. Morgan's in charge."

We bite back giggles and then explode into laughter. Vandana's inability to do anything useful with a stove other than turn it on is the tiniest flaw in her lacquered perfection.

And damn, it feels good to laugh and have the malaise lift.

But, alas, not everything is resolved.

We fall out of eye contact and Vandana clicks her taupe acrylic nails, a nervous habit that manifests before any public speaking. Or before she speaks her mind.

"What is it, doll?"

I have a pretty good idea of what's bothering her. She can't chase from her mind what she saw. Before Dallas and I disappeared into the bedroom to sleep for most of the flight, her ashen face never once mustered a smile.

And now she takes a moment to collect herself, breathing shallow but controlled, like her words. "I will never push you to do anything ever again."

I rub the top of her slender thigh. "Oh, doll. You can't blame yourself. None of this is your fault."

"Let's call it what it was," she insists. "I guilt-tripped you. For my benefit." A tear escapes and leaves a glistening trail on her flawless skin. "I would have never forgiven myself if anything had happened to you. I'm sorry. I'm sorry for everything," she stresses. "I never handled it well."

I tilt my head, confused. There is something behind that statement. "What are you talking about?"

She swipes under both eyes. So used to being the poised one. Breaking down is for me and Flynn to do.

"When I saw you in there," she says, "it made me think of how scared I felt after our night with Chase. When we…"

She trails off because we both know the night. How could I ever forget? Second year at Stanford, nineteen and swilling champagne and smoking contraband cigars before my best friend buried herself between my legs. And poor Chase. His first foray into sexually reckless Vandana-land, and he was a goner. Nothing but gibberish spilled out of his mouth, so turned on at the sight of her going down on me. His cock pounding into the tight, dark hole of her perfect white arse seemed beside the point.

"I handled it all wrong," she continues. "But I was scared of what it all meant. That maybe …. Well, you know my parents."

The Republican nightmares who wanted her to sign a petition to ban rainbow flags in their Laguna Beach neighborhood? I sure do know them.

She swivels her head. Those beautiful dark brown eyes latch onto mine. "And you and I were so close. I didn't want our friendship to be ruined."

I admit it messed me up a little. I sat in a fog the following morning when Vandana stumbled downstairs at her usual eleven a.m., mascara smeared, hair a sexy mess. She plunked herself on the sofa, unaware her hot-pink Victoria's Secret bathrobe had splayed open to showcase all her fabulous long limbs. She mumbled hello, clicked on the TV, and started to skim through the channels while I tried not to stare at her flat tummy or the sweet curve of her implants. She caught me looking, and I turned away, mortified.

She yawned and stretched with a lazy smile. "Fun night, huh?"

Snap the book shut and move on.

But it wasn't so easy for me.

Thoughts of her and us infiltrated my mind for months. Then one day, the pleasure of the world's most momentous orgasm faded away, and I churned through a rotation of lackluster boyfriends, thinking, *This is it? This is the best you have in the sack?*

Did I sabotage all my relationships with men because of her? Maybe. The thing is, we never talked about it. I had no idea she still carried this around with her.

And it sparks a theory I once had but never voiced until now.

"Is that why you placed an ad for a third roommate?"

She nods, guilt blooming in her eyes. "I was worried," she says. "Like, really worried. Me, you, and your fabulous tits alone in the house … I thought a different dynamic would keep things chill."

Vandana had signed the lease on our Palo Alto rental, so I went along with her decision to farm out the third bedroom. We interviewed several candidates and unanimously chose Flynn on the spot. A tall, bright, and well-spoken but shy girl hiding behind her tumble of curls. She moved in with one suitcase and kept to herself at first. We had no idea about the past she'd run away from. We had no clue until a few months ago.

"Does Flynn know she's our surrogate love child?" I ask.

Vandana cackles, and that's how I know she's back. The public never gets to hear that raucous laugh. "Maybe that's why I always view her as our baby sister." She tucks a lock of hair behind my ear with a reflective expression. "I had to clear the air. It's bothered me for years. I hope you don't hate me."

"Hate you? I love you forever, you naughty bitch. And for what it's worth, you would have made a fine lesbian."

Hearing the L word, her eyes flash. "Promise me you will never tell Morgan. He already thinks our little trio is incestuous. And I'm beginning to wonder about his man crush on Chavez. He bought a *poster* of him," she whispers scandalously, like Morgan harvests organs as a side hustle. "And hung it in the living room!"

I stifle a laugh. "Hopefully, in a nice frame."

"It's a beautiful frame. Beautiful like you." She playfully squeezes my right boob. "And you still have fabulous tits."

I smack her hand away. "Sorry, you had your chance."

A brief hitch in the conversation stretches out until she asks, "What's happening with you and Dallas after all this?"

All this.

When will I tell my besties what unfolded in Argentina? I need to sort myself out first before that story gets told. But I can be forthright about my feelings for Dallas. Flynn loves to use the word destiny when describing how she and Chavez came together, and it fits the bill with me and Dallas. Who else could I be with after a lost decade and the craziness with Navarro? Not to mention, a certain someone stole Vandana's title of giving me the most earth-shattering orgasm. Usually, I share everything with my besties, but some things are better left unsaid.

I wink and kiss her cheek. "I could do worse, right?"

Chapter Thirty-Seven

OF ALL THE DEADLY SINS, SLOTH IS THE CORROSIVE LEADER OF THE pack and one I rarely indulge in. But my afternoon of lying about with Vandana and Morgan leaves me restless and eager to get at it. I can only stare at the four walls of my house for so long before going stir-crazy. And Dallas is debriefing Nikki at Evener Equity this morning, so I pull on my big girl pants and head to the office.

The staff has organized a surprise welcome-back celebration, and our boardroom table heaves with cookies made by Kate, and we all bump up against giant silver balloons tied to the chairs that spell out GREEN TIME. I put on a brave face but feel discombobulated, like a veteran with shrieking noises of war in their head, forced to smile through a ceremony in a suburban mall.

I peel away from the festivities to attack the day, but Mark catches me staring off into space when he drops by my office thirty minutes later.

"You have a sec?" he asks.

"Of course," I say. "Come in."

My corner office is a southeast-facing, all-white affair, and Mark, dressed in all black, passes through the brilliant sun like a shadow. He shaved off his sad excuse for a goatee and could be a young David

Beckham with his swooped-back, newly blond hair. He won't always be so damn fresh-faced. Not with triplets on the way.

"Good news," he says, taking a seat on the sofa I bought for catnaps and have used all of three times. "Prime Produce, the big lettuce grower up in Salinas? They just called. They want our technology. I'm hopping on a plane tomorrow to meet the president."

"Wow. Well done. Fantastic effort."

It sure is. All it takes is one industry giant coming on board for momentum to snowball. So why do I feel absolutely nothing?

He munches on his donut, swallowing the lump of sugared dough without chewing properly. And he wonders why he has stomach issues. The silence stretches on, and his eyes are shifty, not landing anywhere.

I want to scream, *Get on with it!* Because he's here for another reason.

He clears his throat noisily. "I want to apologize for what I said before you left. You gave me a chance when no one else would. I learned everything from you. You're my hero, so I hope you can give my whine-fest a one-time free pass."

"I appreciate that, Mark. No hard feelings. We've all been there."

He appraises me, surprised at his good fortune of being let off the hook. Was he expecting a lashing? "If you need me to step it up, just say the word. I got your back."

The bite mark in his apple fritter; that missing half-moon percolates disturbingly in my brain. I make an incoherent noise and nod. I wish he would stop staring at me.

"Are you feeling okay?" he asks. "You seem a little out of it."

"Tired is all. It was a whirlwind trip." I tug on the sleeve of my blazer. The angry red on one wrist has dulled into a light pink that could still be a possible conversation starter. "And I have a ton of work here, so…"

"Yeah, sure. No problem." He bounces up from the couch as if I tasered him. "And, uh, by the way," he adds. "I talked to Cliff yesterday after he called you. Sounds like those two women are angling to settle out of court. That's good for us, right? To have it blow over."

Blow over.

Like ruptured lives can be dusted away like bunnies.

If only.

"I think we'll be fine," I say with my brightest fake smile.

$

THE REST of the day passes by in a blur. I've scoured through the dense wall of emails. Returned the urgent calls. Vandana, still in shock that I lugged my arse into the office, touches base at five p.m. asking if I'm going to meet Dallas for dinner at his house as planned. If so, she and Morgan will order in sushi.

I say yes, but message Dallas to confirm. He hasn't reached out since this morning.

There's no reply to my text, and a follow-up call goes straight to voicemail. Evener Equity reception says he left the office hours ago. The world starts closing in, and my mind will not behave.

His texts from last night keep rearing their ugly heads.

That he couldn't sleep with all the ambient city noise. That he was too afraid to shut his eyes.

DE: If I open them and we're back in there, I'm going to go fucking crazy.

With still no word out of him at five fifteen, I hop in my car and speed to Venice.

Déjà vu swirls around me as I ring the doorbell. Was it just last week I stood here? It feels like an entire lifetime has come and gone. After a fruitless two minutes with no response, I depress the door handle and push.

I pause in the foyer, my ears perked. There's a certain sound in a room when no one's in it.

"Dallas?"

My voice echoes high up in the vaulted ceiling.

No response.

I kick off my heels and poke around the main floor. The kitchen looks untouched. Pillows on the sofa plumped and magazines fanned just so on a coffee table. Tucked at the back is a home office, neat as a pin and decorated in tasteful shades of dark grey with thick Persian rugs underfoot and black-and-white landscape prints mounted between bookshelves. I can see his backyard from here. There's a lap pool and a substantial patio built for entertaining. No grass. All that concrete makes me realize we never discussed who would take the dogs.

There are many things to discuss.

Is that why he's gone into hiding?

I'm about to leave when I see it sitting in front of the daisy-chained triple monitors on his desk.

A piece of stationery with a photograph perched on top.

I'm not one to snoop, but curiosity gets the better of me. I round the desk for a better look, and my heart stumbles.

The selfie of Dallas and Navarro is grainy with age and taken somewhere on the Oxford campus, based on the stately buildings in the background. They're sitting on a round of grass with the sun shining brilliantly, Dallas's arm outstretched at a high angle to capture Navarro kissing his cheek. They glow, bright and magnetic and impossible to ignore. Two fools in love.

And Dallas looks so young without the beard.

I blink back the sting of tears. I shouldn't be so affected, but my hand trembles when I reach for the letter. The folds in the creamy yellow paper mirror the photo dimensions—a loving crypt to hold the memory intact. I skim the brief sentence written in the watery strokes of a fountain pen.

L'amore non è senza amarezza, ma io ti amerò per sempre.

Oh, Jesus.

No wonder Dallas knew what those words meant. Based on the date of the letter, he's had years to decipher one sentence. And at one point in the dungeon, he had interpreted the phrase for me.

Love is not without bitterness, but I will always love you.

I set the letter and photo down and take a micro-step back, my heart thumping. If Dallas spent time with these two mementos, he'd be unglued. I hurry to the base of the floating staircase that introduced me to Ally and her impossibly perky boobs and shout his name.

A long silence passes and then, a response. In a dead, flat tone. "Can you come up?"

The polished concrete steps curl up to the mezzanine, and that's where the smell hits me. A stupendous intake of single malt. The fumes lead me into the only open doorway at the far end of the hall. It's hot and stuffy in his bedroom. The blinds are drawn against the early evening sun. An uncorked bottle of Dalmore sits on the bedside table, and his rumpled sheets look like he wrestled with them before he curled up like a snail to face the far wall, fully clothed, trainers still on his feet.

My first instinct is to touch him, and yet, it's like he's buzzing with dark radioactivity that screams, *Go away.*

"Is there anything I get for you?" I ask. "Some water?"

In a strange, calm voice that doesn't match his tightly coiled frame, he says, "They found him. I saw it on the news."

Something cold slithers up my spine. Found, in this context, means inert and no longer breathing. I sit down heavily on the edge of his bed and forget how to breathe.

"Where?" I ask.

"In a dumpster outside of Buenos Aires."

I shut my eyes. Numbness fills every bone. "Oh my god, Dallas. I'm so sorry."

He rolls over to face me, eyes red-rimmed and wild. "For what?"

"Because you two were close."

"I'm not talking about Navarro," he says, his voice hitching. "They found Dick."

He searches my face for understanding, but it's as blank as my mind. If Dick's dead, that can only mean…

"Then where did he go?" I ask, a brain-dead question if there ever was one, because the *where* doesn't matter. What twists Dallas's features into a ball of anguish is the *why*.

Why Navarro never came back for us.

"You heard what he said," Dallas mumbles. "Escape into the jungle where no one can find him." His chin start quivering, and I can barely understand what he says next because he curls away from me, his words drowning in a flood of despair. "I'll never see him again."

And Dallas of the precious Brioni suits, chauffeur, and weekly facials, the one who maintained the stiff upper lip when I tipped over the edge into hysteria at my darkest point in the dungeon, dissolves into deep, racking sobs. Swallowed alive with hurt and betrayal.

Mum once said it wasn't the silence of an empty house that distressed her after Father died. His presence, knowing he was around, even when he was at the pub with his army mates, comforted her in ways she never understood until he was gone. Dallas and Navarro lived their lives separated by continents and circumstances and conflicts deep within them, but Dallas confessed that he always felt strangely connected to him because Navarro was, in theory, a phone call away.

This, of course, made wonkier with the desire not to be any closer.

The body and mind can find a balance between opposing forces. The heart, however, is not a master juggler. And all the emotional balls Dallas kept in the air are crashing down in a torrent of grief.

I swing my legs onto the bed and inch closer until we're spoons tucked tightly together. Tremors convulse through him, and I feel his anguish in my bones. I hold him in my arms until the racking quakes subside. Navarro's final disappearing act must feel like the cutting off of a limb for Dallas. The permanent loss of someone he once loved.

And maybe still does.

I think of the photo in his office, and my heart bursts.

Love throws us into the deep end with no guarantees. We flail. We sputter. Sometimes we find our bearings and swim to safety.

And sometimes we drown.

"June," he says, his voice a strangled hush.

I pull my arm tighter around him. "I'm here. What is it?"

His body contorts into the tiniest possible variation, burrowing against me as if he wants to disappear.

"Don't ever leave me. I'll never survive if you do."

Is it a plea, a command? Or does life as he knows it no longer make sense? I can't say for sure. He wanders lost in the wilderness with night bearing down, and one day soon, this will all catch up to me. On a sunny, benign morning, the manager at Ralph's will come running to console a woman who has collapsed on the floor, hyperventilating and clutching her broccolini like it's the only thing she has left in the world.

And since Dallas would come for me, no questions asked, I will be here for my dark prince. Now and forever.

I kiss his hair, press my lips onto the softness of his neck, and whisper, "I won't."

Chapter Thirty-Eight

THREE MONTHS LATER

"Watch the potatoes!" I warn. "Keep them moving, or they'll burn."

I taught Dallas how to flip the skillet—a gentle flick with the wrist to keep food circling up and back into the pan. But after three hours of dinner-party prep, it is two hours and fifty minutes longer than he spends in a kitchen at any one time. He panics and uses too much wrist. A Yukon gold potato wedge launches from the pan and freefalls to a buttery death.

Our resident hoovers jump to life and attack the freebie. Rodolfo gulps down his prize, leaving Mimi to whinge for her own snack.

I nudge them away with my foot and a stern voice. "You two are menaces. Go off then to your beds. Dinner is coming soon."

They hang their heads and sulk off into my living room like chastised children. Our therapist has questioned our decision to keep the dogs. Fair enough, considering the thousand dollars an hour he collects for untangling the thorny mess of Navarro in our minds. To him, a daily reminder is nonsensical. But whoever said humans make sense?

Dallas slides the frying pan off the heat and cuffs sweat from his brow. "Next time," he says, "I'm calling a caterer."

"If you want to host a dinner party, it does mean cooking."

"Can I pretend to be a guest? Technically, I don't live here."

I playfully snap his butt with a kitchen towel. "I believe sleeping in my bed five nights a week pushes you beyond guest status."

He can't help smiling at that. "Your bedroom has a better view than mine. And it comes with you."

With one arm around my waist, he captures me for a kiss. The tease of his tongue sweeps over mine, and I fall back against the counter, my British heart beating wild and free. Our bodies call to each other, and I press against his warmth and hardness.

Stupid me once thought rejection was protection.

File that under horseshit.

Dallas shoves my beaded mini-skirt higher and mutters, "I need an appetizer. You on the counter?"

Over his shoulder, the microwave clock reads twenty-past six. Vandana, Morgan, Chavez, and Flynn are on their way in Dallas's Rolls Phantom for a six thirty arrival, and I don't fancy a rush job. That being said, our record is under two minutes. Me so hot and horny, all it took was a few devilish lashes of his tongue to unleash a hell of a storm. The sex between us is so addictive that we both know we can never let it go.

Okay dances on my lips just as the doorbell rings.

Dallas groans, "Fuck!"

Mimi and Rodolfo are on it, bounding to the door and barking at us to get a move on. Dallas pins me against the counter, his hand sliding between my thighs. He knuckles my wet, bare pussy with an audible sound of anxiety.

"How am I supposed to behave?"

I trawl along his erection with my fingertip. "Who said anything about behaving?"

"How about we don't answer the door?" he suggests in a hopeful tone.

As if our barking sentries will ever let that happen. And as if I would ever not embrace my dearest friends on such a momentous night. I grab Dallas by the hand, towing him out of the kitchen. He's wearing dark denim and my favorite black dress shirt, an inky black the same color as his hair. Well, most of his hair. I told him the grey moving in makes him look distinguished, and he's trying it out.

The other thing he's wearing is a smile, and that's a good thing.

Today has been a good day, and not all of them are. But slowly, we are healing. Therapy three times a week, and dear Flynn bought us both journals. Our left-brain, spreadsheet minds shunned them at first, but now we scribble furiously every morning. We work out at the gym on the weekend and spend our evenings as aroused as possible. Part of the charge is in the excess. Finding salvation one delicious love-making session at a time.

Before I open the door, I cross-check to ensure my tank top and skirt cover everything. I told my besties tonight was casual, and Vandana interpreted this to mean movie-star shades, a jungle-print Versace dress, strappy heels, and Morgan getting suited up like a banker. One limo ride away from the Met Gala. But look how cute Chavez is in a button-down, jeans, and a megawatt smile. And Flynn, absolutely radiant in a velvet jumpsuit with cork wedges. I make a mental note to ask who does her facials because that is some serious glow.

We run through all the hugs and congratulations and chatter excitedly en route to the kitchen. Dallas insisted his chauffeur round everyone up so we could celebrate and drink without worry. Chavez won the US Open five days ago, and tonight we live large. Two Grand Slams in one year? Unreal. And it all happened under the tutelage of his adoring Flynn.

"Babes!" Vandana exclaims, reaching for a skewer of olives on the charcuterie board. "It smells uh-mazing in here. Do you also cook?" she asks Dallas.

"If you like the taste of refrigeration and surrender," he quips. "I'm your guy."

Morgan laughs and sets two bottles of red wine on the counter. "I heard steak was on the menu."

"And we brought the champagne!" Flynn reveals a bottle of Dom Perignon from the tote bag she carried in. "Pre-chilled and ready to go."

"I'll get the flutes," Dallas offers.

I'm impressed he remembers what cupboard to find them in. There is hope for him yet.

Morgan pops the champagne—he is a master at it, given it is essentially water where he lives—and expertly tops up the flutes. One by one he hands the glasses off, knowing to bypass Chavez, the non-drinker.

But Flynn also holds up her hand. "None for me, please."

She and Chavez steal a quick, furtive glance. He rubs her belly, and both of them bite back smiles.

What?

Vandana and I swivel our heads in unison to gape at one other. She finds her voice first and gasps, "Oh my God, Flynn! For real?"

Chest puffed out like a gorilla, Chavez confirms it. "We just hit the three-month mark."

The shock dissolves, and I throw my arms around my dear, willowy, beautiful friend who swore she would never have children. "Congratulations, doll! But why did you keep this a secret?" I scold. "Haven't you learned your lesson?"

Her cheeks redden. "Chavez didn't want to jinx anything."

"Trust me," he chimes in. "She wanted to blab *right* away."

"Incredible news. Another tennis player, perhaps? We should be so lucky." Morgan throws a chummy arm around Chavez, and does he linger a touch too long? Or maybe he hung a poster of Chavez in his living room just because.

Vandana wipes away tears of joy before her makeup smears. "Our baby, all grown up. Marriage, kids. I can't even."

"I'm only a year younger than you two," Flynn reminds us, for the umpteenth time.

"But you'll always be our little sister," I add, flashing a wink at Vandana.

Dallas, quietly imbibing his Dom asks, "Boy or girl?"

Flynn grins shyly. "It's a girl."

"Her name is Estrella," Chavez announces, already the proud father. "It means star in Spanish. Because Flynn is my sky, and Estrella will shine bright in our universe, won't she, Miss Flynn?"

And if I need more proof of how utterly adorable Chavez is, he plants the sweetest, softest kiss on her cheek. But there's no more green-eyed monster clawing up my throat now that I've found my own champion.

I smile warmly at Dallas, but his body language has stiffened. This baby reveal is bittersweet. We visited his father in Seattle a few weeks ago and sipped coffees one morning in a park near our hotel. A father roughhoused with his two young sons on a field across the street, and a muscle tightened around Dallas's jaw as he watched them.

We've never talked about kids.

No need to, based on his condition.

In those endless hours when we had nothing to do but confide all our dark secrets to each other, he admitted he was sterile. And he choked up saying it, because if kids were on my agenda, they were the one thing he could not deliver on.

Truth be told, the idea of children never crossed my mind. But then again, Dallas and I together was also a far-fetched fantasy. Things change all the time.

And sometimes for the better.

So I silently remind him with my eyes, *It's okay. We'll be okay.* Because if push comes to shove, there are other ways to have children.

"Baby news aside, we also have a tiny favor to ask," Flynn says.

She and Chavez exchange impish grins while we hang on to that sentence. And I thought Vandana had cornered the market on dramatic pauses.

"Since we fell in love in Europe," she continues, "that's where we want to get married. Chavez has a two-week window in early October. Could you help us pull it together?"

She directs this question to Vandana, who reacts with a hand to her chest and a stunned, "Me?"

"It's super small." Flynn uses her little girl's voice reserved for when she really wants something. "Our immediate families. You guys. That's it."

"We don't want a circus," Chavez adds, a warning more than anything. For a guy bathed in the tennis spotlight, he aggressively avoids needless exposure.

Forever dishing out the advice, Vandana now seeks it from Morgan. "What do you think, babes?"

He shrugs and says what all of us know to be the truth. "I think there is no one better for the job."

She blinks away a round of fresh tears. For someone who spent years composed as the perfect PR queen, Vandana has let herself go in the emotions department.

"I'm so flattered," she blubbers. "It will be an honor. But where?" She voices this concern to no one in particular. "It's such short notice."

Dallas shoots me a look. I gesture back with a nod. *Yes, it's time.* Chavez and Flynn aren't the only ones with news.

"I know the perfect place," Dallas says. "My villa in St. Tropez. June and I are relocating there for a few months. We'd love to host."

Flynn slaps her hands on the counter and wails, "Noooo! You're moving too?"

"For a while. Not forever," I reassure her. "We need a time-out. And you're jet-setting all over the place these days, so I'll likely see you more in Europe than here."

Vandana squeals and click-clacks over to hug the life out of me. "Seriously? That's so close to Monaco. Oh my God, I have *every-thing* planned for us."

"I have to crack the whip on Morgan. Make sure he's working on my yacht," Dallas jokes.

Morgan tips his champagne flute. "The initial designs will be ready in a month."

I balked at having my night of mortal embarrassment commemorated so permanently, but Dallas insists on christening our new yacht *The Blue Moon*.

"What about your companies?" Vandana asks.

There's that too.

Green Time is in great shape. Once Mark inked the deal with Prime Produce, our growth exploded. Revenues have surpassed our projections, and we're just getting started. Evener Equity took a board seat but relinquished the controlling position. (Dallas apologized for being a dick but reminded me disclosure is still one of my weak points.)

And with Green Time back in my hands, I did the right thing and handed Mark the reins. He didn't cry when I told him, but he came close. I taught him well, so I know he can handle it. Me? This CFO is thrilled to crunch numbers from her pole position on a sun bed overlooking the Mediterranean.

Dallas followed my lead and made a similar offer to Nikki, who pounced all over the opportunity to oversee Evener Equity as the interim CEO. She's a firecracker and a new friend, likable and relatable, and in her own words, "Bowed down to Jesus" that Dallas and I sorted out our tangled relationship mess. Apparently, he had a mad crush on me for years.

Go figure.

So many changes and new beginnings for all of us, and my heart swells in direct proportion to the loud grumbling in my empty stomach.

Leave it to a Frenchman to sum it up so perfectly. "All this good news is making me affamé," Morgan says. "Anything I can do to help?"

$

Long after the food and wine, laughter, and tears, it's just me and Dallas and a magical Malibu night. We're on a lounger overlooking the ocean, a fingernail moon high above us and the tang of salt hanging heavy in the air. Nestled between his legs, with the thrum of his heart-beat on my spine, we pass a joint back and forth. Turns out he does have access to the good stuff, and relaxing is my new black.

Dallas blows out a smoke ring, and we watch it drift and spin into the sky thick with stars. "What a great night," he says. "I'm so lucky to be part of your crew."

"Everyone adores you, and thank you for going the extra mile," I say. "You were helpful, attentive, and funny."

"You mean I was my usual brilliant self?" he jokes.

He hands off the joint to me for one last puff before I snuff it out in the ashtray. I admire his fingers, the deviant creatures that they are. Always finding their way into places that make me shudder.

"I was thinking of getting a piano," I say. "It would fit in the corner by the bar. What do you think?"

My favorite nights are when he plays for me at his house, and the music becomes a physical thing that makes my senses vibrate. I still love the Einaudi piece best. Every time I hear it, I close my eyes and see his muscles bathed in the beams of sunlight, his half-naked body and lounge pants utterly out of place amid the ornate salon.

"Maybe I'll just move mine here," Dallas says.

Something flips inside me. After weeks of going back and forth with the dogs, I wondered if this conversation would ever crop up.

When I don't reply, he sounds a bit panicky. "Does that freak you out? Living together?"

Nothing can freak me out anymore, is what I want to say. But that would drag us backward. The lesson from three months of therapy is to always move forward.

"Not at all," I say. "If you play your cards right, I'll give you a deal on the rent."

His chest rumbles beneath my back with rolling laughter. "I have another way of compensating you that you might prefer."

"Does it have anything to do with the giant zucchini pressing against my arse?"

"Hostile takeover?" he suggests.

"I was thinking mergers and acquisitions."

"Spread your legs, you dirty little wench," he whispers. "Knowing you didn't have panties on all night made it hard to focus."

I splay my thighs open and he buries his finger into my welcoming slit. I moan, feeling nothing but a constellation of sensations sparkling between my legs. His breath is hot in my ear, promising that he plans to ruin me here, under the stars.

The dogs, snuggled together on the deck and exhausted after socializing and begging for steak scraps, stir with the noises coming from their owners/slaves. Their curious, innocent gazes make me feel self-conscious, and I yank a nearby blanket over us.

"Why do they always look at me like that?" I ask.

Dallas nuzzles my neck and draws slow, lazy circles over my clit with his thumb pad like the rotter that he is, eliciting another groan. "Because you sound like an animal in heat whenever I touch you."

"Is that what I sound like? A half-mad wildebeest?"

"A beast, for sure," he says, and I can feel his smile against my neck. "And a little wild. Just the way I like it."

"Do you want me to get the shoes?"

He loves it when I ride him wearing stilettos. We've found new ways to play after he went cold turkey with the handcuffs. I half-expected there to be a weaning-off process, given the need to restrain was born in such a deep-rooted part of his psyche. But let's face it. He never wanted the tables turned and then had his whole world turned upside down.

"Nah," he says. "Your sweet pussy is all I need tonight."

He finger-fucks me slowly and a little rough, and I surrender to the wave of pleasure using nothing but my body to communicate. There will always be something dark inside Dallas, and I respond to it every time. We have reached a place of absolute trust in the past few weeks, fucking and therapizing our way to understanding the positive and negative spaces we inhabit.

It won't always be easy, but damn, we have fun figuring our shit out.

Dallas coaxes me higher, his greedy finger making me wet and ready. I feel loose and weak but not uncertain. Not when it comes to us. *This.*

My eyes fall shut, lost in the endorphin rush. "That feels fantastic. Keep going, please."

His cock, angry and impatient, twitches against my backside. "I want to make love to you out here. Are you okay with an audience?"

"Yes. But I want to be on top."

He chuckles. "Of course, you do."

He pops his finger free and lets me taste myself, before peeling off my tank top. He frees my girls next, cupping his hands beneath them to hold the heft. Some nights he fucks them, and my nipples prickle with arousal at the risqué thought.

I wriggle out of my miniskirt and maneuver onto my knees to pull off his jeans, stripping away his boxers while he removes his shirt. Framed against the endless ocean and propped high on balls swollen and full, his manhood looks especially impressive. He lies back and holds himself upright in his hand like a five-p.m. cocktail—hold the tail.

Ready driver one.

"Come sit on me," he murmurs.

The dogs are now very interested in our erotic tableau, and I bite back a laugh before straddling his muscular limbs, sharply defined under his olive skin and glowing in the moonlight. The soft night breeze wraps around us as I spread myself and wet the tip of his cock with my warmth.

His eyes roll back with a groan. "Not slow. Not tonight."

"Okay, then."

I slide down his smooth, naked flesh until our pelvic bones collide and he fills me completely. A gruff sound buzzes in his throat. His eyes are sharp and clear and bore right into mine, but I realize he's shaking when his hands clamp against my hips.

"What is it?" I ask.

He licks his lips nervously. Confusion and hurt once threatened to hang forever in the depths of his pupils, although the longer we are together, the less I see them.

After a hard swallow, his voice is thick as clotted cream. "How do you feel about marriage?"

The shock of it. That it rolled out of his mouth just like that. Before I can think properly, I blurt out, "Uhm…"

"I'm not asking," he's quick to say. "Not now, like this, but what do you think?"

"I think Flynn and Chavez need to have their day first."

His eyes darken. "That's not an answer, June."

Does he not get how gobsmacked I am? Can he not feel how I'm gripping his manhood in response to the surprise?

"I, I know," I stammer. "It's just–"

"And I don't want to mess with their day," he interrupts. "But I've been thinking about marriage because … I love you."

A muscle around his mouth twitches. I start to tremble, processing what he just said.

"Is it okay that I love you?" he asks tenderly, vulnerably, and so utterly lovelorn. One day, I'll tell him how unnecessary that question was. We might even laugh at the fumbling moment in the future.

But the fact we have a future is why I start crying.

"Yes, it's okay. It's more than okay. And I love you too."

I lean forward, he lifts his head, and the kiss that seals us together starts a little clumsy but melts into a sensual twirling of tongues. I can feel him throb and grow bigger inside me. When I break the kiss to catch my breath, he wipes the tears from my cheek with his thumb.

"Don't cry," he says. "It's all good."

And it is. No messing around. Maybe just us a little messed up because of the security detail trailing us 24/7. Even though Navarro insisted his family would know nothing of our visit or the cash, Dallas isn't taking any chances.

Not after the letter arrived.

I remember every detail of that day in vivid Technicolor.

The sweltering heat of August. I left the office early to walk the dogs and prepare a birthday dinner for Dallas. My mind traveled across continents when I found an envelope postmarked from Manaus, Brazil in the mailbox. Two glasses of ice wine went down like water before I ripped it open. I had to lay it on the counter to read because my hands shook so violently.

Principessa,

I hope this note finds you both well. How wonderful that Green Time has achieved such success. I had no doubt I backed the right horses.

I'm writing partly to assuage the demons in my head but also to set the story straight. I did return to the castle, only to find you two gone. I'm sorry that I took longer than promised. Dick proved to be a formidable opponent, but in the end, youth over age.

In retrospect, it's better that I didn't return to LA with you. And I have no intention of intruding on your lives in the future. Thank you for looking after Mimi and Rodolfo. I feel better knowing they have a loving home and that a little piece of me can remain with you.

I suppose Carolina either nicked or returned your earring because I could not find it before I left. Forgive me for sounding like a romantic fool, but I wanted to have a memento of you. It was an absolute pleasure to meet you, although I wish it could have been under different circumstances. I did enjoy our private moments, misguided as they were. You are in far better, and more deserving, hands and we both know that.

Please give my love to Dallas. I apologize for not writing to him directly, but whenever I put pen to paper and think of him, I fall apart.

Fondly,

Navarro

His voice, melodic and sweet, curled around me like a piece of silk, but it was like reading a letter from the dead. Dallas came home later that evening, sensed how shaken I was, and paled when I told him. He refused to see or touch the note but eventually asked me to read it, laying on the couch to stare blankly at the ceiling before he excused himself to sit on the deck until the first light of dawn. I joined him, bearing coffees and the duvet, and we snuggled together in silence to watch the sun turn gold over Malibu.

Dallas made one comment about the letter during therapy—an offhand statement that Navarro will likely resort to plastic surgery to keep himself hidden. I found it apropos that he chose the word *hidden* because our lives will be forever marked by the eras BN and AN—before and after Navarro.

He is the invisible tattoo inked on our skin.

Visible to no one but us.

"June?" Dallas asks, snapping my attention back. "Everything okay?"

His eyes are dilated, and I remember the first time they were like this. I flash, like I sometimes do, on that time-stopped moment when Dallas dipped me during the tango, and we shared the kiss of the century—the beginning of a life-altering love I craved but never thought would find me.

And somehow, it did.

"Yes, I'm okay," I whisper, my throat closing in. "It's all good."

And then we get down to business because it's what we do best and because, sometimes, there is nothing more to say.

Thank you and free bonus!

I hope you enjoyed *The Closer!*

Reviews are the lifeblood of an indie author's success. I'd be honored if you took a moment to post a review on any of the sites below. If you're not comfortable putting your thoughts into words, a star rating works just fine.

Amazon

Good Reads

Book Bub

$

Guess what? *The Closer* playlist is dark and sexy, just like Dallas! Scan the QR code below for the Spotify link.

The Closer Playlist

$

What to read next? Dive into books one and two of The Hustlers Series or fall in love with the fabulously sexy Trenton brothers in The Trenton Troublemakers series! Save 25% on all eBooks by buying direct through my Rowan Rossler Shop. All eBooks delivered immediately through Book Funnel. Signed books also available, mailed with love & bonus swag!

Scan to Shop!

Also by Rowan Rossler

The Hustlers Series

The Cruiser (book 1)

The Challenger (book 2)

The Closer (book 3)

This jet-set romance series stars three BFFs navigating dreams, desires, and all the beautiful complications of falling in love. Glamour, spice, and sexy drama. Pack your bags and follow your heart!

The Trenton Troublemakers Series

My Grape Crush (book 1)

My Cherry Duet (book 2)

Book Three (coming soon!)

Three brothers and the fiery women who tangle with them star in a trio of interconnected but standalone romances brimming with sibling drama and shameless fun. Trouble always comes in threes…

Acknowledgments

Where to start? The journey of this book is the wildest ride of my career. What began as a light and breezy boy-meets-girl eventually transformed and became my most layered work. Many thanks to the following people and places who helped shape this story directly or indirectly.

The first props belong to Mahendra Ramsignhani for writing the enjoyable and informative *"The Business of Venture Capital."* A treat to read, Mahendra managed to turn what could be an incredibly tedious subject into a real page-turner. As Dallas explains, by investing in ideas, VCs can and do change the world. I've invested in many junior companies and been on the winning end of some great successes.

As always, hugs to my beta readers and editors for weighing in with helpful notes. Your insight made this story shine. An extra special shout-out to Jennifer Rainnie for reading an early version of this book. Your comments were bang on and forced me back to the drawing board to craft a more compelling tale of June and Dallas.

The rewrite of the book introduced the Italian mafia and the character of Navarro, both of which fascinated me the deeper I started to dig.

In June 2023, I traveled through Southern Italy by car to get a taste of the region that birthed the mafia. From Sicily to Calabria to the gritty streets of Naples, I learned so much from the people I met and the places I explored. While the average tourist will never see or experience the silent influence of the mafia, the deadly and corrupt force is alive and well.

Born out of the need for Italian clans to bond and protect their families from invaders of Sicily, the mafia is now so entrenched in the culture and legitimate businesses of Italy that the influence is almost impossible to eradicate. South America, Argentina in particular, is a critical destination for the mafia drug trade. An estimated eighty percent of the cocaine that enters Europe comes from the mafia operations in Argentina. And yes, those illegal profits are mostly laundered in London, England via numbered accounts and shady capital companies.

Despite the bluster of Italian politicians about change and ridding society of the mafia, they gladly line their pockets with kickbacks and payouts from the very criminals they deplore. Navarro embodies the slippery power of this criminal underworld, but I also wanted to humanize the deep-rooted conflict that the mafia conjures for many Italians. Navarro's sexuality created an extra layer of inner turmoil, and I hope you found him as captivating as I did.

A special thank you to Dallas for being one of the most complicated male characters I have ever written. His tangled, tormented feelings for Navarro broke my heart. Certain relationships shatter us on a cellular level, and his pain and fears of abandonment, and trying to control those emotions through the use of handcuffs, made his flaws that much more real.

And this story would be nothing without my inner boss babe, June Allison. I crown her the First Lady of the Hustlers Series because she was the inaugural female character and the one I aligned with the most. The first seven years of my career took place in the financial world, and being the only female in an office full of men was never easy. (I hear ya, June!)

Last, but definitely not least, thanks to all the booksellers, readers, and especially my fans. You have a choice of thousands of books to read and I'm always grateful when mine make the cut. Thanks for being you.

Love,

Rowan

Xo

About the Author

Rowan Rossler is an Amazon Top 100 bestselling author and travel junkie living in Vancouver, BC. She loves bringing bold and flawed characters to life in her contemporary romance tales. If you're a lover of sultry moments, sexy drama, and heartfelt emotion, Rowan is your one-click author.

A lifelong book lover and former financial planner, her pivot into TV production inspired her to put pen to page. If she's not writing, you'll find Rowan stage left at a concert, cooking, whipping her abs into shape, or enjoying la dolce vita on one of her many travel adventures.

CONNECT WITH ROWAN: